PHANTOM
INSTINCT

ALSO BY MEG GARDINER

The Shadow Tracer
Ransom River

JO BECKETT NOVELS

The Nightmare Thief
The Liar's Lullaby
The Memory Collector
The Dirty Secrets Club

EVAN DELANEY NOVELS

China Lake
Mission Canyon
Jericho Point
Crosscut
Kill Chain

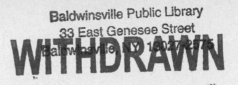
MEG GARDINER

PHANTOM INSTINCT

DUTTON
⟶ est. 1852 ⟵

DUTTON
— est. 1852 —

Published by the Penguin Group
Penguin Group (USA) LLC
375 Hudson Street
New York, New York 10014

USA | Canada | UK | Ireland | Australia | New Zealand | India | South Africa | China
penguin.com
A Penguin Random House Company

LIBRARY OF CONGRESS CATALOGING-IN-PUBLICATION DATA
Gardiner, Meg.
Phantom instinct / Meg Gardiner.
pages cm
ISBN 978-0-525-95431-6 (hard cover)
I. Title.
PR6107.A725P63 2014
823'.92—dc23
2013048812

Printed in the United States of America
1 3 5 7 9 10 8 6 4 2

For the teachers,
who unlock the power and joy of reading and writing

1

When it started, Harper Flynn had a fifth of vodka in her hand, six shot glasses lined up on the bar in front of her, and a stinging cut on her arm from a broken beer bottle. Music rained through the refurbished warehouse, a sheet of noise. Harper poured the martini into a chilled glass. Down the crowded bar, a banker waved his empty highball glass and a twenty. She nodded. Macallan, neat, with a Stella back—she'd get to him. She'd get to them all. Eleven P.M. and she was halfway through her shift.

She slid the martini glass toward the man in the suit. "Fourteen-fifty."

He frowned and shouted over the band. "For an ounce of vodka and an olive?"

She smiled. "For turning you into James Bond." *And for not spitting in it.*

The dance floor was a swerving mass of spangled people. On the walls, flat screens projected glossy music videos. In booths and at tables along the balcony, cooler customers leaned back, holding court over bottles of Bollinger. The stage lights skewed the space between white glare and murky corners. The warehouse windows were milky with moonlight, pierced by occasional Los Angeles headlights.

The suit stroked the stem of the martini glass. "I'll pay four bucks."

"Fourteen-fifty," Harper said, still smiling, but both hands on the bar now.

She wore a black cotton blouse, sleeves rolled to the elbows, and black jeans he couldn't see, because he was too busy trying to Jedi mind-trick her buttons open. Next to him, a woman leaned back, laughing, hand to her chest.

From the crowd, Drew appeared behind the suit. Eyes on Harper, shoulders square, as though he was lining up to head-butt the man.

Drew leaned toward the guy's ear. "How's your drink?"

The man looked up at him, several inches. Noticed the black shirt, the chilly eyes, the cornerback's body.

Harper said, "His drink's about to be paid for."

Maybe half a second the guy held on, wanting to yank her chain again. Then he slapped fifteen bucks on the bar and skulked off.

Drew smiled. "He thought I was your boss."

That smile was wicked, and overtly pleased.

"Never," she said. "Not even when we play dress-up later on."

He didn't work there. He only worked his way under her skin, into her thoughts, her days, her nights. Now he was laughing. She nodded at the far end of the bar and walked down. He followed.

He slid her employee swipe card into her hand. "Thanks."

She clipped the card to her belt, quietly, her back turned to the club's CCTV camera. "What's it like outside?"

"Zoo. Line around the block, security's wanding guys and carding teenage girls."

"But they're still letting people in?"

He raised his eyebrows. The walls seemed to bulge under the press of the crowd. Fire limit was twelve hundred. That many seemed to be clamoring for drinks.

Harper said, "Your sister's not out there, is she?"

He laughed. "Piper might be able to fake her way past security, but she knows you're working. You're scarier than any bouncer."

"That's my motto. Now buy a drink. And tip me big."

Drew had borrowed her swipe card so he could avoid the hassle of security at the front entrance when he came back in. He eyed the bottles arrayed behind her.

She added, "And no, you may not challenge me to mix the worst drink possible. I will not serve you an Antifreeze. Or a Brain Tumor."

"An Old-Fashioned," he said.

She wiped her hands on her apron. "Bourbon or rye?"

"What's the most old-fashioned?"

She set a glass on the bar. "You stir it for eighteen minutes to muddle the drink." She dropped in a sugar cube, added Angostura bitters and water, and stirred with a spoon. "That's how Al Capone demanded it."

She filled the glass with Wild Turkey, shoveled in ice cubes, and nudged the glass at him.

The band hit a final chord. Definitely Arson was the hot ticket that had drawn this whooping crowd to the Valley on a Saturday night. In a booth near the stage, a glass broke. A woman squealed. An ice bucket tipped over.

One of the other bartenders, Sanita, said, "High roller. Vegas millionaire, I heard."

Harper glanced at the booth. Everything seemed brilliant and shadowed.

Across the dance floor, at the main entrance, a man came up the stairs. He stopped in the doorway. Hands at his sides, jacket open. For a second, he struck Harper as a gunslinger, readying himself to draw, waiting for an opponent to rise up from the swirl in front of him. A woman came in the door beside him, a blonde, same urgency, same eyes.

The band launched into a new song. Down the bar, a man whistled and shouted, "Cuervo."

At the door, the harsh-eyed man and woman surveyed the room in slow tandem, like twin Terminators. Drew leaned on the bar, rattling the ice in his glass. Harper took the Cuervo Gold from the shelf.

The first sound was a muffled pop. The man and woman with the gunslinger eyes turned toward the high roller's booth. Harper's skin prickled.

A second report hammered beneath the drumbeat. It was unmistakable, a noise she knew from the firing range and a thousand TV shows, a sound it seemed she had been expecting all her life: gunfire.

2

Aiden Garrison turned at the noise. "Shots fired."

From the doorway, he scanned the club. With its heaving swirl of dancers and the thunder of the band, it might as well have been a riot. Beside him, Erika Sorenstam drew her weapon. The stage lights flashed against her blond hair and the badge hooked on her belt.

"Where?" she said.

People continued dancing, arms upraised. It was a jungle, swaying as though under the force of the beat, and he couldn't see the snakes.

Across the club, the man in the booth by the stage—heavyset, young, and sweating into his two-thousand-dollar suit—pointed at the crowd. Arliss Bale, Vegas hotshot, known meth wholesaler. His bodyguards rose and stormed into the crowd.

"They're going for Bale." Garrison shouldered his way onto the dance floor. His weapon was already in his hands.

Beneath the crash of cymbals, a third shot reached his ears. So did the first scream.

The scream barely cut through the blare of the singer and guitars. Harper's palms went clammy. Drew turned toward the sound.

In the booth by the stage, bodyguards lunged to their feet. They dragged Mr. High Roller from his seat. Another shot echoed.

Harper shouted, "Gunshots. Everybody get down."

The band kept playing. The crowd kept dancing. Then screams

came like a rock slide, pebbles at first, rolling, escalating, until noise and fear cut through the center of the floor, an avalanche. The music dribbled to a stop.

"Go," Harper shouted. "Get out. *Now.*"

Without music, the screams took over. The customers at the bar scattered. People spilled out in all directions, frantic, eyes round. The booth near the stage had emptied, bodyguards rushing into the crowd, Mr. Big on his knees, reaching into his suit jacket for a weapon or his valet parking ticket, something to transport him out of there.

On the dance floor, a woman tripped and fell. Three feet from Harper, Sanita swiped her card to lock the register. She was punching the screen when the shot hit her in the chest.

She keeled back against the bottles behind her and dropped.

"Sanita," Harper cried.

Drew leaned across the bar and grabbed Harper's hand. "This way."

Harper resisted. "Sanita's hurt."

Sanita sat, legs splayed, hand pressed to her chest. She stared astonished at the blood seeping between her fingers.

Two people dived across the bar and rolled to the floor, taking cover. Drew pulled on Harper's arm. Behind him, a man huffed as if he'd been hit with a sledgehammer. Blood erupted from his shoulder.

People were stampeding, hands out, some looking back. For a moment, the dance floor cleared and gave Harper a clean view of the room.

A man in a hoodie, wearing gloves and a gas mask, was advancing toward the high roller's bodyguards, arm extended, firing a pistol. He seemed unhurried.

Drew tightened his grip on her arm. "Come on."

The gunshot took him high in the back and knocked him against the bar.

⁓

Aiden Garrison and Erika Sorenstam forged through the crowd, shoving against the tide. Garrison held his weapon with both hands. The lights flipped blue, strobing, women in iridescent dresses racing past. One shied and screamed at the sight of his gun.

"Sheriff's department. Move," he said.

Sorenstam's face was washed blue beneath the lights. She spoke into her shoulder-mounted radio. "Shots fired at Xenon."

She held her weapon aimed at the hardwood floor. The strobes flashed in her eyes. Garrison continued to scan the room.

Two bodyguards from the booth headed into the melee—suits, glass stares, earpieces, shoving people aside.

One of them went down in the crowd as though he'd been nailed by a shark. Garrison eyed the trajectory the shot had taken. He saw the fleeting profile of a man in a hoodie, wearing a mask. And behind that man, another. Heading toward the bar. Guns in their hands.

Garrison plunged after them. "*Sorenstam.*"

She didn't respond. Alarm jacked through him. He fought against the stampede and passed a man who'd been shot. The man lay face-down, motionless, getting kicked like a rugby ball. Garrison knelt briefly, trying to form a barrier. He put two fingers to the man's neck. No pulse.

He stood. Between fleeing people, two gray hoodies wove their way across the floor, a counterflow, methodical. Another gunshot boomed out. He turned. Who had fired? Where was Erika?

A woman bumped into him, hands out. Beyond her was a shooter, dark hoodie, face covered by a gas mask. The shooter raised a silver pistol. The hoodie rode up his back. Chones hanging out over sagging jeans. Pale white rind of skin visible around his waist. He stalked toward the bar.

Where a young guy in a black shirt had been hit and lay splayed across the counter. And Garrison saw the young bartender.

~

"Drew," Harper said.

She could barely hear herself. Her field of vision had collapsed into a bright shriek. Drew lay crashed across the bar, gasping. His fingers clawed the wood. Blood spread from the exit wound in his chest. Behind him came the reflected flash of silver, from the handgun pointing directly at him.

Dark figures moved against the turbulent flow of the crowd. Shadows, golems, men in masks. One turned her way. The plastic eyeholes of his gas mask glittered under the stage strobes.

Drew tried to straighten, but slid backward toward the floor.

Harper grabbed his wrist. "No."

He looked at her, distantly, seemingly surprised by pain.

A bullet shattered the mirror behind her. Harper flinched. Glass waterfalled to the floor. Sanita cried out and curled into a ball. The man in the gas mask was closer.

Drew slipped another inch. Harper's system flooded with adrenaline. Hanging tight to his wrist, she scrambled onto the bar and across.

Sanita cried, "Harper—no."

Harper jumped down on the far side of the bar. Drew slid to the floor.

She dropped to his side, heart thundering. "Come on."

He swiped a hand in her direction. "Can't breathe."

"Hold on." She worked her arms around him and labored to her feet.

Cover, she needed cover. The main door was a hundred fifty feet across the dance floor. The staff entrance—the door Drew had used earlier—was closer. She turned toward it. A shooter stood in front of it, aiming at the high roller's booth. *Dammit.* Groaning with effort, she turned again and hauled Drew toward the end of the bar. She had to get behind it. His heels dragged on the wood. His shirt gleamed wetly.

Hundreds of people were still trying to get out of the club. The shooter turned in her direction. The eyeholes of his gas mask looked black and void. Harper's skin, her bones, the air around her, felt electric.

She lugged Drew backward, arms aching. He didn't rise, didn't help her, sank lower in her arms. "Westerman, come on, man. *Come on.*"

The man in the gas mask reached inside his sweatshirt. When he pulled his hand out again, Harper stumbled.

He held the worst drink ever invented. The Molotov cocktail.

He jammed his pistol into the waistband of his sagging jeans, took out a lighter, and lit the rag in the bottle. *Hell*, Harper thought. *Oh, hell.* Chaotic flames illuminated a crawling black tattoo on his hand and reflected in the eyeholes of his mask.

Then, deep in the crowd behind him, another figure became visible: the man with the Terminator stare. He raised a gun. He was shouting. Maybe *Don't move.* Maybe *Freeze.*

Gas Mask turned his head sharply. Turning back, he pitched the bottle against the wall above the bar. It burst with a clattering chime. Gasoline bloomed into flame like a sightless orange eye.

Harper staggered. "Jesus."

Liquid flames spilled and flared. Gas Mask tipped his head up as they climbed the wall. Insect-quick, he lobbed something else into the fire, ducked, and disappeared back into the crowd.

Smoke boiled onto the ceiling and curled over on itself. Sanita crawled from behind the bar, aided by another bartender.

Harper called to them. "The door—gotta get out."

With a percussive *crack*, the bar exploded. Red-white flames starburst and shrapnel flew. Harper cringed against Drew, gasping. She inhaled caustic smoke. Choking at the smell and taste and fearful heat of it, she coughed and inhaled even more.

Lock it down. Basic training came back to her. *Hold your shit together, and get out.*

The fire inflated. It boiled up the walls, engulfed the bar, and streaked along the floor. The smoke alarm tripped, a solid high-pitched shriek. Drew hung heavy in her shaking arms. She looked over her shoulder. The main door was one hundred twenty feet away. Beyond it, the stairs were jammed. A cry lodged in her throat. The stairs were packed so solid with people that none of them could move. They were yelling, writhing like worms.

The CO_2 fire suppression system activated. But across the club, a man smashed a window with a chair. Oxygen gushed in. The flames welled and roared across the ceiling. The heat swelled appallingly.

A fleeing woman tripped into Drew. He blinked but didn't move. Harper checked the other direction, the staff door at the back of the club. Black smoke nearly obscured it. Dozens of people were trying to shove through it. But gliding her way were three hooded figures. Amid the panic, they appeared impervious. The blaze seemed to burn from within their gas masks. Smoke enveloped them, then cleared around the one in the center. Under the light of the flames, the crawly black tattoo seemed to writhe. The silver pistol in his hand swept slowly across the room, gradually closing in on her and Drew.

Garrison tracked the shooters through rushing people and flashes of white flame and lowering black smoke. Hoods, masks, strutting across the dance floor. One raised his gun and aimed at the young brunette bartender. The pistol straight out, shoulder hunching, almost a parody of a gangsta pose, sweatshirt riding up, stalking across the floor, ignoring the fire he'd started.

Garrison barged toward him, coughing, trying to get a clear shot through the crowd and smoke. The shooters progressed in a straight line across the club, maybe sweeping the room for their original targets. They neared the wounded young man and the bartender, a slight woman who was straining to drag him to safety. Her hair was falling in front of her face. Her eyes were huge and desperate, but not craven—they glinted with firelight. She meant to save the young man even as the shooters and the fire bore down on her.

Garrison took aim. "Sheriff's department. Drop your weapons," he yelled.

The shooter didn't respond. Garrison kept advancing. The gunman had a clear shot. He himself didn't. The smoke billowed, obscuring all three shooters. Then, with a gust, it cleared. Garrison had an unobstructed field of fire. He squeezed the trigger. One of the gunmen went down. Garrison held his breath and swept his weapon right, and a second shooter was spinning in his direction, gun coming up. Garrison fired again.

Then, with a loud crack and a slithering shift in the floor, the world ended.

The wall of heat seemed to radiate through Harper. The fire bellowed, yellow, sliding around the room. Sparks and glass and the floor creaking. She turned frantically toward the staff exit. The smoke had lowered almost to the floor. Scurrying feet ran through the door, to the back hall, and it snapped shut.

She wrestled Drew toward the exit, groaning. The floor shifted beneath her. In front of the flaming bar, two shooters were down. From out of the smoke emerged the man with a gun and a badge.

She kept moving, even as the noise in the room turned to apocalypse, even as she knew the door was close, but too far. The cop was coming for her.

The floor opened up beneath him. With a flare of sparks and tearing wood, it collapsed. The wall came down with it. The club, the shooters, the night, her life, all disappeared into it. For a second, she caught the cop's eye, until smoke and flame and the falling floor swallowed him. She felt Drew slipping and thought: *I'm only a minute behind you into death.*

3

A hawk drifted overhead, poised, dipping on flared wings. The sycamores rustled in the morning breeze. Down the hill, the Pacific sparkled with firework brilliance. Richard Westerman read from prepared notes.

"My son loved the outdoors. He loved this park."

Though Westerman spoke up, his voice was buttoned down. "So today, in his honor, we dedicate the Drew Westerman Memorial Grove."

Harper stood at the back of the gathering. Twelve months, almost. Three hundred sixty-two days Drew had been gone. Three hundred fifty-six since he'd been put in the ground. The hawk rose on a brush of air.

"We hope that everybody who comes here and walks in the shade of these trees will find . . ." Westerman looked up from his notes. "Find some . . ."

Harper steepled her fingers against her lips.

Drew's mother, Sandra, stepped up and took her husband's hand. "Our family hopes that everyone who comes here will take heart from this beautiful view, the sky, the ocean my son loved so much. Thank you."

Applause pattered. The trees seemed to join in, leaves trembling. Richard and Sandra Westerman leaned against each other. Nearby, Drew's sister, Piper, blinked against the sunlight.

The crowd shuffled toward them, a ragtag receiving line of neighbors, family, Drew's friends from the software firm, and his father's colleagues from the bank. Harper recognized a few people who had been at Xenon that night—fellow survivors. A photographer skirted the gathering, camera to his eye, shooting. Down the hill, the Malibu coastline shimmered in the salt air.

Yeah, this was the spot. Drew had relished sunny days and a good surf report. And the trees, with their roots digging into the ground, gnarling and strengthening, viscerally reinforced the truth that Drew had gone down and was buried.

He had gone down with the collapse of the floor and left Harper hanging on the edge of nails and splintered wood, screaming. That night, she was ten inches on the right side of living. Drew was on the wrong side.

Harper had recovered from the smoke inhalation and lacerations and the burns caused by flaming debris. She had largely stopped hurting. She was still trying to stop asking *why*. That question was a trigger. It sucked her into a recurrent loop, where memory became a kind of recidivism.

Worse, asking *why* seemed to get her nowhere.

The hawk rode the air above her, wings tipping back and forth, hovering as if tethered with a kite string.

Across the lawn, people huddled around the Westermans. Richard and Sandra stood hip to hip, hands locked. Piper stood apart, awkwardly greeting people. She looked like she needed a teammate. Harper walked over.

A woman in a salmon-tinted suit was smiling painfully at the teenager. "A lovely memorial. Your brother's certainly smiling down on you today."

Piper brushed her hair behind an ear. "Glad it's sunny. Better view for him."

The woman's smile weakened. She glanced at Harper, maybe seeking assurance that Piper wasn't toying with her.

She did a double take. "You're . . ."

"Harper Flynn."

The woman had crow's eyes, flat and searching. "You're the girl-friend."

She touched her pearls and glanced at Piper. Volumes in that glance. *Poor kid.*

Piper's eyes flashed. Often the girl hid her gaze behind a down-turned chin and sandy hair that formed a parenthesis in front of her face. But when she stared, it was frank, a paint-stripping glare.

She grabbed Harper's hand. "We're going to get the Ouija board and find out if my brother has a view of traffic on the freeway home. Excuse us."

She turned toward the grove of sycamores, but the woman stepped in front of Harper.

"You're the one he saved," she said.

Piper's mouth tightened. "She'll spell out *thank you* on the Ouija board."

"I'd hope so. My God. To have somebody give his life for you." The woman tilted her head as though examining a specimen, trying to see Harper slantwise. "I hope you live in a way that's worthy of what Drew did for you."

The sun felt jaundiced and overbright. Harper said, "I'm working on it."

Piper pulled Harper into the trees. Under her breath she said, "What a special brand of bullshit people shovel at a gig like this."

"I'm used to it," Harper said.

"I can't take it. Before you walked up, she told me, 'God needed an angel, so he called Drew home.'"

As if a fourteen-billion-year-old god needed to call Drew home that night, via blood loss and blunt force trauma, instead of letting him live out his life. "God didn't do this."

"No shit."

Piper stopped beneath a tree and slumped back against the trunk. "I'm the girl whose brother died. That's plenty to wear every day. You're the one he died for. How's that feel?"

Feel? Grief wasn't a feeling. It was a thing that visited. It was a weight, a lead wall, and it pressed on her lungs and settled a shadow across her mind, until the only way she could inhale was through a gasp of anger. Fleetingly, she saw a barricade of fire, smelled the phantom reek of smoke.

How did it feel? Impossible to live up to. Because it was a myth.

In her statement to the sheriff's department, which she wrote from the hospital, Harper had drawn a diagram and explained where she and Drew were standing. *He grabbed my hand across the bar and said, "Come on." Then the round hit him in the back.*

To his parents, those terse words became the testament of Drew's heroism. Drew had tried to lead Harper to safety. Shielding her, he had blocked the gunfire with his own body and sacrificed himself.

"I take it as a mark of respect for Drew," she said.

"You're trying to earn it, aren't you?" Piper said.

"Maybe."

Piper's hair fell in front of her face. Her razor stare was beneath. "You're going to graduate and get a job with Homeland Security or Protect-Your-Shit Incorporated, and keep watch over everybody in the country, aren't you?"

"To start."

Definitely. Pointlessly. She could scrub her life so clean that it gleamed like the alabaster statue of a saint. To Drew's parents, nothing she did could outshine their son's martyrdom.

With Xenon out of business, she had scrabbled a job as a barista to make ends meet while she finished her degree at UCLA. But she could do nothing about the rest of it—the *why* and *what the hell?* She'd learned way back: You can't control what other people do or how they see you. You can only control your own reactions. Life owed you nothing. Life came upon you. You built what you could.

But she was struggling to do that, because the investigation by the Los Angeles Sheriff's Department, and the L.A. Fire Department, and the BATF had concluded that Xenon was attacked by two gunmen:

hired enforcers, settling a score between criminals over a deal gone bad. The dead men were local lowlifes, convenience store robbers, assholes in crime. Both were killed at Xenon. One was shot dead. The other died when the floor caved in.

Two shooters, not three.

The report noted unverified reports from several survivors who claimed to have seen more than two gunmen. It noted that a civilian witness asserted she had counted three hooded men in gas masks, one of whom brandished a silver pistol. But it found insufficient corroboration to validate her claim. In other words: The authorities thought that in the mayhem, overcome by terror, Harper had imagined a bogeyman.

All dead. So said the police. Harper heard that as a taunt.

She had spent four years in the Navy doing a job that boiled down to threat analysis. Before that, she had survived her teens by knowing how to recognize and avoid danger. Yet nobody believed what she'd seen the night when danger became immediate and personal. Her eyewitness testimony had been relegated to a footnote. That was what nearly made her bleed bile. Her experience had been reduced to an asterisk.

"Don't worry about me. Your snark's at championship level. Doing okay?"

For a second, Harper thought Piper might, finally, cry. But she forced a smile. "Ready for this day to be done."

Harper put an arm around her shoulder. Overhead, the hawk took a last lazy turn over the trees. With a burst of wings, it swooped down the hill toward the water.

Harper missed the sixteen-year-old that Piper had been before Drew's death: impish, precocious, sunny; smart-alecky with the older brother she had idolized. The slicing stare, the sarcasm, were new, her emotional Kevlar.

"Ready to face the crowd again?" Harper said.

"If you'll block for me," Piper said.

Arm around Piper's shoulder, Harper headed back toward the gathering. Across the park, moms were pushing kids on the swings. On the lawn, two young men tossed a Frisbee. A brindled dog watched them, panting. In the grove, the leaves trilled in the breeze. Light and shade scurried across the ground.

Then a deeper shadow seemed to move.

A man stood in the shadows among the trees. Harper saw him in silhouette, backlit by the morning sun. He was thin, in a loose jacket and baseball cap. Shoulders ratcheted up, hands in his pockets. He slid from behind one tree and along the ground, his stride seeming to snap as he kicked up leaves. His head was turned in the direction of the Westermans and the people gathered around them.

Piper said, "What?"

Harper stopped. So did the man, shadow across his face, dappled sunlight falling on his shoulders.

"Harper?" Piper said.

Though she couldn't see his eyes, Harper could feel him staring at her. She tightened her grip on Piper's shoulder. The man held still, watching.

"What's the matter?" Piper raised a hand to point. "Who's that?"

Harper pushed the girl's hand down. "Go to your mom and dad."

Hesitantly, Piper headed for her parents. Harper turned to the grove of trees.

The man was gone.

Her palms were sweating. A pinging seemed to emanate from the center of her head, sonar, seeking a return. The shadows gave nothing back.

Clenching her fists, she walked back into the grove. Leaves crunched beneath her feet. Checking her peripheral vision for motion, she headed deep into the trees, to the spot where the man had been standing. On the ground, in trampled grass, were three discarded cigarette butts.

Her mouth felt dry. She scanned the grove and the park beyond, but the man had vanished. Skin prickling, she crouched and examined the cigarette butts. One was still smoldering.

He'd been standing there long enough to smoke three Marlboros. Watching the memorial service. Feeling half crazed, half foolish, she got an Altoids tin from her purse. She dumped out the mints. Crushing the hot end of the smoldering butt with her heel, she scooped all three into a tissue, dropped them into the tin, and almost furtively stuck it in her purse. It was evidence.

She hurried back to the Westermans. Richard, speaking to a well-wisher, lifted his chin. Sandra's face was sanded smooth, maybe walled up behind the mortar of Xanax.

Piper said, "Scare away the ghosts?"

Her mother looked at her sharply. "Inappropriate."

Harper seemed to see the day through a scrim of yellow light. For a second, she held her tongue.

Then she looked at Piper. She turned to Sandra. "I think it would be a good time to go."

"Really?" Sandra said.

"Somebody was in the grove, spying on the ceremony."

"Spying," Sandra said.

"Yes. I think—"

"Of course you do." Sandra's face paled. Red patches glowed on her cheeks. "And you're right. It's a good time for you to go."

"Mom," Piper said.

Sandra raised a hand to silence her daughter. To Harper she said, "Really. We don't need this foolishness."

"*Mom*. Some guy was watching from the trees. I saw him."

Sandra stared at Harper. "'Some guy.' No, you think it was him. Again."

"Mom, chill," Piper said.

But Sandra was winding up. "You think it was this elusive third shooter. The nonexistent killer. For Christ's sake."

Harper said, "I'm concerned that a man surreptitiously observed the dedication, then took off when he was spotted."

"This is not the time to indulge your sad fantasy. For the love of God, this is supposed to be about Drew. Don't make it about you."

"Sandra, please, believe me—"

"Believe you? That's what you're asking?" Sandra spread her hands. "How? You insist that you see somebody who doesn't exist. Who can trust you?"

Taking Piper's hand, Sandra strode away across the lawn, leaving Harper to bear the glares of the crowd. The scrim of yellow light brightened painfully. Harper clenched her jaw and walked to her MINI Cooper. She climbed in and slammed the door.

Ghosts. Piper might be right. She started the engine and pulled out. In the rearview mirror, she watched the trees.

4

Harper drove down the hill out of the park, trying to quiet the pounding in her head.

Little forensic evidence had survived the fire. The flames destroyed fingerprints, blood evidence, and the building's CCTV cameras. Cartridge casings were recovered, sifted by crime scene techs with shaker trays, like archaeologists winnowing a dig for artifacts. The brass was largely melted. Nine millimeter ammunition, .40 caliber ammo, and magnum loads—at least four weapons were fired during the mayhem. Some witnesses insisted they saw one of the gunmen firing two-fisted. Others reported return fire from the target's bodyguards. Everybody agreed that the shooters had been firing at Arliss Bale, high roller, meth mogul, the guy who escaped without a scratch.

That was another reason the Westermans held Harper accountable for their son's death. Xenon had let a drug dealer through the door and served him champagne. *That kind of place.* Who would work there? *That kind of woman.*

The round that hit Drew went through and through. Forensics couldn't determine which of the deformed bullets they collected from the rubble had hit him. The fire had melted all ballistic markings.

She shifted and accelerated along the road. The coastal mountains rose behind her. Sunlight striped through the trees.

Four weapons at least. The truth, which the authorities refused to believe, was that there were three attackers.

Two gunmen had been killed. The third had slipped out in the chaos. Maybe he ran out the back door. Maybe he yanked off his mask and mixed with the fleeing crowd. But the man with the silver pistol, the one who shot Drew, had escaped.

And now she'd seen a figure in the trees who moved the way the firelit gunman had moved that night. Snapping, sliding, staring without a face.

She had seen him. No doubt.

The Westermans thought she was telling tales. Was she? She'd been raised by the world's tale-telling champ. Her mother's stories had reached Guinness Book territory. *"This guy at the gas station was such an asshole. Yelling at other drivers to move so he could fill up."* Harper had listened, fearful and wide-eyed, as the story expanded, until Lila was waving her arms, going, *"He fired at their feet and said, 'Drive.' When I told him to stop it, he made me dance a little, too."*

Later, Harper retold that story at a friend's house, her fingers twisting with worry. Her friend's mom said, "Honey, are you sure? Because there were no police calls about gunfire at the Shell station." Her friend's mom was a police dispatcher.

She had learned whose stories she could trust: nobody named Flynn.

At the bottom of the hill, she stopped behind a truck that was waiting to turn onto the highway. When she saw the driver through the back window, she honked and flashed her lights. A second later, she got out of the MINI and jogged to his pickup.

He lowered the driver's window. Beard and a trilby. "Yeah?"

"You were photographing the dedication ceremony," she said. "I need to see your photos."

He took more convincing but eventually picked up his camera. A minute later, scanning his camera roll, Harper said, "Stop."

On the display was a shot of the Westermans and, behind them, the grove of trees. In the trees, a figure lurked in the shadows. Harper's heartbeat kicked up.

"Can you zoom?" she said.

He tapped the screen. The figure came into crisp definition. Harper put a hand on the frame of the truck to steady herself. The man in the trees was lean and wiry. His face was too indistinct and shadowed to make out, but his hands were visible in the dappled sunlight. His right hand and arm bore a crawly black tattoo.

"Can you send me that photo?" Harper said.

The photographer looked at her askance. "The Westermans hired me."

"So can you?"

"What's this about?"

She already had her wallet out. "It's about twenty bucks. Forward me the photo."

A minute later, the photographer pulled away and Harper paced by the MINI, phone to her ear.

"Los Angeles County Sheriff's Department. How may I direct your call?"

"Detective Erika Sorenstam," Harper said.

Sorenstam wasn't in. Harper asked to be put through to another deputy. Two minutes later, she wished she'd simply hung up.

"Can you describe the person you saw?" the deputy asked.

"Vaguely." As soon as she said it, she knew she was going down the wrong path. She'd had enough experience describing suspects to law enforcement agencies before. "He was in the shadows."

"It was a male?"

"I couldn't see the person's face."

A pause. "Was this person behaving in a threatening manner?"

"Lurking in the shadows. At a memorial event for one of the victims of the Xenon shoot-out and fire. And when I approached, he disappeared."

"Ms. Flynn, you were also at the club the night of the attack, I understand?"

"Yes." She waited, and there was a significant pause on the line. The deputy, she feared, was reading some note in the file about her. "Please, will you log this in the file and pass the information on to Detective Sorenstam?"

"Of course, ma'am."

She ended the call. The sun felt hot. On the highway, two teenagers walked toward the beach, wearing board shorts, sucking on giant drinks.

Dead end. That's what everybody told her. That's what everybody called her attempts to clarify the events of the night of the attack. They were close to locking the doors on her and calling her an obsessive who couldn't accept the truth.

Maybe they were right. She got back in the car and pulled onto the road. She got another mile toward a pale brown lens of smog when her phone rang.

Piper. She pulled over and picked up.

"You set Mom off but good," Piper said.

"I want you to be careful," Harper said.

"It's the anniversary coming up. It's making everybody insane. But I was kidding about seeing ghosts."

"It doesn't have to be ghosts. There are people who get off on tragedy. They can get obsessed. Sometimes they believe they have a connection with people who are bereaved."

Piper quieted. "You think that guy we saw . . . ?"

"Your mom thinks I'm hallucinating monsters. But I want you to be careful if people contact you about Drew."

"I don't take candy from strangers."

"Seriously, Piper." She hated to scare a kid who'd been through hell in the last year. But she was scared herself. "Not just gamers or flamers or trolls. In real life, too. Not everybody who expresses sympathy has your interests at heart."

Piper sighed. "You need to take a vacation."

Harper's blood pressure had to be sky-high. Himalaya-high. "We all do, kid. But for now, I want you to be vigilant."

"You sound as determined as that sheriff's detective," Piper said. "His report reads like yours. Third shooter. Still out there. Watch out, everybody."

"Maybe that's a good thing."

"I love how you want to fight for Drew. But maybe it's time to take a break."

"Keep your eyes open." Harper dropped the phone and put the MINI in gear.

But instead of pulling out, she stared at traffic. *That sheriff's detective.* She knew the one Piper meant. Sorenstam's partner.

Santa Barbara was sixty-five miles up the coast. She could be there in just over an hour. She pulled a U-turn and headed north along the highway.

5

The tide was with the *Carolina Gail* as she drove toward Santa Barbara Harbor. Two pelicans glided above the water's surface. The sea was alive with rolling sunlight. Aiden Garrison stood at the bow and let the salt spray cool his face.

In the wheelhouse, his brother, Kieran, steered the boat around the breakwater. At the stern, Kieran's deckhand spoke on the phone to his girlfriend, telling her he'd be home soon. Their hold was full of bonito. Aiden was exhausted, and glad of it.

The flags along the breakwater snapped in the breeze. Beyond them the mountains, crisp and green in the clear air, muscled up to the shore. Aiden inhaled. He ached, head to toe. His hands were sore and callused. This was good. All systems were working. He could walk, and talk, and haul line, and banter with Kieran. Behind the sun-splintered windows of the wheelhouse, his older brother looked weatherworn and wise-eyed and, as always, quietly competent.

The thirty-five-foot *Carolina Gail* was Kieran's boat, Kieran's business, his mortgage payment and groceries and school clothes for the kids. It was Aiden's life preserver. He had no illusions about that. He was an amateur at the commercial fishing business. Kieran always thanked him for busting his ass to haul the day's catch. But Aiden knew: This was a stopgap. It was *He ain't heavy, he's my brother.*

They rounded the breakwater. Nearby, Stearns Wharf stuck into the harbor like a long black finger, pilings tarred and swollen with barnacles. Ahead, the ocean calmed to a gentle blue swell. Breakers shrugged onto the beach.

Kieran guided the *Carolina Gail* past a thicket of masts, reversed the throttles, and eased alongside the dock, where cranes and hoists and refrigerated trucks waited for the commercial fleet to unload.

She was standing on the sidewalk outside Brophy Brothers, watching.

The boat's bumpers nudged the wood. Aiden grabbed a mooring line. He checked his balance, as he always did now, and jumped onto the dock.

She waited while he tied off on cleats, fore and aft. He didn't need binocs, or a handshake, or to check her ID. Even two hundred feet away, he recognized her. Even a year away, even though he'd first seen her through gunfire and smoke and panic.

She was slender, almost coltish, in skinny jeans and a white blouse, her near-black hair pulled back in a loose ponytail but fighting free in the breeze. Her hands hung at her sides. Her eyes, glinting in the sun, were patient and watchful.

Kieran cut the engines and leaned out of the wheelhouse. "You know her?"

"Yes."

"Really?"

"Unquestionably."

Kieran raised an eyebrow. "So what are you waiting for?"

"You sure?"

"We're good. Go on."

Aiden touched the brim of his baseball cap in thanks, knowing that this was another sign his brother didn't really need him on the boat. When he finally reached the foot of the dock, she extended her hand.

Her skin was cool, her grip solid. "Detective Garrison."

"Ms. Flynn. It's Aiden." The rest was on hold.

"Can we talk?" she said.

"How did you find me?"

"Don't you want to know why I'm here?"

"I know. I just wanted to postpone the inevitable for at least thirty seconds."

He gestured at the path along the harbor and led her into the afternoon sunshine, trying not to limp.

⁓

"I read the investigative report." She sat at the sidewalk table and tapped her fingers on its surface. "I read your statement."

He eased into a chair, holding the table with both hands. "I read yours."

"As for how I found you, you're in the phone book. Your next-door neighbor told me you're working on the *Carolina Gail*. 'Getting your legs back underneath you,' she said."

"Bless her talkative self."

She seemed to pay no attention to his caution with movement, or to the care he took to line up every step like a target. She wasn't eyeing him like a specimen. But she was eyeing him. He didn't know what to make of her yet.

Slow breaths. She was a fellow survivor, not a trigger. He smelled the whiff of smoke and burning plastic, but confronted it. *It's not real.*

"Why did you track me down?" he said.

"Because you told the investigators there was a third shooter at Xenon and that he got away. You told them exactly what I did. That this guy had a silver semiautomatic. He threw the Molotov cocktail and the magnesium flare. He fired the shot that hit Drew." She breathed. "You saw him. I read it. I read your statement a hundred times."

"I dictated that statement eleven months ago. Why are you here today?"

She pushed her drink aside. Her skin was pale and her features fine, but she wasn't delicate—a frame of taut cabling seemingly ran beneath the soft white blouse. Her gaze seemed a thousand years old.

"Today, Drew's parents dedicated a memorial at Clearview Park. I saw him there."

"Him."

"The man who doesn't exist."

Flames reflected in a gas mask, hood pulled up like the Reaper. Aiden leaned forward. "Why do you think it was him?"

She laid her phone on the table and showed him a photo. He was staring at it, nearly hypnotized, when she opened an Altoids tin. Inside were three cigarette butts.

"Found them where he'd been standing. Maybe they contain DNA," she said.

He set that idea aside for the moment. "This photo."

"The tattoo on his right hand."

He looked up. "I didn't see that tattoo."

"I know. You saw him from the back. I saw him from the front." She tapped the photo. "That's him."

"And nobody will listen to you."

"I hope you will."

"I will. But it won't do any good."

"Why not?"

"Because I'm the guy nobody listens to anymore. Aiden Garrison, head case."

6

Harper's expression remained searching. "If you're a head case, so am I."

"I doubt that."

"You were there. You saw him," she said. "You're here now, and you still agree that you saw him."

Her eyes were blue, bright, piercing. Gulls wheeled overhead. The salt air was so sharp, Aiden could taste it on his tongue.

"I know you were injured. Bad," she said. "I know it didn't affect your eyesight."

His heart beat heavily in his chest.

"Did it?" she said.

"You're blunt."

"The internal limiter on my mouth blew out after the sheriff's department told me I was imagining things. On this topic, I have no inside voice."

She was deadpan. He set down his mug.

"I saw him. I had him in my sights. But the crowd was running between us, and I had no shot," he said. "Then the floor opened up. Drew and I and those two men . . ."

"I know."

Along with Drew Westerman, two other civilians had been killed when the floor collapsed.

"Sheer luck that I was ten feet away from them," he said. "The heaviest debris missed me."

He kept his voice flat and mentally repeated the mantra he had learned during recovery: *Remember it without reliving it.*

The collapsing floor had pitched him into a void. He had tried to roll, calling on his combat jump experience. But training was useless against walls and beams and splintering floorboards. He hit and broke his shoulder and elbow and collarbone and four ribs and his left leg. One rib shattered and punctured his right lung. The building's CO_2 fire suppression system had kept the flames from reaching him. But smoke inhalation and internal bleeding did a crapload of additional damage. And there was the head injury.

"I got bunged up pretty solidly," he said. "I didn't see the shooter escape."

"I understand. I'm glad you're on the mend."

"Getting there."

Two weeks in ICU. Six more in the hospital. A season. A life, a sloughing off of one skin, leaving him raw and shiny, unready for the outside world. He didn't tell her that the finish line forever seemed to recede, always out of reach.

"How about you?" he said.

She attempted a smile. "I was ten inches luckier than you. Minor injuries."

He had seen what she was made of and knew she didn't need his problems on her shoulders. That night, as gunfire tore through Xenon, she had forsaken her chance to escape. She could have dropped behind the bar and shielded herself before running out the staff exit. Instead, she went over the top and risked herself to try and rescue one of the wounded.

She was a hero. He couldn't bitch to a hero.

"Why do you think the person you saw in the trees today was the third shooter? Besides having a right-hand tattoo."

She breathed and spoke dispassionately. "I know he was just a shadow, but . . . the way he moved. The—"

"You know the gunman was male?"

"Heavy shoulders, slim hips with boxers exposed above sagging blue jeans. Plus, he had a thick line of hair running up his stomach."

"Fair enough."

"And that night, the strut. The black hoodie—I think one of the other men wore green. That hand with the tattoo, holding a silver handgun. It caught the light." She looked at him. "Then I saw you behind him, coming toward me through the crowd. I *saw* you. I . . ." A breath. "I thought—*please let him get the guy.*"

She put her hands between her knees.

Aiden said, "That's the guy I saw. But we won't convince the sheriff's department. I told the department all of this. They took my statement in the hospital, as soon as I was able to talk."

"You're a detective. A sworn deputy. An experienced investigator."

He exhaled as though the air was being pushed from his lungs by a heavy hand.

"What do you think he was doing at the memorial?" he said.

"You believe me?"

"What do you think he was doing there?" he said again, gently.

She took a second. "Watching." Another pause. "Stalking."

"For what reason?"

"I don't know."

Her voice remained strong, her eyes clear.

"What do you want me to do?" he said.

"Back me up. Help me get reinforcements. Because that guy's out there."

"And he killed your boyfriend."

"He killed my boyfriend." She colored. "And he's *back*. He's sniffing around people who lost loved ones in the attack, and . . ." She pressed her fingers to her eyes. "What the *hell* was he doing there? What if he wants to target survivors? What if he's some psycho who's been biding his time before picking off people who made it out alive? Jesus, does he want to hurt Drew's family?"

"The Xenon attack wasn't random. They sprayed gunfire, but they had targets."

She said, "You have to have an idea of who it is."

He shook his head. "I don't. And the LASD doesn't either. And there's no way to tie the bullet that hit your boyfriend to . . ."

She flinched.

"Sorry." He reminded himself that she was a victim, not a cop. "There's no way to match rounds fired to the weapons recovered at the crime scene. The barrels were heat damaged. They couldn't be test-fired."

"I need your help to convince the sheriff's department I'm not hallucinating. I know you're on medical leave, but . . ."

"You didn't drive sixty miles to ask me to be your sidekick. What do you want? Revenge?"

She colored.

"Do you?" he said.

"I want this bastard found and arrested," she said. "He was there. Watching us. I want him caught before he does something bad."

He stood and walked to the counter at the snack bar and refilled his coffee mug. When he returned, he said, "I've seen him."

She stilled with surprise. "When?"

He held on for a second and finally decided: Screw it.

"I've seen him several times since that night. I've been absolutely convinced."

"Are you serious?"

"Dead. Once, I was sure I saw the shooter in a crowd near the docks here." He gestured at the harbor.

She knew something was off. "You haven't told the police, have you?"

"They'd say what other people have told me: It's a delusion."

"Because you were so badly injured?"

"Because it's true." He smiled now, without humor. "I see ghosts."

The clatter of plates grated on the man's ears. The waitress was clearing the next table at the sidewalk café, piling plates one on top of the next, cheap thick china that scritched and plinked. Seagulls hovered overhead, shrieking for scraps. The sky was hard with sunshine. The palm trees along the boulevard gave no shade. He cupped his hand over the display on his phone and flipped through the photos he'd shot at Clearview Park.

So many sad pandas. The photos suffered from being shot deep in the trees, but he'd *snapped snapped snapped* and captured every face at the memorial. Rich people. Pretty people. Scared people. All boohooing, including Mama and Papa Westerman, who spent the family's banking money to dedicate a rock to their son.

The waitress scraped half-eaten fries into a busboy's bucket. At the next table, a couple held hands. Their twining fingers looked like sea anemones, soft and wriggling. The whine of traffic saved him from hearing their smiley smug talk.

Nobody from the L.A. Sheriff's Department had attended the dedication. Their investigation was closed, done, shoved in a drawer. The cops had looked away.

They wouldn't look back again.

The field was open at last, unobstructed and ripe for picking. Finally, finally. He sent a text. Event was badge free, target rich.

Picking up his knife, he poked the last of his sausage onto the point and flicked it onto the sidewalk. The seagulls descended. Before they could nab the sausage, the dog stirred. It lolled over and snaffled the tidbit from the concrete.

The smiley smug couple glared at him. The woman's mouth went prissy. She pointed to a sign on the restaurant wall: PLEASE DO NOT FEED THE BIRDS.

"This is Sambo's, not the sultan's palace," he said.

"The gulls are a problem," she said.

"I'm not feeding the gulls. I'm feeding my dog."

She scowled. He scrolled, examining each photo. He recognized six people who had been at Xenon that night. Staff, customers, even the drummer from the band. What were they, bored? Did they like wallowing in grief? He didn't get it—why people kept coming back for more.

But if they wanted more, he'd give it to them. Nobody was looking at the Xenon fire anymore.

Except.

His final photo showed her—lots of brown hair, dark glasses, white blouse, no bartender's apron today but yeah, her—holding on to baby sis Piper Westerman and staring into the shadows where he had stood.

He took his cigarettes from his pocket, tapped one out, and stuck it between his lips.

Prissy Mouth said, "You have got to be kidding."

He paused and pulled the cigarette from his lips. She smirked and returned to dabbing at her food.

He grunged a ten-dollar bill from his jeans pocket and dropped it onto the remains of his fried egg. He took a last look at the photo on his phone. Center of the frame, she was staring straight at him but didn't see. Just like she didn't see him now, a hundred yards away, across the wide boulevard and the moored boats at the Santa Barbara harbor. He took a second to watch her and the sheriff's detective huddling over coffee at a dockside table.

He stood up, whistling at Eagle. The dog slowly roused itself, haunches rippling as it raised all its hundred pounds to its feet. He stuck the cigarette between his lips again. Prissy Mouth turned, but he said, "I'm going," and waited until she and the man stopped staring. People always lowered their eyes eventually.

He grabbed a crust of toast from his plate and flicked it into the air above their table. It landed between them. The seagulls dove on it, squalling and biting. The woman shrieked. The man shoved back, waving a napkin like a panicky matador.

He took one more look across the boulevard. She hadn't moved. The brunette still huddled toward the sheriff's detective, her hair witching in the breeze.

He snapped his fingers at the dog and strolled away to the sound of beating wings.

7

Harper gave Aiden the deadpan tone and the piercing gaze. "Want to explain?"

He stood up. "Let's walk."

She left her coffee. He led her along the edge of the harbor, past the commercial fleet, toward the sailboat marina.

"There's a reason the sheriff's department and fire department and ATF won't listen to me," Aiden said. "And it's not because I broke my leg in three places."

She glanced at his leg. *Don't limp*—the orthopedist, the physical therapists, and his mother all hectored him about that. Limping, favoring an injury, could make his condition worse. Could unbalance him in other ways.

Too late.

"I'm back to eighty percent, physically. Eighty-five percent on a good day."

"Great. But?"

"But physical recovery is one thing. A traumatic brain injury is something else."

"What happened?"

"Coup-contrecoup injuries."

"Meaning?"

"The head comes to a sudden stop. The brain slams into the skull. Then it bounces back and hits the opposite side."

"I know the term. I meant—what happened? Debris hit you?"

"I hit the debris. A floor joist."

"Blunt force trauma." Her head was down, eyes on the sidewalk, hands in her jeans pockets. "Excuse me if I seem ignorant. You have use of all four limbs. You can see. You can talk. You can hold a conversation and have a sense of humor, or at least you're trying to."

"It could have been much worse. I know that." Then he realized. "I know I'm among the fortunate. And I'm sorry for your loss."

She glanced up at him. "Thanks."

"I apologize if I sounded self-pitying. I shouldn't. Your boyfriend's gone. I'm here."

"So am I."

She raised her chin and waited, while he got it.

"Understood," he said.

They walked on. Yeah, he was Mr. Lucky—two Afghan tours with nothing worse than insect bites, then six healthy years with the sheriff's department. Until.

"TBI can screw you up without you knowing it at first. It doesn't always look like a stroke or paralysis. It . . ." *Talk.* "Sometimes it manifests as changes in personality. Issues with anger and impulsivity. Depends on which part of the brain is damaged, and how tethered and healthy you were before the injury."

Traffic lazed past along the seafront on Cabrillo Boulevard. On the beach, kids ran along the wet sand near the surf line. Harper listened with attentive reserve.

"For months, I felt like I'd been knocked sideways through a wall, into a dimension that ran on a different frequency. I had double vision, tinnitus, problems with my memory."

"Memory. That's why they discounted what you told them?" she said.

"One reason. The other reason didn't manifest right away. When it did, nobody understood it. Least of all, me."

"Aiden, just get down to it. What's going on?"

"It's called Fregoli syndrome."

"What's that?"

"I have a problem with facial recognition."

Her lips slowly parted. "You can't recognize people?"

"Ninety-nine point nine percent of the time, I recognize people just fine. You, my brother, the guy who served us coffee. But my brain got beat up and now sometimes it misfires," he said. "It glitches. And I think that a person I'm looking at is actually somebody else."

She looked at him sharply. "Excuse me?"

"Yeah. It's also known as the Fregoli delusion."

He waited for a response, but she simply looked concerned. "It's named after a quick-change artist, Leopoldo Fregoli. It leads you to believe that the people you're looking at"—he gestured at the beach-front boulevard—"are actually other people in disguise. A patient could see his father and think it's actually his wife disguised as his father."

He'd read the literature. Looking for a cure, an explanation, an escape. *Patients with Fregoli syndrome think that the people around them are capable of changing their appearance, dress, and gender in a few instants, with only nearly imperceptible clues to their real identity.*

"And this happens to you?" she said.

"It does."

"You seem calm about it."

"I'm not." Not calm at all. Almost never. "I'm good at putting on a front myself."

"Aiden, I'm sorry."

He nodded. "Thanks."

"So the authorities dismissed your entire statement in retrospect. Jackasses."

"Appreciate that."

"Did you see the third shooter or not?" she said.

"I did."

She squeezed his arm. "All I need to hear."

He kept walking, his throat tightening. He forced himself not to hesitate. *You're going for it: Just go.*

"I saw the same man you did. No doubt. That's not the problem." He blinked at the sun. "The problem is, at unpredictable moments, I can become convinced that a random person—a neighbor, or somebody crossing the street—is the shooter."

"Jesus God."

"It's an injury to the temporal lobe. My wiring sees faces and tries to map them into familiar-unfamiliar . . ."

"Identify Friend or Foe."

He nodded. "And sometimes it blows a circuit."

"What's your status?"

He let out a non-laugh. "I feel like I'm in *The Thing*. Like maybe next time, I'm going to see my nemesis in the face of a dog." He glanced at the sailboard masts in the marina. "It's treatable. To an extent. It rarely resolves."

"Define *treatable*."

"Kept in check." He eyed her. "Most of the time. They're still dinking with my meds."

Cars drove past, windows down, hip-hop thumping. She said, "What a truckload of shit to get dumped on you."

"More kind words. You were raised to say thoughtful things no matter how bitter the situation, I'll bet."

"I was brought up without a single concern for manners. And the Navy taught me to tell it like I see it."

He faced her. "So what do you see?"

She turned to him. "You're telling me this injury will disqualify you from returning to duty."

"The department feels insecure about issuing me a firearm, when at any moment I might decide that the kid checking my groceries is actually a killer in disguise."

She didn't laugh. He looked at the sun flashing off the ocean.

"I'm still on medical leave. But my job as a detective . . ." He spread his hands, as though sand were running through them.

His colleagues were withdrawing. Even his allies and friends. They thought he was off-kilter at best, ruined at worst. His career was in the shitter.

"That's why the department excluded so much from your statement," she said.

"They only trust the testimony that was corroborated by my partner."

Her hands clenched. He recognized the signals: frustration, even rage.

"They might have believed me—if there'd been any physical evidence. But you know the score. No forensics. No video."

The CCTV cameras at Xenon had burned. So had the hard drives that stored recorded video. Hundreds of people in the club had been carrying cell phones, and the cops had recovered dozens of photos from them, but only a few photos had been taken after the shooting started, by people in the heart of the panic. No photos captured the shooters entering the club. Certainly, none showed a masked shooter leaving. He was a ghost. Smoke. Just . . . nothing.

"Aiden, he's *back*," she said. "We have to find a way to convince the department to listen."

He started to shake his head, but she said, "When did you first see the third shooter? How did you identify the guy that night? Tell me everything."

"Detective Sorenstam and I followed Arliss Bale to Xenon, surveilling him. Sorenstam saw a car drop off some guys by the alley. It felt wrong."

"How many guys?"

"She saw two. I know there could have been a third she didn't see. Doesn't matter—I went to check but found no sign of the car or the guys. So Sorenstam and I went in the front door. Five seconds later, the shooting started."

Harper's hair lifted in the sea breeze. Her eyes were hard.

"I saw him through the crowd, advancing in a straight line," Aiden said. The guy had been walking, while everybody else was running, pushing, screaming. "He raised his weapon in the direction of the main exit. It was jammed with people. He was almost strutting. Movie gang-banger style. You know?"

She lifted her arm as though she was holding a gun.

"Exactly. Up on his toes like a boxer, the pistol turned sideways in his hand. When he raised his arm, the sweatshirt rode up his back. It exposed about six inches of skin around his waistline. The tattoo stood out," he said.

"Tattoo?"

"In gothic script. The letters ran sideways up his spine. Like a word climbing his back. They were three, four inches tall."

"Could you read it?" she said. Her eagerness was palpable.

"I only glimpsed it. A portion of a word in black ink: *E-R-O*."

She didn't react.

No, that wasn't right. She stilled so completely that it was the opposite of a reaction. It was a negative, a disappearance somehow.

"Harper?"

She was there, but absent. Her face had paled. Even her blue eyes had dimmed.

"Harper, what's wrong?"

She turned to bolt. He shot out a hand and grabbed her arm.

"Hey."

She tried to pull away. He found his balance, got both hands on her, and said, "Stop. What's wrong?"

Her shoulders were tight and shaking. He held on.

"Not cool. What's going on?" he said.

She was as white as flour, breathing hard. "The tattoo. It doesn't say *E-R-O*."

"What?"

"It says *ZERO*."

"You saw it?" he said.

She shook her head. "No. I mean yes."

He held on tight. "What? You saw the tattoo and only now re-member?"

"I've seen it before. Not that night." She blinked, tears brimming. "I know who it is."

8

Harper shivered under the warm sun, held in place by Aiden Garrison's hands on her arms. She shouldn't have hesitated. She should have spoken without prompting, or else run, hard. She shouldn't have made him force it out of her. That was a mistake. That blew her cover. And if there was anything she knew, it was to maintain her cover. Button it down. Head to toe.

"You know who the gunman is?" he said.

He held her still, Mr. Headcase, eyeing her as though she was the one who had gone bug-nut crazy. Except he didn't seem like a head case. He seemed like a cool guy with a pitch-black sense of humor, sharp and tough and good-looking, a solid cop, a man who seemed compassionate and smart. The only man who had believed her. And now this.

She nodded. "His name is Eddie Azerov."

His pulse beat visibly in his neck. "You know him, personally?"

"We went to high school together." Her throat tightened. *Tell him.* "Azerov—his nickname's Zero. Yeah, I know him."

"High school?" he said.

Harper wanted to pull away but felt as if she'd been stung numb. "In China Lake, up in the high desert."

"Who was he to you? Your neighbor, boyfriend, what?" Aiden said.

Revulsion nearly gagged her. "Not a boyfriend, never."

"Who, then?" He cut a glance at her. "Identify Friend or Foe."

A harsh laugh escaped her throat. And Aiden thought Zero was *his* nemesis?

His gaze cooled. "School bully?"

"For starters."

"He hurt you?" Aiden said.

Her cheeks heated. "I wasn't the only one."

"You knew this guy. Face-to-face. For four years in school?"

"Yes. Are you asking me whether he recognized me that night at Xenon? I hope not. God, I hope not."

"You've seen that tattoo."

She nodded. Her mind wheeled, trying to put it together.

Aiden stared at her. "Do you think it was a coincidence, Azerov being there that night?"

The sidewalk seemed soft beneath her feet. *Zero.* If he was the third shooter, the attack on Xenon hadn't been bad luck and trouble. It wasn't the shit end of the universe randomly dumping on Drew, and Aiden, and everybody else who had suffered that night.

She shook her head. "If you saw Eddie Azerov, then it was no coincidence. Zero and I have a history."

"You think the attack had something to do with you?" he said. "Why?"

She opened her mouth, but no words would come.

"What are you scared of?" he said.

At that, she straightened. *Pull your shit together. All the hell the way together.*

"Chaos," she said. "There's a pit, and it's got a thin covering on it, but it's there, and I have a feeling I just tore a gash in it. I don't want to fall in. You either."

His eyes were serious, but his mouth looked wry. "Ms. Flynn, I fell a long time ago." He nodded at her car. "We're going to the sheriff's department. Come on."

9

In the lobby of the Lost Hills Sheriff's Station in Agoura, Harper paced while Aiden spoke to the civilian staffer at the front counter. She bit her nails.

He hurt you?

Zero went about his rages silently. If you were quick, you'd see him, a flick of motion as he approached from behind. If not, you just heard his voice in your ear. Like that day when she was fifteen, and he came so close that his breath brushed her neck and his words clicked against her skin.

"Make your life simple. Do what we tell you."

So close, too close, his teeth visible. Eddie had tilted his head and tried to poke his index finger into the stitches in her scalp. She jerked away. Her head thundered and nausea coiled through her, from the concussion and from Eddie's ultimatum.

His eyes were flat. "Your choice."

But the figure behind him had moved into the light and circled her, slowly. She knew it wasn't a choice at all.

Now Aiden walked over. "It'll be a minute. Chill. You're acting like you're in a cage."

She jammed her hands into her jeans pockets. The station, which covered northwest L.A. County and Malibu, was bright, airy, and spacious. Outside, golden hills rolled into the distance. But she felt hemmed in. She sat down on a blue plastic chair, crossed her legs, and jangled her foot. He watched her.

"Aiden?"

A woman strode into the lobby. She was blond, wearing black slacks and a tan V-neck sweater. She was the woman who had been with Aiden at Xenon.

His face became studiously neutral. "Thanks for making time."

"Not a problem." She extended her hand to Harper. "Detective Erika Sorenstam. Come on back."

At her desk in the detectives' pen, Sorenstam said, "I got your voice mail, Ms. Flynn. And the photo you sent, of the man in the trees at the memorial service."

Aiden said, "Harper wanted me to see the photo, possibly confirm the ID."

Sorenstam picked up a pencil and leaned back. The pose should have looked thoughtful but instead reminded Harper of a slingshot being pulled back—as if Sorenstam was ready to launch herself. Skyward, maybe, like an ejector seat. She seemed cool and put together, and her eyes, pale gray, looked like glass. One-way glass—she was assessing Aiden as he spoke, from behind an emotional screen.

He measured his words, an experienced cop relaying information that might become evidence. But Sorenstam was resisting it. A block of concrete seemed to weigh on Harper's chest.

Zero. The idea that both she and Eddie Azerov had ended up at Xenon that night by sheer coincidence was a shiny bauble she wanted to grab. But she couldn't.

"Fail, and Zero will find you."

She hadn't failed, not at first. They found her anyway, looking at the sky as if it were an avenue to freedom. As they pulled her onto a side street, Zero had leaned close and said, "Nobody's gonna help you."

In the detectives' pen, the air conditioner rattled. Sorenstam continued eyeing Aiden from behind her smoked-glass gaze. Harper jangled her foot again, stewing over something Aiden had said earlier. *Sorenstam saw a car drop off some guys by the alley. It felt wrong.*

That night, nobody was supposed to get into Xenon without a ticket or a swipe card—and without being searched for weapons. But the gunmen didn't break in or storm past the security checkpoint.

How did they gain entry? Several possibilities: They came in unarmed past security and grabbed weapons they'd stashed in the club earlier. They came in armed, and security missed it. Or they came in through a back door—such as the staff exit into the alley. From Aiden's description, that was almost certainly what had happened.

The club's back doors should have been locked. Perhaps an employee had opened the door from the inside and let them in—but nobody thought that. Perhaps an employee had propped open a door while going out for a smoke, and the shooters had taken advantage of it. Or perhaps the door had been unlocked by an employee swipe card.

She saw it again: Drew, asking to borrow her card. *Just for a minute. I left my camera in the car. I don't want to have to go through security again.*

And she had given it to him. He'd been gone ten minutes. Ten.

Had he forgotten to pull the door closed when he came back in? Had he left it open?

On some level, she had wondered this all along. But she'd never let the thought form fully. Until now, when she knew: They got in through the door Drew had used only minutes earlier.

Did he know they were coming? Did he have something to do with . . .
She shifted. *No.*

Her swipe card. An oily fear seeped through her: If the building hadn't burned, if the data from the door lock had survived, she would have been implicated.

The light slanted through the window behind Sorenstam. The woman's blond hair looked like a corona. Her gray eyes were as liquid as a slick of mercury. Harper locked her fingers together, to hold herself still.

Aiden said, "The tattoo—Harper recognized it from my description."

Despite the radiant sunlight, Sorenstam seemed etched with dark edges. Her liquid gaze slid to Harper.

"Is that so?" she said.

"Aiden described the partial tattoo he saw that night. I recognized it. The entire tattoo reads ZERO."

"You've seen it before."

"Yes."

"I can't recall any mention of it in your statement."

"I didn't see it that night. The shooter was coming toward me. The tattoo's on his back."

Sorenstam rolled the pencil between her fingers and finally tossed it on her desk. "I know about Zero."

Harper straightened. "How?"

"Eddie Azerov? He's a known lowlife."

"Nobody involved in the investigation has mentioned his name or linked him to the attack," Harper said. "If you had—oh, my God. I could have told you a year ago that I knew who he was."

Sorenstam sat forward. "How is it that you know Azerov, Ms. Flynn?"

Aiden said, "They went to the same high school."

Sorenstam looked at him.

Harper said, "Detective, have you known since the beginning that he was involved?"

Slowly, Sorenstam turned to Harper. "He's not the gunman."

"Say what?" Harper said.

"Eddie Azerov was not at Xenon the night it burned. Two shooters entered the club that night. Both of them died. Neither of them was Azerov."

"Because he escaped."

"Ms. Flynn, you are, I am afraid, mistaken."

Sorenstam's voice was flat, clear, and definite. A bolus of anger swelled in Harper's chest.

"I'm not mistaken."

"Azerov wasn't there. I'm sorry you've come all this way and that you've brought Detective Garrison along to present your theory, but it's incorrect."

"Why are you dismissing me?" Harper said.

"I'm not. I take you at your word that you know Azerov and would recognize the tattoo should you see it. But you didn't."

"Aiden did." She pointed a thumb at him.

Sorenstam continued as if Harper hadn't spoken. "I will make a note that you reported seeing an unidentified person lurking at the memorial. We'll keep the photo on file. But we can't use it as evidence that the man at the memorial was also at Xenon. There's no evidence from Xenon to compare the photo *to*."

"Aiden saw the tattoo. A tattoo that was not found on either of the dead shooters."

Aiden said, "Harper, stop."

She turned to him. "Why?"

His face was crestfallen. "It has nothing to do with you."

"It has everything to do with me."

He looked briefly at Sorenstam. His eyes seemed to sink into his skull. "You could have collared Azerov and brought him here in shackles and it wouldn't make a difference to Detective Sorenstam." He stood up. "Let's go."

Baffled, Harper grabbed his hand. "No. What's the problem?"

Sorenstam said, "The problem, I'm afraid, is that Aiden—Detective Garrison—has inadvertently misled you."

He turned to Sorenstam. The look on his face could have cut rock from a cliff face. The shine in Sorenstam's liquid eyes dulled.

She said, "Detective Garrison knew about Eddie Azerov's existence before the shoot-out at Xenon."

Harper's lips parted.

Sorenstam's gaze drifted to Aiden. "Right?"

He didn't answer.

The dark edges on Sorenstam's face grew sharper. "Azerov was a suspect in an armed robbery eighteen months ago. Sporting goods store—the robber took six grand in cash and a dozen Remington shotguns."

Harper held on to his arm. "Aiden?"

He shook his head. "Stop."

Sorenstam said, "He's confused, Ms. Flynn."

"So am I," Harper said.

"Erika," Aiden said.

"He is misconstruing what he saw at Xenon. Because you conjured a demon where there is none," Sorenstam said.

Harper said, "You think he imagined seeing Zero that night?"

Aiden said, "Erika. Let it go."

Sorenstam had stopped looking at him. "He didn't see Zero that night. He's imagining it *right now*. And it's because you planted the idea in his mind today."

"But I didn't," Harper said.

He pulled free of Harper's grasp. "Enough." He raised his hands and backed away from the desk. "I'm done."

Harper and Sorenstam both said, "Aiden."

He turned and strode across the room and out the door.

Harper stood to follow.

"Wait," Sorenstam said. "You need to give him some space."

"That was cold."

"I mean a lot of space. As in, put some distance between you."

Harper's pulse thumped in her ears. "Are you deliberately trying to sound cruel? The man has a traumatic brain injury. And he just drove sixty miles to offer you evidence in an unsolved murder."

Sorenstam got to her feet. "Ms. Flynn, I know that you were close to Drew Westerman. I understand your confusion and your wish that there was something more we could do in this case. But going down the rabbit hole hand in hand with Aiden Garrison is a bad idea."

"There's no rabbit hole. I didn't plant the idea that he saw the tattoo. He told you about it a year ago."

"Yes. While he was hospitalized, he told us he'd seen a partial tattoo. He was severely injured and heavily drugged. He told us all kinds of things."

"Such as?"

"You need to trust me on this. I've known Detective Garrison for four years. You've known him for four hours."

"I know he's trying to do the right thing," Harper said.

"Do you know that he's paranoid?"

"So am I. I bet you are, too."

"I'm not joking," Sorenstam said. "And you'd do well to pay attention to people who have superior information. Or are you an inveterate kitten-rescuer?"

Harper's vision pulsed. She clenched her hands at her sides to keep from taking a swing at the woman. "Aiden told me about the Fregoli syndrome. That's not paranoia, it's a temporal lobe injury."

"More precisely, it's a diffuse lesion of the fusiform gyrus—the portion of the right temporal lobe that deals with facial recognition. And it's not the only consequence of his TBI."

A cold finger seemed to scrape down Harper's back. She remembered what Aiden had said earlier. *Sometimes it manifests as changes in personality. Issues with anger and impulsivity.*

"You're telling me he has other serious issues?" she said.

"I'm telling you who Aiden is." Sorenstam lowered her voice. "He perceives threats everywhere he turns. Maybe because he spent the last decade doing jobs where distrusting other people kept him alive. Add a catastrophic head injury, and everything that was burning beneath the surface erupted."

Harper shook her head. "No. That . . ."

"He got hurt. It unlocked a cage." Sorenstam picked up the pencil again, seemingly to orient herself. "You need to see something."

From her desk drawer, she took a thumb drive. Tersely, she loaded it into her computer and brought up a video.

And Harper understood.

10

Sorenstam queued up the video and turned her screen so Harper could watch.

It was soundless, a black-and-white video that showed a corner of the detectives' pen and Sorenstam's desk. Harper looked up. The camera was tucked near the ceiling.

The date and time ran at the bottom of the video. Eight months ago. A man sat at the desk beside Sorenstam's, white shirt, dark tie, holster on his belt. Nearby, another detective, heavyset, with a mustache, was on the phone, taking notes.

On-screen, Sorenstam walked past the camera, wearing a slim skirt and heels, talking casually to somebody. A second later, Aiden walked into view.

Even with the middling-quality video, his recovery clearly wasn't very far along. He looked thinner. His face was drawn. He held his left arm carefully, close to his side, and walked slowly, eyes on his path. He touched the back of a chair to preserve his balance. Serial tasks, not multitasking. Not like he was now.

She wondered if she should go and find him.

Sorenstam said, "He was scheduled to come back to work part-time, ride a desk while he got his strength back. This was a day he stopped by, just wanted to see people, show his face."

On the video, Sorenstam leaned against her desk, chatting with Aiden. The detective at the next desk stood to shake Aiden's hand. Bracing himself as though he were on the deck of a pitching boat, Aiden let go of the chair, smiling. *"Good to be here. Great to see you, too, you bastard."*

As they shook hands, Aiden glanced at the guy on the phone.

Harper wasn't prepared for what happened next.

Aiden turned sharply to Sorenstam. Said something, and nodded at the guy on the phone, jerking his chin. Sorenstam said, clearly, *"What?"*

Aiden pointed at the guy on the phone and called to him. *"Hey."*

The detective whose hand he'd been shaking took a step back, looking uncertain. Sorenstam raised her hands—a calming gesture. *"Whoa."*

Again, Aiden called: *"Hey."*

The detective on the phone glanced up from his call. Aiden launched himself past Sorenstam, straight at him, and attacked.

Harper touched her fingertips to her forehead. "Oh no."

Aiden shoved the guy's chair back from the desk, on its rollers. The man pinwheeled for balance, but Aiden had height and momentum. He tackled the guy to the floor. He was yelling. Yelling directly in the guy's face. He was completely, corrosively, unequivocally losing his shit.

The detective and Aiden wrestled on the floor. Sorenstam waded in. Her face was lit with confusion and embarrassed horror. She grabbed Aiden's collar. The third detective pried Aiden loose. The guy from the phone sat confused on the carpet, saying, *"What the hell?"*

Aiden had doubled in pain, but he pointed at the guy he'd dumped on the floor.

"Him," he yelled.

Now Sorenstam stopped the video. "He thought Detective Perez was the third shooter. He kept shouting, 'It's him. It's the guy.'"

"Oh, God," Harper said.

"He was completely convinced. Nothing we said, nothing we did, could dissuade him."

"What made him think . . ."

"It was a hallucination. Fregoli is part of a constellation of disorders called delusional misidentification syndromes. You just saw what that means. His brain throws a gear, and he loses control," she said. "He thought the shooter had wormed his way in here to destroy evidence and ruin our investigation."

Sorenstam stared at the frozen image on the computer screen. "Did he tell you?"

"He tried to explain." Shock and fear and empathy pinballed through her. "That was . . ." Awful. Goddamn horrible to see. "Painful."

She tried to shove everything back behind the wall. "But it doesn't negate what I've been telling you about the shooter who escaped. Aiden and I both know it was Eddie Azerov."

"You don't understand, do you?" Sorenstam said. "Detective Garrison didn't simply mistake another detective for the third shooter. That's not his only delusion. His delusion is *that the third shooter exists.*"

A weight seemed to press on Harper's shoulders.

Sorenstam said, "There is no third shooter. Gunman Zero is an illusion."

Harper wanted to say more, but Sorenstam crossed her arms and planted her feet wide. She became a wall built of conviction and anger. And Harper knew that nothing good came of arguing with cops who were fueled by rage and certainty.

Still, she straightened her shoulders and stood as calmly as she could.

Finally, Sorenstam said, "I am truly sorry that you have been swept up in all of this. This year must have been difficult for you."

"Kind of you."

Sorenstam heard the chill tone that slipped between Harper's teeth.

"And I will make sure your report of an unidentified man at the memorial is noted in the investigative file. But you need to ease down. Getting Aiden mixed up in this will not help either of you."

Investigative file? The case was closed. They had no intention of moving forward, not even if she drove into them from behind with a battering ram.

Sorenstam was waiting for her to leave. Instead, from her bag Harper took the Altoids tin containing the cigarette butts she'd collected at the park.

"He dropped them. They'll have his DNA. If Eddie Azerov is on file . . ."

Sorenstam's face said she wasn't about to spend lab time and departmental funds testing the cigarettes. Harper paused and dug deeper in her purse. She took out an artifact. It was dirty, as was the lanyard on which it hung. She held it out to Sorenstam.

"What's this?" Sorenstam said.

"My employee swipe card from Xenon."

Sorenstam took it. "Why?"

"After the fire, I went back to work. For one day. To prove I could do it," she said. "They gave everybody new swipe cards but never collected our old ones. So many were lost or damaged in the fire, they never bothered."

"And?"

She breathed. This was a risk. Once Sorenstam started looking, she might peel back the layers.

"I know you suspect that the shooters accessed Xenon through a back entrance. If they did, how? Did they have a key, or a confederate, or dumb luck? So check my card out."

Sorenstam held the lanyard carefully, as if it might contain a virus. "You think it was used to open the door for the shooters?"

"I have no idea."

"How can that be? Was the card out of your possession?"

"Just check it out. If there's any evidence that my card was used to access the building . . ."

"Why have you waited until now to come forward with this?"

"Because the final report was only recently issued. It concludes that the investigation could not determine how the shooters got in. But today, Aiden told me you saw a car drop people by the back alley, just before the shooting started."

"No evidence suggests that the shooters accessed the building with an employee's swipe card." Sorenstam looked severe. "You're telling me different."

"I'm saying my card is damaged, but maybe you can pull data off of it."

"Why are you doing this? Did you let the shooters into Xenon?"

"No."

"Then why would your card have data showing that they used it to access the club?"

Drew's face appeared before her. For a second, she considered telling the truth. She balked.

"I'm offering it to you for whatever you can get from it. Even one byte of data," she said. "Because the shooter is back."

She turned and walked out.

Her cheeks were burning. She had no idea whether she'd just saved herself or cut the strings on her parachute.

Did she want to believe there was a connection to her? Did she want to believe it was Azerov?

She didn't look over her shoulder. She feared that if she did, she'd see Sorenstam throwing the swipe card in the trash.

She opened the door, stepped into the sunshine, and looked around for Aiden. His truck was gone. So were her hopes.

❦

Sorenstam watched the door close behind Harper Flynn. She had a bitter taste in her mouth. The swipe card the young woman had given her was scratched and worn. The lanyard was grayed with soot.

What did Flynn expect her to find? Fingerprints? Electronic evidence? Of what? She dropped the card on her desk.

On her computer screen, the image of Aiden's attack on Perez remained. She yanked the thumb drive from her computer, not caring when it said she hadn't shut down the device safely. Nothing about this last year had been shut down safely.

She sat, and forced herself not to put her head in her hands, or to think of the partner Aiden Garrison had been and should have remained, had the universe been just.

Personality changes. Depression, psychiatric issues. She'd studied the secondary symptoms of closed head injuries. *Delusional misidentification syndromes.*

She looked at the door as it slowly closed, wondering if she really wanted to see him outside, receding into the distance, ever farther. She turned away.

She picked up the lanyard. The swipe card swung back and forth. It was a plain white card with the name FLYNN, H. and an employee ID number printed on the front. On the back, below the magnetic strip, was printed SPARTAN SECURITY SYSTEMS INC. She looked up their phone number. Then she opened a search.

Harper Flynn.

⁓

Across the street from the Lost Hills Sheriff's Station, a man sat at the bus stop. A dog lay at his feet, panting. The woman from the architectural firm in the business park clicked up the sidewalk, sun in her eyes, holding the Chihuahua's leash. Traffic was light. The dog at the bus stop was a red brindle, big, all muscle aside from its huge head. Its leash lay loose on the sidewalk beside it. Its master had his arms spread across the back of the bench.

She was twenty yards from the bench when the brindled dog sat up, eyeing her and little Gigi. What was that thing? A pit-bull-brown-bear mix? It had half an ear torn off and a crescent bite scar across its face. It wore a studded black collar. Its hackles bristled and ears flattened. The woman eyed it and sped up, her dog ticking along on tiny paws, like a speck of grease jumping in a skillet.

The man lounged, arms stretched along the back of the bench, legs wide. He was facing away from her, gazing across the street. His dog growled. The man let him. What did they call this—a status dog?

He checked the time.

The red brindle growled again, a low, rattling sound.

She stopped ten yards from him. "Your dog's off the leash."

The man ignored her. He seemed more fascinated by the woman across the street, a brunette who stormed to a MINI Cooper and got in like some kind of typhoon, before racing past, engine revving, hair blowing in the open window. At his knee, the brindled dog continued to snarl. Drool leaked from its jowls.

"Excuse me," she said. "Please curb that thing. He's frightening Gigi."

The MINI raced away around a long curve. The man watched it go.

"I said your animal is behaving aggressively."

The man half turned his head, with the speed of a spring snapping. "So get yourself a dog instead of a piece of Kleenex on a leash."

He stood up. The brindle did, too. It lowered its head and padded forward. One step, two. She scooped the Chihuahua into her arms and backed up.

The man simply stood with his back to her. His T-shirt had a grotesque drawing on the back: a man with half a face, half a bloody skull. Beneath the image, it said, GUS FRING: CLASSY TO THE END. She backed up some more. The Chihuahua squirmed and began to yap at the red dog.

The bus pulled up, wheezing to a stop. The door sighed open. The man picked up the leash. "Heel." He and the dog climbed aboard.

11

The next afternoon, Aiden pulled into the carport and turned off the truck. He listened to the F-150's engine tick, listened to himself breathe, listened to nothing. Sunshine glared off the hood, white against black.

Another flash of glass reflected in the mirror: Sorenstam's Accord pulling into the driveway behind him.

Twenty-four hours, he thought. She'd waited a full day to come calling.

She wore sunglasses, a vision of Swedish Californian cool, watching him. The perfect cop, waiting for the guy in her sights to make a move.

He pulled the keys from the ignition and got out. The wood-frame house was crammed under heavy oaks and bottlebrush trees on Foothill Road, near Mission Canyon. He rented it from his uncle. A gnarl of bougainvillea climbed the wall by the carport and spilled across its roof, papery red leaves shaking in the afternoon wind with the force of a rattler's tail.

Sorenstam climbed out. Aiden reached back into the cab of the F-150 for the SIG Sauer and the Heckler & Koch.

She walked up the drive. "Firing range?"

"You really are a detective."

He flicked the remote to lock the truck and headed for the house. He was limping and couldn't hide it. After fishing with Kieran, he had gone running, two miles up Foothill and the brutal rises along Mountain Drive. And back down. That's what had killed his leg, the downhills.

Downhill, that's what was killing his life.

After the run, he still felt wired and useless, like a spinning top that was beginning to wobble. He had needed something to straighten him out, something he could aim at in a direct line. The firing range, in the mountains up San Marcos Pass, was where he'd spent many Saturday mornings with his dad and Kieran in high school, and where he'd practiced after college, when he was getting it into his head that the Army and a career in law enforcement were the things that would set his heart pounding and swelling with righteousness.

He unlocked the kitchen door. "Keeping my skills up. An hour running the roads, an hour at the range."

The burglar alarm beeped. He silenced it. Checked the house for strange shadows, papers out of place, the sound of intruders breathing from their hiding places.

Sorenstam followed him in. The house was warm. The main windows faced west, and all the red energy of the day gathered itself and permeated the kitchen and living room. He took a lockbox from a cupboard shelf and let Sorenstam watch him safe both handguns, ejecting the clips and checking the chamber before setting them inside.

She worried, he knew. She wondered what would happen to him if his brain glitched while he was at the range and tricked him into thinking that the Xenon gunman was standing next to him disguised as another sports shooter.

"Beer's in the fridge."

He walked to the living room, opened the patio door, and whistled. The dog came bounding from the trees and leaped up the steps, a black blur. Cobey was a Labrador/flat-coat mix. Aiden scratched him behind the ears. Back in the kitchen, he poured the dog fresh water. Sorenstam hadn't moved from the door.

"Is this surveillance?" he said.

He walked to the sofa. It was covered with a red-and-black Navajo rug. He sat heavily and propped his leg up, hoping she wouldn't notice, wondering why he cared. They weren't partners any longer. They wouldn't be again.

"We've been through this already, Erika," he said.

She bypassed the beer and walked around in front of the sofa. "I'm not here to put the same old song on repeat."

"Then what?" He draped an arm across the back of the sofa. His shoulder ached. His arm and ribs ached. It started deep and seemed to moan from within the bones that had been broken. He didn't tell her that his hour on the roads had covered only four miles.

He stared at her. "You played Flynn my greatest-hits reel, didn't you?"

She crossed her arms. "I drove an hour out of my way to come here, and my workday is only half over. How about you grant me the courtesy of listening to what I have to tell you?"

Right then, he wanted quiet. Instead, he had Erika, planted three feet away. If not a lecture or a warning, what was it?

"Please," he said.

"What do you know about Harper Flynn?"

He shrugged. "Bartender at Xenon. Before that, she was Navy enlisted. She's finishing college on the G.I. Bill."

She took a second. She always took a second. She liked the suspense. It was a good cop trick. After a while, on a personal level, it became less amusing.

"Erika. What?"

She brushed her pale hair over her shoulder. "I know you believe in the escaped shooter theory with all your heart. But you're wrong."

"You didn't drive all this way to reiterate that."

"And worse, you're being played. Harper Flynn is not who she claims to be."

"What?"

Sorenstam looked implacable under the sharp sunlight. "Bartender, veteran, student—yeah. Add convicted felon."

Something seemed to fray deep inside him. Some wire that kept him moored. He didn't move, but he felt as though he had begun to slide across the room.

"Prove it," he said.

"She's only walking free because she committed her crimes as a juvenile."

"Who told you this?"

"Flynn admitted she went to high school with Eddie Azerov. She left out that when she was fifteen, she and Azerov were part of a crew of thieves."

Aiden lowered his sore leg to the floor and hung his hands off his knees.

"They had a modern Fagin's gang up in China Lake. Tenth graders working for an adult boss. Shoplifting. Pickpocketing. Home burglary. They worked eastern Kern County and the Antelope Valley."

She crossed her arms. "It didn't stop there. She wrecked a car, driving underage without a license. With two bricks of marijuana in the trunk. She's also suspected of being a money mule—a heist where hackers stole credit card data and sent out a cash crew to withdraw as much as they could from ATMs. The guys running the operation didn't even have to launder that cash. It came out clean."

He looked at the floor.

She paused, until he looked up. "Eventually, she drove the getaway car for an armed robbery."

He stood and walked to the window. Sorenstam followed.

"They robbed a jewelry store in China Lake. Eddie Azerov and another youth from their after-school crime club went in with sledgehammers. Harper waited at the curb. Somebody called 9-1-1. Harper and the boys fled, but she managed to drive directly into an oncoming police car and get them all captured."

Aiden stared at the square of sunlight angling across the floor near the window. "Sure you don't want that beer?"

"Aiden?"

"Because it's your last chance. Otherwise, I'll drink for both of us."

He walked to the kitchen, his leg throbbing. He took out two beer bottles, wedged the edge of one cap under the other, and popped it open.

He turned back to Sorenstam. "How'd you uncover information that should have been sealed?"

"Small-town cops have excellent memories. The China Lake PD really hated the people involved in this racket. They took pride in busting it. And in reliving the bust." She walked into the kitchen. "I'm sorry, Aiden."

He spoke quietly. "Why did you tell me this?"

I don't want you to save me, he meant.

"You deserve to know. Letting Flynn run over you would be a piss-poor thing for a former partner to do."

"That's it?"

She ran her gaze up and down him. "She wasn't just playing you. She's still working an angle."

"You think she came to me in an effort to get to you? That she wanted to use me as a front, so the department would believe what she was saying?"

"Maybe."

"Then she's hardly the criminal genius you're making her out to be. Only an idiot would think Aiden Garrison is her ticket to believability."

She blinked as though he'd spit at her. "I assume she figured she could use you, and thereby use me. She needed an introduction, and you provided it."

"Why does she want to use you?" he said.

"Did she tell you what she did in the Navy?"

He shook his head.

"She was a translator."

"So?"

"Russian," Sorenstam said. "They sent her to the Defense Language Institute at Monterey. You know why the Navy does that, right? It's not so they can train swabbies to interpret chit-chat at diplomatic dinners."

"Intelligence?" he said.

"Cryptologic technician. She worked with the spooks," Sorenstam said. "And now she's finishing a college degree in linguistics. She's going to apply for jobs in security. She has clearance, for God's sake."

He leaned his hands on the counter, trying to slot the information into comprehensible compartments. "So what? Why would she draw attention to herself now?"

"Did she tell you about her employee swipe card from Xenon?"

"What about it?"

She took that as a *no*, which it was. "She gave it to me. Asked me to check it out. She suggested I try to pull evidence off of it. She didn't mean fingerprints."

"Do you know whether it's actually her card?"

Her eyes glinted. He'd exposed himself, revealed his still-living sense of himself as a detective, and shown that he doubted Harper's truthfulness.

Sorenstam said, "I have no idea whether it's actually her card. She asked me to find out whether it was used as a key."

"Key to Xenon?"

She raised an eyebrow. "She certainly wasn't implicating herself. I took her to mean that somebody else used it to grant the shooters access. She left it to me to figure out who she was pointing at."

"What do you make of it?" he said.

"If you decipher it, tell me." Her gaze lingered for a moment. "You take care." She headed to the door. Hand on the knob, she paused. "Ask her what happened to Susannah."

She left. When he heard her car back out of the driveway, he tilted the beer bottle to his lips. It was cold, but not as cold as he felt.

Harper Flynn. For the last twelve months, he had seen her as a hero. Hell, he had *watched* her leap over the bar into withering gunfire, in a manic bid to pull Drew Westerman to safety. Harper hadn't just seemed heroic during the attack. She had been heroic. Unquestionably.

Convicted felon.

He looked out the window. The swipe card. It would record a bartender's transactions across a work shift, plus entry and exit. Harper, he guessed, had asked Sorenstam to check whether the card had been used to access the back door.

He then understood Sorenstam's implication: Harper had turned in the swipe card in an attempt to pin the blame on somebody. But she had lied. If somebody gave the bad guys an access card, it wasn't another employee, or the boss, or a friend to whom she'd lent it—who would almost certainly have been Drew Westerman. No. If Harper was playing Sorenstam—and him—the person who swiped the door open for the shooters was Harper herself.

Through the living room window, the sun poured over him. The sharp light felt like a knife.

If Harper had let the bad guys in, she was the person who got Drew killed.

Then why hand over the card? It implied that she was on the verge of exposure, and trying to weave and dodge and deflect the blame onto the dead guy.

He had another thought, a worse one. If Harper was working with the bad guys, then her valor was smoke and mirrors. Because she would have known they weren't actually shooting at her. The heroic leap over the bar was nothing dangerous. She knew she wasn't a target. She was protected.

He picked up the beer bottle and threw it against the wall. It shattered in a starburst of glass and foam.

"Son of a bitch."

If Sorenstam was right, he was a tool, nothing but a toy being wound up and set loose to totter across the floor and knock down the Tinkertoy castle.

He stared at the walls, and at the photos on his bookshelf. His mom and dad, his brother and sister. At least those photos didn't lie to him. Those images didn't suddenly seem false, concealing a shadowy figure with a silver pistol in his hand.

Screw it all. No matter what Sorenstam said, or whether Harper Flynn was lying, he knew one thing. He had seen the third shooter that night.

The man was real. He was still out there. And now, Aiden had to think, the shooter might be working with Harper. Working on *him*.

He grabbed the keys to his truck. Whistling for the dog, he stormed outside.

12

The wind lifted damp strands of hair from Harper's neck. She focused on the trash can a hundred yards up the beach and ran, pumping her arms. Her lungs burned. The whitecapped ocean was gilded in the afternoon light. The sand churning under her feet was hot. On Pacific Coast Highway, traffic slurred past. She tried to pick up her pace, but her legs felt like wool. She slogged to the trash can and stopped, wheezing.

The Santa Monica Pier glittered in the surf spray. The sun shone on surfers and sunbathers and palm trees. She hated it all right now.

She spit onto the sand. "Dammit."

She had thought running after work would clear her head. But bent over, hands on her knees, she only felt her fears confirmed: She had blown it. Cajoling Aiden into going with her to Sorenstam had been a disaster. And she had exposed herself to whatever winds were rising.

Distantly, a vehicle door slammed shut. A moment later, a dog loped up to her, tags rattling, a beautiful black mutt that gazed up at her as though beguiled. She heard a whistle.

"Cobey, sit."

She straightened. Aiden was walking toward her across the sand.

She wiped her forehead with the back of her hand. "My boss told you where to find me? Turnabout, I guess."

He walked up. "I followed you along the road for half a mile. You didn't watch your back."

The sun glared from his shades. The wind smelled of salt.

"I'll be more careful," she said. "Are you here to talk about seeing Zero that night at Xenon?"

"Forget Xenon. I'm here because I can't stand being lied to."

She dropped her hands to her sides. "I didn't lie to you."

"Bullshit. You weren't Eddie Azerov's victim. You were his accomplice."

A bright hum rose in her ears. His face was flat with anger, his shirt blowing against his frame. An urge to disappear overcame her. Drive north to the desert, up the eastern side of the Sierras. Vanish into the backcountry.

She had thought Los Angeles would be the backcountry. She came here to hide in plain sight among nine million people in L.A. County. Aiden's hands hung open, but tense, as though ready to curl into fists.

She was well and truly hosed.

"My juvenile record was sealed when I turned eighteen," she said.

"You and Zero had a hell of a run, until you crashed a getaway car. Is that why you didn't tell me earlier? Because you botched the escape?"

The humming in her ears rose to a roar. The light took on a searchlight gleam. Sorenstam had managed to dig it all up.

Why had she thought her history could be kept secret? Records were records. They might be sealed, but they never evaporated, any more than memories or pain.

Say something. Say the right thing. The gleaming light seemed to turn her numb.

"Eddie Azerov is a nightmare. He's . . ."

"*Sssuu . . .*"

Azerov's voice, hissing and hot, filled her mind. His flat eyes, his tiny teeth, the way he cocked his head as he leaned in and whispered threats in her ear.

"You think I wanted to spill everything about him fifteen minutes after I met you? No way. And to hear you give me information that he was involved—"

"Stop it. Whatever you're trying to pull, just stop it."

She nearly raised her hand to slap him. Ten years earlier, she would have. "I'm not pulling anything. Why would I do that?"

"That's the jackpot question. You want the sheriff's department to provide you with official cover for something? You're out to get Azerov and think you can worm his whereabouts out of the department? Barricading yourself against some attack that's in the wind?"

"I'm trying to convince the department that the third shooter exists and is back."

"Then you're going to have to convince me."

His eyes were hidden by the sunglasses, his face clenched with some cool bitterness. Sorenstam had planted a seed of suspicion, and it was growing twisted roots. Harper felt she was on the edge of something very bad. It was circling. She had only a little time to get out from under it, or her last chance to come out of this the right way would be gone for good.

"You want to know the truth? I'll tell you. And Sorenstam can dig up the court records and rip open everything that was supposed to be confidential. You can corroborate everything I'm going to tell you. But—"

"No *buts*."

"But you have to tell me everything about your traumatic brain injury. The issue with misidentifying people. Straight up."

"I have."

"Now I call bullshit."

"Stop deflecting. You tell me the whole story, and I will damn well verify every syllable you speak."

They faced each other, neither moving back. The dog stood at Aiden's side.

He glanced at the ocean. "Sorenstam's wrong. I did see the shooter's tattoo at Xenon that night."

"You saw Zero."

"I am one hundred percent positive." He looked back at her. "My vision is screwed up. Not my memory of that night. I saw him."

The crash of the surf cut through the humming in her ears.

"Then we have a huge problem. Because as far as bad times go, Eddie Azerov is only the advance guard." The breeze chilled her skin. "Something's coming."

13

W hat's coming?" Aiden said.

The searchlight sun turned the ocean and sky a flat white. Harper breathed. "Them."

He eyed her from behind his sunglasses. "Azerov?"

"And the guy who holds his leash."

"Start talking."

"Walk with me."

She couldn't let the words pour out and stay standing in them. Nodding at the cliffs above Pacific Coast Highway, she headed for the pedestrian bridge that crossed the road. Aiden clipped a leash to the dog's collar and followed.

"I didn't join the crew for kicks. China Lake's isolated but not that bad," she said.

"So why? Your daddy ignored you and your momma was cruel?"

"Dad died when I was a kid. China Lake's a naval air weapons testing facility. They blow stuff up in the desert, and one day, things went wrong." She climbed the steps to the bridge. "Mom drank."

Aiden didn't look at her. "And you became a bartender."

"I also joined the Navy. I wasn't afraid I was duplicating their lives."

Still, she could see her mother staring blankly out the kitchen window, as though watching for her father's ghost. She could hear Lila's monotone. *"Stop spying and get Mom a beer. And don't make me drink alone. Get yourself one."*

Harper didn't. She was twelve.

Now she climbed toward Ocean Avenue, eyes forward. "And I learned early how to cut people off."

"Does that go for dealing drugs?" Aiden said.

"I never dealt."

"Didn't keep you from working as a courier."

Abruptly, the date palms, beachfront apartments, the manicured lawns blooming with jasmine and hydrangeas, looked like a cardboard front—a Potemkin promise of freedom from the life she had fought to escape. A hot stone heated inside her.

What was the point in telling him? *I hate drugs because my mom mixed booze with pills and larceny.* It would come off like a sob story—liquor stores where Lila slipped a pint flask of whiskey into Harper's jacket. Being nudged down the aisle at Walgreens to shoplift Excedrin because Mom had a hangover but no money. At the health clinic, being told, "*Just grab it from his desk. I'll keep the doctor talking in the hall and you take the prescription pad.*"

She stopped walking. "I can warn you about what we're dealing with, or you can keep up the verbal beatdown. Your choice."

Aiden shortened his grip on Cobey's leash and peered at the ocean. On the horizon, a haze blurred water into air.

"There's a real threat. It doesn't come from me," she said.

Finally, he looked at her. "Then from who?"

"His name is Maddox."

"First name?"

"Travis."

"Is he in the system? Have an arrest record?"

"Yes."

He took out his phone. "He ran the crew?"

"His dad did. Roland Maddox, better known as Rowdy."

He keyed his phone. "You may be a redneck if . . ."

"He'd been a pro wrestler. It was his ring name." Her voice was a scythe. "You can call him Fagin."

He looked up. "How did he turn you into the Artful Dodger?"

"Mom moved in with him. They called it a common law marriage. That started it." She nodded at his phone. "Taking notes?"

"Mind like a steel sieve. I'm searching for Travis's arrest record."

She resumed walking toward Ocean Avenue. "Maddox was a balls-to-the-wall crook. He got Mom to ferry stolen property out of China Lake to L.A., then make the return run carrying cash or bricks of dope."

"You knew?" Aiden said.

"Just that sometimes Mom left while I was at school. Sometimes, she arranged for me to sleep over at a friend's, then didn't come home for two days."

Nobody ever invited her back to their house a second time. Eventually, when Lila left, Harper locked herself in her bedroom at Rowdy's half-built mansion in the desert south of town.

Aiden said, "The car wreck."

She eyed him.

"Sorenstam's thorough," he said.

Like a flamethrower was thorough. The familiar script lay at the back of her throat, ready to recite. *The car crashed on Highway 14, south of China Lake. I ran it off the blacktop into a ditch. I didn't have a driver's license. A trucker stopped and called the highway patrol. They found the bricks of weed in the trunk.*

"You were ferrying dope to Maddox," Aiden said.

"The dope was on its way to him."

He turned to her. "I have nothing but time. So stop holding back. What's the real story? Eddie Azerov was driving but split before the flashing lights turned up?"

Her cheeks heated. What could she lose at this point by admitting how much she had lied?

"It was my mom."

He looked at her.

"She fell asleep at the wheel. Woke up when we barreled into the ditch."

"Your mom ran and left you there," he said.

"I had a concussion and needed stitches. She said the trucker would get help."

His expression turned skeptical. "How come she didn't take the dope?"

"She loaded probably a dozen bricks in my backpack before she ran. She didn't have time to grab the last two."

"And she reminded you that you were a minor, while she couldn't afford to face charges for, what, the third time?"

"Fifth." Harper's face was burning, heat pouring from her palms.

"Pretty damned vicious," Aiden said.

It was the first sympathetic remark he'd made since he arrived. She'd take it.

"We wrecked near an abandoned factory. She headed cross-country and hunkered down there. She said she'd be watching—like she was a guardian angel. But . . ."

Calm down. It was old news—a scar, not a scab. She could put a flame against the story and it shouldn't hurt. She held her hand out to the dog. Cobey padded silently, his black coat rippling in the sunlight.

"The wreck isn't what matters. It's what happened afterward," she said. "Zero and Travis Maddox found me. Travis told me I was going to start working for Rowdy. That if I didn't, he'd anonymously call the cops and tell them Lila was at the wheel. My mom would go to prison, and the water would just be over my head."

Travis had slowly circled her. Zero poked at the stitches in her scalp, his breath brushing her neck. *Make your life simple. Do what we tell you.*

Aiden took off his sunglasses. His expression was pained. Somehow it softened him.

"So they inducted me into their crew," she said. "Commercial burglaries. Auto theft. Household B and E. Phishing schemes—e-mails tricking people into revealing their credit card numbers and PINs. An ATM cash-and-dash with stolen debit card data."

Aiden said, "You didn't have anybody to talk to? A teacher, a minister?"

"First rule of an addict's household: Say nothing. Ever. Besides, when you resisted, Rowdy got his belt."

Rowdy, six-two and juiced. *"Disobedient bitch . . ."*

They crossed Ocean and walked to Caffé Nero, where she worked part-time. She stopped on the sidewalk. The dog stood at her side, panting.

"Rowdy left welts, but nothing else. He had us kids to do the dirty work. We were the ones who left fingerprints."

"How many kids?"

"Including Travis, seven or eight."

He held up his phone. "This him?"

The sun glared from the screen. The mug shot was everything she remembered about Travis Maddox: sullen eyes and a caustic teenage stare.

She nodded. Aiden continued to hold up the phone, as if brandishing a crucifix at a vampire. His voice was low.

"What happened to Susannah?"

The noise of traffic brushed over her. After a long moment, she said, "She's gone."

Aiden continued to brandish the phone, waiting for more than that.

She nodded at the photo. "Because of him. Susannah's gone," she said. "I got rid of her."

14

Erika Sorenstam gulped her coffee and spun the steering wheel with the heel of her right hand. She pulled the unmarked car into the parking lot at Spartan Security Systems Inc.

The Spartan complex was a cluster of blue glass and steel buildings at the west end of the San Fernando Valley. Sorenstam got out, pulling her black suit jacket over the holster on her hip. Beyond a screen of eucalyptus trees, traffic whined on 101. Toward the coast were the hills covered with golden grass and live oaks famous from *M*A*S*H* and a hundred television westerns.

She buttoned her jacket and slid her hair back over her shoulders and walked to the door. She entered a lobby of black stone floors and blue-tinted light. She tucked her sunglasses into her jacket pocket. At the front desk, she badged a receptionist who had the flat calm of a mannequin.

The woman eyed Sorenstam's star, seemingly counting all six points. "Do you have an appointment?"

"Tom White."

"One moment." She touched a screen and spoke mildly into her headset mike. She would have made an excellent front for an evil mastermind's lair, or a dentist's office. She said, "Someone will be down."

While Sorenstam waited, she strolled around the empty lobby. Big-screen televisions mounted on the wall were playing promotional videos. Alarm systems. Manned guarding. CCTV. Cybersecurity.

Spartan Security Systems' headquarters was in Laurel, Maryland.

The company was a vast and tentacular organization, founded by a former Army Ranger who cut his teeth in private security as a contractor in Iraq. It had a squeaky-clean corporate record. Sorenstam suspected that was because its overlords knew exactly how to rebrand themselves to disassociate from legal troubles overseas. It employed six thousand people worldwide. The wall-mounted screens showed photo montages of happy children and the American flag.

A door buzzed open. When she turned, a man was approaching, his hand out.

"Detective. Tom White, Corporate Security."

He was in his thirties and was white indeed, tall and neatly pressed into a black suit, his hair cut close on the sides. He could have been a fashion-upgraded sheriff's detective. He even had the searching eyes. His smooth demeanor was the kind that would give suspects the willies. He smiled. It was winsome. His teeth were bright.

"How can I help the sheriff's department?" he said.

"It's about the shoot-out at Xenon."

The smile remained bright. His eyes were astute. "Come on back."

He got her a visitor's badge and punched a code into the door lock, which opened with a pneumatic hush. They passed open-plan departments partitioned behind thick glass. He escorted her to a conference room. On a gleaming cherry tabletop, a tablet computer was waiting for him.

He closed the door. "Tell me."

"Tell you what?"

He spread his hands. "The case is officially closed. If you're here, there's a new angle that nobody's reported yet."

"You sound curious."

"Absolutely. Spartan wants any and all information on the incident so we can debrief correctly, game out future scenarios, and offer improved security in similar situations."

The investigative report did not fault Spartan for the breach at the club. Spartan's remit that night was to provide unarmed guards at the entrance, who were to check all guests for tickets, over-twenty-one IDs, and weapons. Spartan was already Xenon's plant security provider—alarm systems, electronic locks, CCTV. The report speculated that an employee had failed to securely close the back door on the alley. Two kitchen staff had died in the fire, so there was no way to question them about it. The shooters' route into Xenon remained an open question.

And White had to know that.

He smoothed his tie. "We didn't control hiring at Xenon. We didn't perform criminal background checks on its employees, though we could have. An integrated security solution might have prevented what happened."

Sorenstam let him finish his spiel. "We're sweeping up the last specks of sawdust. Double-checking whether Spartan collected data from Xenon's employee swipe cards."

"From that night?" He shook his head. "Everything was destroyed. The CCTV cameras, the magnetic card readers in the door locks, and, I hate to remind you, most of the cards themselves. It wasn't a pretty scene."

"If I supplied a swipe card, could you retrieve data from it that had been uploaded to your system?"

She had asked a forensic tech in the sheriff's department lab about recovering data from Harper Flynn's swipe card, hoping to track Flynn's movements that night. The lab was backed up, and the tech had said: No way. To begin with, the card was damaged. Beyond that, it was not designed to record and store an employee's movements. The magnetic strip contained the cardholder's name and employee ID. Each time the card was used, it might or might not create a record. But the card itself didn't contain that record. It was dumb.

Harper Flynn had to be aware of that. Sorenstam didn't understand why she had given the card to her. But the word *nefarious* lodged in her mind.

"Xenon was on a basic contract," White said. "We supplied the manpower for special events, but we were limited by their budget. And we were limited by their facilities. The electronic door locks were an older design. The swipe cards were primarily intended to monitor employee access to the cash registers, to prevent theft. Same with the CCTV cameras—they were all aimed at the registers, to watch for bartenders slipping money into their own pockets. Same with the fridges and the stockrooms in the basement." He shrugged. "As for the door locks, they had electronic keypads that anybody could open with a code. The swipe cards just sped things up. The locks, as far as I know, didn't register the particular ID on the card when an employee swiped a card."

"As far as you know."

"I didn't install the system. And you're the first person who's personally asked me that question."

"Can you find out?" Sorenstam said.

"Happy to inquire." He looked eager but slightly edgy. "Any particular card you're looking for?"

The card was in the evidence locker at the station. Sorenstam handed White a high-resolution photo instead.

"The name and employee ID number should get you started," she said.

He nodded in acquiescence. "Understood."

She said, "We'd like to look at your records again."

"I can arrange for you to speak to Legal about access." He turned quizzical. "The sheriff's department has seen our records before. And didn't you see the state of the club after the fire?"

"I was there," Sorenstam said coolly. "As I said, we're covering all the bases."

"Yeah, you had a deputy injured, didn't you?"

"Indeed." She waited, pulse threading through her wrists, for him to mention Aiden's name.

He leaned back. "Sorry. Didn't mean to rub pepper in an open wound."

"If I may ask, Mr. White—what's your official capacity at Spartan Security?"

She had checked his entry on the Spartan website, but little was available beyond his title.

He raised his hands as if surrendering. "You got me." His smile looked rueful. "I didn't handle the Xenon account. The manager who did has since left Spartan's employ. I'm filling in. I'm in corporate cybersystems, mainly."

"You don't handle physical plant security?"

"I have and I do. But my role here is primarily in safeguarding companies from cyberintrusion." He pulled out his wallet and handed her a business card.

TOM WHITE. CYBER SOLUTIONS, CORPORATE SECURITY DIVISION.

He set his hands on the polished conference table. "Spartan handles cybersecurity for both digital files and physical plant access. As you probably know, many businesses put their control systems online. Door locking systems. Power plant programs. Dams that have automated sensors to determine whether to open or shut the floodgates."

"Nuclear power stations," Sorenstam said. "Hospital intravenous drip systems."

"Yes. We manage data protection, but so many companies have integrated physical and cybersystems that they're not fully aware of, that's where I come in."

"Not fully aware?" Sorenstam said.

"Companies sometimes put control systems directly onto the Internet without a firewall or password protection. Putting shutdown protocols directly onto the Net with a raw IP address, for instance. And certain search engines can locate things of that nature."

"Are you suggesting that Xenon had a vulnerability like that?" Sorenstam said.

He shook his head vigorously. "Hardly. Xenon had a standard system. Not that sophisticated. It worked for them perfectly adequately. Until it didn't."

Sorenstam considered it and tapped the photo of the swipe card. "Can you find out what data this card could have transmitted?"

He nodded. "I'll check it out."

"I presume you have a list of Xenon's employees, and of everybody who was injured or killed, and of all the people interviewed in connection with the shootings and fire."

"I'm sure we do. Any names in particular you want me to investigate?"

"Bar staff."

"Will do."

"And if you have staff photos on file, I'd be interested in any that show tattoos. Right hand." She stood. "I'll be back in touch tomorrow."

He saw her out. As she walked to her car, she felt that a thousand electronic eyes were watching her from behind the blue glass windows. She turned and surveyed the building, to let it know she wasn't blind. She drove away without another glance.

15

Harper and Aiden climbed the stairs at her apartment building and she unlocked the front door. "I'll get water for Cobey."

Aiden scanned the apartment. The kitchen was sized for an Easy-Bake Oven, the living room barely big enough to hang a Georgia O'Keeffe print. He walked to the balcony door. Outside, a Moreton Bay Fig spread green shade across the street.

"Nice cave."

"G.I. Bill, plus my student loan, work-study, and my job, means I can cover the rent. I can live here and finish my degree, instead of tossing a bedroll on the floor of a storage container."

"Lemons, lemonade."

He stuck his hands in his jeans pockets. He was waiting for her to explain about Susannah. Harper filled a water bowl and set it down. Cobey lapped gratefully.

She walked over to Aiden. "I get that a lot. People told me the shootout and fire were a message from God that I was meant do something with my life."

"People are assholes."

"I asked them, what was God's message for Drew, then? Die, dude?"

A look crossed his face, as if she'd splashed him with ice water. His expression brightened. "I doubt the Lord of the Universe burned down a packed building to nudge you toward self-improvement. If that's God's way of text messaging us, he's an incredible bastard."

"Amen."

She handed him a laminated card she had taken from deep in a kitchen drawer.

He examined it. "This is?"

"My high school student ID."

"That's not an explanation."

"You asked about Susannah." She nodded at the card. "That was her."

He eyed her slantwise. "Susannah Flynn. You."

"Not anymore."

"You changed your name."

"I changed my name, I bugged out, I dropped chaff behind me to scramble their radar so they couldn't follow. I knew they'd want to come after me."

"Because?"

She took a pitcher of iced tea from the fridge and filled two jam-jar glasses. "Because of what I did to escape."

She handed him a glass and led him onto the balcony.

"Back on the beach, you asked why I didn't talk to somebody about my situation. You meant, why did I go along?" she said.

"You were coerced. I get that."

The breeze stirred the leaves of the fig tree. She gave him an astringent smile.

He said, "But you didn't run."

"Not for a long time." She sat down. "You know about the ATM heist. Maddox obtained stolen debit card numbers, sourced blank cards, loaded them with the stolen data, drove us to Vegas, and put us on the street to empty cash machines."

"I know some. What don't I know?"

She remembered it as she told him. The heat in the van had been stifling. When Maddox pulled to the curb, he said, "You will be standing on this corner when I return. Fail, and Zero will find you."

The younger kids, Jasmine and Oscar, looked panicked. The Strip: a million watts of neon and a river of cars and trucks. Zero had confiscated their phones, cash, and wallets.

Four hours later, Harper rushed toward the meeting point, her backpack stuffed with thousands of dollars, her nerves like frayed electrical wire. Overhead, an airliner screamed past. She wanted to grab it by the tail and let it carry her off.

Now she looked at Aiden. "Zero and Travis were waiting on a side street."

They grabbed her from behind and marched her away from the Strip into a neighborhood of broken sidewalks.

"You looked at that jet like you wanted to fly away," Travis said. "You planning to steal Rowdy's money?"

"No. Of course not."

Her voice trembled, and Zero smiled. Travis stared, the light in his eyes strange and hungry. A cold heat settled in her stomach. They shoved her across a vacant lot humped with weeds and trash, to the edge of a ditch. Zero pulled off her backpack.

"No, Eddie, don't . . ."

"You even think of running, you end up here." He leaned in. "Nobody's gonna help you."

They threw her into the ditch and ran with the pack. She hit hard and slid into rank mud. Shaking, she got to her knees.

From the bushes beyond the ditch, a young voice said, "Are you okay?"

It was Oscar, twelve years old, smart and scared and skinny as a chopstick. He was covered in ditch mud, too.

"You can hide here with me," he said.

She wobbled to her feet and held out her hand. "No. We have to get to the meeting point."

As soon as they limped back toward the Strip, Maddox's van crawled up the street. The window came down and he said, "Get in."

Now, she held Aiden's gaze. "They were always watching."

He sat and leaned forward, elbows on his knees, and was quiet.

"I'm not asking for forgiveness," Harper said. "I'm not offering excuses. I'm telling you how it was."

"I don't ignore context."

She tried to slow the pounding of her heart. His eyes were gray, almost pewter, with a metallic sheen that flecked brightly when the leaves dipped and the sun caught his face. Leaning on his elbows, shoulders filling his shirt, he looked open and accepting. She had an urge to reach over and brush his hair back from his face.

"Good to know," she said.

His smile was dry. "Meaning, for a paranoid cop, I'm not half bad?"

"My outlaw years are in the past. I've stopped mistrusting lawmen."

"Also good to know." His gaze hung on her.

So trust him. "Sorenstam told you about the armed robbery."

He nodded.

"It happened September, my senior year. During the day, I went to physics and read *Macbeth*. At night, I held the bag, literally, while Zero broke into warehouses," she said. "Travis was taking classes at the community college and cranking out phishing schemes. His dad had developed a taste for white-collar crime."

"It's a trend. Even street gangs have realized they can make money without butchering each other. Plus, sentences are lighter for cyber-theft than bank robbery."

She held tight to her jam-jar glass. "Rowdy had a computer shop. Travis was his tech, the guy who did installations and helped mom-and-pop businesses set up their systems."

"Travis hacked their customers."

"Mostly installed malware. Viruses, worms, Trojans. Then he'd charge them to remove the infection."

"And if they didn't pay . . ."

"They paid in other ways." She set her tea on the deck. "I could deal with nighttime burglaries. They scared the hell out of me, but nobody got hurt. Travis had a contact at an alarm company who gave him deactivation codes. It was relatively low risk. The thing was, Zero liked breaking things. He saw no reason why the world should be allowed to stay whole. On jobs, he"—she forced herself to slow down—"he smashed framed family photos. He stopped up toilets and flushed them. Once, he poured a kid's aquarium into the kitchen sink and turned on the garbage disposal."

She paused. She could still hear Zero laughing. "He was always going to escalate to violent crime."

"What a prince," Aiden said.

Heat poured from the palms of her hands. "Travis decided to rob the jewelry store because the owner had threatened to sue Rowdy for infecting his computers. It was going to be in and out, smash and grab," she said. "They told me I was going to do the driving."

"Why you?"

"Because I was good at it."

She'd learned to drive in the desert. She could handle cars, pickups, dirt bikes. On the asphalt or off-road. Boondocking. Street racing, on hot nights when the roads were just empty enough to make it risky but doable.

She stood and walked to the balcony railing. Beneath the trees, traffic was desultory.

"I knew the robbery would be the start of a fast slide to a ditch I could never climb out of. Some people have no bottom, but armed robbery was mine."

"But you did it," he said.

"I did it like nobody's business," she said. "Necessity is the mother of invention. Desperation is the author of crazy-ass exits."

She turned and faced him. "They didn't search me. Before we got in the car, they handed me a ski mask and sunglasses and a baggy sweatshirt. I was a skinny, flat-chested chick. Covered in polyester and Ray-Bans, I looked like a teenage boy at the wheel of a stolen Camaro. But I had a cell phone taped to my calf."

"What'd you do?" he said.

"The store was in a strip mall—wide open, nothing but four-lane blacktop and green lights all the way to Nevada." She thought of Zero, jacked up. And Travis, coolly setting a sledgehammer on the floor by his leg. "The plan was, the guys get out. I drive around the block so nobody gets suspicious about a car idling outside a jewelry store. I come back, they get in, we drive away."

"But?"

"I'd learned some of Travis's tech tricks—like how to spoof phone calls so they seem to be coming from other numbers. I drove around the block, stopped and dialed 9-1-1."

"You called the cops."

"I spoofed the call so it appeared to come from a pay phone. Then I threw the cell phone down a storm drain and hauled ass back to the strip mall."

"That was—ballsy."

"When the guys came out, the cops were racing up the street. China Lake PD, coming like a couple of Sidewinder missiles. Zero and Travis jumped in, and I floored it, straight into the flashing lights," she said. "I rammed a police car."

He eyed her. "Deliberately."

"The cops swerved across the road to block the Camaro. They left six feet of daylight between them and I could have threaded the needle, but the guys didn't know that. Travis was screaming at me. I was going seventy-five when I threw it into a skid and slammed sideways into a black-and-white."

"You purposely got yourself arrested."

"I thought it was my only chance," she said. "I still do."

For a long moment, he looked at her, his face unreadable.

"I'd gamed out a dozen escape plans. Getting arrested was the only scenario where I came out alive. I couldn't simply run. Travis and Zero would have come after me. I needed to pen them in. Jail was the only thing that would protect me."

"Harsh form of rescue."

"When was salvation ever painless?" she said. "I pleaded guilty and was sent to Kern County Juvenile Hall in Bakersfield. The last time I saw my mom was the afternoon I was sentenced."

"Brutal."

"Could have been much worse," she said. "Kern County had a school for juvenile female offenders, the Pathways Academy. I begged them to take me. The court ordered me to eight months in Pathways, then sixteen weeks closely supervised release at home. But I petitioned for legal emancipation."

"You got it? Under those circumstances? Don't you need . . ."

"I had a cousin in Sacramento. She agreed to take me in. The judge looked at my family history, granted my petition, and said, 'Good luck.'"

Aiden picked up the student ID card again. The photo looked ordinary, taken before homeroom on a chilly desert morning. She wondered if Aiden could see the pain and confusion barricaded behind her sleepy teenage eyes.

He handed it back. "You remade yourself from the ground up."

"Nobody can change the clay they're made from," she said. "But I broke from China Lake, completely. Harper's my grandmother's maiden name. When I turned eighteen, I petitioned the court to change it legally. I petitioned to have my criminal record sealed. And I joined the Navy."

"Maddox?" he said.

"He cut me off. My mom called my cousin a couple of times, sniffing around. Becka never told her where I was." She smiled. "Patron saint of family battle lines."

"Travis and Zero?"

"State prison. They were eighteen—tried as adults. Travis got forty-eight months. Eddie shattered the store owner's ribs with a sledgehammer and got six years."

The sun flickered through the leaves of the fig tree. A car cruised past, stereo thudding. Across the street, a dog stood panting in the sun, a muscular red brindle.

Aiden said, "Did they know you set them up?"

"They had to suspect."

"You think they've been looking for you?"

"I think they've found me."

She tried to keep her voice level, but nauseating dread threaded through her. Aiden stood and came to her side.

"If Sorenstam won't listen, I'll find someone who will," he said.

"They're going to come after me, and they won't care who's in the cross fire." She pressed her fingers to the corners of her eyes. Her voice dropped. "Zero *likes* cross fire. Travis will set it up and let him pull the trigger."

"Hey."

"We have to find them and shut them down. Because they won't stop. Jesus, *Xenon* wasn't enough for them."

He stood close and leaned in. "I'm going to get on it."

His face was grave. The assurance in his voice calmed her. She nodded wordlessly.

He headed for the door. She followed, wiping her eyes.

Halfway out, he paused. "Lock up behind me. Don't let anybody in unless you know who it is."

"I won't. I have a class later, but I'll be all eyes."

Heat was radiating from him. They held for a second, looking at each other.

She touched his arm. "Thank you."

"For?"

"Believing me."

He put a hand over hers, squeezed, and rubbed his thumb against the back of her wrist. She felt unbearably hot. She impulsively raised up on tiptoe and gave his cheek a good-bye kiss.

His stubble brushed her skin. When she stepped back, he put two fingers to his forehead in a jokey salute. Then he was gone.

16

From the lobby at Spartan Security, Tom White watched Sorenstam drive away. He watched until her car disappeared behind the screen of eucalyptus trees.

White had trained himself never to hesitate—not with other security specialists, not at passport and immigration control, not when speaking to law enforcement. *Present a confident aspect.* One of the seven rules he lived by.

He returned to his office and closed the door. Sorenstam was keen to pry open a can of worms that had melted shut in the Xenon fire. Employee swipe cards were an issue. He wondered how she had obtained this one.

Bar staff. He pulled up Xenon's records and found an employee ID photo: bartender, girl with coffee-colored hair pulled back in a loose, sluttish clip. Spare makeup, eyes like tarnished coins. Face that could fool the savviest man. She had survived, he knew. The two staff members who died were men.

He got his cell phone, the pay-as-you-go, and called a number from memory. After a second, a grating voice picked up.

"Just got a visit from a sheriff's detective," White said.

"Who? The woman?"

"Sorenstam."

"Huh."

White waited but got nothing more. "That all you have to say?"

"She was there that night. She must feel personally invested."

"She asked me about an employee swipe card."

"Did she? She should have asked about it a year ago."

"Stop playing games," White said.

"Then why did you call?"

A year back, the swipe card would have been a valuable piece of evidence. The night of the shoot-out, it had been key—White had no doubt. But when the club went up in a Molotov and magnesium blaze, the cards became nothing but warped, sooty plastic. They were of no use to him now. They were nothing but trouble.

He said, "I want to know why Sorenstam showed up today. The card she obtained belongs to"—he looked again at the ID photo on the computer screen—"Harper Flynn."

"Sheriffs know Flynn is connected to the Westerman family. Got to."

White watched the news like everybody else. The Westerman family had to loathe the bartender who had crawled out of Xenon alive, while their son had died.

"Keep eyes on surveillance," he said. "But for Christ's sake, be careful."

"Ain't I always?"

White could have choked him. "You're as careful as an avalanche."

"And as effective." He hung up.

Tom White stood by his desk, phone hanging in his hand. Sorenstam had no cause to suspect that he cared about anything besides selling security software and earning his Christmas bonus. If she did, he would get backup from his bosses. They'd vetted him. They trusted him.

I'll check it out, he'd told Sorenstam. He didn't need to. He already had a handle on the issues.

He had from the start—from the day he interviewed for the job at Spartan. He had walked in and told the HR interviewer about the vulnerabilities of their client list and how he could electronically and physically exploit those vulnerabilities to clean their clients out. Then he told the interviewer to call the Spartan CEO, a dark prince who had earned his millions as a bagman delivering cash to US toadies in Iraq and Afghanistan. Tom White told the interviewer exactly how he would hack into Spartan's secure server to expose their kickback list and their back-channel money drops, and to reveal how negligibly they screened the guards they hired, and where their warehouse was, the one with the illegal firearms and RPGs that they exported to conflict zones for their own profit.

The interviewer turned the color of an egg white.

When Tom White said he could plug the holes in the company's security and screw their competitors, they shook hands.

The interviewer said, "Welcome to Spartan."

The military-industrial complex was a beautiful beast. And White had figured out how to get himself a teat to suck on. Spartan profited by sowing rumors of war and chaos. Bump up people's fear. Persuade them they needed ever more sophisticated and expensive protection. Turn the ratchet ever tighter, and never release it. Convince them they were always on the verge of losing it all—violently, catastrophically— and that a robust, even vicious response was their only salvation.

It worked for him. He lived in an apartment in Marina del Rey. He drove a BMW. He had Lakers season tickets. Last year, Spartan had flown him to the Super Bowl to schmooze some of their big clients. He was now the guy Spartan counted on to keep their clients' data and money safe.

And he did keep it safe. Usually.

Spartan's clients didn't think of themselves as criminals. They saw themselves as hard-nosed business people. They might employ Spartan's dark ops to damage their competition with malware and industrial espionage. Then blame the Chinese, always. But they didn't countenance open violence. That didn't square with their self-image.

So they never expected him to countenance it and subvert them from within. Neither did Spartan.

He always wore a white dress shirt and a rep tie. He cut his hair as though he were a few months out of the Marines. He talked bro-talk and drank beers with his colleagues after work. He told PG-13 jokes. He was a White Hat. Squeaky clean.

But this thing with Sorenstam. That worried him.

She struck him as a digger, Sorenstam. All that Scandinavian cool, the black suit with the holster beneath the jacket, the slick way she slid the photo across the table with her pearly manicured nails. She was probing into the Xenon shooting—a case that should have been closed.

He needed to know what was going on.

No—he needed to shut this down. Now. Before it began to unravel.

And it might, because the sheriff's investigative report was essentially on the money. That night, the shooters had gone to Xenon to deal with Arliss Bale. Tom White had sent them.

White worked for Spartan Security, but he also worked for himself. He maintained a network of private clients who paid him to liberate information from Spartan's secure servers. They used that information to conduct business in the black economy. Sometimes, their business involved fraud, extortion, and illegal movement of funds through countries that don't follow UN money-laundering protocols. And on one occasion, it had involved a transaction with Vegas meth marketer Arliss Bale.

Bale, shabby gangster that he was, had entered a contract but failed to deliver. Tom White's clients had therefore needed redress. *Consequences*. White was adept at meting them out, from a distance.

How wonderfully excited he had felt when he realized that Bale could be lured out in public, to a hot club where he would be surrounded by a thousand revelers. At Xenon. Damn, that was karma giving Tom White a French kiss.

Send a message. That was his remit. Frighten Bale, put a semiautomatic to his head and remind him to honor his commitment. Maybe pistol-whip him. *Clock's ticking, asshole.* But the shooters had ignored the mission parameters. They didn't believe in rules of engagement. Aside from: Fuck 'em all.

White shook it off. Regret was pointless. Action was everything.

He scrounged change from his pocket and strode down the gray-carpeted hall to the break room. He nodded at a drone who was texting and sipping a diet soda. He dropped coins in the vending machine. A PayDay bar clattered into the slot.

He tore open the wrapper and stalked back to his office, chewing. He dropped into his desk chair and again examined the photo on the screen. Her employee identification number undoubtedly matched the card that had been issued by Xenon to Harper Flynn.

He'd made sure they matched. He had gone into the database and verified the employee ID and the alphanumeric that tied this bartender to the card she was required to use at the club.

Now Sorenstam was sticking her nose into things.

Sorenstam seemed to enjoy coming off as a Valkyrie. Choosers of the slain, weren't they? He found that ominous. She had come to him. She might not stop there. She might talk to somebody else at Spartan. She might have other sources.

He needed to make sure this didn't go any further.

White finished his PayDay bar and balled the wrapper and three-pointed it into the wastebasket. That damned swipe card. He started making calls.

17

Aiden unlocked his door, disarmed the alarm, and checked the house for signs of intrusion. He let Cobey into the backyard and tossed his keys onto the counter.

Harper Flynn checked out. Robber, scammer, thief. And true confessor—if he could trust the story she told, stony-eyed. *It's only teenage wasteland.*

His bones ached. His face, where she'd kissed him, seemed to throb.

He had liked it. He had liked her. Way too much.

Online, he checked the searches he'd been running. No luck with the tattoos. Eddie Azerov's ZERO tat was not in the database. Which, admittedly, was spotty, running to gang tats and Russian prison ink. The search for photos matching the tattoo on the hand of the man in the trees at the memorial had returned fourteen hundred hits. The photo, and the search parameters, were too vague.

His searches for the current whereabouts of Azerov and Travis Maddox caused him greater concern. Azerov's last known address was the halfway house where he had gone after his release from prison four years earlier. Maddox's last known was his father's decrepit McMansion south of China Lake, which, according to one of Aiden's contacts, was abandoned and in the process of being condemned. Travis was in the wind.

Aiden didn't like it. Threats seemed to flicker from every corner, but when he looked for them, they dissolved into shadows and air.

He took his lockbox from the kitchen cabinet and headed out back to the picnic table. In the shade of the live oaks, beneath the looming mountains, he stripped and cleaned the HK and the SIG. He needed something he could rely on.

⁓

The key rattled in the lock. When the door opened, noise from the freeway grated into the living room. The dingy sunlight silhouetted the man in the doorway. He pocketed the key and took two steps inside before spotting that he wasn't alone in the room.

He stopped. "How did you—"

"Hello, Feliks."

Feliks Galkin drew in on himself, shoulders rising. "Mr. Maddox, I didn't—"

The shadow that had been standing behind the door stepped into the light. "Didn't expect us?"

Feliks jumped.

The shadow's face was half-lit beneath the brim of a Dodgers cap. A shiver visibly rippled up Feliks's back. In the light that filtered through the yellow curtains, his face looked like a wilting hatchet. Travis sat facing him in an easy chair, legs crossed, hands tapping the armrests.

Feliks cleared his throat. "Is there something I can help you with?"

Travis continued to tap the armrests. Feliks glanced toward the bedroom.

"We sent your girlfriend away," Travis said.

"Okay. Yeah."

Feliks ran his hands up and down his thighs, wiping away sweat. He didn't ask if she was injured when she left, or whether she would ever come back. He stood in his own living room, hunching as though he'd been stripped naked and dowsed with ice water.

Behind him, the shadow leaned in. And sniffed. "You been drinking on the job?"

Feliks's shoulders ratcheted tighter. "Never, Eddie."

Eddie Azerov began to rock back and forth, sharply, like a metronome. Feliks looked at Travis with something approaching pleading. Good.

"We have questions," Travis said.

"Of course. Sure."

He couldn't have looked less sure, or more confused.

"Xenon," Travis said.

Anxiety ignited in Feliks's eyes. "Yeah?"

"You haven't spoken to anybody about it, have you?"

"Of course not. No way." He wiped his palms on his jeans again.

"Has anybody contacted you about it?"

"No. How could they?"

"Because you were the one who spray-painted the cameras in the back alley, Feliks. And if your face was at all visible, they could have you on a security video."

"Unh-uh. Impossible." His knee started to jitter. "I did exactly like you asked. I wore the mask, the . . . the . . ."

"Balaclava."

Feliks nodded frantically. Behind him, Zero rocked, his tempo increasing. From the kitchen came the sound of a slow gathering and claws ticking on linoleum.

"Your assignment was to provide a clear path."

"I carried out my assignment, Mr. Maddox. Completely."

"We have a report that the cops saw you in the alley."

"Bullshit. That's impossible."

Travis stood up. "Are you contradicting me? I don't make statements without evidence."

Feliks raised his hands in placation. "I did what you asked. I checked that no vehicles were in the alley. That nobody was out there. I sprayed the camera. They couldn't have seen me."

"They?"

Feliks's mouth hung open.

That was all the evidence Travis needed. He glanced at Azerov. Eddie's metronomic rocking ceased.

Travis walked toward the door. As he passed, Feliks turned, be-seechingly, and grabbed his arm.

"Mr. Maddox. Wait. No, I swear . . ."

Travis shook him off. "Don't swear. Not at me, ever."

"But—no, but I . . ."

Eddie stepped up behind Feliks. In his hand, he held a red cylinder the size of a stick of dynamite. He jabbed it against Feliks's cheek. Feliks cringed.

Eddie said, " 'But-but-but.' Let's talk about what that means, in terms of your impeccable assignment. Really talk. 'Cause this flare bu-bu-burns hot."

Travis smoothed the sleeve of his jacket where Feliks had grabbed him. "Five thousand six hundred degrees Fahrenheit, roughly. Tell Eddie what he needs to know. In full."

He opened the door. Into the slit of yellow sunlight, the dog walked out of the kitchen, rippling, almost tiger striped, the sun turning its dime-size eyes to ingots.

The door swung noiselessly shut behind him. Feliks's whimpers soon faded beneath the drone of freeway traffic.

18

Harper hoisted her backpack over her shoulder. Scanning the street, she locked the MINI and hiked toward her apartment building in the reddening sunshine. She had three hours of reading and research ahead, if she could keep her nerves contained. She wanted to fortify her apartment with sandbags and an antiaircraft missile battery and maybe a decoy, in the form of Detective Erika Sorenstam tied to her balcony railing. But she couldn't ignore her classes. Computational linguistics. Structure of Russian. Topics in Computer Security.

Nobody at the university knew about her background—in the Navy or on the street. Her classmates in mathematical cryptology had no clue she had passed trigonometry while incarcerated, or that at another secure facility ringed by razor wire, she had translated intercepted signals traffic. Keeping that information quiet was easy. She'd been trained all her life not to open her mouth.

Scrubbing away the rest of her teenage training was harder. She consciously avoided doing things the way she had in China Lake. She drove the MINI, not a muscle car. She never counted money like a bank teller, or a thief. Instead, at work she forced herself to switch hands when she counted cash, swiping from a pile of bills in her right hand with her left thumb. Her memories sometimes nauseated her, but very occasionally they produced a taste on her tongue like excitement. She worried that she was like an animal that had been conditioned to respond to an illicit rush. A devil slept on her shoulder, she feared, and if she drifted, even for a moment, it would wake and slide beneath her skin and whisper guiding evils to her once again.

Outside her building, a blue RAV4 was parked at the curb. She found Piper sitting at the top of the stairs, laptop open on her knees, phone in her hand.

"Hey. Everything okay?" Harper said.

Piper stared at the phone, thumb scrolling. "Needed some air. And cookies."

She pointed. Her backpack was slouched against the wall, spewing textbooks and a copy of *Catching Fire* and a bag of Oreos. She wore skinny jeans with ballet flats and a baggy black sweater with sleeves so long they almost ran past her hands. It looked Dickensian.

Harper bent and kissed her cheek. "Come on in."

Piper hit a bunch of keys on her laptop, rapid-fire. "I cadged access to your Wi-Fi. You should change your password."

"I'll keep that in mind, vixen." Her password was strong, but she had given it to Drew. Piper must have gotten it from him.

"'Vixen'? What are we, in a film noir?"

Harper unlocked the door, smiling. It warmed her that she was someone Piper turned to. She'd had few people like that in her life when she was sixteen. And she wondered why Piper looked so lonely.

"Thought you had yearbook after school today," she said.

Piper followed her in. "Please. Lame. I quit last month."

"Dance team?"

"Do I look like I belong on the dance team?"

"Auto shop?"

"Now you're messing with me."

"Repairing engines is a useful skill to have," Harper said. "What do you want to drink?"

Piper strolled, half aimlessly, to the living room. "What are you having?"

"Coffee."

"Then I'll have coffee."

Harper started a pot. Piper stood by the plate-glass windows, gazing at the trees, biting her thumbnail.

Harper walked over and put a hand against her back. "What's going on?"

Piper shrugged. She looked at the room. "You get lonely living by yourself?"

"Not usually. I'm busy, and around people all day on campus and at work."

She tried to read Piper's mood. Something was jagged underneath the surface. "What's up, kid?"

Piper looked at her bitten thumbnail. "I can't even breathe at home. Mom and Dad won't hear anything I say. I try to talk about Drew, and they glaze over, like they're *American Gothic*." Her face flushed. "If Drew . . . would you guys have lived together? Would you have gotten married?"

Oh, sweetie. "It's impossible to say." She gently rubbed Piper's back. "I thought Drew was the greatest. I really did. We totally dug each other."

Piper rolled her eyes. "Don't talk teen. You're speaking the wrong dialect."

"Sorry. Drew and I were close. But, honey, we hadn't been going out that long. Anything's possible. I like to think . . ."

"Of what might have been?" Piper's eyes had a glass gleam in them. Maybe tears.

Harper steadied herself. This wasn't about her. "Drew's in my mind and . . ." She touched her chest. "Here, too. But I have learned that hindsight is twenty-twenty, and thinking of what might have been will make you blind. With rage or regret or grief."

"So you don't wonder?" Piper said. "Not ever?"

The fragility in Piper's voice choked Harper up. "Sometimes. But if I let myself do it too often, I'd lose my shit."

Piper raised an eyebrow and said, "Huh."

Harper put an arm around Piper's shoulder. "I lost your brother. Building an imaginary life with him, only to see it evaporate when I opened my eyes . . . that would be self-inflicted cruelty, and more than I could bear."

"But maybe if you at least imagined it, you could keep him alive in a way."

"Oh, Piper." She tightened her arm around the girl. "That's punishing yourself. You can't do that."

"It takes the pain away. For a while."

"I know. But if you immerse yourself in an imagined world where Drew's living, then every time you pull back from the fantasy, you rip open the wound again."

"I want to."

"I understand. But, Piper, you have to learn how to remember him without reliving the moment, the pain."

"It's how I see him most clearly."

"But you'll make yourself sick that way."

Piper exhaled. "Do you at least dream about him?"

"Yes."

"In the dream, do you know he's dead?"

"Yes."

"Do you ever tell him?"

"No."

Piper looked up. "See—you don't want to break the spell either."

Harper's breath caught. For a second, her pulse pounded in her ears. She wrapped her arms around the girl. "I know."

Piper grabbed hold. Beneath Harper's embrace, her skin was soft, her elbows and shoulders hard.

When Piper stepped back, pink patches heated her cheeks. She picked up her backpack.

Harper said, "Don't go."

Piper shouldered her pack. "I'm fine. Going to try out for cheerleading."

"Oh, my God, you have a fever. Maybe a brain-eating amoeba."

Piper smiled, but it looked melancholy. She kissed Harper's cheek and headed out the door.

When the latch clicked shut, Harper ran her hands through her hair. She walked to the plate-glass windows and out onto the balcony. The RAV4 disappeared down the street.

Could she have said something different? What did Piper need? How could she get her arms around a kid who was so riven with pain?

She leaned on the balcony railing and looked down.

A dog stood on the sidewalk directly below her. It was a red brindled animal, sleek and huge. Its mouth was open, and it was breathing hard through sharp teeth. Its leash dragged on the sidewalk, hanging from a studded collar. Its tiny eyes squinted up at her.

She held still. She'd seen the same dog across the street earlier. It bristled with muscle. Its ears were cropped into stubby triangles, tortilla chip ears. A deep set of teeth marks disfigured its face—fighting scars.

I know you, she thought.

She'd seen it here twice. And once at the memorial garden, after Drew's dedication. Slowly, she straightened and looked up and down the street. Nobody in sight. She stepped back from the railing. The dog grunted and its hackles rose.

She reached into her back pocket for her phone. The dog growled.

Abruptly, its head swiveled. It looked up the street, Dorito ears twitching. It spun and broke into a muscular lope toward the corner.

Somebody had called it. Harper bent down, looking through the trees. The dog ran straight toward the corner, leash trailing. Somebody had used a dog whistle.

Near the bus stop, a man stood on the sidewalk facing the dog. He was about a hundred yards away, hands in his jeans pockets, Dodgers cap pulled low on his head. Harper went rigid.

His face was shadowed beneath the brim of the cap. He wore a sweatshirt, big and baggy. White guy, skinny, with a ragged strut.

Her hands seemed bolted to the railing. He whistled, an eerie sound, then laughed and strolled lackadaisically away. The dog dug in and accelerated.

Focus, Harper. Don't see things that aren't there.

Dammit.

She ran inside, found her keys, ran out the door, and pounded down the stairs to the sidewalk. She ran along the street toward the man in the cap.

Was it him? The strut, the hands-in-pockets pose, the don't-give-a-shit laugh about a vicious dog running loose . . . it was him.

She ran under the trees, trying to punch the passcode for her phone. Take a photo of him, she thought. Evidence. Get something to show Detective Sorenstam that she wasn't hallucinating.

Something to give to Aiden to convince him he wasn't crazy.

Zero. Right there, in the open, a hundred yards from her apartment. What the hell was he doing?

She got a few yards from the corner when her warning system squealed *Stop.*

Don't let him see you. Stay in the shadows. That's what she'd been taught all her life. *Nobody sees.*

Hands shaking, she ducked behind a hedge. Through its leaves she peered across the street in the direction the dog had run. It was nowhere in sight. Neither was the man. But he had to be nearby.

Behind her, she heard a rustling sound.

She spun. "*Jesus.*"

Ten feet away stood a woman with pruning shears and gardening gloves. "I beg your pardon?"

"Sorry."

Harper ran out onto the sidewalk again, looking up and down the street. She ran two blocks before she gave up.

She stopped and turned in a slow circle. She felt both ridiculous and exposed. The sun was bright, the palms purring in the breeze. Her phone hung in her hand, ready to take a photo of . . . what?

A truck cruised by in traffic, sun flashing off the windshield. She stared at the driver. He stared back. Sunglasses and a hat. Chilled, uncertain, she brought up the phone and snapped.

Then the truck was gone.

19

The pounding on the front door was rapid and sharp. Through the fish-eye lens, Aiden saw her standing on his porch.

He safetied the SIG Sauer and jammed it into the back of his jeans. He flipped the tail of his work shirt over it.

He unbolted the door. "Harper."

Her hands were tense at her sides, fingers working. She looked like a jack-in-the-box about to spring. "Thank God you're here."

He gestured her in. "What's wrong?"

"I talked to Sorenstam. She didn't help."

"Slow down." He shut the door. "Talked to Sorenstam about what?"

"I saw him. Eddie Azerov. Today. Up the street from my apartment building."

"Time out. When?"

"Two hours ago. He was a hundred yards away."

"You can positively identify him?"

"Yes." She winced. "No. I chased after him. I tried to get a photo, but he had too much of a head start, and—"

"Chased him?"

"He was watching my place. Had to have been. I'd just gotten home from campus. He—"

Aiden put his hands on her shoulders to hold her still. "You thought you saw Eddie Azerov, so your first reaction was to chase him up the street?"

She paused, lips parted.

"You didn't lock the door and call the police?"

"No. He was leaving. He had a dog, it was off the leash, a fighting dog, running loose . . ."

"Harper?"

"I wanted proof," she said.

He held on to her shoulders. "Can you give a description?"

"I gave it to Sorenstam. And a photo, truck with a partial license plate."

"Not to the Santa Monica police?"

"I don't have any connections there."

He shook his head and stepped back. She looked confused.

"What?" she said.

He didn't know whether to high-five or shout at her. "You saw the man you claim is stalking survivors, and your reaction was to run toward him? Without any backup—and, I presume, unarmed?"

She took a beat. "My neighbor was in the bushes with pruning shears."

He pinched the bridge of his nose. "God help you." He laughed. "You are something else."

"Yeah. I'm scared shitless, and I got nothing to show for it."

He put a hand on her shoulder again—reassuringly, he hoped. "Come on. Let me get you something to drink. Tell me all about it."

In the kitchen, he got a bottle of Pepsi from the fridge. He popped the cap with a bottle opener and handed it to her.

"Cheers," she said, and drank, greedily, tilting her head back.

Her neck was long and lovely. Her hair fell down her back in waves. He shut the cabinet door, hoping Harper hadn't seen the prescription bottles. They returned to the living room. She walked to the patio doors and gazed at the mountains.

"Sorenstam said if I have evidence that somebody is stalking me, to file a report with the Santa Monica PD. But I heard the skepticism in her voice." She looked openly frustrated. "I got the impression that she thought I was trying to pull something on her."

"So you drove all the way up here to try it out on me."

Her face sharpened. "Jesus, no."

He spoke evenly. "Don't take offense."

"How can I file a complaint against a guy I haven't seen face-to-face since I was seventeen? A guy who hasn't contacted me by phone or mail or Instagram? Somebody the sheriff's department thinks is a figment of my imagination? How do I get a restraining order against a delusion?"

He reached out. "Hey."

She swatted his hand away. "Ain't gonna happen."

He raised both hands in surrender and backed off a step.

She flushed. "Sorry. I don't mean to sound so brusque."

Now he smiled. "*Brusque*. You've been working on your vocabulary."

"Sounds worse in Russian. *Grubo*." In Mandarin, *cūbào*. She smiled back. "Let me start again."

She crossed to the sofa, sat, and leaned forward, pressing the Pepsi bottle to her forehead as if cooling a fever. Aiden sat down beside her. Cobey padded in, tail wagging.

She said, "I can't be sure it was him. Maybe I did imagine it. I'm on edge, and I can't trust my own reactions anymore."

"So you came to me because . . ."

She looked at a loss.

"Harper, why? Because I'll tell you what you want to hear? Back up your delusion?"

She took a second to calm herself. "Because you're the man who wears a star on his chest."

Cold water seemed to pour through him. "You really are cynical about law enforcement."

"I'm serious. You're not on active duty, but you're a lawman. That's who you are."

"I've hung up my spurs and six-shooter. And . . ." He stopped, his voice tightening. *Don't do this.*

The light in her eyes was silvery. She put her hand on his arm. Her skin was cool and smooth. Her grip was reassuring.

"Hey," she said.

He just looked at her.

"Sorry. I'm rude sometimes. No, I'm an idiot."

"Hardly."

He stood up and held out his hand. "This house feels too small. Want to get dinner?"

For a second, she held back. Then she took his hand and let him pull her to her feet. Her eyes glowed silver and gold, reflecting the sunset. Her pulse pounded near the hollow in her neck.

She said, "Yeah. But not yet."

Harper stepped closer and felt the heat pouring off of Aiden. She held hard to his hand.

"I shouldn't have brought up your badge. It was thoughtless," she said.

"No, it's okay. Nobody asks me about my life. Not really, not anymore."

All at once, she felt ashamed. Ashamed of herself for barging in on him. For thinking so much of herself, of her roiling fears, the memory of blood and fire, that she had seen only her own pain. When in front of her stood a man who'd lost a part of himself, and with it, the world he had tried to forge.

She looked at their intertwined hands. His grip was sure. From her fingers to the small of her back, she felt electrified. She pressed herself against him, eyes on his.

He wrapped his arms around her. He was strong and lean and the heat and assurance in his embrace seemed a promise, safe harbor. His chest rose and fell against hers. He leaned down to kiss her.

She kept her eyes open and pressed her lips to his. Then her arms vined around his shoulders and she raised up on tiptoe and tilted her head and didn't want to break away, not even to breathe.

His hands snaked into her hair, and he kissed her again. Then he picked her up and swung her around and carried her to his bedroom. She felt a moment of doubt, heard a whisper back in her head saying, *Careful*, like a train crossing coming down, telling her to stop and wait and watch out. He kicked the door shut. The curtains billowed in the breeze. And she said nothing, felt like she was ignoring the clanging lights and warning signs, gunning the engine instead, racing for the tracks.

He set her down on the bed. She reached to work the buttons on her blouse, and he pulled her hand softly aside. She waited for him to undo them, but he dropped to his knees in front of her and leaned in and kissed her neck and the V in the open collar of her blouse. She breathed a hard *ahh* and felt a shiver down her legs. She shut her eyes.

The past bloomed vividly, and she saw everything again—Drew, his empty eyes, his life pouring red and running out through her hands. She smelled smoke and saw the world turn to flame. And she saw Aiden, indistinct at first, trying to reach her. She saw their lives collapse in thunderous noise.

She opened her eyes and saw him now, slate-eyed and warm, his mouth heating her skin, his hands cradling her shoulders. He was beautiful, and careful, and had a smile that could make the devil spit with envy. Her emptiness, her loneliness, dropped away like a scrap of cloth.

She grabbed the front of his work shirt, hauled him onto the bed, and pulled him on top of her. She didn't want to wait. Didn't want caution, or care, or tender exploration. She needed touch, sensation, raw blank sex to overwhelm her circuits. She held on to him, and they were all arms and elbows and grasping hands. She tried to pull his shirt over his head without letting go of him. She didn't want to talk—to talk would be to break the spell, the new thing that was happening, herself coming back into the world, with another damaged person as her guide.

He wrestled his shirt off and she tugged on the buttons of his jeans. Then her shirt was gone and his hands ran down her ribs. His lips traced the centerline of her abs, breastbone to diaphragm to her navel, and his breath on her skin gave her goose bumps. He reached for the nightstand and came out with a Trojan. She took it from him and was breathing so hard, her heart pounding, that she could barely see the packet. They both tried to tear it open and had to get another one, and she laughed and knew things would be all right. Sometime after that, she remembered shouting, and at some point, the lamp on the night-stand got kicked over. Then they were lying side by side, panting, spent, and the curtains waved as though in applause.

She rolled onto her back. "Okay," she said. "Now I'm ready for dinner."

20

They took his truck downtown to Joe's Cafe on State Street. Aiden walked into the restaurant loose-limbed and self-possessed. In a booth by the front windows, they drank beer from bottles and ordered steaks bloody rare. Harper observed him. In the evening light, his face was angular and strong, his eyes calm. The tension that had thrummed through him, like a string tuned too sharp, was gone, at least for now. He looked at her with what seemed like wonder and an open thirst. She wanted to finish their dinner and drive back to his place.

He held out his hand, palm up, smiling. She took it. He closed his fingers around hers and rubbed the ball of her palm.

"Coffee?" he said.

"I don't need caffeine to get me going again."

"Speed metal music?"

"Who seduces to speed metal?"

"F-16s strafing a landing strip?"

She laughed. His eyes sparked.

"You look good when you're happy," he said.

"Then keep it coming, boss."

She turned his hand in hers. A fine line of scars ran toward his elbow.

"The fire," he said.

She squeezed his hand.

"You can ask. You were there."

She hesitated. To ask meant uncaging memories that had claws. "Do you have nightmares?"

His smile thinned. "You know zombie movies? The scene where they swarm a person's car. Dozens, hundreds, moaning, slapping, biting, just everywhere."

She nodded. "The main stairs at Xenon. I still see them. Flailing like worms."

"In the nightmare, I'm swarmed by shooters and I can't fire my weapon. I can't get my finger on the trigger. Can't find Sorenstam." Eyes on her. "Can't find you."

Heat spread up her neck to her face.

"It happened when I got back from my second tour, too. Meet the new dream, same as the old dream." He shrugged and peeled the label from his beer bottle. "Were you deployed?"

"Menwith Hill, England."

His gaze grew shaded. Maybe he knew that Menwith Hill was a listening post.

"I spent my assignment in a Charlotte Brontë novel," she said.

"Got it. Of course you did. You don't have to send the commando sheep from the Yorkshire moors to kill me."

Smiling, he peered out the window. On the busy street, red neon and headlights lit the view. In the next booth, a group of people laughed and snapped photos, the flash from their cameras strobing. Aiden shut his eyes and looked away.

"Covering your six is standard for you, isn't it? You were trained to worry," Harper said.

He paused before looking up again. "I was trained that in combat you do not get second chances. So pay aggressive attention to detail, execute flawlessly, and expect the unexpected." He glanced at the street. "You can't turn it off."

"Hypervigilance."

"I could hardly remember what safe and calm felt like. I was more comfortable pissed off and on edge."

She took his hand again. No wonder he had paranoid tendencies. Quietly, she said, "Any triggers?"

He continued to watch the street. "Heat."

Her throat constricted.

He turned to her. "You?"

Thinking of Drew's last moment was a trigger. So were loud bangs, screams, the smell of smoke, and the smell of bourbon.

"Yeah. It's a feed from an electric wire, and you can't shut off the power," she said. "How do you handle it?"

"When I came home from Afghanistan, I joined the sheriff's department. Being a cop—okay, sure, there's a thrill. But I was trying to lower the volume. Coming out of combat, I wanted a job, something I could be good at, someplace where I could make a difference. But I wanted to dial it all down, back to normal range." He looked at the street, orange with sunset and lengthening shadows. "Thought I had. Tried to. For a while, anyhow."

He had turned somber. "Since the injury? Cognitive processing therapy. In rehab, I learned ways to unwind the anger from the depression. You have to fight the cascade of impulsive and irrational feelings. The first line of defense is to slow down, cool off, and think. That helps get an edge." He looked at her. "So does talking to you."

She rubbed her hand along his arm. He drank his beer and swept the street again with his gaze.

"And if we ever face a zombie attack?" she said.

"Carry blunt objects," he said. "But I think you're the one who's going to be prepared. How many jobs are you applying for, once you get your degree?"

She leaned back. He had her. "Homeland Security. FEMA. Air National Guard. Risk Mitigation Associates. Metro Disaster Preparedness, Inc. Spartan Security. Advantech Systems." She shrugged.

"FBI?"

"No. No law enforcement agencies."

"Your background as a cryptologic technician, fluent in Russian—

you'd be an asset. Cyberthreats, especially from the former Soviet Union, are a huge portion of the bureau's current focus."

"I can see myself as a White Hat but not a cop."

She meant to sound offhand, but as soon as the words left her mouth, she flinched. He was being forced to see himself in those terms, and she knew it hurt.

"That came out wrong," she said.

"Forget it." He held her gaze. "You haven't asked me about the video Sorenstam showed you. What I did at the station that time."

"When you went after the other detective."

"Ask."

Okay. "What the hell was that?"

"Misidentification. It happens when the brain fails to keep an uninterrupted view of the world." He set down his beer. "The brain normally processes images and predicts what's coming, so we have instant focus. It's a steady cam that helps us see straight. That day, the camera crashed."

"So what did it feel like when you saw Perez? A roll of film slipping off the reel?"

"A disconcerting feeling. Like déjà vu," he said. "You saw—Perez's in his fifties, with that gut. But when I saw him, I felt with crystal certainty that I was looking at the shooter in disguise. Complete confidence. It was like an electric jolt that hit me in the head and flew out my fingertips."

"Even though Perez looked nothing like the shooter. And you knew that."

"You're trying to be logical."

"I'm trying to understand how this works."

"I thought he was taunting me. I thought the shooter was a mad genius who had perfected a disguise so that nobody else could recognize him. It was blowing my mind." He watched the street. "So I tackled him. I was unarmed, but what I wanted was my service pistol, maybe a Taser and a telescoping baton." He turned to her. "So now you understand. The department isn't going to trust me with a duty handgun when at any moment I might decide that Santa Claus at the mall is actually a hired killer."

"Have you done that?"

"There's time. I'm making a list and checking it twice."

Outside, people strolled along the sidewalk, chatting and laughing. Traffic brushed past. She saw a low swirl of red-brown, canine motion. She refocused.

Aiden followed her gaze. "What?"

Up State Street, in the middle of the pedestrian crowd, a heavily muscled dog stood on the sidewalk.

"The dog." She leaned forward, trying to see the dog through a stream of people and headlights shining on the road. "Hundred yards away."

Aiden stood up, flipping the tail of his shirt down. "I see it."

He stalked to the door and out of the restaurant, intent, a hitch in his step.

She grabbed her things, threw some bills on the table, and ran out the door after him. People swirled past her on the street, music flowing out of a club, loud guitars and an amplified wail. Half a block ahead, Aiden forged through the thick evening crowd. Beyond him, the dog raised its heavy black head. It spun and ran off.

He crossed a street against the light and kept going. At an Italian restaurant, people sat at sidewalk tables. Music rolled from the open windows. A group stood waiting outside the door.

Aiden stormed toward them, the hitch in his step more pronounced. Harper hurried. Aiden plunged into the group. Harper heard a shout and a glass breaking as it hit the sidewalk. She broke into a run.

Somebody cried, "Hell are you doing?"

Aiden grabbed a man and threw him across a nearby table. A woman screamed. Glass and plates flew, hit the sidewalk, and shattered. Chairs tipped over backward as people scattered. Aiden went down with the man, fighting.

Harper ran into the fray.

"Fuck is this?" a man yelled.

She shoved through the crowd. Aiden was on the ground, kneeling on a man's back. Skinny guy, jeans, a hoodie askew over his head. The guy was thrashing. Aiden had one knee in the small of his spine and was twisting his arm back behind him, as if ready to cuff him.

"Shut up and don't move," Aiden said, breathing hard, his face dark.

The guy in the hoodie kicked and tried to buck out from under Aiden's grip. "Get off me, asshole."

Harper forced her way to his side. "Aiden."

Aiden pressed the man's head to the concrete. "Call 9-1-1."

Confused, she fumbled her phone from her pocket. Behind her, a woman said, "I already called."

From the restaurant, a young man pushed through the crowd, face dull with anger. "Get off him."

Harper said, "Leave him alone. He's making a citizen's arrest."

He shouldered her aside and pulled on Aiden's shirt. It exposed the pistol in the waistband of his jeans. Skittishly, the man stepped back. "He's got a gun."

The man pinned beneath Aiden clawed at the concrete. "Get off me."

Harper knelt at Aiden's side, heart pounding. She pulled the hood of the sweatshirt off the man's head. He continued to thrash.

Aiden reached around to the small of his back. Harper's fear ran out of her fingertips like sparks.

She grabbed his hand. "No. *No.*"

Aiden gave her a look, seemingly taken aback by her reaction. Then he moved his hand away from the gun. Faintly, she heard a police siren.

Aiden pressed his hand to the man's neck. "That's them. Flag them down."

"Aiden," she said.

He bent to the man's ear. "Did you think you could get away with it forever?"

She took hold of Aiden's shoulders. "Who is this?"

Breathing hard, Aiden said, "Him."

Harper's scalp tingled. The man beneath Aiden's grip was in his early twenties, with East Asian features.

The sirens grew louder, and flashing blue lights cut across the crowd.

Harper said, "Aiden, I don't know who this guy is."

Aiden looked up. "Him. Zero. It's Azerov."

21

The music pounded from the makeshift stage in the beer garden. The wind rattled the hanging lightbulbs, and a crowd slammed pitchers on the worn picnic tables under the trees. Out front, a rank of motorcycles was parked on the dirt, mostly Harleys. In the deepening night, Rosalita's was hopping. People came from up and down the coast to this two-lane strip in Ojai to eat and dance and knock back some of Rosalita's thirty varieties of tequila and four brands of beer. The band was hammering at outlaw rock, the guitarist bent over his ax like Stevie Ray Vaughan. In the kitchen, Jasmine Hay dragged a trash bag from the can, tied it off, and lugged it out the back door.

Behind the restaurant, she slid the bolt on the gate and hauled the rattling trash bag down the alley. She chucked it into the Dumpster. When the lid banged closed, she wiped her hands on her waitress's apron and took a pack of Winstons from her pocket. It wasn't officially her break, but her feet ached and her ears were ringing. She cupped her hand to light a cigarette and stood in the alley, blowing smoke at the dark sky.

The fence muffled the music. The foothills that separated Ojai from the coast loomed pale in the moonlight. She smoked the Winston and stamped out the butt and headed back up the alley.

Outside the gate, the saucer she regularly filled with food for the alley cat had been kicked over. She righted it. The manager of Rosalita's didn't want employees feeding strays. The manager didn't want employees boosting cash from the registers either, but Jasmine was smooth.

She had learned not to be greedy. That's how she had kept the job for nine months. Keep things quiet. Just slide by and nobody notices what you're really doing. Besides, she needed the cash. The other waitresses had husbands and parents and boyfriends. She had only herself to count on. At minimum wage, that didn't cut it.

She peered around for the cat, making a kissy sound to attract it.

She heard the click of tags rattling on a collar. She turned. Down the alley, near a streetlight, a dog padded into view. Three heavy steps, and it stopped.

She stood there.

It was half-visible under the streetlight, a soot-faced ghost that cast a heavy shadow. Something hung from its mouth.

She didn't want to know what that thing was. She knew what it was. She took a step toward the gate.

The dog took a step toward her.

The thing in its mouth swung heavily. Feet limp, tail dragging on the pavement. The dog held the cat by the neck, clamped tight in its teeth. She felt a lightning moment of nausea.

She looked around for a rock, something to throw. Nothing. When she looked back, the dog was closer. It didn't seem to walk, just to be nearer. It was breathing easily, its eyes glittering under the streetlight.

Her nausea spread into fear. Unreasoning blank *get the fuck out of there* fear. She backed toward the gate and grabbed the handle.

It wouldn't open.

"Shit." She rattled the gate. It was locked.

The dog was closer. Standing there with the cat in its mouth, back feet dragging on the road. She rattled the gate again. Something was jammed into the latch on the other side. She thought she might be sick.

She pounded on the gate. "Hey!"

She shouted it, but the restaurant's back door was securely shut and the band was thrashing away in the beer garden. Unless someone happened to be standing directly on the other side of the fence, nobody was going to hear her. And all the businesses on the other side of the alley were shut for the night.

She backed away from the gate, slowly. To escape from the dog, she would have to back all the way out of the alley and run around to the front of Rosalita's. The dog stood in a shadow, and its tags rattled, a cold sound. It appeared again, closer. She could see its teeth now. It looked at her and never blinked. She kept backing up. The exit from the alley was about sixty yards away.

Behind her came the purr of an engine and the crunch of car tires on broken glass. She looked over her shoulder.

The dark outline of a car blocked the exit from the alley. Headlights off. Inside, behind the wheel, the red tip of a cigarette glowed as the driver inhaled.

Jasmine looked at the dog. It dropped the cat, watching her.

Into those teeth, or the grille of the car?

She knew who was behind the wheel. Knew why he was here. Had told herself—for a year—that everything had gone quiet, that the fiasco was over with and forgotten because nobody wanted to mention Xenon ever again. As long as she stayed under the radar and didn't get arrested for shoplifting or receiving stolen property, as long as she didn't get a speeding ticket, as long as the car she had driven that night remained at the bottom of Lake Casitas, nobody could connect her to what had happened. Nobody had seen her driving Zero away from the burning club. Nobody had seen her drop him in Hollywood. Nobody even knew about it. The only person she'd told was Feliks Galkin, and he for damn sure wouldn't talk. Would he?

Idiot. She stood in the alley.

If she didn't move, she had about sixty seconds until she was dead. The car was old, a granny's car, big American thing with a huge hood that drooped toward the ground, maybe a New Yorker. Two tons, probably. It filled the alley. She couldn't squeeze around it.

The dog stood over the cat, facing her, panting. Drool slid from its jowls to the pavement. The music thudded from the distant stage. She inhaled and tensed.

Jasmine turned and ran straight at the darkened car. Fifty yards, forty-five. Her only chance was to leap onto the hood and climb over the roof and jump off the trunk before Zero managed to accelerate and hit her at a speed that would kill her. Forty yards. Tires spun and the engine gunned and from the darkened interior, the cigarette glowed hotter. The car slowly gained speed, looming in front of her. She sensed more than heard the dog behind her, coming.

Fool. This was inevitable, she knew that now. Zero, Rowdy Maddox, Travis—they went back years together, and she was only a street kid, somebody they'd used for their own purposes. *Drive. One night only. Don't even have to be outside the club. Wait two blocks over. We'll cut out the back door and down the alley and over the cement wall. Meet us at the vacant lot. Nobody will see you. In and out. Dump the car. Go on about your business. Five hundred bucks.*

She ran, gauging it. Thirty yards. The car was closing, gaining momentum. The music continued pounding in the beer garden, but she heard only the roar of the engine, saw the hood, and prepared to jump.

She dug in, twenty yards.

The dog sank its teeth into her ankle. She cried out, shocked, and went down. She heard its growl and felt an agonizing pain, teeth biting down on her Achilles tendon. She tried to roll and kick free, but the dog held tight, jaws clamped, ripping her, holding her in place while the car roared toward her. She screamed.

The car braked sharply. Three feet away from her, it stopped. The dog continued tearing at her leg.

She screamed again and knew that nobody heard her: 110 decibels from the amplifiers on the stage, two electric guitars, mikes turned all the way up. Noisy kitchen, the only other place somebody might take notice. Mariachi music from a portable stereo there.

"No," she yelled. "Get off me, you fucking thing."

She tried to roll and kick the dog away. She cocked her knee and booted the dog heavily in the head. Its grip weakened. She kicked it again. It squealed in pain and let go.

She rolled and tried to stand, and her foot was useless. She started crawling.

The door of the car opened. The cigarette came out first, hitting the ground with a confetti of red sparks. Then two boots hit the ground. She could see only legs beyond the open door. She crawled, gravel digging into her palms. Then a heavy object appeared, hanging beside the man's leg, swinging from his hand. It was a sledgehammer.

22

Beneath a sky fading to deep blue, Harper sat on a wall outside the Santa Barbara Police Department. The Spanish-style building glowed white under spotlights. A dying redwood stood sentry behind her. She crossed her arms against the chill.

When the station's doors opened, she was relieved to see three men emerge: Aiden; his brother, Kieran; and the lawyer Kieran had called.

She stood up. The men approached slowly, talking in low tones.

The night felt dead. The palms hung limp. The tall antennas above the building faded into the night. The street was empty. Only a meter maid's electric cart was parked at the curb. The flashing lights and noise and dismay from the downtown sidewalk had ebbed but lingered around her like a sickly scent.

The man Aiden had tackled was named Derek Wong. He was a sophomore at UC Santa Barbara. He'd been waiting outside the restaurant for a table, there to celebrate his fraternity brother's birthday, when Aiden plowed into their party and steer-wrestled him to the ground. Wong had bruises and abrasions from hitting the pavement. The police were an unhappy bunch, perplexed and wary about Aiden.

"He's a killer." Aiden had shouted the words at Wong as the cops shoved him, handcuffed, into the back of the patrol car. "You're letting him escape."

Wong just pointed at him. "Dude is crazy."

Now, winding his way down the ramp in front of the police station, he looked drawn. The lawyer talked. Kieran looked around, hawkish, seemingly for threats, or targets Aiden might attack next. Harper felt desolate. And afraid.

She hung back when the men reached the sidewalk. The lawyer raised his hands in a calming gesture. He was a young guy wearing a button-down shirt and jeans, after-hours clothes. He was in a wheelchair. He had a matter-of-fact manner that couldn't disguise the misery of the situation.

"Lay low. Stay calm," he said. "I'll talk to you tomorrow."

They shook hands. The lawyer said good-bye to Kieran and headed up the sidewalk toward the parking garage.

Aiden watched him go. When he was out of earshot, he said, "You sure about him? He's a kid."

"I've known him since he was sixteen. He worked on my boat one summer in high school. He's smart, and tough as a cast iron skillet." He crossed his arms. "Plus, you're standing on the sidewalk, instead of in a cell or on a psychiatric hold."

Aiden raised his hands. "Noted."

Kieran squeezed Aiden's shoulder. Kieran's expression spoke of loss and futility. Then he glanced at Harper. He seemed unsure why she was still there, and maybe whether he should trust her and Aiden on their own.

She approached. "Glad to see you both."

Aiden put his hands in his jeans pockets.

Kieran said, "I'm sorry I wasn't there when it happened." He cut a glance at his brother. "Not that I could have kept an episode from—"

"Kieran, you couldn't have," Aiden said. "Let it go."

Reluctantly, seemingly at frayed ends, Kieran nodded. "I'll give you a ride back to your truck."

"My weapon," Aiden said.

Kieran looked almost theatrically at the police station. "When we get to your pickup, man."

The drive back to the parking garage was silent. So was the ride in Aiden's F-150 back to his house on Foothill Road. In the dark cab,

Harper watched the headlights scroll along the white lines on the road. Aiden's face was lit eerily by the dashboard lights, edged red. When they pulled into his driveway, she was struck by the heaviness of the foliage, the oaks leaning over the roof, the manzanita and hibiscus overgrown under the eaves. As if the house were hiding, pulling a cloak over itself. In this hilly neighborhood, where the winds scoured the ground, and the fire station posted signs warning that the fire danger was high, he had let it grow like kindling.

He turned off the engine. She got out before the moment could stretch. In the chilly air, she found her car keys. He climbed out. His door closed. She waited, but he said nothing. He stood by the truck, staring into the darkness.

She felt a draining sensation, as though a plug had been pulled. She couldn't get into her car without saying good-bye. She felt vulnerable and frightened and knew he couldn't help her the way she had wished for.

She told herself: *Straighten up and fly right.*

She walked around the pickup toward him. "You gonna be okay tonight?"

"I'm not going to get drunk, if that's what you mean. Celebrate my first arrest with tequila shooters and a piñata."

She was more concerned that Kieran had handed back Aiden's SIG Sauer. She stopped six feet from him.

He stood under the wind. The oaks dipped and hissed, and the manzanita scraped against the walls of the house. In the backyard, Cobey barked.

Aiden said, "I'm sorry you saw it."

"You don't have to explain."

He spread his hands. "This is where I am. This is it."

"It's okay, Aiden."

It wasn't. He knew that. He smiled, and it was a look as unhappy and cutting as anything she'd ever seen.

She didn't know if he wanted her to come in, or stay, or whether he was testing her, waiting to see which way she jumped. She didn't like the uncertainty. She knew that was a fault of hers, and right then, in the dark, on an empty road with a man carrying a gun, she didn't want to find out.

"I'll call you in the morning," she said. "It's a long drive home, and I have class at nine."

"Sure."

She stepped toward him and he raised a hand. "It's all right. We'll talk."

She reached for his hand, but he gave her a thumbs-up and walked toward the house. The door shut behind him with a hard click.

Aiden stood in the darkened kitchen, leaning on the counter. He heard her engine start, and then the headlights of her car swiped across the walls of his living room. She gunned the MINI into the night. Cobey barked again to be let in.

He opened the cabinet and took out the prescription bottles. He popped the lids and tipped pills into his palm and swallowed them with lukewarm water from the tap.

Don't blame her.

He stood there, lights off, moonlight floating through the windows, the trees brushing against the roof.

Two days off his meds. He'd been sloppy. He'd been arrogant. Feeling strong, feeling seduced. Feeling too much pride to let a woman see him downing the chemicals that kept his half-broken brain from frying a circuit.

He'd been so sure.

The guy he tackled, he'd been positive. This time especially. The hoodie, the jeans, the way he laughed and looked at him, eyes cold.

He shook himself. At least he hadn't blacked out with a seizure.

Even now, he could rely only on the word of the police, and his brother, and the can't-get-away-fast-enough Harper Flynn. He'd been one hundred percent convinced.

He still was, somehow. Logically, he knew the evidence was against it. But his heart and his throbbing, craptastic mind told him: Zero had tailed them. And he had disguised himself with a look that nobody would doubt—younger, Asian, laughing at Aiden and Harper all along.

But Derek Wong was not Eddie Azerov. Aiden had to believe that for now. That attorney—he found the guy's card, Jesse Blackburn—had been direct with the cops, and ready to go, and didn't look at him funny, not even for a moment. Guy with his own issues in the way people perceived him, Aiden was sure. Experienced, Kieran said. Blackburn was ready to defend him but didn't believe for a second that Derek Wong was Zero. Aiden had no chance of convincing any of them.

But if Azerov wasn't in Santa Barbara, where was he?

Cobey barked.

And Harper. Angry and confused and he saw her eyes, the way she'd looked at him, trying to pull him off the man. A look brimming with raw knowledge and fear. Harper was gone.

He opened the back door, and Cobey bounded in. Aiden dropped onto the sofa. Cobey whined and set his head on his knee.

"Christ, what a fuckup I am," Aiden said.

23

Even with his headphones on, Oscar Sierra heard barking. He was listening to a TED talk online, but the stereo speakers were also booming out Taking Back Sunday, and the TV was running a *Doctor Who* marathon. The barking was sharp, demanding, and close. He paused the TED, stopped the music, muted the TV, and slipped off the headphones. The wind brushed against the trailer. The dog barked again.

He stood up, wary. He didn't have a dog.

He padded to the window and peeked through the curtains. Outside, things were dark—no headlights on the dirt road. His closest neighbor lived two miles away. Distant scattered dwellings were just twinkles on hilltops, like fireflies in the desert night.

He couldn't see a car parked outside, or a motorbike, or even a freakin' mule.

More barking. Definite, like a summons. This didn't sound like a stray ready to get into the garbage.

None of his business.

Except, who knew? An ashtray sat on the burnt-orange shag carpeting, full of roaches. He should probably throw them away. But his gaze strayed across his rig, the computers stacked across two tables and the desk in a corner of the living room. Four hard drives, two monitors, a laptop, and the stolen Cray, connected by cables that spread like the tentacles of the kraken. And beneath the table, the card encoders and the cardboard boxes that contained five thousand blank plastic magnetic stripe cards.

Another bark. Could be a police dog, some kind of drug sniffer or electronics sniffer or ninja German shepherd with frickin' laser beams attached to its head.

He couldn't make his rig disappear, but he could dump the roaches. Unless opening the door would mean exposing himself to police spotlights and the night scopes of fifteen DEA agents lurking outside in the cactus.

Shit, dude, you're getting paranoid.

The dog barked again.

Gingerly, Oscar opened the door. The sky was steaming with stars. Sand hissed against the rusting walls of the trailer. Ten feet from the foot of the steps stood a busted-face fighting dog, rippling brown and black, piggy-eyed, posing there like a sleek fur statue.

Whoa, he was really baked.

He inched back, and the dog growled.

"Gonna ask him in?"

The voice came from behind him in the hallway. Oscar jumped and turned, hand on the doorknob.

"Whatever. Sure." Oscar wiped his hand under his nose. "Kind of a crap practical joke, man."

Dude walked out of the back hallway into the living room. He must have climbed in a bedroom window. Hadn't knocked, hadn't been invited in. Oscar would have remembered inviting Eddie Azerov in. Oscar didn't think he was *that* baked.

Azerov slid around the room, eyeing the TV and computers, sniffing the air. He glanced at Oscar, flicking his head around locustlike.

"Skunky weed, Oscar."

Another growl rolled from the darkness at the foot of the steps. "What is that?"

Azerov whistled. "Eagle, come."

The dog bounded up the steps into the trailer and trotted to Azerov's side. It moved like silken, weighty meat. Its jowls sagged, teeth visible, gleaming with drool.

Oscar stepped back. "He have a saddle, or you ride bareback?"

"Close the door," Azerov said.

Oscar did as he was told. He was mightily surprised. China Lake was a solid two-and-a-half-hour drive from L.A. and not a spot you dropped into on a whim. It was off almost every highway, a deliberate twenty-mile detour into the desert any way you came at it.

"Something going on?" Oscar said.

Eddie Azerov strolled to the kitchen and opened the fridge. He pulled out a bottle of Stoli. Found a clean glass in the cupboard. He came back to the living room, dropped into the Naugahyde chair, and poured himself three fingers of vodka.

He pointed at Oscar with the bottle. "Sit down."

Oscar looked at his furniture. The sofa now sported the dog, sitting upright and alert on the center cushion, eyeing him. He took the desk chair.

"Things are cool," he said. "I breached the firm in Hyderabad. It's the one that processes debit card transactions for Samaalbank in the United Arab Emirates. Got the account data. I already eliminated withdrawal limits."

Eddie set the vodka bottle between his legs, propped against his crotch.

"We got the blank cards sourced," Oscar went on, pointing at the box under the desk. "Target gift cards. I just need to program 'em with the Samaalbank data. We're solid." Still no response. "So, once you get the cashing crews organized, you're ready to rock."

He wiped his nose.

Azerov said, "Yeah. I know. That's not why I'm here."

"Then what?"

"That thing last year."

Oscar squinted to focus. "Which one?"

"Xenon."

"Okay."

"Your work—you know."

Oscar leaned on his knees, trying to keep Azerov's face sharp in his vision. It was distracting, having the dog right there, jowls drooping, showing its teeth. It licked its chops, so loudly that it seemed to be speaking to him.

"I know. My work was spot-on," Oscar said.

Zero smiled, a quick flash that reminded Oscar of good times. He got up from the recliner, holding the vodka bottle by the neck.

"I love you, Oscar. Never lived outside the Indian Wells Valley and you talk like an Englishman." He crossed the room and affectionately patted Oscar's cheek. "You're my own little Doctor Who."

Oscar rubbed his cheek. The dog opened its mouth. Its breathing was noisy.

"Why is he so insistent?" Oscar said.

Zero set the bottle on the desk and leaned over the computer. "Who?"

"The dog. He keeps talking to me."

Zero was absently playing with the keyboard. He half turned.

"Careful, man, I got some stuff running," Oscar said.

Zero raised his hands, like *no harm, no foul.* "What's Eagle telling you?"

Oscar looked at the dog. Its tongue lolled from its jowls. Its eyes were unequivocal.

"He's telling me to jump off the Rock Creek Bridge or he'll eat my heart out."

Zero tilted his head. Sharp, like a click. "Oscar, what was in the last joint you smoked?"

Oscar shrugged. "What's got you and Eagle so twisted up that you had to come out here in the middle of the night?"

"Remember that card you mocked up last year?"

Oscar nodded. "Which one?"

"The employee swipe card from Xenon."

"Right. Man, that turned into something surreal. I saw the news. It was . . ." What was it? The dog's breathing grew louder in his ears. "What about the swipe card?"

Zero said, "The information I gave you, to encode. You deleted it?"

"Harper Flynn? Her employee ID number, that?"

Zero turned all the way. "You remember the name?"

"Not that common. And it reminded me of, you know . . ." He shrugged. "Flynn. That last name."

Zero nodded. Oscar got a weird feeling, like a bee stinging him at the base of his skull. The dog hadn't moved, but its eyes were talking to him again. Oscar blinked and rubbed the heel of his palm over his own eyes.

"Sierra," Zero said. "Did you delete all the data?"

"From my machines? Absolutely, man." He smiled, thinking: *But not from my brain.*

The dog stirred. Oscar felt the stinging deeper this time. *Uh-oh.*

Zero stared at him, seeming to calculate something.

Oscar's mouth went dry. "It's gone from my rig, my rack, from the cloud, poof, obliterated. Sayonara. I'm on to the next big thing, Zero. Hyderabad, Samaalbank. Want some pizza?"

His tongue was sticking to the roof of his mouth. The dog said, *Think you're tougher than him?*

No. Not hardly.

He pointed at the kitchen. "Meat lovers' paradise, delivered from Papa John's at lunchtime, it's still fresh. I'm gonna heat it up."

He walked himself to the kitchen. His back itched. He could hear the dog breathing and thinking, and Zero watching him. The watching, he could hear it like a crackling in the air.

He said, over his shoulder, "Check my in-box. It's afternoon in India. Maybe Dev's had some luck. But if he's online, don't chat with him."

"How come?" Zero said.

Oscar rounded the corner into the kitchen. "He's skittish. Won't talk to anybody but me."

His entire body itched, a psychic itch, with a sound like teeth grinding against each other in a dog's mouth. He clattered a plate out of the cupboard and slid two curled slices of pizza onto it and slammed it into the microwave and turned the thing on, giving it two minutes at high power. It hummed like a lawn mower. He tiptoed to the door.

He called out, "There's cake. A whole sheet cake from the supermarket bakery; they were going to throw it away."

"Stop dicking around," Zero said.

His voice came from the desk chair. Hand trembling, Oscar turned the knob and opened the flimsy door wide enough to slide through. He twitched down the wooden steps, eased the door shut, and tried to widen his eyes to gulp down the vast black night. The light from the windows dribbled in a pool about thirty feet ahead of him. Ducking low, he speed-walked into the desert. Thinking: *Quiet, feet. Quiet. Quiet.*

Twenty yards from the trailer, he gave up and ran. He ran to get out of the light, away from the dog's words, away from Zero's gaze. His legs seemed like caramel, soft and wobbly, and he knew Zero was coming before he heard the kitchen door flip open and hit the wall of the trailer and heard Zero pound down the stairs, before he heard his own breath and the sound of panting in the air and paws tearing through the sand. He ran.

24

Harper eased off the clutch and sludged forward in Westwood's morning traffic, inching toward campus on Wilshire Boulevard. Her eyes were red from lack of sleep. Her hair fell out of a sloppy updo with a big clip. Her jeans, she saw, had a coffee stain. She hadn't called Aiden.

The morning news droned from the radio. She turned it off when the announcer said, "Police are investigating mysterious burns to a man's face and arms, which may have been caused by a road flare." Then, unsettled, she turned it back on. Road flare. Magnesium flare? But the report was over. She parked and schlepped her book bag onto her shoulder. As she hiked toward the Linguistics Department, she phoned Erika Sorenstam.

"Ms. Flynn."

Sorenstam didn't even simulate enthusiasm. Harper said, "I was calling to see if you've learned anything from my swipe card."

"I'm on it."

Harper walked through busy bicycle traffic and clots of young people half-asleep and intent on getting to class. The sky was robin's-egg blue.

"Ms. Flynn? Is there something else I can help you with?"

I'm afraid I've been a fool. I'm afraid I've blown any chance I had to get through this unscathed.

"No. Thank you, Detective."

She hung up, thinking: *exercise in futility.* She picked up her pace toward a cluster of redbrick buildings. They sincerely attempted to project gravitas, something never quite possible on a sunny Los Angeles campus surrounded by freeways and beaches and Hollywood. She hurried around a corner, started up a flight of steps, and saw the girl leaning against the balustrade.

Harper slowed. "Piper?"

Piper smiled and looked abashed. "I didn't know where else to find you."

"What's going on?"

"You in a hurry?"

Harper tried not to look at her watch. The plaza was emptying out, the last few students hurrying to class. She had maybe four minutes. Her professor would be unforgiving. Her professor, the one she hoped to ask for letters of recommendation.

"I have time. What's up, kiddo?"

Piper straightened. "I acted like a douche yesterday. I'm sorry."

"Oh, sweetie. Thanks," Harper said. "What else? You're all tied in knots."

"Nothing. School. Drew."

The last word came out half whispered. Harper slid her arm around Piper's shoulder.

"He laughed at me two hours before he headed to Xenon. Then, *it.* Gone. No going back, no trying again, no breathing or thinking, no nothing. And he never expected it, I never imagined it, and why did he go to Xenon that night?"

She clenched her fists and pressed them against her mouth. Harper held on to her. The plaza had emptied.

Piper inhaled, shoulders shuddering. "Sorry. I know you don't have any answers."

"Except to keep living. Breathe in, breathe out. Get up every morning."

"One day at a time."

"I don't want to sound saccharine."

"No, it's sweet." She sighed. "Overly sweet, with sparkles on it. But sweet."

She reached into her backpack and took out a small folded piece of black paper.

Harper said, "Origami?"

It was a horse, angular and striking. Piper set it in Harper's upturned palm.

"For you."

"Thank you. It's lovely," Harper said.

"Figure you deserve something for putting up with an annoying teenager."

"I'm here, hon. Whenever you need me."

"And I'm not skipping school. I don't have first-period class on Thursdays." She grinned. "I could tell it was killing you. I bet you never missed school in your life. You were the teacher's pet."

"I'll let you picture me that way."

"Somebody killed my brother."

Harper held on to her. "Some asshole absolutely did."

"Are you getting anywhere with the sheriffs?"

"I've been . . . diligently calling Detective Sorenstam."

"Pestering, you mean."

Harper squeezed Piper's shoulder. If the girl still had a sense of sarcasm, she wasn't too far gone. "Relentlessly."

"You think she's a good detective?" Piper said.

"As far as I can tell."

"Hope so. My parents said that at Xenon, Sorenstam was probably concerned about the other sheriff instead of the people who were injured. That guy, Garrison."

"He was her partner."

"Yeah. 'Partner.'" She made air quotes.

Harper felt a dump of adrenaline. "Sorenstam and Aiden Garrison?"

"Yeah, lovers. What's the matter?"

She shook her head. "Nothing. I just hadn't heard that."

"Is something wrong with it?" Piper said.

"No. They're adults." She picked up her backpack. "No, nothing's wrong."

"Then how come you're acting like a scared bird? You're all ruffled."

She hucked her backpack onto one shoulder. "Everything about this ruffles me. And if Sorenstam and Garrison were . . ."

Son of a bitch.

"If they were a couple . . . then, nothing. They're professionals."

Piper's gaze was acute. The girl was going to see through her like light through a waterfall.

"Mom and Dad said they should have been evacuating innocent bystanders but instead maybe they were just covering each other's backs."

Why hadn't Aiden said anything?

Piper kept talking, but Harper barely heard her. All at once, she understood the tension between Aiden and Sorenstam.

"Right?" Piper squinted against the sunshine. "You don't think Sorenstam would try to make Garrison look bad, or promise to do something for him and then half-ass it because she's getting back at him? You know, because they broke up?"

It had never occurred to Harper. Now it did. "Absolutely not."

Yeah. Because nobody in Harper's life had *ever tried to get back at someone over a personal issue, ever.* She felt light-headed.

Piper looked worried. "What did you tell her?"

Harper put a hand on the girl's shoulder. "Every single bit of information I can remember. That's what the authorities ask witnesses and survivors to do."

Piper's face paled. "Survivors. But what if Drew saw something?"

Harper felt as if she'd been scratched across the face with a farm implement.

"What if he saw something important? What if he was the key?" Piper said.

"There's no way to know that now."

"I know. It's just . . . we're talking about my brother." Piper scrubbed a hand across her cheek. "You're missing your class, aren't you?"

"I'll sneak in the back."

"Thought you told me it's better not to find excuses."

"You're not an excuse. You're a friend."

Piper seemed to assess that and decide that Harper had passed her test. "You're the only person I can talk to about this. The only one who doesn't treat me like a kid. Sorry if I unload on you."

"You going to be okay?"

"It's a sunny day."

She turned to go. Harper did, too. But she turned around.

"Yeah, it is. So let's take advantage of it."

Piper tilted her head, curious. Harper took out her car keys. "Girls' day out."

⁓

The smoke boiled off the tires, and the view slid past the windshield. Concrete, weeds, dirt, back to the concrete, facing the sun. At the wheel, Piper squealed.

The MINI spun around and stopped, jolting Harper against the seat belt. "Gas. Go."

Piper punched it.

"Clutch," Harper said.

Piper let it off too sharply but better than before, and they leaped forward.

"Yes." Piper virtually bounced with excitement. "*Yes*."

Harper couldn't help smiling. "Again. That was better but still sloppy. Look where you are on the track."

Piper stuck her head out the open window and howled. The wind blew her hair. Harper laughed.

"Come on. You're getting it. Let's go again," she said.

Piper stopped at the end of the old runway, downshifting this time, braking with the engine the way Harper had shown her. She eased the MINI around and faced the centerline again.

She took a large breath and gripped the wheel. Her face was flushed, her eyes determined.

"Ready?" Harper said.

"I get this one, you'll let me drive in the hangar?"

"Get it precise and I'll buy you an ice-cream cone."

Piper glared up the runway at the traffic cone Harper had set out, two hundred yards ahead. Harper scanned the perimeter one more time. Past the taxiway and scrubland, the perimeter fence listed slightly. Nobody seemed concerned that she'd managed to get a bright blue MINI Cooper onto the shuttered airfield at the north end of the Valley. The lock on the gate looked secure, too.

"Okay. Line it up six feet to the right of the centerline."

Piper goosed the gas and eased the MINI over. Harper aimed her hand at the windshield like a hatchet.

"Go."

They squealed away, not perfect but fun, and that was the point.

"Shift," Harper said.

Piper jammed it into second, much better than a half hour earlier. They passed the orange line of cones Harper had set up as an obstacle course.

Harper eyed the tachometer. "Third."

Piper's face was set, focused, but joyous beneath. Harper's own heart felt full. This was the girl she'd known before Drew died, the sharp kid eager to lap up new experiences.

Piper smoothly shifted into third.

"Beautiful," Harper said. "Hold this line. Get it on the money and I'll buy you a puppy."

"Pony." Piper looked like she wanted to laugh but couldn't spare the distraction.

They raced toward the cone in the center of the runway. Fifty yards, forty.

"Hands," Harper said.

Piper slid her left hand over the top of the wheel and grabbed it at three o'clock. With her right hand she gripped the parking brake.

"Remember, brake and clutch," Harper said. The cone grew larger in the windshield. "Now."

Piper braked. A moment later, she remembered to depress the clutch. The tires squealed. The tip of the grille drew even with the cone.

"Turn."

One-handed, Piper raked the wheel left.

"Pull," Harper said.

Piper yanked the hand brake. The car shrieked, and the rear end swept around.

"Off again," Harper said, watching as Piper released the hand brake. "First. Go."

Piper let go of the hand brake, grabbed the gearshift, hit the gas, popped the clutch, and the MINI bounded away. It was a pretty damn fine hand-brake turn.

"Yes, *yes*," Piper shouted, laughing. She nodded at Harper. "Forget the pony. Make it a unicorn."

Harper clapped. Piper raced along the runway, shoulders more relaxed than Harper had seen in a year.

Piper said, "You learned this . . . where?"

"The Navy."

Piper's mouth pursed.

"Menwith Hill, England," Harper said. "Why do you think I got a British car when I came home?"

Harmless lies wouldn't hurt, not right now, in the sunshine. Harper said, "They taught us all sorts of things."

"One more?" Piper said.

Harper patted her on the shoulder. "Next time. I need to leave some tread on my tires."

"Do we have to leave?" Piper said.

Harper again scanned the perimeter. "We've been lucky. They don't have an on-site guard, and their security patrol hasn't shown up."

She could have taken Piper to a local racetrack, but they would never have let the sixteen-year-old behind the wheel, and they would have blown a lobe to see Harper teaching her stunt driving.

"Let's not press our luck," she said.

"I get the feeling you've been doing that a long time."

Harper's cheeks burned, but she just smiled and nodded. "Switch places. I'll teach you something else."

They swapped. Harper told herself *just this once*. "Buckle up."

Piper clicked her seat belt. Her eyes were shining.

"Evasive driving 101," Harper said. "Hold on."

She shifted into reverse and hit the gas.

"Whoa," Piper said.

Eyes on the rearview mirror, Harper accelerated backward along the runway, holding a line and keeping the orange cone at the edge of the mirror. The MINI handled with quick responsiveness. It was a rugged little thing, so low to the ground that she always felt as if she were driving a go-kart. Its suspension was virtually nonexistent, but it cornered like a champ. Her heart pumped vigorously and she felt her reflexes slide into a rhythm, the feeling of syncing with the car. Piper's mouth opened. The speedometer reached twenty-five mph. Both hands on the wheel, Harper turned her head and looked out the rear window.

"Who are we evading?" Piper shouted over the wail of the engine.

"FSB. Russian intelligence." Harper held the wheel. The car was tight, had great balance, the four-cylinder engine revving hard. But the road surface was dry, and she hadn't done this in a long time.

"Why is Russian Intelligence after us?"

"Because you're too good at stealing Wi-Fi passwords and getting into clubs underage."

"They'll never recruit me. But what about you?"

"All you need to know is, they aren't going to catch us. Repeat after me: *Vy ne mozhete ostanovit' nas ot pobega*."

"*Vy ne mozhete . . .*"

The cone flashed past. She came off the power and felt the weight transfer to the back of the car.

Harper rapidly turned the wheel, three-quarters around. She double-clutched, *bam-bam*, reverse to neutral to first. Piper squealed. The car kept turning, the hood whipping around. Harper reduced the steering wheel lock and straightened it out.

Breathlessly Piper tried: ". . . *mozh . . . ot pobega* . . . Jesus."

Harper finished the J-turn, sloppy and rough, stomped on the gas, and spun the wheels squealing away in first, headed straight for the hangar.

"Yeah. Try it again, Piper—*Vy ne mozhete ostanovit' nas ot pobega. Poka, suki.*"

"*Poka, suki* . . . huh?"

"You cannot stop us from escaping. So long, bitches." The car gathered itself beneath her, intoxicatingly. "*Yob tvoyu mat'.*"

"*Yob* . . ." Piper gave up and looked at her for the translation.

"Famous Russian expression. Fuck your mother."

Piper's mouth widened into an O. Then she shoved a fist skyward out the window. "*Yob tvoyu mat'. Poka, suki.*"

Harper grinned. Ahead, the doors of the hangar were wide open. "On three, Piper." She raced inside, into shade, onto slick concrete. The engine noise echoed off the walls. "One, two, three. *Moio sudno na vozdušnoy poduške polno ugrey.*"

"*Moio* . . . oh, forget it. What's that mean?"

Harper braked again. As she was pushed against the seat belt strap, she flung the wheel and sent the car into a raucous donut. "My hovercraft is full of eels."

Piper was bracing herself, trying to hold her head still. "Monty Python. Excellent."

The engine droned, and the noise bounced off all the walls and the roof and the smooth, shining concrete floor. They spun until Harper began to feel dizzy, then she straightened it out and raced back into the sunshine.

Piper said, "Forget the unicorn. Teach me Russian."

They sped along the runway, the sun gleaming off the hood. Piper looked out the back window. "I see a truck, way back beyond the hangar. Looks like a private security vehicle."

Harper's heart gunned in time with the engine as she shifted gears. The gate they'd entered was half a mile ahead. "Get the Silly Putty from the glove compartment."

"You're sure they'll never know?" Piper said.

"Listen, kid. When somebody's after you, the best exit is the one they don't ever see."

At the gate, Piper jumped out and opened it for Harper to drive through. She quickly shut it. Harper got out, ran the chain and padlock back through the hasp, and stuffed a wad of Silly Putty into the lock. When she jammed the shackle into the lock, it held. It would hold for months, maybe years. As long as the security detail didn't check the lock itself and see that a screwdriver had been jammed into the mechanism to open it, they'd never be the wiser. And the gate would look secure.

Just this once. They jumped back in the car. Piper was flushed and so energized that she was practically fizzing. Harper pulled across the dirt to the road and drove onto the asphalt.

"What if they do see us?" Piper said.

"Then you'd better be fast."

They pulled away.

⁓

Back in the parking garage on the UCLA campus, Piper leaned across the MINI and hugged Harper tightly.

"Thank you," she said.

"Drive safely on your way back to school. No hand-brake turns."

Piper smiled wickedly and kissed Harper's cheek. "We'll see."

She grabbed her backpack and hurried to her RAV4. Harper

honked and waved as she drove away. Her entire system felt highly charged and filled with hope.

Ten minutes later, she ran up the stairs in the Linguistics building, working on the excuse she planned to offer her professor. From the stairwell below her came a harsh whisper.

"Flynn."

She shivered in the warm air. Hand on the stairway railing, she looked down. A face peered up at her from the basement level.

She stared, petrified.

He stepped from the shadows. "Don't scream. You gotta help me."

"Oscar," she said.

25

When Harper was fourteen, a new kid came into Rowdy Maddox's orbit. Ten years old, scrawny as a broomstick, with Pepsi-colored hair that fell over his eyes and hand-me-down surfer T-shirts that were never quite clean. He could hold as still as a sculpture for long stretches of time. Except his fingers. They were always moving. And his eyes. They flashed, taking everything in. At first, she thought he was watching for his opportunity to steal something, or for Travis or Zero to lash out at him. As if he thought that was how life went, and constantly expected punishment. And she was right. It took her longer to find out that Oscar Sierra was absorbing every scrap of information from his environment, then running it through some mental algorithm that helped him figure out how to survive in hostile, unloving territory. Give him a computer, and he could work magic. The kid was a genius.

Rowdy Maddox realized the same thing, and turned Oscar Sierra into his personal digital master thief.

Now Harper looked over the staircase railing, two flights down, at Oscar huddling in the shadows. Hair still tumbling over his eyes, collarbones still protruding from his T-shirt beneath a ratty green army fatigue jacket. Fear in his eyes.

"Please, Zan," he said.

Her breath snagged in her throat, and the air around her seemed to thicken. Nobody had called her by that nickname in years, not since she'd been released from juvenile detention and gone to court in Bakersfield to erase it from her life.

He looked abject. Her warning systems blared red. *Trap.*

She turned and jogged down the stairs.

When she reached the bottom of the stairwell, Oscar retreated into the shadows. Voices echoed from the hallway above.

"What the hell are you doing here?" Harper said.

"Trying to keep my heart beating, obviously," Oscar said.

"How did you find me?"

He hunched, arms crossed beneath his armpits. "I can find anything."

True. Her palms started to itch. She didn't like this, didn't like being down in the bottom of the stairwell, didn't like this nervous, nose-wiping figure from the past appearing in front of her.

She listened to the voices overhead. Oscar looked cold.

"It's just me. Nobody else," he said.

"Better be."

"If Zero was here, I wouldn't be. I'd be dead back at my trailer or chewed to pieces by his dog."

"His dog. Brindled thing, cropped ears . . ."

"Stares at you with those little eyes. I swear he talked to me last night, and . . ."

Harper's nerves changed to excitement. She grabbed Oscar by the arms. "You saw the dog. And Zero came with him."

"That's what I said. Last night, they showed up at my place. I am still creeped out up to *here*." He raised his hand overhead.

She said, "Let's get out of here."

"It's quiet down here. And nobody can see us."

"And the only way to get out is up the stairs, because that's a janitorial closet, and it's locked. I don't want to get cornered in a dead end."

Oscar glanced around, seeming to notice her point for the first time. His face was strangely unmarked by years of lawlessness. He still looked like the hungry kid she had first met before his voice changed.

Yet he was the one who'd never been caught. He could hide his location from everybody online. Zero had never exposed him. Neither had Rowdy Maddox. He was their most valuable player, and he managed to slip silently through life in the wide, high desert. But here he was. Pale and exhausted and openly frightened.

"Where's the last place you saw Zero and the dog?" she said.

"In my living room."

"You split? Got away from him?"

Oscar nodded. "I ran. Lost them. I don't know how. Maybe the dog told Zero to track me in his car."

A long-suppressed and familiar feeling overcame her: frustration held in check by helpless affection. Oscar had never been able to lie to her or anybody. He was guileless. He knew what he was doing and made no apologies. If he had regrets, he dulled them with reefer.

"This way," she said.

"You're whispering."

"Damn right. You don't want to be seen? You don't want to be heard, either."

She led him up the stairs, listening for untoward sounds. Oscar looked like he wanted to blend into the wall. She found an empty classroom and nudged him inside.

"Talk." She dropped her pack on a desk, unzipped a pocket, and ferreted till she found a granola bar. "Calories. Consume. Spill. Make it snappy."

She tossed the granola bar to him. He tore it open like a rabid spider monkey and funneled it into his mouth.

"How long since you ate?" she said.

He wet his finger and dabbed at the wrapper to get the crumbs. Then he eyed her up and down. "You look amazing."

She waved a hand to brush his remark aside. "Why did you track me down?"

"No, Zan, really, you're looking like, whoa." He held up a hand, Boy Scout style, to indicate his sincerity. "Sleek and academic. One of those sexy teacher calendar models. Don't stab me with that pen. Put it down."

She continued to aim her BIC at him. "Don't call me Zan."

"What, then. 'Harper?' Where'd that come from?"

"None of your business."

He looked hurt. "I'm interested, that's all."

"Stop. Oscar. Look at me. How many pens am I holding up?"

"I'm straight and sober."

"Is that what Zero's dog told you last night?"

"That was then. Right now, I'm telling you fear has a way of cleansing your system of substances. And I was freakin' fearful."

"I see that."

"Okay." He flopped in a seat. "You want to hear? Sit down and listen."

He spent ten minutes outlining his previous evening's activities. She listened, learning that he was more or less the same guy she'd known in high school, only now more savvy and more stuck in his ways. Living in a trailer he'd inherited from his grandma. Working with super-high-speed connections he'd scrounged from the phone company in a nowhere town in the high desert that had extremely robust Net connections because it was built next to one of the Navy's most exotic high-tech weapons testing facilities.

She said, "You still work with Zero?"

"Not often. He's . . . worse."

That chilled her. "Does he still live in China Lake?"

He shook his head. "Just shows up now and again."

"Why did he come to your place last night?"

He looked up. "To kill me."

Her throat tightened. "How come he didn't?"

Oscar shrugged.

"Seriously," she said. "He could have waited for you to fall asleep." Or pass out, she didn't add. "Then come in and kill you where you slept. No fuss, no noise."

"Jesus, Zan. That's a horrible image. How can you think up such things?"

"Oscar. I've been doing nothing but thinking about Zero for a while now. I think he killed my boyfriend last year. He shot him in the back in cold blood."

"Oh, my God." He blinked. "When? Where?"

"At Xenon. Right before the club was set on fire."

He leaned back. His face was pasty. He had dark gray circles beneath his eyes. His T-shirt said, THERE ARE 10 KINDS OF PEOPLE IN THE WORLD. THOSE WHO UNDERSTAND BINARY, AND THOSE WHO DON'T.

"He wanted to talk about some work I did for him last year," Oscar said.

"Which was?"

"Is this conversation confidential?"

"No."

"Isn't there, like, a university honor code?"

"Against cheating, not confession."

He squirmed on his seat. "He wanted to talk about a tech project I did last year. No names were involved. I never knew what the project related to or what I was doing it for. Except now I do."

She felt as though she was pulling his teeth one at a time. How could somebody who was so focused when working with ones and zeroes be so scattered when dealing with human beings?

"What was the project about?" she said.

"I think he wanted to talk about you."

She'd expected his answer, but nevertheless a falling sensation overcame her. "Did he mention my name?"

"No." He wiped his nose. "He's never mentioned your name since he got back. Not once."

"From prison, you mean?"

He nodded. "The job was a special ticket. One off. Usually, he wants stuff in bulk. You know, like the blank debit card thing. I deal in volume."

"What was the job you did last year?"

"Cloning the magnetic strip on a swipe card."

She nearly jumped and hit the ceiling. She felt both sick and victorious.

"Zero paid you to clone a swipe card?" she said.

"Basic white plastic card stock with an embedded magnetic strip. Zero got the data from the original card, and I did the rest. The software, the physical embedding of the information."

"Just one card?"

He nodded. "Zero didn't want me to see the data that was going on the card. I understood his reasons, but I needed to read it to verify that it had been cloned correctly. Didn't want any glitches showing up on a screen in a secure environment, tripping alarms or anything."

"And?"

"It was a very simple card. Employee ID number and name. Designed so there's a record and the management can compare it against—"

"I know how it works," Harper said.

"It was also programmed to access certain points of entry at the place of employment. Doors, etcetera."

"What was the name of the employee?"

"Harper Flynn."

She leaned back. "And Zero set this up."

"But Harper Flynn was just a name. I didn't know it had anything to do with you. I may have said something about *Flynn*, but he shut me up. Said coincidences happen all the time."

"This wasn't one," she said.

"You're telling me."

"And it's been a year, but Zero didn't show up at your place until last night?"

"Asking if I'd told anybody about the card, what I recalled about the information."

"And that's when you decided he was there to kill you?"

"Yeah."

She dug her phone from her backpack. She could barely swallow.

"What are you doing?" he said.

"I need to tell the cops about this."

And she had to tell Aiden. Aiden had been right from the beginning—Zero was behind things. It wasn't a hallucination.

"No fucking way." Oscar reached for her phone. He looked frantic. "You can't involve me."

She kept the phone out of reach. "Then what are you doing here? You're involving me. You didn't come to L.A. to warn me. You could have done that from China Lake."

"Zan—sorry, Harper . . ." He threw up his hands.

"Why did you find me?"

"To warn you. Really. And . . ." He wiped his nose again. "Okay. I got nowhere else to go."

"You want me to help you."

He looked at her like *Duh*.

"How?"

He shrugged. He hadn't thought that part through. "If Zero's after me, then I got nothin'. Nobody in China Lake's gonna help me. And I got nobody else."

He looked at her with eyes like a half-drowned bunny.

"Oscar. Snap out of it."

He appeared as if he was trying to keep his bottom lip from quivering. He pressed his mouth tight.

Harper felt as though a series of tiny gears were grinding against each other inside her, about to break and spew teeth. She didn't need this revenant from her youth turning up, even if he looked charming and lost.

"If you want me to help you, you have to do several things for me," she said.

"I . . ."

"Then forget it." She stood and headed for the door.

"Zan—Harper—no."

He scooted around her and blocked the door. "Let me think about this."

"I'll help you if you help me."

"Okay, okay. I just need someplace to stay."

"Not at my place."

"'Course not. Never." He looked so obviously disappointed that she almost laughed. "Where?"

"There's a public restroom at Zuma Beach. I hear the last stall in the men's room is roomy and fairly unlikely to be broken into."

"That's . . ." He rolled his eyes. "You haven't changed so much after all."

"Listen closely. Zero knows where I live. I've seen his dog outside my building."

Oscar's face fell. "Shit."

The gears spun ever faster. "I don't want to go home. Much less take you there."

"We could get out of town. Together."

"I'm not going on the run with you, Oscar."

He scraped his fingers into his hair. "Then what am I supposed to do? You can't go to the cops. No way."

"You mean Susannah Flynn would not have gone to the cops. But we need protection. We need help."

"I thought you would be the one to help. You always tried to."

Her heart seemed to clench at that. "Do you have a phone?"

He patted his pockets and eventually found it.

"What's your number?" she said.

He recited it, and she wrote it on her forearm with a pen. He shook his head.

"Just enter it in yours," he said. "And give me your number, too."

The mischief Oscar might do with her phone number, she didn't need to imagine. Malware. Spoofing calls and making it look like she'd made them. She didn't even want to put his digits in her device, lest they activate a secret code and begin to burn through the electronics and turn her phone into an incendiary device.

She capped the pen. "No way."

He nodded, as though imbibing the deepest secrets of the universe. "That's hurtful, but I can respect it."

"Good."

"Dude. So who can help us?"

She heard people in the hallway. Classes were getting out. They needed to go.

"You ever been to Santa Barbara?" she said.

26

Harper slipped out of the classroom into the hallway and closed the door behind her. On her instructions, Oscar followed ten seconds later and headed in the opposite direction. She wanted nobody to see them together.

She hurried from the building to the parking lot where she'd left the MINI. She tried again to reach Aiden. Again got voice mail. She texted him as she walked.

Call me. Urgent.

She debated leaving a more detailed message. But *Forgive me. You were right all along* didn't sound compelling in text-speak. Neither did *Are you okay? Still attacking innocent bystanders?*

A few minutes later, at the wheel of the car, she rounded a corner in Westwood and saw Oscar a block ahead, walking along the sidewalk. His head was down.

Oscar had figured out her identity from the cloned swipe card. As a hacker with a series of powerful search software tools and no scruples, he found out she was enrolled at UCLA. How he figured out her class schedule was a different matter. She needed to alert the registrar that their system had been compromised.

She edged through afternoon traffic, eyeing the mirrors for vehicles following her. Her countersurveillance skills were rudimentary. She turned the corner and zigzagged through village streets, past boho shops and restaurants and a movie theater. When she came around again, from the opposite direction, Oscar was crossing the street, just as she'd told him to.

She swerved to the curb. He hopped in and she punched it, rounding the corner as the light turned red.

"Anybody jump the light?" she said. "Anybody follow us? Anybody on foot watching to see where we're going?"

Oscar craned to see out the back window. "Clear. I think."

She shifted gears and swung into an alley, bouncing along the rough concrete. "You think, or you're positive?"

He kept watching. "Positive." He turned around. "Nobody's coming."

She barreled along the alley. Despite her nerves and anxiety, she felt stoked. The streets looked brightly etched, high-focus, and the traffic ahead seemed to ribbon into a smooth flow. She could see holes opening up, lanes where she could swing in and pass slower cars. It was like slaloming on a glass track. She accelerated.

She skimmed the corner and came out on Veteran, heading for Wilshire and the 405 freeway.

The channel scintillated with light that kicked off the surface of the water. The ocean was a deep, cold blue. The *Carolina Gail* pushed through, ten miles offshore, heading for the harbor. At the stern, Aiden stowed gear. The wake spilled white behind the boat. Alongside, slipping fast just beneath the surface, two dolphins swam in tandem with them.

He didn't look at the wheelhouse. Kieran drove the boat toward shore, tired behind his sunglasses, and silent. His brother hadn't said five words to him all day.

Aiden was sore. Beyond. His shoulder didn't so much ache as stab every time he moved. His cheek was abraded. He didn't want anybody to comment on his black eye.

His phone buzzed. He waited for it to stop. He'd ignored three calls from her. She'd left three voice mail messages. But this one was a text.

Call me. Urgent.

What did Harper want with him? Was she trying to break through his stubborn silence, or did she really have news for him?

The boat dipped in the afternoon swell and rose again. The bow lifted, spraying white water. He could see Kieran's silhouette, still and steady at the wheel. Seagulls followed the boat.

Harper. Maybe she wanted to play around. Maybe she just wanted to play him.

She always came to him with questions. With inquiries. Did she just want information? If so, she should know by now that he had no more information to give.

Did she want to use him for his connections to the sheriff's department, to find out what the department knew?

If she was involved in the events at Xenon, why would she do that? Did she want to screw it up?

Did she want to steal information about the evidence the department had collected? Did she have plans that none of them knew about?

Urgent.

Ex-thief with a new name and a clean reputation. And the way she had used that when she was released from custody was to become a cryptologic technician—stealing information from foreign governments. It was robbery wrapped in the flag. A hell of a rehabilitation.

Just happened to be on scene the night the club was attacked and destroyed. Just happened to claim to know the man he oh-so-helpfully told her he'd seen.

But maybe Erika was right. Zero didn't exist, except as his hallucination. What did you call that—a nonexistent nemesis?

Had Harper actually wanted to plant that idea in his head?

It didn't make sense to him, except that it was happening. And the woman who'd run from him the second his mind had let the monster out . . .

He guessed he couldn't blame her.

He watched the birds circle behind the boat.

27

Forty miles northwest of Los Angeles, driving along the freeway through the flat strawberry fields of Camarillo, the MINI's fuel light came on. Harper checked the mirror for tails. She waited until the last possible second to veer across two lanes and hit the off-ramp. Oscar braced his hands against the dashboard.

"Dude."

She downshifted sharply and took a right toward a big-box mall. Catty-corner from it, she pulled into a service station and drove the MINI to the center of the pumps, where she was surrounded by pickups and RVs.

Oscar leaned back. "Paranoid much?"

She climbed out. "Three minutes."

Oscar got out. "Men's room."

He looked frazzled, his hair flailing in the salt-laden sea breeze. His eyes seemed feverish, the circles beneath them darker.

"Get a sandwich," Harper said.

Oscar headed inside the service station's mini-mart. Harper hoped he didn't plan to ingest other substances in the men's room. Maybe she should have searched him. She jammed the nozzle in the tank and began filling up.

She hadn't heard from Aiden.

She scanned the station forecourt and the road as the pump hummed in her hand. She took out her phone. No replies.

She finished filling up, replaced the nozzle, and headed inside to pay with cash. She didn't want any record of the transaction to go into a database. Walking across the forecourt, she knew she was on CCTV. But a silent, grainy film from a Southern California video camera wouldn't go anywhere, most likely. A credit card transaction would be easily accessible to the cops. Or to folks like Oscar.

Paranoid? Very much.

Inside the store, the door closed slowly, light and color sliding across the glass. She got in line to pay and called Erika Sorenstam.

Her stomach clenched. How had she walked—no, leaped—into a love triangle, even a broken one, with Aiden and Sorenstam?

The phone rang. She approached the register. The clerk, a woman in an orange top, said, "Number 12?"

The phone was answered. "Yes?"

Harper was fishing her cash from her front pocket. She put the phone between her shoulder and her ear. Another customer passed by, brushing her shoulder. The phone squirted out and dropped to the tile.

She tossed a wad of bills on the counter and bent to pick it up. "Detective, sorry," she called.

When she straightened, Oscar was standing in the hallway by the restrooms, his eyes as round as quarters.

Sorenstam said, "Ms. Flynn?"

Oscar turned and disappeared down the hallway.

Damn. She ran after him. "Hang on," she said to Sorenstam.

The back door to the mini-mart was closing, a hot slice of sunlight shrinking as it hissed on its hinges.

If Oscar got away, she had no proof of Zero's involvement. None. She ran down the hallway, hit the door before it closed, and slammed it open. Oscar was already across the street, running toward the mall, his green fatigue shirt beating behind him like a cape about to shred.

She ran across the street and into the mall parking lot with the phone in her hand. Sorenstam's voice swung back and forth, tinny.

"Hey, Flynn."

Oscar's flapping green shirt vanished through the doors at the mall. Harper put the phone to her ear.

"I'm here. Got . . ."

A car passed nearby. She pulled up and veered.

"What's this about?" Sorenstam said.

The driver honked at her, long and annoyed. She kept running.

"I have evidence that Eddie Azerov was involved in the Xenon attack," she said.

"What now?"

"The swipe card. Somebody cloned it. With my employee ID."

"Who? What evidence do you have?"

Harper bounded toward the mall entrance. People were streaming in and out the doors. She ran inside, into echoes and air-conditioning and Muzak. The place was packed—with families ambling with strollers and hanging banners advertising a chance to win a new Corvette and a popcorn vender at a kiosk in the center of the concourse. The mall had three levels and escalators, and the noise and crowds extended overhead. A wallpaper version of the Chili Peppers's "Give It Away" was playing. Briefly, she felt the urge to hunt down whoever had recorded it and beat them senseless with a shoe.

Harper hated malls.

She hated crowded public places, hated people pushing against her, and amplified music, and the smell of anything burning, even the cheap-ass popcorn being shoveled, greasy and yellow, into paper bags directly ahead of her.

Oscar was barely visible a hundred yards ahead, heading for the department store at the end of the concourse.

She barreled after him. Sorenstam was still on the line.

"I'm chasing a guy I knew back when. Hacker. Turned up this morning."

"Who?" Sorenstam said.

"Oscar Sierra."

There was a pause.

Harper kept running. "He told me he'd been hired to clone my employee ID." Still no answer. "Detective?"

Sorenstam said, "Where are you?"

⟡

At her desk in the Lost Hills station, Erika Sorenstam heard ambient noise and Harper Flynn's hard breathing. Sounded like she was running.

"Harper, where are you?" she repeated. She got no reply.

She muted her end of the call so Flynn couldn't hear her. Staring at her computer screen, she picked up her cell phone and dialed the number for the Kern County Sheriff's Office.

"Detective Erika Sorenstam, L.A. Sheriff's Department. I just got your bulletin. I may have a lead on your missing person."

"Oscar Sierra?"

"What more can you give me?"

The Kern County deputy ran it down. An anonymous tipster had phoned 911 to report that a friend's mobile home near China Lake was trashed, the friend's car on fire. The friend was missing. When deputies arrived, the trailer's door was pried open. A car outside the trailer was smoldering, nearly burned out. They could find no sign of Oscar Sierra.

Sorenstam asked if they could send their report to her.

The Kern County deputy said, "You say you have a report of Sierra's whereabouts?"

"I have a woman on the other line who claims Sierra is alive. She says she's pursuing him."

"Name?"

"Harper Flynn."

The Kern deputy said, "Flynn. You sure?"

"Positive. Why?"

"That name has come up in our investigation."

"Can you be more specific?"

Sorenstam's computer pinged. She opened the files Kern County had sent and saw photos of the scene: a trailer home, run-down even by desert trailer-home standards, door off the hinges. Inside, sofa sliced open, cushions gutted. Chairs overturned. Computer monitors all smashed, cables pouring onto the floor like viscera. What looked like blood on the wall, near a bent door frame.

The Kern deputy said, "We found evidence at the scene that links to Harper Flynn. Messages in a cell phone we found in the trailer. Indicating that Harper Flynn was waiting for a delivery—of cash, drugs, we don't know what—from Sierra. And asking him to be at the trailer last night between eleven P.M. and one A.M."

Sorenstam straightened. "What time did you get the 9-1-1 call?"

"Eleven forty-five."

"You think Flynn set Sierra up, making sure he was home when somebody came knocking?"

"That's our working assumption. If you have Flynn on the line, I suggest—"

"I'm on it. I'll report back to you."

She hung up and returned to the call with Harper. She clenched her jaw and slowly exhaled to modulate her voice.

"Harper," she said. "Are you still there? Is everything okay?"

"He's trying to get away," Flynn said.

Sorenstam snapped her fingers to get the attention of two other detectives nearby. They looked up. She motioned them to her desk and pointed at the computer screen. Grabbing a pen, she scribbled on a piece of paper: *Triangulate this call.*

28

Phone pressed to her ear, breathing hard, Harper ran through the mall. "Detective?"

A woman emerged from Victoria's Secret, pink shopping bags in her hands. Harper dodged but sideswiped her. The bags went flying.

"Jesus, you crazy—"

"Sorry."

Bras and panties spewed into the air and rained to the glossy tile floor. She kept running, toward the department store. Her heart was thudding, and a heavy rock seemed to sit in her stomach. Oscar had vanished.

Sorenstam said, "Ms. Flynn. Where are you?"

"We're not in L.A. County," Harper said.

"Where, then?"

She ran into the department store. A young woman with a bottle of spray cologne stood at the entrance, wearing a white lab coat.

"Miss, would you like to try—"

"In hell." Harper ran past. "Detective . . . what kind of assistance can you get in Ventura County, and how fast?"

"What's going on, Harper?"

The tone of Sorenstam's question sounded off, her voice too sharp. Harper's warning radar sparked to life. *Say nothing. If you have to say something, lie.* But without help, without getting Oscar to officials who would listen, she had zip.

"Lemon Tree Mall, Camarillo. I'm chasing Oscar into Macy's. Can you get a patrol unit here to help me?"

"Help you do what, exactly?"

She slowed near the escalator, looking around. Glitz and bling and displays of makeup and jewelry. She glanced up.

Saw the green shirttails disappear at the top of the escalator.

"Harper," Sorenstam said. "Has Oscar Sierra committed a crime?"

"I don't judge." She turned and ran up the escalator, legs heavy. "Detective, please."

"Stay there. I'll see what I can do."

Sorenstam hung up. Doubly uneasy, Harper reached the top of the escalator. Women's Clothing. She jogged around the escalators, looking for him.

Oscar, Oscar. Where would you go?

She jogged to the fire door. When she opened it, she heard nothing in the stairwell, no scuffling feet, no labored breathing or sniffling.

Online, Oscar was brilliant at covering his tracks. He could dip into a protected account, drain it, slash to the bone the information it contained, and slip away again without leaving anything but the slightest evidence there'd been an intrusion, much less his digital fingerprints. He knew how to plant bots deep in a system's code, curled up so tight they were nearly invisible, even when they activated and misbehaved. He was expert at inserting himself into a system and hiding there.

Not so good at running. Not so skillful in the physical world. Still, she couldn't find him.

She spun around. Women were browsing the racks. At a desk, a salesclerk pulled the security tag off a violet dress for a waiting customer. Harper hurried over.

"Seen a man come past here? Young guy, dark hair, green fatigue shirt?"

The clerk looked at her peculiarly. "You have a bra hooked on the back of your shirt."

Harper grabbed the Victoria's Secret stowaway and tossed it aside.

The customer said, "He headed toward the dressing rooms."

"Thanks."

When she reached the dressing rooms, she paused. Carpeted, they were hushed. Most of the doors were closed.

She caught her breath and waited till she could proceed without panting. She walked down the row, glancing under each door. The fourth door was closed. She tried the lock. It wouldn't budge. Nobody complained when she rattled the lock. She checked again: no feet visible inside.

Checking that nobody was coming, she dropped to all fours and peered under the dressing room door.

On a stool, feet propped against the wall, a middle-aged woman was sleeping. She wore a store name tag.

"What the hell?"

The voice came from behind Harper. She retreated and stood up. A sales assistant stood at the end of the hallway, mouth gaping.

Harper pointed at the dressing room. "Heard moaning. Thought something bad was happening inside. Or really good."

She speed-walked toward the young woman, hoping to get past. *Stay calm and don't admit anything.* Rule one of getting out of a store where you're suspected of wrongdoing.

The sales assistant braced herself, as though she might throw a low tackle.

Harper raised her hands. "I'm looking for this idiot friend who asked for a ride, then took off on me." She pointed over her shoulder. "Your colleague's asleep inside, snoring."

The young woman's head swiveled toward the dressing room. Harper hurried past her.

Out on the sales floor, she looked around. Her stomach was cramping. Sorenstam was supposedly calling the local cops, but she didn't know how long that would take. And if they actually showed up, she'd better have Oscar with her, or she was screwed.

And she hadn't liked the pauses on Sorenstam's side of the conversation. The detective had been thinking—too much for Harper's comfort.

Behind her, the sales assistant said sharply, "Hey. Come out of there."

With a click, a door opened. Harper looked over her shoulder.

The sales assistant stood outside the dressing room where the woman was asleep. The door was still closed. She rapped on it. "Lucy. Get off your ass."

But two doors down, another door stood open, and in the doorway stood Oscar.

He saw her and jumped like a hamster. He started to close the door again, thought better of it, and bolted out. She was running at him.

He turned and ducked into the employees' stockroom. She followed. He cut between racks of clothing and out onto the sales floor through another door. She launched herself at him. They tangled at a display of short shorts and slid across the lacquered countertop like air hockey pucks.

They thudded to the carpet. Somebody nearby squealed.

Harper straddled him and pressed his shoulders to the floor. "Hold still. Stop behaving like a squirrel."

He looked up at her, spent. "But I am a squirrel."

Customers shied away from them. Peripherally, Harper saw a clerk with a headset, clicking her walkie-talkie.

Harper pressed her hands against Oscar's shoulders. "We're going to get up and walk out of here together."

The walkie-talkie clerk said, "Miss, sir—get up. I've called security."

Harper held Oscar down. "We're leaving."

She swung to her feet, hauling him up by his lapels. He looked around with a gaze that could only be described as shifty.

The clerk said, "Security is going to escort you out of the mall."

"No need," Harper said. "My brother is getting back in my car and we're going to his dentist's appointment now."

Oscar looked at her askance. She pulled him toward the exit. At the top of the escalator, a burly man appeared, lumbering toward them in a shiny blazer, his faux Secret Service earpiece twisting wormlike down his neck.

Harper tightened her grip on Oscar's sleeve. "Care to take it up with Mr. Muscle? Because he'll lock you in his office and fantasize about playing Jack Bauer with you until the local cops show up. You want that?"

Oscar stared at the floor. "No."

The security guard raised a hand. "Hold on, folks."

Harper slowed but nodded at the escalator. "Give us a hand? We need to get outside as soon as possible."

"I need to see some ID," the man said.

Harper didn't even dignify that with a raised eyebrow. "I need to get him into the open air even more than you need us to leave the premises. Come on."

"What's the problem?" the security man said.

Oscar looked at her, too, curious.

She led him onto the escalator. He automatically stopped, but she pulled him down the stairs.

The security guard followed. "Ma'am? The problem?"

She tried to think of something, but all that came to her was *I am a squirrel.* Then they passed beneath the banners offering a chance to win a free car.

"Corvette's syndrome," she said. "Similar to Tourette's, but the involuntary compulsive behavior isn't verbal. It's prey behavior. Begins with flight—hiding, then fleeing. You saw that."

"Corvette's?" the guard said.

"It escalates rapidly if an episode occurs in a confined space with droning ambient noise. Such as Muzak, and, really—'Love in an Elevator'? Come *on.*" She tugged Oscar down the stairs. "Once it reaches that stage, disrobing quickly follows. I need to get him to his doctor's office."

"Dentist," Oscar said.

She yanked on his sleeve. They reached the ground floor. Harper glared at him, pointedly.

He flinched. Then he began twitching his fingers, snapping them, flapping his hands.

The guard said, "This way."

He led them toward a door to the parking lot.

Oscar twisted his head and pulled on the collar of his T-shirt. "Hot."

Harper yanked. Hot didn't count.

"Tight," Oscar said. "Too tight." He scratched at his shirt.

"Oh, no, you don't," the guard said.

"Faster," Harper said.

Oscar tried to wriggle out of his fatigue jacket. "Need to lighten the load."

Together, Harper and the guard rushed him out the door into the sunlight, the guard chugging intensely, as if Oscar might detonate.

"Where's your car?" the guard said.

"Thanks," Harper said. "I can take it from here."

"He ain't gonna strip on mall property. Get him onto the public sidewalk."

Oscar was pulling his T-shirt over his head. Harper said, "Gas station."

The guard held tight to Oscar's arm and together they got to the gas pump. Harper nudged Oscar into the passenger seat. While the guard stood watch, she ran around and got behind the wheel.

"Will you be okay?" the guard said. He looked half serious, half dubious. But at this point, it didn't matter.

"I'll be fine. I have a fifty-thousand-volt stun gun under my seat for when he gets too hard to handle. It'll put him right out until I can get him tied down."

She started the engine. "Thank you."

The wheels chirped as she pulled away.

29

Harper overrevved the car up the on-ramp onto the 101. Oscar said, "Stun gun. Very funny."

"Don't try me. You want to get hit with it?"

He cut a look at her. "You were never this mean."

"You never tried to leave me high and dry."

"You're the one who called the cops."

"I wasn't going to turn you in," she said. "I need the lead detective on the case to know there's evidence pointing to Zero. It's how we protect ourselves."

She took out her phone to redial Sorenstam.

Oscar pushed her hand down and turned sideways in his seat to face her. "You don't get it."

She accelerated into traffic. A gasoline tanker passed them, the sun glaring off its curved silver flanks.

"What don't I get?" she said.

"If the cops knew about me being with you, they'd take us both in."

"That's off the wall."

"When did you get so naive?"

"Oscar, stop it. You came to me for help because you're in danger. And you're part of an ongoing shitstorm. We need to protect ourselves."

"I thought going to Santa Barbara was protecting ourselves."

Harper flushed. Her phone felt heavy in her hand. Aiden still hadn't returned her call. Maybe this was a wild-goose chase.

"Harper, you need to think on this. I ran last night. I took off with just the clothes I'm wearing and the phone in my pocket. If I didn't know the backcountry near my trailer, Zero would have caught me for sure."

"You were lucky. Be grateful."

"But after I got away from him, what do you think he did?"

She watched the road. Malls and car dealerships alternated with strawberry fields and windbreaks of eucalyptus trees.

Her stomach knotted. "He went back to your place."

"Undoubtedly."

"And . . . damn."

"He would have messed the place up. He probably ruined everything I have there. Stole as much of my shit as he could carry." He shook his head and put a hand to his forehead. "My stash."

"Forget your stash. What would he have done?"

"You know him."

Her phone rang. Erika Sorenstam.

Oscar peered at the display, shook his head, and made a slashing motion across his throat. Anxious, Harper let the phone ring. Finally, it stopped.

She drove for a minute, thinking. Then she punched the voice-to-text command on her phone. "Text Detective Erika Sorenstam." After a second, the phone pinged. Harper dictated. "Found Oscar Sierra. All under control. Don't need police assistance. Will come to you."

She sent the message. Oscar looked at her expectantly.

"I didn't say when we'll go to Sorenstam," Harper said. "I'm not going to dump you in the sheriff's station parking lot. Chill." But the knot in her stomach tightened. "Zero. What's at your trailer that he can use against you? And against me?"

"Lots. Listen. Last year, Zero paid me to clone your swipe card—to forge a new one."

"You're saying that he wanted *my* card specifically. He wanted to plant evidence against me."

"And he didn't succeed. Not a year ago."

"So he came to you trying to kill you?"

"I was one of those loose ends, you know. Like you always see on TV."

She drove, frustrated, the engine revving. "Something doesn't make sense."

"All I know is, I did the card thing for him. Heard nothing for a year. Then last night he shows up at my place, asking all kinds of questions, and getting ready to—" He shut his eyes. "I don't like thinking about this. It hella scares me."

"Me, too." She tried to keep her voice measured. "What do you think he did at your place?"

"Besides search for clues that would help him hunt me down?" He raked his hair back. "He could plant evidence. Papers, notes, something with your name on it."

"Messages. E-mails."

"Texts."

"You have your phone in your pocket."

He looked at her. "I have *a* phone."

"Crap."

She thought about it. The road scrolled beneath the car, tires droning. She found Aiden's number. Hit it and put the phone on speaker.

A second later, they heard a busy signal.

Harper said, "I have a bad feeling about that."

⌒

Aiden cautiously put the phone to his ear. "Erika?"

The boat was about a mile offshore, angling toward the harbor. Briefly, Kieran glanced out the window of the wheelhouse. His expression was unreadable.

"Aiden," she said. "Have you heard from Harper Flynn today?"

That was not what he was expecting. He had presumed she was calling because she'd heard that he'd been arrested.

"What's up, Erika?"

"Some sketchy things. Possibly criminal and related to people from her past."

"Could you be more vague, please? I can still see through the fog."

"She's playing games with me. I think she's trying to cover her tracks about her involvement in the attack on Xenon. It's not working."

"Playing what kind of games?"

"Trying to alibi herself."

"For what?"

"A missing persons case in Kern County. China Lake."

Aiden held on to the port railing as the boat rose, plowing through the swell. His leg ached beyond pain, but he didn't want to sit down, didn't want to let Kieran see him hurting.

"Who's missing, and for how long?" he said.

"Guy named Oscar Lamont Sierra. Report was filed with Kern County last night. Harper called me an hour ago and said she has Sierra with her right now."

"I don't get the twist you're putting on it," he said. "Or why you're calling me."

"It's extremely convenient that Harper called. The Kern deputies found her name on some incriminating evidence at Sierra's residence."

Shit.

"And?" Aiden said.

"And as far as I can determine, nobody except Harper Flynn has actually seen Oscar Sierra. It's all smoke and mirrors."

"Again—why are you calling me?" he said.

"When she phoned me, Flynn said she was in Ventura County heading north on 101. Why might that be?"

"You think she's coming to see me?"

"Is she?"

"I haven't spoken to her." *And I hate the accusatory tone in your voice.*

Sorenstam waited, almost as though hoping he would confess. He felt a free-floating sense of shame and anger. Sorenstam didn't believe in him anymore. The woman he had been closest too for the longest time in his life had given up on him. Even worse, she now seemed to view him through a heavy pane of glass, as if he were an animal to be kept penned, or a suspect to be observed and monitored with disdain. And Harper . . . she had literally turned away from him. If she was coming his way, he didn't know what to think.

The spray off the bow wave shimmered in the air and cooled his face. But the heat of his confusion and anger seemed to turn the view red.

Finally, Sorenstam said, "Aiden?"

"What do you want, Erika?"

"If Flynn contacts you, or shows up, would you let me know?"

"You'll be the first."

"Great. Thanks."

He ended the call without saying good-bye. As soon as he lowered his hand, the phone rang again.

Harper Flynn.

After a long moment, he answered it. "I'm aboard the *Carolina Gail*. And if you're on your way to Santa Barbara, turn around and go home."

He heard road noise on her end and hard silence. Then she said, "I'll be there in half an hour. I have somebody with me who is going to confirm everything you've been saying about the involvement of Eddie Azerov."

"Who's that? Oscar Sierra? Put him on."

A second later, a man's voice came over the phone. "This is Oscar."

"Good try. I have work to do. I'll talk to you another time, Harper. And whoever you have in the car with you."

He hung up. The phone rang again, and he silenced it. He made his way to the wheelhouse.

"Kieran. What's that lawyer's phone number? I've been an asshole. I'm sorry. I'll call and tell him I'll plead to whatever the cops want."

Kieran eyed him from behind his Oakleys. "Thanks. We'll give him a call as soon as we dock."

30

Dammit." Harper glanced at the phone and back at the road. "What the hell was that?"

The freeway stretched ahead beside the coast, a concrete river that rolled along the narrow line between the chaparral-covered foothills and the frothing surf.

Oscar said, "That was cold is what it was. Sorry, dude."

Her face stung. She felt as though Aiden had tossed hot coffee at her. Oscar tapped her shoulder.

"Forget it," she said.

"Here."

She glanced down and saw a folded white handkerchief in his hand. She took it and dabbed at her eyes. "Sorry."

"This guy, Aiden, you two, you know . . ."

She blinked again, clearing her vision. "That took me by surprise."

"I'm chivalrous," he said.

She nearly laughed, despite everything. "You are, sir. I meant Aiden. I didn't think he'd shut me out."

"So what now?"

The road scrolled onward along the coastline. There wasn't another exit for miles.

"We're almost to Santa Barbara. I don't want to turn around."

"Then I'm with you," Oscar said.

She scrunched the handkerchief against her eyes again and put both hands on the wheel. "Then that's where we're going."

"Except you know something's going on in the background, right?"

"Yes."

"Because why else would this Aiden guy know I'm with you?"

"You were right. Somebody in law enforcement knows you're not in China Lake anymore."

"Okay, then."

She pulled out and passed an RV, rounding a bend toward the shimmering lights of Santa Barbara.

In a conference room at Spartan Security Systems, Tom White sat taking notes while one of his colleagues clicked through a PowerPoint presentation. "Developments in on-site personnel management." Christ on a pony, kill him now. On the table, his phone buzzed. Blocked Call.

He stood up. "Sorry, emergency."

His colleague paused, annoyed. White swiveled and hurried from the room. Shutting the door snugly behind him, he marched down the hall, phone to his ear.

"Never. Not ever. Do not call me during working hours."

"Got it all working, though."

"What, precisely, is *it*?"

"The setup. Ducks in a row."

"And Oscar?"

"About that."

White's blood pressure bumped up. His eyes throbbed. "Do *not* tell me you missed him."

"You want the truth or not? Thought you were in the security business."

He rounded a corner. Two people were walking his way, coffee mugs in hand. He bulled past them, letting their surprise stand for confirmation that he looked like an executive on the rampage.

He lowered his voice and pushed through the fire door onto the stairs. He jogged down. "Tell me."

"Oscar is not as slow to respond as we imagined. He's in the wind."

He shoved the bar on the door and stalked out into the warm sunshine. Noise from the freeway brushed over him.

"He's gone? Is that what you're saying?" White said.

"Long gone. Got there and his trailer was trashed."

"I do not accept that. Jesus, this is a disaster. How could you—"

"It's a good thing. It's an opportunity. Shut up and listen."

And there was the rub. Ignore him, and he got nothing. He got more trouble. Catch-22. "I'm listening. Make it count."

"Oscar can't tell the truth, and he can't keep his mouth shut. He's got a reputation, and it isn't good. He's out there like a loose cannon. We just need to use him the right way. And I've already got a head start on that."

White exhaled. "Explain."

He listened. And was surprised. It might just work.

"Get on it, then," he said.

"Already am."

"This time, there's no backing out."

"Not for any of us. Got that." He hung up.

31

Harper was sitting behind the wheel of the MINI, parked around a corner from Aiden's house, when his black pickup pulled into the driveway. The sun flashed off the windows. He eased it under the carport. She put her car in gear.

She gunned around the corner into the driveway behind him as he climbed out of the truck. He paused, but only a second. He locked up and headed for the kitchen door.

She turned off the engine and pulled the keys out. "Wait here," she said to Oscar.

Oscar squinted at Aiden. "What happened to him?"

"Life." She opened the door. "Trying to save mine, mostly."

She got out and followed him toward the door. He looked like he was trying hard not to favor his left leg. She had seen the black eye.

"You might as well talk to me, because I'm not going away," she said.

He climbed the steps to the door. Painfully, it seemed. His hair was blown crazy by the wind. He was sunburned. He hadn't shaved. She could tell he was already tired, had worked a long day despite being battered. He didn't want to give in, and it was taking its toll.

But she needed this. "Aiden."

"Or what?"

She approached him. "I don't understand."

"Talk, or what? You'll keep stalking me?"

"Hey." She stopped behind him. "Cut it out."

He turned. "You're awfully late turning around and coming back here."

She flushed. "Dish it out. I deserve it. But then listen to me."

He looked abashed. He glanced at her car. "Who's that?"

"The guy I told you about, or tried to, on the phone."

That, finally, piqued his curiosity. "Oscar Sierra?"

"He needs to tell you what happened to him last night."

"Why?"

"Because Zero tried to do it to him."

He looked at the keys in his hand. She wondered if he had a gun stashed in the small of his back, tucked into the waistband of his jeans.

He said, "Come on."

They settled at the picnic table on the patio, staring at each other warily, like well-armed poker players in a saloon. Birds sang darkly from the oak trees.

Aiden said, "Don't wait for me to ask questions. Explain what this is about."

"It's about whatever Zero started last year coming back around again," Harper said.

Aiden looked at Oscar. "You know Eddie Azerov?"

"Dude. Come on." Oscar turned to Harper. "You didn't brief him?"

Aiden raised a hand. "Just give it to me in your own words."

Oscar nodded and looked at the trees and hunched forward. "Zero came to me last year with a project."

It took him ten minutes to run through it. Aiden didn't interrupt. He listened, maybe trying to piece together a coherent narrative from Oscar's fractal take on the world.

Harper sat with her hands knit together. When Aiden finally looked at her, his face was inscrutable. She waited, hoping. Wondering. *Please say something. Please believe me.*

"And you told Erika about this?" he said to her.

Thank you, Universe. "I told her everything I could. Oscar doesn't want to talk to the cops. But we need to do something."

A gust lifted her hair from her shoulders. The wind was rising, a dry rattle through the trees. The birds squealed and shook their wings and rose into the sky.

"Last year, Zero wanted to pin the blame for the attack at Xenon on me," she said. "I don't know how he would have arranged it, exactly. He didn't need to do too much, it seems—get Oscar to clone the card, use it on the back door once they reached the club, then the authorities would have checked it out and connected it to me. Except all the evidence was destroyed."

Aiden nodded. "You two say Zero—'he' did it. But he didn't act alone. He isn't the alpha dog, is he?"

Oscar rubbed his thumb along the grain of the wood in the table. "No. You have a point."

"He was the muscle. The sharp end of the spear," Aiden said.

"Except things escalated and he threw a Molotov cocktail with a magnesium flare chaser," Harper said. "I can't believe that was part of his orders."

"Orders?" Aiden said. "You think it was that strict?"

She was thinking of other things. Of Zero's standing in the pack, and of her fleeting suspicion that Drew had been involved. She felt a lump in her throat.

"So why did they wait a year?" Aiden said.

She looked up, breaking the spell. "Because of the fire. It got out of control. It became felony murder. Citizens died—innocent bystanders. Zero walked into Xenon with a gun in his hand. But whoever sent him there wanted to remain in the background. And that means it's somebody out there with something to lose."

"Travis Maddox?" Aiden said.

She felt oddly off balance. "Somebody who . . ." She ran a hand through her hair. "Somebody who was biding his time. Travis—yeah, of course. Who else would wait for a year?"

He reached across the table and set a hand on her forearm. "Hey."

She felt the heat in his hand. She felt startled by the gesture, thrown off guard. Didn't know if it was meant to hold her still or offer her comfort. Or more. His eyes were alight.

The off-balance sensation intensified. "I think I set in motion a chain reaction."

"How?"

"When I went to Sorenstam with you. When I gave her my employee swipe card. I thought . . . I thought that card had been used to give the shooters access to the club. But if it was cloned, that's even worse."

"You didn't start anything," he said.

"Sure I did. When I was sixteen." She got up from the table and paced to the back fence, arms crossed, then back. "Going to Sorenstam seems to have poked a hornet's nest. Otherwise, Zero wouldn't have gone after Oscar."

"That seems a given," Aiden said.

"And now Zero's after me and Oscar both. I have to presume he's coming after you, too."

Aiden looked at Oscar. "What do you make of all this?"

"I don't know, man. I'm dying for a glass of water, though. I ran about two miles through a mall in Camarillo with Zannah here on my tail." He pointed his thumb at Harper. "I'm thirstier than hell."

Aiden said, "Zannah?"

"Don't even," she said.

In the kitchen, he got her a soda and turned on the television, a news channel. He got Oscar a cold glass of water. He poured another for the dog. Oscar drank his greedily and said, "Can I use the john?"

Aiden pointed down the hall and watched hawk-eyed as Oscar headed into the bathroom. When he shut the door, Aiden continued watching.

"Do you trust him?" he said.

"No," she said. "Do you trust my answer on that?"

He glanced at her. "The jury's still out."

In the background, a reporter said, "Police are hunting this afternoon for a murderer who attacked an Ojai woman with a sledgehammer. Jasmine Hay was found bludgeoned to death in an alley behind the restaurant where she worked as a waitress. We go now to Rosalita's, where . . ."

The Pepsi bottle slid from Harper's hand and shattered on the floor.

The sun had sunk behind the trees in the west, glaring gold, a firefly sunset through the leaves. Harper stood at Aiden's living room window, fist pressed to her mouth. On the driveway, he paced, phone to his ear. She heard snatches of his conversation with Erika Sorenstam. She felt as though electric worms were crawling beneath her skin.

Aiden ended his call and came inside. He closed the door softly. "I told her you'd phoned me. That you heard the news report, that you knew the victim back in China Lake and were afraid there's a connection to Azerov. I said I hadn't seen you."

"Did she believe you?"

"At this point, I don't know. But I don't think she's sending SWAT here to arrest you."

Harper pressed her fingers against her eyes. "Jasmine. Oh, my God."

She hadn't seen Jasmine Hay since before going down for the jewelry store robbery. She remembered a thin thirteen-year-old with intimidating physical bravado, who kept a Beanie Baby bear in her school backpack.

Aiden said, "How's Oscar?"

She looked out the back door. He was sitting at the picnic table, head in his hands. He knew Jasmine better than she did.

"Are you kidding? He's devastated. And scared. So am I." She ran her hands over her face. She was close to shivering. "A sledgehammer. Aiden, that's Zero. It's the robbery all over again, but a hundred times worse. It's . . ."

Her stomach coiled. "Excuse me."

She hurried to the bathroom, hot and nauseated, pressing her hand to the wall to steady herself. Inside, she grabbed the toilet, but nothing came up. She leaned on the sink and splashed water on her face. Her hands were shaking.

In the mirror, she saw Aiden appear in the doorway. He took a towel from the rack and held it out. She accepted it and buried her face in it, hiding hot tears that welled out of abject fear.

"Hey."

His arm went around her shoulder. She hupped a breath into the towel. He gently took it from her, tossed it aside, and wrapped both arms around her. When he pulled her in, she pressed her face to his chest. She felt completely clenched. *Don't cry. Cry and you'll weaken. Weaken and you won't be ready for whatever's coming.*

He held her close. "I gotcha."

She nodded tightly. She couldn't even breathe. His arms seemed all that were keeping her from screaming. She squeezed her eyes shut and felt his chest rise and fall. He rocked her, just rocked her.

"You're not alone," he said. "You're not."

She raised her face. His eyes, weary and bruised, had a look in them like iron. Want, and gratitude, and overwhelming need poured through her. She opened her mouth to speak, but nothing came out.

He put his cheek against hers and murmured in her ear. "You. Are not. Alone."

He kissed her neck. She nodded and tightened her arms around him. For a second, she felt safe. She knew that he had her back. He believed her. He was in, all the way.

The wind had risen, black and hissing, and was bearing down on her. But she knew now: She couldn't let it blow her away. She had to hold on.

She put a hand to his face. "You aren't alone either."

She raised up on her toes and kissed him, hard and with a ragged edge. Then she shut her eyes again and clutched him, finally managing to breathe.

They stood in the doorway for a good minute, until Oscar appeared at the end of the hallway.

"Dude. Harper, your phone's ringing."

⟋⟍

She went outside and took her phone from her backpack. She didn't recognize the number. "Hello?"

"Flynn."

But she recognized the voice.

She stood beneath the oaks, the wind sweeping around her, her tongue abruptly thick and useless. Her fingers tingled. Her face felt numb.

The man breathed, almost a laugh. Though she couldn't see him, she sensed his leer. Sensed his eyes running down her body, felt the electric crackle of his presence beside her in a getaway car just before he pulled on a ski mask and got out and ran with Eddie Azerov into a jewelry store, sledgehammer in hand.

"Good to hear your voice, too," he said. "Bitch."

32

Harper stared at oaks that were bent against the wind. They seemed vague, seemed to be dissolving into gray mist. On the phone, Travis Maddox spoke to her, live and in thundering black and white.

"I'm sending you a link," he said. "Open it."

She couldn't move. The noise in her ears was no longer the wind but the pounding of blood through her veins.

Her phone beeped. A URL appeared on the screen. She got out her tablet and copied the link into its browser.

A video feed loaded. It looked like a live view from a camera located outdoors somewhere in urban Southern California. A busy street, traffic flashing in the sunshine. Across the road, a flag waved on a flagpole.

"Are you watching?" Travis said.

"What do you want?"

The camera slowly panned. Foothills in the distance, green, threaded with curving streets and houses. Los Angeles. Harper's stomach tightened. She didn't look up from the screen but waved at Aiden. *Get out here.*

The camera continued to pan past apartment buildings and cozy retail stores, to a parking lot and neatly mown lawns. School buildings. It stopped.

North Hills High School.

Travis said, "I can hear you breathing, Zannah. You're getting worked up."

Harper's temples pounded. It was Piper Westerman's school.

Aiden appeared at her side. She put her index finger to her lips. A second later, Oscar walked over. Aiden gave him a *zip it* motion.

Harper set the tablet on the picnic table and put her phone on speaker. She foraged a notebook and pen from her backpack, scribbled, and held up the message so Aiden could read it.

Travis Maddox on phone. Piper's high school on video. Call Sorenstam.

On the video feed, the main doors of the high school building opened. The sound was poor—wind and traffic and distant voices.

"What are you doing?" she said.

"Just watch."

Aiden took out his phone and strode into the house, punching numbers. He shut the door behind him.

On-screen, Piper pushed through the door into the sunshine and practically skipped down the steps. She headed for the parking lot.

Oscar chewed his thumbnail. Abruptly, he pointed at the screen.

Harper saw it: the dog. It was standing in the middle of the parking lot. "God."

"That's more like it," Travis said. "You should—"

She hung up on him.

Vision pulsing, she scrolled through her contacts, found Piper's number, and dialed. It began to ring.

On-screen, Piper crossed the school lawn and neared the parking lot. The dog stood facing her. From her angle, she couldn't see it.

Piper's number rang in Harper's ear. But on the video feed, Piper kept walking. She didn't seem to hear the phone.

"Dammit, her phone's on silent," Harper said.

She spun toward the house. Inside, Aiden had his phone to his ear. He chopped the air with his hand as he spoke. He saw her and shook his head. He was getting nowhere.

Harper pointed at Oscar. "Call 9-1-1."

"I can't do that."

She turned a death gaze on him. He backed up, hands in the air, and fished out his phone. "What do I say?"

"Tell them there's an emergency at North Hills High School on Wilshire in L.A. You got a report that an armed man is stalking the parking lot. Tell them you saw it online. Social freakin' media, he's bragging about it. Just goddamned call them."

"From my phone? I'll have to dump it."

"Do it, Oscar."

On the video feed, a city bus passed in front of the view. It cleared. Piper was drawing closer to the dog, still seemingly unaware of its presence.

She paused and looked at her book bag.

"Yeah, your phone's ringing. Answer it, Piper," Harper said.

A cement truck crossed in front of the camera. When it passed, Piper was fishing in the book bag.

"Answer, come on, come on," Harper said.

Oscar punched 911 and said, "My emergency is a weird one and you need to get firepower on it ASAP."

On the screen, Piper pulled out her phone and looked at the display.

"Pick up pick up pick up," Harper whispered.

The camera zoomed on Piper. Somebody was manning it. Travis, probably.

Travis Goddamned Maddox. Always breathing in the depths of her life, speaking for his father, curling around her fears and squeezing her heart and lungs like smoke. It was always going to be Travis.

On-screen, Piper finally answered the call. "Hey, Harper."

"Piper, turn around and run," she shouted.

On the phone, Piper said, "What's—hang on, Harper."

"No. *No.* Piper, get out of there. Run. Run back to the school building. Don't stop, don't—*dammit.*"

On-screen, Piper lowered her phone. She had stopped at the sight confronting her twenty yards ahead: the dog. She backed up a step.

"Piper, *run,*" Harper shouted.

Piper spun, aimed herself back at the high school, and took off. The dog did the same, tearing after her.

Ahead of her, a car pulled into the parking lot. A nondescript sedan,

American, beige, old but with plenty of horses under the hood. The kind of car Harper would have boosted when she was fifteen and told to steal something for a hot getaway.

It drove straight toward Piper. She was caught between it and the charging dog.

Oscar, still on the phone with 911, said, "You gotta get people to the high school like right now, Jesus, man, it's going down, hurry."

Harper said, "Piper, God."

Piper pulled herself to a stop, looking frantically for a way out. The door of the beige sedan opened. A figure wearing a hoodie over a baseball cap jumped out and grabbed her. Piper kicked and fought, but he held her tight and flung her into the car. The dog raced at the vehicle and leaped in after her. The hooded man jumped in the driver's seat, slammed the door, and took off, burning twin lines of rubber into the asphalt. He roared out of the parking lot, headed for the back streets and wooded neighborhoods beyond the high school.

On Harper's phone, the call from Piper went dead.

"Oh, my God," Harper said.

Oscar lowered his phone. "No. Oh man. Oh no." A dispatcher's voice tinned from his phone. "Sir? Sir?"

Aiden threw open the back door and hurried, limping hard, to see the screen. "Yes. North Hills High. Main entrance, the west side parking lot . . ."

"Too late," Harper said. "They got her."

~

Aiden put a hand beneath Harper's elbow. "I'll get LAPD. You saw it. We'll get them on it."

But Harper shook her head. "How? Look. There's no sign of it."

She pointed at the screen. Piper was gone. The car was gone. Nothing had been left to tell the tale.

Aiden made another call. He spoke rapid-fire to somebody in the LAPD.

Harper stared at the computer screen. "Oscar, can we trace that video feed?"

He frowned and waggled his hand. "Maybe, maybe not."

Into his phone, Aiden said, "Do it." He hung up. "LAPD is sending a unit to the scene."

She grabbed his arm in thanks. To Oscar she said, "Can we trace the IP connection? A phone number?"

Same face, same gesture. "Live feed, no recording."

The video feed was abruptly cut. The screen went black.

Her phone rang. Despite herself, she jumped. Hand trembling, she answered the call.

33

Harper put her phone to her ear. The oaks rattled under a gust of wind. Aiden stood close, his face flat, eyes keen.

The sound of Travis Maddox breathing through the phone raised the hairs on her arms. She didn't wait for him to speak.

"I know how this works. I know how to fuck you up. Let Piper go right now and I won't come after you."

Aiden and Oscar stared at her.

"You're darling," Travis said. "You're a diamond in the pig shit that is the world. But you don't know where I am. Now shut up and hear what you're going to do."

His voice had no joy in it, no hint of mercy. Just the same dry certainty he'd always spoken with, the ego and desire for command. She kept her knees locked. Aiden's hand steadied her. She held tight to her voice.

"Talk, Travis."

"And forget about tracing this call. The number will be dead as soon as I hang up. You know this drill, but let me state it in case you are busy pissing your pants. You will not contact Piper's parents. You will not contact the police. You will not phone them, Sam I Am."

Acid rose up her throat. He was enjoying himself. "Get to it."

"Turn yourself over to us, or little sis will die."

She heard a whine in her head, the sound of a heated wire, getting louder, filling her ears.

Her knees were readying to give way. "You can't think I'm going to do that."

"You want Piper to live? You want to see her breathing, with four working limbs, without her face burned away?"

"Stop it."

"I have nothing to do with it. But Eddie, you know . . . he likes to zero things out. And even if he's in a mellow mood, Eagle is almost impossible to control when he gets the scent of prey." His voice turned lively. "Eagle being his dog."

Yes, asshole, I know. "What do you want from me?"

"Nothing. I just want you to understand what you've wrought."

"Really?"

"God, you still have that sarcastic edge to your voice. It's like a bone saw, grinding against my shins." He paused, seemingly waiting for her to jump in again. She forced herself to stay quiet. "This will unfold in my time, not yours. What do I want? Oscar, for starters. The rest is easy. Your full confession."

"I did my time, Travis."

"Fuck you did. You know what the pressure of a dog's jaw is, on a human jugular? Even if he doesn't rip her throat out, he hasn't been vaccinated for rabies. Forget the disfigurement. All that has to happen is for her to stay hidden for the incubation period. There's no cure once symptoms manifest, you know. And even if it turns out the puppy doesn't have rabies, God knows what kind of staph infection he might transmit through his filthy mouth."

"I'll confess anything you want, Travis. Just tell me where to exchange her. But you're not getting Oscar."

"Sure I am. Instructions will follow. Keep the phone line open," he said. "Ticktock."

34

Harper stood with the phone hanging from her hand, her eyes shut. The wind rattled through the trees. Aiden put a hand on her back. She flinched. She wanted to jump like a vampire straight through the oaks, hit the sky and scream on through the atmosphere, past air and blue and people to the dense empty black beyond, where light would hit her in a vacuum, silently, and none of this would matter.

"Harper," he said.

She opened her eyes. "They have Piper."

Oscar said, "And? What do they want?"

She looked at him. He shook his head, slowly at first. Backed up a step.

"No." He raised his hands. "You can't. I won't."

"Of course not," she said.

He continued to back away, his gaze flitting between her and Aiden. "You can't turn me over to him. To them."

"Oscar, it's okay." She held out her hands, and knew she was almost gesturing as though patting out a fire. "Nobody's turning you over to them."

"Shit shit shit—oh, God, I should never have taken that job. They were playing me behind my back and I should have known."

"They were playing all of us," Harper said. "Now we figure out what to do."

She had to keep him from bolting again. If she could get him invested in a solution, he would get distracted and forget about running.

That was the thing about Oscar: The project was everything. Creative problem solving, a win at the end—the goal was all. A number. Cash in his pocket. Like a video game with a real outcome, which generally meant pride and some good dope. A hackathon. But now, for the first time in years, it was becoming real for him.

"Oscar, I drove you up here to keep you away from Zero. Do you hear me? I will not turn you over to him."

He pointed at Aiden. "How about him?"

Aiden shook his head. "Not gonna happen."

Aiden looked serious, but she imagined that all his cop training had prepared him to look serious with people he was trying to calm down before he got close enough to Tase them and cuff them.

Oscar nodded. "Okay. I believe you."

Aiden turned to Harper. "The LAPD unit is en route. And I left multiple messages for Erika. They'll put out BOLOs on that beige sedan. But if Zero is the one who snatched her, presume he parked a switch car nearby and that he's already abandoned the vehicle you saw on the video."

Her stomach and hopes began to drop. And they were already low. "They'll check for the spot where Travis was filming, too? It had to be across from the high school parking lot. Somebody must have seen him."

"They'll check."

"We've got to get to the scene, gotta do something to help them. . . ."

He took hold of her shoulders. "You are not going to the scene or anywhere near it. You are not going anyplace close to Zero and Travis Maddox."

"I have to. This is on me."

"Bullshit. You're not doing anything that will give Zero and Maddox a chance to get hold of you. Or that will give the cops a whiff of suspicion about you."

"I already had you call it in," she said. "That has to be two strikes against this already."

He frowned, but only for a second. "Brutal."

"Sorry."

"But true."

"Aiden." She put a hand on top of his. "It doesn't matter anymore what people think of us. Piper's been taken. We have to do everything we can."

His hands were hot on her shoulders. She could feel his pulse beat through his palms. She wanted to wrap her arms around him. The air felt chilly.

"Please. Help me," she said.

"I am."

"I've been myopic. From the time I saw the shadow at the memorial service, I should have warned Piper more forcefully. I should have insisted that the Westermans protect her."

"But you told her to be careful. You told her parents that you were worried."

"Oh, my God."

He put an arm around her shoulder. "Hey." She thought he was trying to comfort her. He said, "You need to suck it up. You care about Piper—I know it, and they know it. And this is all about getting you in their sights."

"Why don't they want me to contact her parents? I would expect them to demand a ransom. The Westermans have money, plenty of it. That is, if . . ."

"Money is their backup plan. It's Plan B," Aiden said.

Her nausea returned, cold and stinking.

Oscar cleared his throat. "Where does that leave me?"

She and Aiden both looked at him. She said, "We might need your skills. You up for that?"

"This girl," he said. "She's a friend?"

"She's the little sister of the guy who died at Xenon."

His face fell. "Your . . . your boyfriend."

She nodded. And she felt a thin line of hope. "His name was Drew. And Zero never mentioned him to you, did he?"

Oscar shook his head. Harper realized: There was no possibility

Drew had been involved in providing the shooters access to the club. She had let her own suspicious nature take over. God. She had blamed him, nearly led Sorenstam to him, and tried to get the detective to look at him, without having said it herself. She felt ashamed.

"We need to get to L.A. Let's go," she said.

She was running to the house when Aiden's phone rang.

"Erika. Yeah," he said.

The warmth and relief in his voice when he said Sorenstam's name sent an ice pick through Harper's heart.

Sorenstam was in a departmental unmarked car, heaving it through freeway traffic toward downtown L.A. On the radio, she had Detective Perez from the station. On her phone, she had Aiden.

"I'm on my way to the high school," she said.

"Thank you," Aiden said.

"Don't, yet. This thing is weird, Garrison. And it's unspooling fast. I don't know what's going on and I don't want to think that you're sending me on a snipe hunt."

"Appreciate it. Truly."

Her stomach burned. She told herself it was because she was entering an arena where everything was uncertain, where she didn't know if she was risking her time on a fool's errand, or heading for a trap. She tried to convince herself it wasn't because of her feelings for the man on the other end of the line.

"Aiden, if this turns out to be nothing, or it smells bad when I get there . . ."

"Understood."

"Harper Flynn can't be ordering us around. If she's after something, I will not put up with it. Got that?"

"Loud and clear."

"I'll call you when I know something." She ended the call and pressed TRANSMIT on the radio. "Perez?"

His voice fuzzed through. "Talked to the Ventura Sheriff's Office. When they arrived at the Lemon Tree Mall in Camarillo, no sign of Flynn or the man she supposedly found. No word from her."

"Okay," Sorenstam said. "If Flynn calls the station again, keep her on the line. Try to get her location. We need to bring her in."

"On what grounds?" Perez said.

"Material witness." Professional pain in the ass. Possible devil. She hit the windshield flasher lights and pulled into the fast lane.

⸺

Thirty miles from Los Angeles, Aiden signaled and pulled the pickup off the freeway at a gas station. Harper followed.

She parked near the pickup and looked at Oscar severely. "If you so much as breathe on the window, much less open the door and get out, I'm going to telepathically contact Zero's dog and tell it to hunt you down."

He frowned. "Sheesh. Chill." Then he shrank back against the door frame. "Don't look at me like that."

She yanked the keys from the ignition and got out. The afternoon heat pressed down. The hills were dry, the golden grass little more than kindling, the huddled oaks almost gray. Aiden stood at the pump, holding the nozzle, watching the numbers spin.

"Any more news from Sorenstam?" she said.

"Not yet."

"She should be at the high school by now."

"She'll call." He eyed her. "What?"

I know about the two of you, she wanted to say. I know that you may have loved her. I know she's still angry at you, maybe because she resents what was taken away from the two of you. I know that when you talk to her on the phone, once you get past the thorns, your voice mellows, and you speak in the shorthand of cops and friends and people who know each other far better than you and I do. I know I'm on the outside.

"It's nothing," she said.

He squinted at her. "We're headed into God knows what. Don't hold back. There's no time."

She listened to the traffic slice past on the freeway.

"You worried I'll have another episode?" he said.

"No."

"You should be. Some of my wiring's been ripped out. Medication can stop the sparks from jumping the gap only so much of the time."

"I understand."

"This thing, Fregoli—the meds help focus my vision, but they can't restore my neurology to what it was before the injury. Face blindness is just the strangest symptom. I've blacked out before. And I can guarantee that what happened last night will happen again."

His face was stark. His gaze didn't flinch. He had decided to be open with her. He looked like he was asking something in return.

"Okay," she said.

"Okay what? You going to tell me what's got your teeth nearly chattering?"

"Okay, you son of a bitch. You want to know the truth? What happened last night scared me half to death. It made me pull back. I saw somebody I was having dinner with—holding hands with—somebody I'd just made love to give a complete stranger an unmitigated beatdown, and it scared the hell out of me."

He didn't look away. "I know."

She waited for him to say something else.

He glanced at the pump. "Do what you want. But if you want to be with me, you have to take me as is."

"All right, then."

"All right."

He kept looking at her. "My turn."

She jammed her hands in her back pockets. She had a feeling what was coming.

He said, "Tell me the rest. Tell me everything and stop holding back. I may not see things right all the time, but I know when something looks wrong. And I can hear it. I can see it in your posture, in your eyes. You may have grown up lying and stealing and sneaking past people's defenses, but I spent years learning how to spot people like you, and years before that carrying a military rifle and figuring out my plan to kill everybody I met that day."

She deliberately avoided swallowing, but inwardly she flinched. His voice was calm, his face intense. The wind flattened his hair against his forehead.

"There's more," she said.

"The rest of the story."

"Yes."

After all this time, it lodged in her chest. The fallout: debris scattered across the desert, across many lives.

"Travis and Zero are out for revenge. Everything I told you about the armed robbery—it's the rock-solid truth. We all went away. All did time," she said. "But that wasn't the only consequence of that day."

His eyes scanned her. Maybe he seemed to think: *No surprise.*

"The robbery was my ticket out," she said. "But I'd been trying to find a way out for a long time. I knew that things were heading down the drain to the sewer, and that I had to find a way to stop what was happening to me. And I was angry and desperate and seventeen. So I talked to Oscar. He taught me some of the things he was doing for the Maddox family."

"He initiated you into his hackerish ways?"

She glanced at the MINI. Oscar was fiddling with the stereo.

"He was literally a kid with toys. And he showed me how he'd set up Maddox's computer security. It was drumskin tight. But Rowdy never even praised his work. And that's what Oscar wanted—somebody who would let him be a kid under the Christmas tree, even if it was in a half-built crime mansion in the scrub desert outside China Lake."

"And you soaked it all in."

She nodded. "I listened. And I thought about it. And later, after Oscar explained something to me—"

"Or you asked him questions . . ."

"Of course. Afterward, I wrote everything down, in a little Mole-skin notebook I hid behind the molding along the floorboard in the closet. I cut a hole in the sheetrock and put the baseboard back over it," she said.

"You knew how to get into Roland Maddox's computer system?" Aiden said.

"For months, I was too scared to do it. I knew that if I ever did, I had to get out or I'd get dead."

He finished filling the tank and replaced the nozzle on the pump.

"That's why Travis is after me. Because that final day, I didn't just set them up and wreck their armed robbery. Before I got behind the wheel, I got into Roland Maddox's computer system and screwed with it."

"What did you do?" Aiden said.

"I ruined him."

She said it and her head rang and her breath felt light in her chest. Travis knew, and Zero and her mother—but she had never broken her silence until now.

"I destroyed his records, some of which were encrypted via one-time pads."

"Whoa."

"He lost millions and couldn't pay his debts to some very bad peo-ple." She looked at the concrete and back at Aiden. Her heart pounded heavily in her chest. "He killed himself."

Aiden didn't move, not toward her, not away. He looked like stone.

"It happened while I was in juvenile detention. My lawyer men-tioned it almost in passing. He thought I fainted because I loved Rowdy. Not because I was terrified and relieved."

"Jesus."

"So you see," she said. "I didn't just cost Travis a big score, or his freedom. I cost him his father."

A man Travis idolized. A man whose assets were either blown away in random bits or seized by the IRS. Travis was left with nothing.

When he got out of prison, even the house was only a sun-wrecked shell, infiltrated by sand and scorpions and claw-rooted desert weeds.

"That's why Travis is determined to punish me," Harper said. "Now you see. And nothing will stop him."

She stood, hands at her sides, hearing her own heart and the blur of traffic from the mindless freeway.

Eventually, slowly, Aiden nodded. "Then we'd better get Piper back before he can hurt either one of you."

The sun seemed to brighten. Despite everything she'd done in her life, he was going forward with her. She was getting one more chance.

"Let's go," she said.

35

Outside North Hills High School, Harper swung the MINI off Wilshire Boulevard into a parking lot. Aiden was right behind her. It was nearly empty, six forty-five P.M. now, the students gone, the teachers, too, except for the principal and other administrators. A black-and-white LAPD squad car was parked in the center of the lot. On the sidewalk, Erika Sorenstam was pacing back and forth, phone to her ear.

When Harper and Aiden pulled in, Sorenstam hung up. Her hair was a near-white sheet in the dusk. She walked toward them.

Harper said to Oscar, "Let me do the talking."

They climbed out, as did Aiden. Sorenstam looked icy. Harper's spirits sank.

Clearly, nobody had seen a sign of Piper. Two LAPD detectives stood by the squad car, coffee cups in hand. A uniformed officer was combing the scene, walking with measured steps, holding a flashlight. Damn, they actually did that.

Harper said, "Any news?"

Sorenstam set her hands on her hips. "You have some explaining to do."

"Anything. Tell me what you need to know."

Aiden approached. Sorenstam gave him a look, brief, and then a longer one. Then she nodded at Oscar.

"Who's this?"

He lifted his chin in greeting. "Oscar Sierra." He tossed his head to clear away his hair from his eyes. "Ma'am."

Harper thought he might just shake so hard his shoelaces would untie.

"Can I see some ID?" Sorenstam said.

He dug his wallet from a sagging jeans pocket and slid out his driver's license. Sorenstam compared the photo to his sorrowful and anxious face. She turned the license to let the sunset catch its edges, checking whether it was legitimate.

"One moment." She took it to her car, leaned in for the radio, and read off the number.

- Oscar wiped his nose. "I am so screwed."

"Just hold on," Harper said.

Sorenstam came back and returned the license. "Mr. Sierra, you know that you were reported missing? You've been with Ms. Flynn and haven't reported your whereabouts to the China Lake police."

"Hey. I reported them to her." He jabbed a thumb at Harper. "She reported it to you. I presume you reported it to—"

Sorenstam waved him off. "I'll get to you in a minute. Don't go anywhere."

"Doesn't seem likely, not with all these cops around," he said.

Harper tried not to shoot him a glance. She knew he would regard escaping from this law enforcement rodeo as a coup.

Aiden said, "Erika, is there any news?"

"Not the kind you're hoping for."

Harper's pulse rocketed. "Oh, God." The horizon tilted sideways against the sunset.

Sorenstam frowned. "Cool down. That's not what I mean."

She felt Aiden's hand on her elbow and the dizziness abated. "You haven't found her?"

"No. But that's not the issue."

"What, then?"

"We have no evidence that Piper Westerman has been abducted."

"You haven't heard from the kidnappers?" Harper said.

Sorenstam crossed her arms. "I mean we have evidence that Piper is fine."

Harper and Aiden reacted simultaneously. "What?"

Sorenstam glanced over her shoulder at the LAPD detectives finishing their coffee. One caught her eye and ambled in their direction. A black guy, late fifties, breathing noticeably under his weight.

Harper said, "She got away? They released her?"

Sorenstam said, "She hasn't been abducted."

"You keep saying that. What do you mean?"

"Piper has contacted her parents in the last hour."

"Oh, my God." She put her fingers to her temples. "Thank God. She's alive. What did she say?"

"She texted them that she was going to a basketball game with friends. School game, down in Palos Verdes. Said she'd be home around ten P.M."

"Text," Harper said. "That's all? Did you—did the LAPD—inform the Westermans about what I saw?"

"See, that's just it. 'What you saw.' You're the only one who claims you saw her being abducted."

Oscar said, "I saw, too."

Sorenstam looked at him with acid disdain.

"Nobody in the parking lot?" Harper said.

Sorenstam shook her head. "And on a sketchy video link. Not in person. From a hundred miles away."

"I told you. They wanted me to see it. They wanted me to—"

Sorenstam raised a hand. "Are you listening? Piper sent a text to her parents *after* the time you allege she was abducted."

Allege.

Harper said, "But Zero grabbed her and everything she was carrying. He got her purse, he definitely got her phone. He could have sent the text."

"Her parents replied to the text. They got a couple of back-and-forths."

Harper felt the evening begin to disintegrate. "The Westermans don't think she's been taken."

"They talked to her," Sorenstam said.

Harper shook her head. "When? What did she say?"

"Half an hour ago. She sounded fine."

This was wrong. Twenty kinds of wrong. "No. It's a trick. I saw it."

"I think not," Sorenstam said. "Her parents aren't the only ones who spoke to her. That detective over there? He got her number from her folks and called, too."

She felt like she was slipping on a crumbling hillside. "No." She looked at the uniform inspecting the parking lot. "What is he searching for?"

And she wondered: evidence that she herself was in on a setup?

Sorenstam said, "Her car isn't here."

"So?"

"You said she was thrown in the back of a vehicle and driven away at high speed. If so—if she was abducted on the way to get in her car to drive to the basketball game after school—why is her car gone from the parking lot?"

"Because the kidnappers got her car keys, same as they got her phone. Oh, my God, don't you believe me?"

Aiden said, "Harper." He reached for her arm and she pulled away.

The LAPD detective arrived. "This Flynn?"

Sorenstam said, "She's the one who set this off."

He glared at her, up and down, gave her a good paint-stripping. "Mind telling us why you've thrown two law enforcement agencies into high gear and set up a couple of parents to face their worst nightmare?"

"I didn't set anything up," she said. "I phoned in a report of what I saw on video. I'm telling you the truth."

He hitched his belt. Sorenstam said, "Give us a minute."

"One. Otherwise, I'm of a mind to take Ms. Flynn to the station for questioning." He glanced at Oscar and Aiden. "And her entourage."

Oscar said, "Not me, man. I'm just along for the ride."

Harper wanted to bite him. The detective strolled back to his colleagues.

Harper said, "I don't know what's going on, but it's a game."

"Sounds about right," Sorenstam said.

"No. Not me." She felt her last hopes slipping away. Aiden was looking at her with reserve. And had he stepped closer to Sorenstam, away from her?

"It's Zero and Travis Maddox," Harper said. "They've set this up so the police won't believe that Piper has been abducted. I know it. They took her, they made sure I saw it via video that couldn't be recorded. They got her keys and drove her RAV4 away before the LAPD arrived. And now they're texting her parents and forcing her to talk to them and pretend nothing's wrong."

"Mighty unlikely."

"You don't know these guys."

"But you do. Oh so very well. You worked hand in glove with them for years," Sorenstam said.

"I'm not working with them now."

"Do you know how improbable that sounds?"

Cheeks burning, Harper turned away. She pulled out her phone.

Sorenstam said, "Who are you calling?"

She scrolled through her contacts and found the Westermans' number. Her thumb hovered over it. "What did you say to Piper's parents? What excuse did the detectives give for contacting them?"

"False alarm. School prank. One that wasn't funny. The principal agreed to go along," Sorenstam said.

"And they told you they'd spoken to Piper. That's exactly what they said."

"Yes."

Harper hesitated. If the Westermans thought Piper was okay, how could she ruin that? They had already faced their worst nightmare. How could she force them to suffer again?

No. This was about Piper. "I was with their son when he died. I'm the one who had to tell them. And I am *not* going to be the one who tells them something horrible has happened to their only surviving child."

She pressed the number. As it rang, she shut her eyes.

Richard Westerman picked up. "Harper. What is going on?"

She started to step away, then realized that everybody needed to watch and hear everything.

"I'm concerned about Piper," she said. "You say you've heard from her?"

Sorenstam threw up her hands and began turning in circles.

"Yes, we have," Westerman said, "The police called us. I take it that's thanks to you."

Harper tried to phrase her words not to sound alarmist. But she had to know. "Mr. Westerman, what exactly did Piper say?"

"She's at a basketball game. North Hills is playing PV. She's fine."

"I just—"

"Listen to me. I know Piper is struggling. We all are. You have no idea. And we've appreciated you providing a sympathetic ear for her. But this has gone too far."

"I'm just concerned about her. Very concerned."

"You think she's run away? She hasn't. She called to let us know where she was going, and then after the police called, her mother phoned her back to verify she was okay."

"What did she say?"

His tone sharpened. "She chatted and laughed with my wife. She was with friends. She didn't sound as though she was being held against her will."

Harper inhaled.

"That's what you're hinting at. Don't deny it," he said. "I don't know why you'd suggest such a vile thing, but it's extremely disturbing. Piper actually said, 'I'm fine. No ransom note. No guys with saws and meat hooks. Jesus, what's going on?'"

"Mr. Westerman, please, just—"

"No. I'm done. You're ignoring my message here. My wife and I have spoken to our daughter twice in the last two hours. She sounded both completely at ease and completely perplexed about why we're so concerned."

"Did she mention—"

"Mention you? Yes. She said you're being very intrusive and weird."

Harper's face heated. Her palms heated.

"It's not funny, Harper. You may think you're being a Good Samaritan, but you're frightening our family."

"No. Mr. Westerman. Richard. Please . . ."

"I'm going to ask you not to call here anymore. Don't call Piper, either. Don't text her, don't e-mail, and do not under any circumstances attempt to see her."

"This isn't about me. I need proof that Piper's okay."

"You are to leave our family alone. Do you understand? From this moment, we want no contact with you. If you attempt to speak to any member of the family, but particularly to Piper, I'll be forced to take legal action against you."

She stood in the darkened parking lot, with everybody staring at her, and felt herself shrinking.

"Do you understand?" Westerman said.

"I hear you."

He hung up.

Sorenstam said, "Slam dunk, huh?"

She squeezed her eyes shut.

Had she been wrong? Had Travis played her so completely that she had fallen for a ruse? Maybe he had hired a teenager to dress like Piper. The video had been poor resolution. Maybe this was all meant to get her crawling down a hole in which she'd become trapped.

She looked up, humiliated. "If I'm wrong . . . about what's going on . . ."

She shook herself. Raising her phone again, she scrolled until she found Piper's number. She called.

It rang. She closed her eyes and hoped.

A voice picked up. "Harper?"

Her pulse pounded in her temples. "Piper."

"You shouldn't be calling me."

She felt as though she were being watched, and not just by the cops. She turned slowly in a circle, eyeing the parking lot, the street filled with evening traffic, office buildings on the far side, and a multistory parking garage. That had to be where Travis had been standing when he shot the video.

She put the phone on speaker. "Piper, are you okay? Where are you?"

"I can't talk right now. I'll call you back."

Harper heard a heated thread of anxiety in the girl's voice.

"Just tell me what's going on," Harper said.

"You know."

Aiden drew near. Sorenstam leaned in, her expression overtly skeptical. She opened her mouth as if to say something; Harper shook her head sharply.

No, she mouthed. *They're listening.*

Oscar stirred and fished a phone from his shirt pocket. His eyes widened. He made a slashing motion across his throat. *Stop talking. Get off the phone.*

"Piper . . ."

"I'll call you later," the girl said, and ended the call.

Harper redialed, but Oscar said, "Don't. They sent me a warning."

Sorenstam said, "What kind of warning?"

"'Get off the phone and get away from the cops or Piper loses her fingers.'"

"Jesus," Harper said.

Aiden put up a hand. "They texted you?"

Oscar shook his head. "They sent me a notification. One-time thing, through a network I set up. It shows up on my screen for three seconds and then fades away. It's not captured and recorded in the phone's system."

Sorenstam said, "You're telling me you just coincidentally got this dire warning and you can't show it to us? You have no proof? It just vanished?"

"Lady, I designed the system myself so it doesn't leave fingerprints, digital or otherwise. It's come back to haunt me."

"Right," Sorenstam said.

Behind them, the LAPD detective whistled. "We're finishing up here. There's nothing to see."

He gave Harper a hard glare. She knew he was half a breath from charging her with filing a false police report.

She made a hard choice. Turning to Sorenstam, she said, "Tell him to go."

Aiden said, "What the hell?"

"Tell him I've been punked by a bunch of lowlifes I used to work with. They set this up to ruin my reputation, maybe get me arrested and kicked out of UCLA, get my security clearance pulled."

"Harper, are you kidding me?" Aiden said.

Sorenstam looked at her askance. Harper said, "Tell them. Let them clear the scene."

Sorenstam looked like she was the one ready to slap Harper now. But Harper said, "Oscar is telling the truth. I know what he's capable of. And everything he built, he built for Travis and Zero." She stepped closer and lowered her voice. "This is an elaborate game. One that is designed to put me square in the bull's-eye. Do you understand?"

Sorenstam parsed her face.

"Please," Harper said.

Sorenstam exhaled and walked over to the LAPD detective.

Aiden grabbed Harper's arm. "Hell's going on?"

She said, "They have her. They know we're here. They let her answer calls from people, but they're monitoring them." She turned again, scanning the view. "They could have a camera out here watching us. We need to get away from the scene. Piper's in danger."

He held her gaze. His support seemed precarious. "Okay," he said.

He headed for his truck, beckoning Sorenstam as he went. Harper and Oscar got in the MINI. She knew what she had heard in Aiden's voice: reproach. The unsaid message: *This is your last chance.* But it wasn't. It was Piper's.

Her phone rang. The display read: Call blocked.

She answered. Travis said, "See? I can do whatever I want to you, and you can't stop it."

36

Fifteen minutes later, Harper paced back and forth by her car in the parking lot outside Eller's Diner in Westwood. Aiden's truck rumbled in. Right behind him came Sorenstam. They parked and walked over to her.

Sorenstam said, "You're about ten seconds from being arrested."

"We're inside Los Angeles city limits. You don't have jurisdiction."

"Try me."

Harper said, "I made a mistake back at the high school."

"Just one?"

"Travis knew I wasn't alone. And then he knew when I was. He waited until I got in the car to call me."

Aiden said, "They had eyes on you."

Sorenstam said, "You believe her? That's it now?"

Aiden gave her a cool look. "I do."

Harper squeezed his arm and breathed a quiet, "Thank you."

Sorenstam said, "Where's the evidence?"

Aiden said, "Harper hasn't developed my delusion. This isn't a folie à deux."

"But you didn't see the video. In Santa Barbara, you heard the supposed phone call from Travis Maddox but can't identify his voice. And we have countervailing evidence—Piper's own words."

"You want evidence?" He nodded at the night. "I'd wager everything I own that the LAPD hasn't found Piper at that basketball game. Nobody will have seen her there. Because she never went."

"They're checking." She turned to Harper. "They consider this a waste of resources. They can sue you for reimbursement, you know. Right after they haul you in for filing a false police report."

Harper said, "Aiden's right. We need evidence."

She looked at Oscar. He raised his hands.

"Not me."

"I'm asking you to help me with some tech."

"Like what?"

"Travis is going to contact me. He has my phone number. I will lay odds that the next time he calls, he'll either ask me to go to a pay phone or to go to a public place where he can observe me from a distance to verify that I'm alone."

Aiden said, "He'll want to make sure you aren't wearing a wire. And he'll ask you to get rid of your phone so the cops can't use its GPS to track you."

"I need another device to mirror my calls and messages. I have cloud services set up. If I can get Travis to text me, the message will arrive on my phone, my tablet, and my computer if they're turned on. I can hang on to my phone and give you the other devices, Detective."

Aiden said, "Erika won't be convinced unless she hears Maddox identify himself, implicate himself, and show himself to her."

"Please, give it a try," Harper said.

Sorenstam said, "Okay." She still looked dubious.

"I don't know why you think I would invent this," Harper said.

"You'd be amazed what people do for their own reasons. And how often they involve the authorities. Ever hear of mailing ricin letters to the president? Then blaming a rival?"

"Please, Detective."

Sorenstam thought about it. "One shot."

"I'll take it."

"If all this is true, these people will try to lure you to unfamiliar ground and isolate you." She glanced at Oscar. "And they'll insist that he accompany you."

He crossed his arms, hugging himself.

"It won't happen," Harper said.

Aiden looked him up and down. "Follow me."

He led Oscar into the diner. Harper turned to Sorenstam.

"I know about you and Aiden," she said.

Sorenstam took a slow second to look at her. "And?"

Don't blow this. "You may know him better than anybody except his brother. I'm relying on him for help. If you can tell me whether that's the right decision, please do it now."

"I've been telling you what to watch out for since the day you came into the sheriff's station."

"You were angry at him that day." Harper looked at the pavement. "And you were on the money. I've seen what happens when things go wrong."

"It happened while you were with him."

Sorenstam didn't phrase it as a question but a statement. Harper nodded.

Sorenstam glanced toward the diner. "Did he hurt somebody?"

When Harper hesitated, Sorenstam dropped her head.

"That's how he got that black eye. And why he's limping," she said. "Later he tried to apologize, but the guy he took down wasn't in the mood."

Traffic rolled by on the boulevard, slow and unobservant. After a second, Sorenstam looked up. "If you've seen it, why are you asking me whether he's okay? You know he's not. You asking if he's dangerous? You have the answer. Why are you asking me whether to trust him?"

"Because I see the expression on your face."

Sorenstam turned her head toward the street but not in time to hide the pain in her eyes. If Harper had ever doubted that Sorenstam still cared for Aiden, she didn't now. Her anger shone with grief at what Aiden had lost.

"I know you're furious at everything that's happened to him, and how it affects him," Harper said. "I want to know if the partner you trusted is still there, somewhere."

"I don't know." Sorenstam turned to her. "I tried, for a long time, to tell myself that the man I knew was going to heal and come back. But that's not the way it works with traumatic brain injuries. Especially not to veterans and cops. TBIs don't scab over and repair themselves. They scar. Sometimes the scars rewire you so you look the same, move the same, sound the same. But your mind has been fragmented, and when it reassembles, the spirit that's there is somebody else."

"Like the flip side of Fregoli's syndrome," Harper said.

"I'm not a fan of painful ironies."

"You still love him."

"I love what we had. I'm confused by this man who looks at me with Aiden's eyes and wants me to love him now."

"Would you still trust him?"

"That's irrelevant."

"Not to me."

Sorenstam's white-blond hair reflected the lights of passing traffic, like a halo. "You hooked up with him. Didn't you?"

"Not a hookup."

Sorenstam blinked. "Okay. You want relationship advice from me?"

"No. Detective—"

"Erika. No point in standing on formalities at this point."

"If I survive all this, it would be fun to get drinks so we can bitch about other people instead of snarking about me. But I need to know if Aiden can stay steady when the pressure hits."

Sorenstam looked conflicted—maybe jealous and hurt. But after a second, she stood straighter.

"Yes. He can."

Relief and hope bucked Harper up. "Thank you."

"His bravery . . . he's the same fearless bastard he always was. The face blindness, altered perception—sometimes he knows it's happening. If he heads that way, the important thing is to stop it in its tracks. Help him understand that he's off on a dangerous tangent."

Aiden and Oscar came out of the diner and walked toward them.

Harper said, "I appreciate it. I hope this discussion doesn't come into play. I hope everything turns out fine."

"You have a fairy godmother?" Sorenstam said.

"Just like you have a magic dolphin you ride to work."

Sorenstam smiled, just for a moment.

Aiden and Oscar approached. Sorenstam said, "It'll work."

Aiden was wearing Oscar's fatigue jacket, T-shirt, watch cap, and sunglasses.

Harper felt both relieved and on edge. "Really?"

Sorenstam said, "Light disguise, and in the dark, if he's a passenger in your car . . ."

"At speed, or at a distance," Aiden said. "That's all we need. Azerov saw Oscar wearing these things last night. And I'm not that much older than he looks."

"Hey," Oscar said. He was now wearing Aiden's shirt. "I . . . wait."

Harper's phone chirped. The skin on her arms tingled. A text notification hovered on her screen.

She stood motionless in the parking lot with lights from the diner throwing them all into sharp shadow.

The text notification stood out starkly on her phone's display. It had no identifying information—no name, phone number, URL, not anything.

> Buy a new pay-as-you-go phone. Activate it. Go to the
> pay phone at the corner of Wilshire and Federal. It will
> ring in 60 minutes. If you don't answer, Piper dies.

> TICKTOCK.

She held up her phone. Her mouth was dry. Sorenstam and Aiden crowded in to see. The notification faded.

"It's gone," Aiden said, "What did it say?"

Sorenstam said, "Answer his call at a pay phone in one hour or Piper dies. Ticktock. Asshole."

"Let's go."

He glanced once at Sorenstam, maybe to see if she was going to stop him. Maybe for other reasons. But Sorenstam was watching Harper.

Harper returned the look. She nodded at Sorenstam. Then she walked with Aiden to her car. They got in and she fired up the engine. Fifty-nine minutes left. She peeled out of the parking lot.

37

The sun had fallen to the horizon. Dusk was dropping a cloak over the electric splay of lights along Wilshire Boulevard outside the street-front shopping center. Harper stood in line at the kiosk in the first-floor promenade, harried by the echo of conversation around her. A hundred yards away outside the doors, beneath a picket line of palm trees, the pay phone caught the pewter flash of headlights. She had eight minutes left to purchase a cell phone at the kiosk, register it, and get to the pay phone before Travis called. Nearby, Aiden prowled the aisle inside a bookstore, watching her through the windows.

Three people stood in line ahead of her. A single clerk manned the kiosk, a twentyish guy in a black T-shirt with boy-band hair, doing his best to help two teens choose between the pink and the silver sparkle phone cases.

Harper checked the time again. Seven minutes. The teens settled on a rainbow phone case. The woman waiting in front of Harper was purchasing a set of earbuds.

Harper said, "Huge favor. If you'll let me go first, I'll pay for those earbuds."

The woman looked at her askance.

"Big hurry. It's urgent."

"You couldn't have thought of that before you stood there squirming and breathing down my neck?" the woman said.

"No."

"What could possibly be so urgent?"

"Friend's been kidnapped. If I don't buy a new phone so the kidnappers can call me, it's going to be a shit show," Harper said.

The woman pulled back a step. "Sheesh. Go ahead."

The teens left. Harper took the woman's earbuds and stepped to the counter. The woman pulled a hands-free headset from the rack and added it to Harper's purchases. "Plus this."

Jaw tight, Harper paid, tapping her foot as the clerk scanned each item. Five minutes. The noise in the shopping center sounded like an avalanche, cascading onto her. She handed over her credit card. The clerk had a merry air. He whistled while he rang everything up.

"There you go, miss. Would you like our three-year extended warranty?"

She grabbed the phone and tried to rip open the packaging. "No."

"May I have your e-mail address?"

She tugged on the plastic shrink wrap. "No."

"Would you like to be kept up to date on our promotional offers?"

The plastic remained slick and impregnable. "I need a knife."

"What?"

"Pair of scissors. Something sharp. Please."

The woman behind her said, "Otherwise, the kidnappers won't get the ransom."

Nonplussed, the clerk found a box cutter and sliced open the plastic casing around the phone. He seemed decidedly less merry. He handed Harper the credit card slip, and she scribbled her name.

"Thanks." She ripped open the packaging and yanked the phone out, scattering plastic and cardboard and coupons and a mini instruction manual across the kiosk, as if stripping a patient in the ER to reach an injury.

"You really like that phone," the woman said.

Clutching it, Harper jogged for the exit. Four minutes left.

The phone had an activation code, but she couldn't read it as she ran. She paused at the door and entered it. The phone acknowledged the code and fired up. Her heart was beating like a piston. Glancing outside, she gasped. Somebody was at the pay phone.

Three minutes. Her new phone lit up and pinged and buzzed and beeped and welcomed her to its fantastic world of voice and data communications. The man at the pay phone continued talking, perhaps clinging to his direct line to 1971. Harper fumbled with the new cell to find the thing she needed most: its phone number.

She found it. Ninety seconds. Pushing through the doors, she ran into a cooling night and street noise. The man at the pay phone was leaning against the privacy hood, speaking with a smile on his lips. She walked up and stood close by him, politely but firmly invading his space.

"I need the phone. Right now," she said.

He glanced at her and lowered his voice. He wore a blazer and khakis and sounded like he was calling a girlfriend, not completing a drug deal. He gave Harper a disapproving look and turned his back. She walked around to face him.

"Some people are going to call this phone and if you're still on that call in sixty seconds, they'll tear this street up."

"This is a private conversation. Get out of here."

"Probably with a bulldozer. I'm not kidding."

Thirty seconds. The guy still hadn't hung up.

From up the street came a piercing, two-fingered whistle. The man at the phone looked up. Aiden was walking toward them, hands at his sides like a gunslinger.

Harper grabbed the receiver from the man's hand and said into it, "He'll call you back."

She hung up. The man glowered at her, bristling.

The phone instantly rang. He reached for it.

"Bad idea," she said.

Aiden continued to come on. The man threw up his hands and backed away. The phone rang insistently.

Harper grabbed it. "I'm here."

"Not good enough," Travis said.

38

Harper grabbed the side of the pay phone. It was cold and grimy. "I'm here. On time. It's a public phone, and somebody was using it when I arrived."

"Not my problem," Travis said.

Traffic pulsed past, lights strobing over her, music thudding from car stereos.

"I'm ready to take the next step. Tell me what that is," she said.

Twenty yards away, Aiden continued walking in her direction, but he blended into the crowd on the sidewalk and kept going. She forced herself not to look directly at him or watch him as he passed. *Eyes on.* She had to presume that Travis was watching her.

"I need Oscar," Travis said.

The phone booth's privacy hood felt cold, but the phone in her hand was warm. The pay phone smelled of grubby metal.

"I need Piper," she said.

"So you're agreed that we'll swap. You aren't so stupid after all. Or so redeemed."

"I'm not going to swap," she said. "We need to make a deal, but I won't just let Zero take Oscar and disappear with him."

"Piper's a grief-stricken sixteen-year-old who had the bad luck to get to know you before you got her brother killed," Travis said.

Harper's throat clenched.

"She's an innocent bystander who loves you unreasonably," Travis went on. "Oscar is a thief and a doper who'd turn on you for the price of a key. Either a kilo of dope or a cryptological key that lets him play in people's accounts online. You know that."

She looked at traffic. The night was growing cold.

"Here's what you're going to do," Travis said. "You're going to put Oscar in your car and drive him to the GPS coordinates I text to your new phone. And you're going to slave your phone to my computer system. I'll send a request and you'll authorize me to mirror your displays and data in real time. That way I will be able to monitor your progress on the GPS. You will follow the directions I give you without deviation. Got it?"

"What if Oscar won't come with me?" she said.

"Convince him."

She slowly turned, eyeing the street. Aiden stood against the wall of a clothing store. The streetlights didn't reach him. He was in shadow, wearing Oscar's clothes and hat, indistinguishable from him.

"Okay."

"That's the spirit," Travis said. "Give me the number for your burn phone."

She lit the display and read it to him. Then she said, "Let me talk to Piper."

"This isn't a cheap action movie. You don't get to talk to anybody."

"No proof of life, no Oscar."

He was quiet a bit. "No, you're right. It would be best to remind you of the importance of doing as I tell you."

She leaned her forehead against the pay phone, her chest tightening. Soon she heard noise and muffled voices.

Piper's voice was thin. "Harper?"

"You're going to be okay." Harper strained to keep her own voice level. "I'm going to get you out of there."

"I'm so scared," Piper said. "These guys . . ."

Harper could hardly bear it. "I'm going to bring you home. Hear me? Piper, I'm going to bring you home."

"They said if the police come, they'll kill me. They took my phone and sent texts to people, like I was fine. They made me call Mom and Dad and say I was at a basketball game so nobody would know they have me. I don't understand, Harper. Don't they want money?"

"Piper. Stay steady. Dig deep and hold on. I'm coming."

"You couldn't get Drew out of Xenon. Can you get me out of here?"

Claws to the heart. Harper leaned heavily on the phone.

Piper's voice filled with tears. "Help me. Please. I'm begging you."

"I hear you. Hang in there. Can you do that?"

The tears were in Harper's eyes, too. She swallowed, and they ran down her throat. "I'm going to help you. Do you understand?"

Piper sobbed.

"Do you understand? Say it," Harper said.

After another sob, Piper said, "I understand."

"You are a strong fucking girl. Do you understand? Say it."

"I am a strong fucking girl."

"I will find you, Piper. Wherever you are. I will bring you home."

There was a pause. "Like the Pied Piper? Hansel and Gretel? Ariadne?"

Harper's mouth hung open. *What?*

"Please, Harper. Please—*omigod, let go . . .*"

Noises erupted on the other end of the line. Piper's voice rose and was abruptly silenced.

"Travis, Jesus Christ, leave her alone," Harper said. "Don't hurt her."

His voice was smooth and about two degrees above freezing. "I take care of the merchandise," he said. "I covered her mouth so nobody has to hear her mewling."

Harper gripped the pay phone. "If Zero touches her, I'll hurt you so bad your grandchildren will feel it a hundred years from now."

In her hand, the new burn phone vibrated. On the brightly lit display were GPS coordinates—latitude and longitude.

"That's where you're heading," Travis said.

She thumbed the burn phone and brought up the physical location of the coordinates on a map.

"That's in Canyon Country," she said.

The map pictured a bright blue pushpin for the destination, on a stretch of road at the far north end of Los Angeles County. Past the city limits, past the suburbs and strip malls and amusement parks and horse ranches, over the pass and on the down slope to the high desert. It was seventy miles away.

"It should take you ninety minutes to drive to those coordinates from your present location on Wilshire," Travis said.

She calculated. Once she cleared the morass of the L.A. freeways, it should be clear sailing.

"Be there in an hour," he said.

"Hey, hell are you trying—"

"You failed to answer this pay phone when I first called it," Travis said. "As a penalty for that failure, you lose thirty minutes."

She slammed the receiver down. He may have continued talking, but she had no time to hear it. She ran up the street, pulling out her car keys. Behind her, she heard Aiden's footsteps.

With her new phone, she quickly dialed Sorenstam. "We're heading north to the desert. Busting ass." She didn't wait for Sorenstam to answer. She just ran.

39

Sorenstam followed Harper's taillights along Wilshire Boulevard, headed for the freeway. The sun was below the horizon in the west, tinting the car windows red. Oscar slouched in the passenger seat, his entire posture a grumble.

Radio to her mouth, she said, "They're going north to the Antelope Valley."

Her lieutenant was curt. "Let them go."

"I need to see how this plays out."

"You've been playing along far too long, Detective."

Her blood slowly boiled up. "What if I let them go and this isn't nothing? Nobody from LAPD or the Palos Verdes Police has actually seen Piper Westerman, have they? She hasn't arrived home yet, right?"

"That doesn't mean—"

"We're talking about a sixteen-year-old girl. If it turns out that she's actually been abducted, do you want to be the one who has to tell her parents, and FOX TV, that the sheriff's department stood down? I don't."

"Detective Sorenstam, I need you to return to the station. We're shorthanded."

"One hour. Give me sixty minutes. We'll know by then if this is for real or not."

He breathed. Finally, he said, "Sixty minutes. No more."

"Thank you." She clicked off and pulled out her phone to call Aiden. When he answered, she said, "You've got sixty minutes. If you want my backup, you need proof by then."

"Got it," he said.

She hung up. Oscar was looking at her.

"Are we going to follow them?" he said.

"From a distance."

"You calling in a surveillance team? Double up?"

She drove. "I'm going to call the Kern County Sheriff's Office to let them know their missing person has turned up safe and sound."

"Nobody who cares about me would call it in the way they did," he said. "My friends would put their name to it."

He looked at her. She understood. She got on the 405 heading north. He slouched lower in the seat, knowing who might lie ahead.

~

Harper kept one hand on the gearshift, changing lanes and dodging in and out of traffic on the long slope down the 405. Ahead, the lights of the valley spread like a vast electric yellow bowl. She was going eighty-five, and if that damned pickup hauling a horse trailer didn't move out of her way, she was going to veer right and pass him on the shoulder. Aiden sat almost motionless in the passenger seat, but his legs were jammed hard against the foot well, as though he couldn't keep himself from invisibly trying to brake.

Forty-five miles to go. The dashboard clock told her she had forty-three minutes left.

The horse trailer signaled and pulled out of her way.

"Finally." She shifted into fifth and accelerated.

Ahead of her was a river of red taillights, all the way to the bottom of the pass and beyond. She kept her foot hard on the pedal. Aiden glanced at the speedometer.

"Don't," she said. "It's this or nothing."

She glanced in the rearview mirror, the headlights hitting her eyes hard.

"If a cops flashes you, what then?" Aiden said. "Pull over and let them give you a ticket, I'd recommend."

That would take ten minutes. "Drive it like I stole it."

"Run from a flashing light and you lose any chance of getting to Piper. They'd catch you live on TV."

"So I'm going to make sure no flashing lights get on my tail. They are not even going to spot us."

He gave her a look like: *Good luck with that.*

"You watch for LAPD or CHP. And I mean with eyes you didn't even know you had," she said.

He continued looking at her for another long second.

"What?" she said.

"I see why people wanted you driving getaway."

She didn't know if he meant it as a compliment. If not, she didn't have time to feel offended. They were in this now, and he would either trust her or not.

"We're going to get her," she said. "We're going to get Piper back."

She hit the bottom of the hill, holding hard to the wheel through what should have been an easy turn at the speed limit. Forty minutes left. Thirty-seven miles.

"We're ahead," she said.

She blew past the 101 and headed north across the valley. Her heart was drumming, her mouth dry. The freeway stayed clear. Until they reached the mountains at the north end of the valley. They saw the red flick of traffic braking ahead of them, accordioning, people coming hard to a stop.

"Shit," she said.

They slowed to stop-and-go. For three minutes, she stayed with it, her hand feeling numb on the gearshift. Aiden glanced at the clock.

He rolled down his window and levered himself out to peer ahead. "Accident."

"No. No." If they didn't do something, they had no chance of getting to the next stop.

He reached into his back pocket and pulled out his wallet.

No—his badge.

"Get on the shoulder," he said.

She hit the blinker and he rolled down his window and stuck out his arm. She wished he had a gumball light for the dashboard. But this was second best.

He looked over his shoulder. "Go."

She swung onto the shoulder, put on her flashers, and eased along past traffic, crunching over dust and detritus. She glanced again in the mirror. She saw lights, bright and relentless. She didn't know whether they belonged to cops or kidnappers or ghosts come to take her.

The red river of electric taillights stretched on for as far as she could see. Thirty-eight minutes.

40

Harper cleared the jackknifed gasoline tanker fifteen minutes later, swerving back into traffic when Aiden spotted the emergency flares and the CHP motorcycle officer in the road with a flashlight, directing traffic. Her pulse felt as quick as the engine's rpm.

Aiden checked the side mirror. "Go."

She put the pedal down.

The road rose into crenellated ranges of hills and mountains that formed the northern barrier of the Los Angeles Basin. The MINI, though quick and light and responsive, still had only four cylinders. It was screaming as she downshifted into fourth and began the climb. It had heart but not a huge amount of power, and she had to shove her foot hard against the pedal to keep the car from losing speed on the uphill.

Thirty-two miles left. Twenty-three minutes.

We're not going to make it.

It was only a whip of a thought, but she must have hissed through her teeth, because Aiden looked at her.

"Just drive," he said.

"You think they won't kill Piper if I'm late?" she said. "Don't kid yourself."

She tried to loosen her grip on the wheel. Her fingers were close to cramping. "They'll punish her to punish me. They'll start killing her slowly. And they'll let me hear it. If we don't get there on the dot, she's gone."

They wound through hills and swung onto Highway 14, deeper into ranch land and scrub country, farther into the ranks of hills. The headlights thinned. The moon rose and spread an eggshell layer of ghostly light across the landscape.

Twelve minutes. They crested another hill. The lights of Los Angeles were deep behind them, a yellow fuzz radiating from the horizon. Harper pushed the car flat out across the broad summit of the grade. Ahead, the road sliced through a canyon down a long slide to the desert floor. They were entering the Mojave, the desolate and ever-distant top corner of the county. They were well beyond the jurisdiction of the LAPD now, into the realm of desert rats and ex-urban commuters and the far-flung outposts of the sheriff's department.

Aiden said, "Exit's in two miles."

"Eleven minutes. How far once we get off the highway?"

"Maybe five miles."

"Come on, baby, come on . . ."

"The road looks a lot rougher once we turn off."

"Of course."

"You grew up out here, didn't you?" he said.

She nodded at the sage and chaparral. "No. This is New York City compared to where I grew up."

The black stripe of the descending highway unrolled for miles to the desert floor. From there, it ran straight north through Palmdale and Lancaster, electric outposts of well-gridded streets and civilization. China Lake was a hundred miles farther on up the road, past the next range of mountains, out in the white nowhere at the edge of a dry lake bed.

"At least here, we're within range of help if something goes wrong. We can see the city down there. We don't have to rely on a highway patrol officer happening upon us from fifty miles away."

"You think help is going to be close at hand?"

"I'm a Pollyanna," she said. "It's within arm's reach."

He put his hand against the back of her neck and held on, reassuringly. She kept driving.

⁓

Aiden held on to Harper's neck, feeling her pulse boom. Under the blue-white glow of the dashboard lights, she looked spectral.

"Pollyanna kicking ass," he said.

The engine was screaming. They were going ninety-plus on the downhill. The road was good and she drove it like she meant to get every ounce of speed out of the car, sure and slick and confident. He didn't doubt her driving ability.

Her knuckles stood out on the wheel, forearms corded. Half in a mutter, she said, "If they hurt Piper, I'll kill them."

"Are you actually willing to trade yourself for Piper if things go bad?" he said.

"That's what I told Travis."

"I mean *actually*."

"I'll do whatever it takes to keep Piper safe. I'll do whatever they want."

"Two different things."

She paused, lips parting. "I'll do whatever I have to."

The road cut through a bulldozed canyon, heading sharply down the long grade. The canyon walls sped past, gray in the moonlight, rock upon endless rock. Nothing upon nothing. Her face was set, lovely and drawn. She had no idea what she was promising.

"If you do whatever you have to, then I'll help you, no matter what," he said.

Again she glanced at him, a brief, searching look. Her eyes were clear and harder than sapphires. She nodded, sharp and definite.

He glanced at the clock. Seven minutes. Ten miles. He wasn't worried about her driving. He was worried about her intentions.

"They want you. Once you're in range, they'll try to take you," he said.

"How far to the turnoff?"

"Half a mile." He turned to her. "They have no intention of letting you drive home with their hostage."

She scanned the road for the exit. It wasn't lit, no streetlights, just a green sign and an arrow. She lifted her foot from the gas pedal.

He said, "Did you hear me?"

"Yes. I know." She downshifted and slipped into the exit lane, hanging on as it curved. "I know, Aiden. So we have to get Piper out before anything else happens. To her or to you or to me."

"Excellent. You have a plan to do that?"

She braked and veered around an outcropping of rock. "I don't."

Of course she didn't. She had been driving like a maniac just to get there, had hardly even been breathing.

"But I will."

She held the car steady as the road narrowed and the good pavement turned to rough old asphalt, crumbling at the edges. "We'll think of something."

He looked at her, and against every wish and hope, he felt a fresh moment of doubt about her goals, and her heart.

As though maybe she'd tricked him into coming along with her on a mission to meet up with people who were . . . what, her confederates, even now? People she wanted to kill, with his help?

Was he meant to be the reliable witness she would use later on, to exculpate herself?

His chest felt hollow. His head was beginning to ache.

No.

Don't do this, Garrison. Stop it.

He pulled back from thoughts that were leaching into his mind like lye. He counted to ten. *Clear your thinking.* Analyze it, and see if you're going down a road that's illogical and self-defeating. *You're being paranoid.*

He noted how upset and shaky Harper was—or had been, at the start. Now she looked intense and ready to go over the edge.

She looked fierce. He watched her, and felt her intensity in the darkness of the car. Was she acting?

No. She couldn't be. She was tuned as tight as a saw blade and ready to cut. Her rage and fear were too real and raw. He knew that Harper was a trickster, a thief, and that she had managed to hide her intentions from Zero and Travis on the day of the armed robbery. She couldn't be *that* good an actor, to fool him this late in the game. Could she?

He said, "What do you know about ambushes?"

"Not much."

"Have you ever taken part in one?"

"No. I've been jumped before. By these guys." Her face looked pained and driven. "But I know all about double crosses."

He didn't have to ask her to spell that one out. She was an expert at it.

"One mile ahead," he said. His phone rang.

She gunned it.

⁓

Near the crest of the pass, just before the highway leveled out and began the long descent to the Antelope Valley, Sorenstam held her phone to her ear, listening to Aiden's number ring. He picked up.

"You there yet?" she said.

"A mile away."

"We have six minutes left in the hour my lieutenant gave me," she said. "If you don't want me to turn back, you—"

"Harper has four minutes left in the hour Travis gave her. We're booming. Just catch up. If you—"

The call went dead.

"Dammit." She redialed but got a *No Service* message. "Stinking desert. They're out of range."

She handed Oscar her phone. "Keep trying him."

He wiped his nose and pressed REDIAL, then shook his head.

"Tell me something," Sorenstam said.

He looked at her with suspicion.

"Harper's employee swipe card. She gave it to me. She suspected that it was used by the shooters to get into Xenon."

"Why would she think that?"

"Why would you think it wasn't?"

He gave her a sidelong stare. Shook his head.

Sorenstam said, "Harper says Zero paid you a visit intending to murder you."

"That's harsh. That word."

"Kill you? Eliminate you? Exterminate? Waste you?"

He raised his hands. "I get the picture. Just don't make me picture it."

She did a double take. Half laughed. "Harper said there's only one reason Zero would be after you. To shut you up because you forged a copy of her card."

"I ain't saying nothing about that."

"Mr. Sierra, I don't care about your role in the swipe card forgery. I just need some corroborating evidence, so I can know once and for all whether Harper is telling the truth, or trying to mess with me and the department for her own reasons."

"Harper has no reason to mess with somebody like you." He was sunk in the seat, but straightened. "She stopped rolling on my side of the street years ago. She went legit. Hell, she's the only person I could think to turn to when I needed help today."

He nodded and then realized this might not send the message he'd intended. "Wait, that came out wrong. She's the person I trusted—not because she's still working for Zero, but because she went straight. I knew Zero wouldn't expect me to reach out to her."

"So what's up with the swipe card?"

He went quiet again.

Irked, she told him to scroll through her recent calls and find the number for Spartan Security Systems. It was past the close of business, but she had him dial Tom White's direct line. She took the phone and put it to her ear. It rang, then the call was forwarded. When it was finally answered, the connection was fuzzy and intermittent.

"This is Tom White. Detective, what can I do for you?"

"Any luck recovering data from that swipe card?"

"Afraid not. Our data forensics team has come up empty."

"Even though you have the employee number?"

"It's been a year since the fire. They don't think there's any way to match it."

"There must be some corresponding data left to compare it to."

"Detective, there's no record of where any swipe cards were used that night. Every device they touched was damaged or destroyed."

He sounded more definite now than he had thirty seconds earlier. She wondered if he was trying to let her down easy, or to give up too easy.

"I'd appreciate it if you'd continue to try." She ended the call.

Oscar was drumming his thumbs against his legs. "About that call."

"What about it?"

He continued to drum his thumbs against his thighs. He seemed to be weighing his options.

"Oscar, I'm your best shot here," she said. "I'm the only one who might be able to protect you—and I mean from Zero and from prosecution. If you provide me with information, you might be able to leverage that."

He squirmed. "Harper's swipe card. I take it you want to know where and when it was used at Xenon the night of the fire."

"Harper suspects it was used to give the gunmen access through a back door."

"If it was—and I'm not saying it was her card, but if a card with all the identifying characteristics of hers was used that night—who's that guy telling you all the data was lost?"

"You heard that?"

"A few words. Hey, I'm offering to help you hack this problem. Don't diss me, man."

"All right. The swipe cards are dumb cards, right?" she said. "They contain identifying data that other devices can read. But they don't build a record of when or where or how they're used."

"That's correct," he said. "What are you trying to find out?"

"Whether Harper's card—either the real one or the clone—was used on the back door around the time the gunmen entered the club."

"You haven't been able to get that information because . . ."

"Xenon's computer systems uploaded all the data only once an hour, to an on-site server. From there, it was sent at the end of each day to a central site owned by the company that handled security for the club."

"Company didn't do such a great job," he said. "They should have some liability."

She gave him an incredulous stare. "Says the man who helped the bad guys get in."

"Whoa." He raised his hands. "Slow down. That's a harsh suggestion."

"You know that's what this is all about."

"I don't hurt people. Not ever. That's not my bag. No way."

"So what did you expect to happen?" she said.

"I'm not saying anything was supposed to happen. Nothing. Nada." His voice rose and he scooted backward. "This is not supposed to be an interrogation."

"You're right. It's not. Stop trying to screw yourself through the seat and into the floor."

They crested the pass and headed into a lightless expanse.

Sorenstam said, "Let's back up. I was talking about the security system at Xenon. Let's stick to technical data."

"Good. Yeah."

He looked at her with dark hurt in his eyes, as if she'd pulled a chair out from under him. Well, he needed to get real.

"You answer my nonaccusatory questions about technical stuff, and then we'll talk about what else you might say and how I can protect you from the people who want you dead."

He hunched again. "I'm not a snitch."

"Of course not. But I'm just a detective with a degree in political science. I need a lesson in Data for Dummies." She squinted at the road. "Spartan Security Systems installed the key card system at Xenon. They lost all the data that evening because the fire destroyed the locks, computer chips, and wiring at the club before it could sync with their system."

"That's what they said?" Oscar asked.

"Their locks were keyed to a central system at the club via Wi-Fi. That was hard-linked in their computer room, and from there to Spartan. We checked. All the video camera footage was destroyed. That's why nobody knows for sure whether there were two shooters, or three as Harper and Aiden claim. Or four, riding the horses of the apocalypse."

Oscar was quiet for a minute. "It doesn't sound right."

"What doesn't?"

"That all evidence was destroyed. No backup systems? Everything on-site? When they had a hard link to the security company? Come on. Every business that has a burglar and fire alarm is hardwired to send emergency messages straight to a central control room at the company. 24/7."

"And that's the way Xenon worked. Except the employee swipe cards were on a different system," Sorenstam said. "They weren't tied into the alarm system. They were designed for inventory control, to prevent petty thievery, and to control access to various entrances in the building."

Oscar was sitting taller, tapping his thumbs harder against his knees. "I don't think so." He shook his head. "No way. You know your smartphone?"

"What about it?"

"Earlier, Harper was talking about cloud computing services. They automatically synchronize between devices. You enter a party in your calendar on your phone and it shows up on your computer at home.

Your game scores sync up. Your books are on all your devices and when you switch from one to the other, your bookmarks are saved, so it opens to the very same page."

"Right."

"Spartan Security saves all their data the same way. Has to. It's all got to be there in the cloud."

"But Spartan only synched once every twenty-four hours."

"You sure about that?"

She went quiet, driving through the empty night. She redialed Tom White and put the phone to her ear, struggling to hear him through the poor connection.

"Got a question," she said.

He hesitated. "Shoot."

"I know you didn't originally handle the Xenon account. Could you go back through Spartan's records and see if there's a chance that data was uploaded to your cloud services the night of the fire?"

"All right." He sounded less enthusiastic than he had earlier. "Detective, I'll get on it first thing in the morning."

"I need it tonight."

After a heavy pause, he said, "I'll call our technician on duty."

"I need it in the next fifteen minutes, Mr. White."

"Really? This can't wait?"

"It's an emergency. I need an answer now," she said.

"Fine. Yes, ma'am. I'll see what I can do."

"Now, as in right now."

"Got it. I'm at your beck and call. Ticktock."

He hung up. Sorenstam kept driving, her hand rigid on the wheel.

"Oh, my God," she said.

⁓

The thrum of the engine vibrated through Harper's hands, into her chest, all the way through her. The headlights swept across the empty road. There was nothing—not even jackrabbits or tumbleweeds. She was overdriving the lights, massively, but didn't slow down. The clock on the dash showed the time.

None left.

Aiden said, "Stop. This is it."

She braked hard, the MINI almost sliding to a stop. The scenery seemed to keep rushing past. Her vision was throbbing.

"I don't see anything. Where are they?" she said.

Aiden scrutinized the roadway in the moonlight, the rocky hillside ascending to their right, the drop-off to their left. The road was pocked with potholes, the white lines chipped and faded.

He nodded ahead. "What's that?"

She edged forward. The headlights caught the reflection of metal and glass in the scrub a few yards off the shoulder of the road.

It was the rusting hulk of an abandoned big rig with a trailer attached. It had run off the asphalt and tipped on its side.

"Keep your high beams on," Aiden said.

"Let them know I'm here, but keep them from seeing into the car?" she said.

"Exactly."

Her new burn phone rang.

"Answer it," he said.

She could hardly see. Forty-five miles in one hour; they'd done it.

She pushed the button. "I'm here. On time."

Travis said, "What do you want, a cookie?"

"You coming?"

"Where's Oscar?"

She breathed deep to slow her heartbeat. Ahead, past the high beams, the road faded to black. They saw nobody, only the icy splash of the stars and the twinkle of electric lights from the floor of Antelope Valley, ten miles to the north.

"He's with me," she said.

She had to play this cool, and now came the moment when she realized that improvising at full speed, with a clock counting down, had left no room for maneuvering. She had no time to think of anything clever, no way to find an out. She had to clear her head and play it right. First time or nothing.

"I'm here. Where are you?" she said.

Aiden was sitting low in the seat, scanning the road ahead, the hills, the view from the side mirror, hoping not to see Zero rise up from the dirt and descend on them. He held his HK, aimed at the floor.

Travis said, "Send Oscar out."

Lie. Balls to the wall. Drive it like you stole it. "Nope."

She opened her door. She got out, walked to the front of the car, and stood in the headlights.

She held the phone to her ear. "Oscar thinks I'm taking him to meet a friend who'll drive him across the border into Mexico. He thinks I'm helping him get *away* from you. If I send him out here into the desert all alone, he'll know something's squirrely." The headlights hit her in the back, just above the knees, and sent her shadow jutting ahead on the asphalt. "So I can't talk to him about Piper. I can't make it obvious that there's going to be an exchange. We need to do this quietly."

"Oscar go quietly?" Travis said. "The guy can't even take a quiet piss."

Did he believe her? "After he smoked his second fatty tonight, he stopped talking and started staring at the stars. You have a small window here, Travis. He's half-baked. But Oscar half-baked is still ten times smarter than most ordinary mortals. Ask Zero how slippery he is and how fast he can run."

Travis was silent. She took that as further assent.

"Show me Piper. Once I see her, I'll tell Oscar to get out, that she's his ride."

Travis seemed to be considering her proposal.

"Here's what we're going to do," he replied, and she knew this was going to screw her. "Let me see that Oscar's with you. Then I'll tell you where to go next."

"Next? Goddammit, Travis."

He didn't actually laugh, just emitted a harsh *heh*. But his voice took on a singsong lilt, cheery and soaked in bile.

"You thought we were going to be waiting for you?" he said. "Aren't you the naive, eager beaver. I needed to make sure you were on your own, that you weren't dragging any cops or police helicopters behind you when you came over the pass."

"Stop dicking around."

"Keep talking like that to me and you'll regret it," he said.

She had to keep talking to him like that. Had to keep strength in her voice, even though her legs felt like yarn, and fear crawled down her arms like a host of spiders.

"I'm here, Travis. I'm about to screw over Oscar, somebody I've known since I was a kid. I'm in a pissy mood. All I want is to see Piper and take her home."

"Then walk over to that wrecked truck."

She hesitated. The hills swallowed the light, even the moonlight. The wreck was rusted and keeling, full of sharp edges and places where Zero could hide.

She started walking, the headlights illuminating her path. Her knees felt loose.

For Piper. For Drew.

She got ten yards from the wreck and stopped. The spiders seemed to skitter along her arms and down her legs. Where was Travis? Uphill along the top of a ridge, with a pair of high-powered binoculars? Sitting on a boulder beside Zero, holding a night scope on a high-powered rifle? She walked another fifteen feet.

In her ear, Travis said, "Smile for the camera."

It took her a minute to see it: a miniature video camera with a green light pinpointed on the top, facing the road.

He wasn't there. He wasn't anywhere nearby. And neither was Piper.

41

The desert night seemed to fold over on itself and capture Harper, pressing down.

"Travis . . ." *You snake. You heartworm.* She forced herself not to scream at him. "You see me. You know I'm here. I have Oscar. Nobody's following. Let's get this over with."

"I need to ask Oscar some questions first."

"Do that and he'll bolt into the desert before I can blink. I told you, he thinks I'm taking him to meet a friend—"

"Who's going to drive him to Mexico for free surfing and endless fine Cuervo Gold. Have it your way. Look under the camera. There's a set of zip ties and enough rags to make a blindfold and a gag. Restrain Oscar and then we'll get going."

How the hell was that supposed to work? "Can't do it."

"You'd better."

She stepped closer to the camera. On the dirt behind it, she saw a Baggie with the ties and rags.

"Travis, take a look behind me. I'm driving a MINI. Even if I restrain Oscar, the car's so small he'd be able to kick me, elbow me, even head-butt me despite a gag and blindfold and makeshift handcuffs."

"Cuff him to the door handle or the glove box."

"No loops to slide the zip ties through. Listen to me. He'd either run us off the highway into a ravine or get the door open and throw himself out. Do you want him dead? I don't really think so. He knows too much you want him to tell you before you kill him. You need him alive."

There was a pause, and maybe a sigh. "Then we'll go with Plan Z."

On the phone came scuffling sounds. A new voice. "Harper?"

Her skin abruptly felt so cold it burned. "Piper. Honey, I'm coming."

"Hurry. God, please, I am so—"

That was all she said. Travis came back on.

"You apparently need motivating, Flynn. So listen to this."

Through the phone came sounds of a struggle. Piper cried out. "No. Omigod, what are you . . . oh Jesus stop, stop . . ."

"Travis!" Harper yelled.

"Shh," he said. "Don't want to spook poor Oscar now."

"What are you doing to her?"

In the background, Piper screamed. It sounded unearthly, riven with shock and fear and some unraveling realization. Harper turned toward the car. The headlights blinded her. Piper's voice crashed into sobs.

"What have you done?" Harper said.

"Given you a choice," Travis said.

"What?"

"To save her life, or not. All up to you."

"Travis."

Piper's broken cries filled the phone. She said, "They cut me."

Harper's stomach coiled. "How?"

"Harper they sliced my wrist and it's bleeding everywhere."

Piper's voice dissolved into panic. Travis came back on the phone.

"So you see? The choice is simple, but it's yours."

"Motherfucker," she said.

"You truly are a white trash she-bitch, Susannah."

"You slit her wrist?"

"Not me personally."

Harper seemed to feel the road slide beneath her feet, as though it was a long ribbon and somebody had yanked on the other end.

Travis said, "A single slice with a box cutter, across one wrist. Her hands are unfettered. Her feet are shackled and bolted to the floor, but her hands are free. She can raise the wrist overhead"—his voice veered away—"that's it, Piper, hold it up, like you're the Statue of Liberty. Clamp the other hand around the wound. Keep pressure on it."

Harper pressed a fist to her mouth.

Travis said, "Huh. I may have underestimated the severity of the cut." He paused, and his voice cooled another few degrees. "I'm not a doctor, but there's a significant amount of blood. Go on, give her— yeah, that rag." He was apparently talking to whoever had cut Piper. "Let her tie it around her wrist." Back to Harper. "Thing about wounds like these, you can estimate how long it takes to bleed out, but it's not an exact science."

Harper heard herself moan.

"But I've seen this before," Travis said. "It can take twenty minutes to empty the veins before the heart stops. And that's a big heart, with both wrists cut."

Harper bent over and put a hand on her knee to keep from vomiting.

"Give her an hour, tops," he said.

Travis's father had committed suicide by slitting his wrists. Rowdy drank a liter of bourbon, downed a handful of Valium, and turned on the faucets. Travis found him floating, eyes wide, in a bathtub three feet deep with blood.

"She won't be able to maintain her strength or hold her hand on the wound much longer than that. Once she drops her wrist, gravity welcomes everything in her veins right back to Mother Earth."

Harper said nothing. Travis had idolized his father. Roland Maddox was terrifying and charismatic, and Travis had tried desperately to please him. When Travis failed, he suffered. Rowdy treated his family the same way he treated business deals: as win-lose, profit-loss. And

Travis finally saw his dad go down hard, losing for good. For that, he blamed her.

"Look on the ground behind the front wheel of that wrecked truck," Travis said.

Head ringing, Harper walked over. She knelt, one hand against the wheel, feeling sick. On the ground, she saw a phone.

"That's your new cell. It will ring with calls from me and nobody else. It will call me and nobody else."

She pressed the power key and stood up.

"Now get Oscar's phone from him," Travis said. "Tell him it's compromised. That the people he's afraid of have the ability to track it. I want to see him throw it out the window."

She walked numbly to the MINI. She knocked on the window and, when Aiden lowered it, leaned down. "Gotta dump your phone, Oscar. Quick. It's compromised."

She hoped Aiden would play along.

It only took him a microsecond. Muffling his voice behind one hand to disguise it, he said, "But if I . . ."

"No argument. Give it to me."

He took out his phone and handed it over. She held the phone up in the headlights so Travis could see it.

"Throw it," Travis said.

She lobbed it into the rocky hillside. "He believed it's compromised because he's the one who set up the program to restrict call access on the phone you put behind the truck, isn't he?"

"You aren't such a dumb cluck after all." His voice had energy, a current of excitement that he couldn't hide. "Is the new phone powered up?"

She checked. "Yes."

"Now throw your burn phone away. Good and hard. Not like a girl."

She didn't bother ending the call. She wound up and pitched it overhand high and hard at the mountainside. Even as she heard the burn phone hit the hillside, sending pebbles tumbling downslope, Travis's new phone rang in her hand. She answered.

"Get in that car and drive, Flynn."

"Where?" Harper said.

He told her. She tried walking, but only because if she'd stood still, she would have gone down on her knees.

42

Sorenstam gripped the steering wheel with one hand. In her other, the phone seemed to emit an electrical shock. Tom White was no longer on the line, but his words buzzed through her. The car felt close. The dashboard lights seemed to pulse. Sorenstam kept rolling, her mind in overdrive.

Oscar said, "You okay? You look . . . like somebody just hit you with a cattle prod."

Ticktock.

She said, "What do you know about Spartan Security?"

"It isn't just an intruder alarm company. They don't call to ask if you're okay when your cat sets off the alarm. I mean, they do, but that's not their bread and butter. I'm talking, these guys are *deep* into the spooky stuff. Iris identification, cloud surveillance, metadata."

Frowning, almost absentmindedly, Sorenstam said, "Spooky?"

"I mean they're run by ex-spooks and mercenaries. They took Blackwater as their template. They have all kinds of toys and techniques, human and algorithmic. They're not Allstate Insurance. And they're not the Boy Scouts."

She felt a sinking sensation in her stomach. "They hire from a significantly broader pool of employees than that, don't they?"

"Plenty of guys have in-theater combat experience, military contractor training, security clearances, sure. The security guards and bouncers they send out . . . who knows what they've got. Mixed martial arts veterans? Ex-bikers?"

"Criminal convictions?"

He turned to her. His expression seemed to be searching to see if she was serious. "I haven't seen their hiring reports, but . . . why not? You think these guys care about an arrest jacket? No way. Bet you fifty bucks they'd hire *me*. Bet you if I cracked their system, then turned up promising to show them the weaknesses in their programming, they'd give me an office and all the vending machine candy bars I could eat."

She accelerated, punching it toward the long downhill to the desert.

"Tell me why you think the company didn't lose all the data on the Xenon attack," she said.

"The very fact that Xenon had Spartan running its security contract meant it was forking out for the latest whiz-bang shit. Electronic key cards, electronic locks, it monitored everything second by second. Video, too."

"Camera on the alley was spray-painted before the attack began. So nobody could tell exactly which entrance they used, or how—with a key, or because somebody inside opened a door. Nobody was monitoring the video on-site."

"Was the video sent digitally to Spartan in real time?" Oscar said.

She hesitated. "I never thought so."

"I bet it was," he said. "If they had downloadable data from the door locks, I bet it was sent in real time, too. To the cloud."

Spartan had told the sheriff's department that the only data they were capable of receiving live from Xenon was an alarm—a breach of physical security because of a break-in. All the rest, the swipe-card information, was limited to the cash registers and the locks themselves. Once the fire cut power in the building, to retrieve data from a particular lock, a technician would have had to physically attach a card reader cabled to a handheld terminal, and download the information from each individual lock. That, Spartan had told the LASD, was the only way to transfer the information from the locking system. And when the building burned, all the history contained in the locks burned with it.

"They told us everything was destroyed."

Oscar said, "I bet that someplace in Spartan's records, there's a trail. Despite what they told you."

"You think they uploaded all data from the club automatically, to their cloud backup."

"Bingo."

Hell.

She felt Oscar's eyes on her in the darkened car.

"Where are we going so fast?" he said.

"To catch up with your pal Harper." And with Aiden.

The car gained speed. She grabbed the radio and called her lieutenant.

"Are you on your way back here?" he said.

"Not yet."

"It's been an hour, Detective."

"There's been a development. I need a background check on—"

"Detective. Stand down," he said.

She wanted to pound the wheel in frustration. "Detective Garrison is in danger."

"Tell me about it when you get back here. You're done. Turn around, Sorenstam."

She was going north at ninety mph, far from home, with no backup, and she knew that tone in the lieutenant's voice. Oscar was watching her, confused.

"Detective? I said, turn around and return to the station. You're done."

The headlights swallowed the road. Her foot rested heavy on the gas.

"I hear you," she said. "Out." She dropped the radio.

Her gut said: Go. *Screw it.* She floored it north on the highway, trying to catch up to Aiden and Harper.

Ticktock.

She'd run across that expression twice tonight. Once from Tom White, sounding harassed. And once on Harper Flynn's phone, in the parking lot at the diner, when the kidnapper told her to get moving if she wanted to see Piper Westerman alive again.

Tom White was Travis Maddox.

Tom White stared out across the desert night. On the handheld video monitor, Harper Flynn ran to her car and drove away.

In his ears, the sound of Detective Sorenstam's voice lingered.

She had no reason to run his name for a criminal background check. If she did, nothing would come up. It would end there, with ninety-nine percent certainty.

If it didn't, he was covered. His bosses would back him up.

T. M. White. Anybody would have changed their name in his circumstances. Going from the dark side to being a White Hat. Spartan had understood. They all called him Tom. He had eight clean years under his belt now. But he'd always have a felony stretch on his record, forty-eight months of real prison time. Four years she owed him.

Travis Maddox White calmed his breathing and thought about how he was going to handle Harper Flynn and the people she'd collected around herself like iron filings around a magnet.

Spartan Security Systems knew about his history. They didn't know how much he had enjoyed it. Living in China Lake with his dad, Lila Flynn, and little sneaky Susannah, figuring out how to crack systems, learning phone skills, blue boxing, old school. In East Buttfuck, if you didn't play football or ride dirt bikes, you had endless time on your hands. As long as you didn't fill it with meth or masturbation, you could learn all kinds of skills.

Such as phishing, and coding malware, and learning how to disarm a simple burglar alarm system so that you could get inside some dumb dick's house and liberate the stuff he should have protected more securely.

Four years in Chino had left him with some catching up to do as far as tech. But it had honed the rest of his skills. He left prison with a cut physique, some scars, and the knowledge that he could survive any-thing. With enough incentive, he could become immortal. He could even use his knowledge as a hacker and a thief to become a security expert—a bad boy, but Spartan's bad boy.

And at Spartan, he bided his time, playing the dutiful office drone. Running his side business sub rosa. And tracking down Susannah Flynn, so that he could collect on the bill that was long overdue.

Susannah Flynn. Little Fly, he had called her, back when she moved into the half-built hacienda on the hill south of China Lake. When he first met her, she had seemed like a meerkat, skinny kid, all legs and elbows and wide eyes that sought danger at every turn. She was no fool. She knew her mom had brought her to a house where she was bottom of the heap, runt of a litter that showed mercy to no one.

It took him a while to figure out that she was adaptable, and quick, and had learned too well the skills his dad had taught them all. Sleight of hand. Smash-and-dash. Pin the blame on somebody else. He should have seen it, but she'd always seemed so frightened of him, even—especially—when he eyed her and saw her lips slightly parted, her smooth face glowing in the summer sun, her chest rising and falling, skin pale where her blouse buttoned on her chest. His dad told him: "Don't touch." Don't mix business and pleasure. Don't shit where you eat. His dad was afraid that Travis would get her pregnant, through love or insistence. His dad would have torn his nuts off. So Travis had kept his hands off her. But he saw the way she acted around him. She was a tease. How else could she have done what she did?

After he was released, it took him a long time to find her again. The California juvenile justice system was serious about protecting the pri-vacy of former inmates. The state might have vindictively voted in three-strikes laws, but when it came to apple-cheeked little white girls, they were still willing to cut Barbie some slack. Finding her had taken lawyers, and money, and patience, and patience, and patience. It had taken his job at Spartan, where he finally had access to mind-blowing data mining software. She had legally changed her name. But she couldn't change her social security number. She couldn't change her date of birth, or who she was related to. Court records, military records, college enrollment records . . . eventually, he located her.

Going to college part-time, grinding out her degree a course at a time, sometimes at night, and working the usual round of jobs. Barista. Waitress. Finally, bartender at Xenon.

He didn't actually mind that she'd gone legit. It would have infuriated him to learn that she had escaped unscathed after their arrest, only to pick up where she'd left off. No, what burned him, among the many things that burned him, was that she had fled, and saved herself at his expense, only to adopt a bog-standard, mundane life. Something so socially *expected*. Something so unworthy and dull and *small*. Of course, it could be an act. She had been expert at playing along, only to send his life up in flames. She could be doing the same now.

Flames. He gritted his teeth.

The original plan had seemed ideal: two birds with one heavy stone. Xenon had drawn him like a neon flower. Both physically and emotionally, it was an excellent place to carry out the plan. And that plan had seemed so elegant. Attack a criminal who hadn't paid his debts—Arliss Bale. Do it at the club where Harper worked.

She had sent him to prison. He would even the scales. A heavy fall this time, not juvy. Clone the swipe card, implicate her in the attack.

Regrettably, Zero's no-rules-of-engagement style involved one of the guy's favorite props: a Molotov cocktail. So easy, so reliable. Zero liked fire. Loved the heat and the instant panic it caused, the chaos, ever building. Loved the power and the knowledge that he was the one who had unleashed such a primal force.

So, that night at Xenon, when the tide started turning and Arliss Bale's bodyguards began firing back, Zero pulled out his showstopper. Cleanse the scene. Distract everybody. Unluckily, he killed some bystanders.

Zero had burned Xenon to the ground. And he had escaped, amazingly, without leaving a physical trace of himself on the operation. The man was smoke itself. He needed to be. And, once the crime scene turned into a murder investigation, so did Travis Maddox White. For a year, Travis had thought it had worked and that any scent of their involvement had evaporated.

But no. The swipe card. The clone was supposed to be the piece of evidence that linked Harper Flynn to the attack. It should have been perfect: An employee illegally provides access to armed intruders who start shooting at a gangster across a crowded dance floor. Harper would have been roasted on a spit.

Instead, flames. Bodies. After the fire, his off-the-books business had dried up, and Harper had gone on her way. Now, Detective Sorenstam not only had Harper's original swipe card, she had her teeth into the case again. And he was now in the line of fire. It was a fiasco.

But he had the trump card that would change everything. He had Piper.

On the monitor, he watched Harper's car spin its tires and race away. He looked out across the shimmering desert night. She was coming. At last.

43

North, into a canyon that cut between the walls of the desert mountains, Sorenstam drove, trying to catch up with Harper and Aiden. The highway had emptied out. She'd called in a request to the station to check on Tom White of Spartan Security Systems—wants, warrants, and aliases, especially the name Travis Maddox. But she was on her own. Even with Oscar Sierra in the passenger seat.

She nodded at him. "Try Aiden again."

Oscar palmed the phone and redialed, but shook his head. "No luck. I'll text them both."

"Either Harper's new phone's been dumped already, or they can't get service."

In the twenty-first century, forty miles from Hollywood, driving through a land where the electric grid pumped out seven thousand megawatts, they had crossed the pass into nothing but sand and space, and might as well have been crossing the frontier with a mule team. The darkness briefly seemed to swell, to encompass not just the car but her, inside and out.

Aiden. He'd been right to trust Harper. Now he was out there, strong but broken, searching with nothing but instinct and guts.

Oscar keyed in a text message. "Doesn't matter if Harper knows Travis is working for Spartan, pretending he's gone corporate. He's gonna do what he's gonna do. The rest is just evidence for prosecution. You're excited about it 'cause it helps you put your case together, but haters gonna hate. Travis is gonna bite, and Harper knows it."

Sorenstam saw it differently. Travis Maddox had used his position with Spartan Security to set Harper up to take a fall for the attack on Xenon. He was setting her up right now. He had Piper, and he wanted Oscar. But he wanted Harper most of all.

"Tom White—Travis Maddox—isn't just out here for kicks. He has access to Spartan Security's assets. He has all kinds of resources at his disposal."

"You think . . ."

"Assume he's going to employ those resources to ambush Aiden and Harper." She held tight to the wheel as the big car gained momentum on the downhill.

Abruptly, her phone pinged. Oscar said, "It's a text from Aiden. Coordinates."

"Call him back. Hurry."

Oscar pressed REDIAL but immediately lowered the phone. "Nada. Not enough signal for a voice call." He thumbed the controls and sent a text, and then threw up his hand. "It failed."

"Keep trying. Just keep trying. Unless we can contact them, Harper and Aiden are driving into an ambush blind."

She felt the pang again, and the anger. That man—a good man torn up from within, unable to see the world clearly. It was not his fault, but the cracks in his perception seemed to prevent him from seeing her heart. His pain, his explosiveness—those things she could have dealt with, if she'd had any hope that he was going to recover, and to become again the person he had been before the injury. She hardened herself to deal with him dispassionately tonight.

She knew she'd lost him for good. She saw the look on Aiden's face when he was near Harper, saw how he moved when he was near her, protective and full of badly disguised want. She saw the look in Harper's eyes, too, desire and nerves and hesitation—as though she were about to walk across the Grand Canyon on a high wire, and knew it would be exciting and beautiful but suspected that the wire was frayed and the bolts holding it to the ground might give way. Harper, she thought, was at the start of a crossing she herself had only recently completed.

And they were all headed toward catastrophe. She drove.

⟋⟍

The clock on the dashboard read ten to midnight. Harper stared at it, as though she could will it to stop advancing. They'd crossed into Kern County a while back. Miles behind them, the scattered lights of the town of Mojave shivered on the desert floor. Ahead, the countryside was completely dark. The highway had narrowed to two lanes. There was nothing out this far but auto wrecking yards and chemical plants and the detritus of industries that had shriveled and died in the desert heat. She downshifted, watching for the turnoff. They were in the middle of nowhere, but a particular part of nowhere that she remembered with granular clarity.

Even under the moonlight, she recognized the landscape, even ten years after she'd run from this part of the state. Ahead rose a ridge of mountains that looked as sharp as a hatchet blade and heated red in the sunlight. Beyond the headlights, not far away, was the spot where her mother had fallen asleep at the wheel, with a fifth of Maker's Mark beneath the driver's seat, and drove a car packed with weed into a ditch.

"It's probably two miles farther," she said.

"Travis is playing an elaborate game," Aiden said. "One that's extremely cold."

"More than just a game."

Travis had directed her to turn off the highway onto a private access road that headed toward the knife ridge of mountains. He was sending her to the abandoned factory where her mother hid after the wreck.

"The factory," she said. "Rowdy Maddox used it for stashing stolen property."

"So Travis knows the layout."

"Inside and out. Rowdy used one of the security guards who patrolled the property after the factory shut down. Paid him off to get inside the gates." She leaned forward, scanning the road. "Soon."

A minute later, the headlights caught the turnoff. She swung the car onto the access road.

"Shut off the headlights?" Aiden said.

"Yeah. Let's not let him spot us until we're ready for him to know we're there."

She flipped the switch and downshifted, engine braking, slowing below twenty mph. After a second, her eyes adjusted and she began to see the road again. Under a crust of moonlight, the car rose along the rough pavement, through sage and yucca, gradually heading uphill. She steered into a long curve, over a rise, and the last trembling lights of Mojave disappeared behind it.

Aiden pulled his phone from his pocket. "Still no signal."

"So whose phone did you have me chuck into the brush back there?" she said.

"Throw-down," he said.

She almost laughed then. She put a hand on the gearshift. He set his hand over hers for a moment. It calmed her. Just enough.

Which was good, because they crested another rise and saw the factory complex in the distance. A chain-link fence glinted dully in the moonlight.

The phone in Harper's hand rang.

44

Harper lifted her latest phone, the one Travis had planted by the wrecked big rig. Something warned her to hold her cards close to the vest. Instead of saying, *We're here,* she said, "We're close. We'll be there in ten minutes."

And she heard another sound—a buzz. It was Aiden's phone.

Travis said, "Take the road to the main entrance. Drive through the gate."

Aiden's phone continued buzzing. Travis wasn't supposed to know that either of them had another phone. Travis wasn't supposed to know that the man in the car with her was Aiden. Harper stared at him wide-eyed as he reached into his back pocket and silenced it.

"We're coming," she said.

She crawled along the road. The factory was still at least a mile away.

"We do this outside the gate," she said.

"You have no say. Drive."

She hung up. "He wants us inside."

"That means he traps us." He cut a glance at her.

She kept going. Slowly.

"You actually planning to go in the front entrance?" he said.

Her nerves began to sing. "Maybe. But Sorenstam doesn't have to. There's a fire road that cuts through the hills behind the complex." She ran a hand through her hair. "If we can reach her. I wish we knew where she was."

"She's coming. Believe," he said.

He got out his phone and sent her a text.

⟡

When Sorenstam crossed the county line, she knew definitely she was outside the fence. Out of Los Angeles County, directly disobeying an order from her commander, she was out of her jurisdiction, without the official sanction she'd had a hundred yards back. She wondered, briefly, if this might work to her advantage.

"Tell me when you get a signal," she said to Oscar.

He shook his head and snapped his fingers. "Comes and goes like that."

The road was narrow and winding, through towering hills. The last text she'd received from Aiden said, Back road. Don't come in the front. Take the fire road. Oscar was sitting with a map on his lap, shining a flashlight on it. She felt increasingly alone, and increasingly outgunned. She picked up the radio and scanned frequencies, searching for the Kern County Sheriff.

They didn't know she'd been told to stand down. They didn't know she was acting against orders. She punched the scanner, getting little but static.

All at once, the radio squealed and a voice broke through the static. She locked the frequency and pressed the TRANSMIT button.

"Kern County Sheriff, come in," she said.

The static returned and the voices disappeared. She braked hard, put the car in reverse, and backed up.

Oscar said, "Excuse me?"

She swerved backward up the road until the static eased. "Need backup," she said. "These guys might be it."

As the unmarked car reversed around a bend, the voices crept back. She stopped and again said, "Kern County, come in."

The voice that replied was faint. "This is Kern County dispatch. Identify yourself."

"Detective Erika Sorenstam, LASD."

She gave them her badge number. She felt a tigerish energy ripple through her.

"I need backup," she said.

Quickly, she told the dispatcher she was investigating a possible abduction. She explained that she'd come to Kern County to check on a possible runaway, a case that now seemed to be more sinister. They wanted to know why they weren't contacted first—why the odd approach?

"The girl is the daughter of a departmental friend," she said. "It's personal for us."

"What do you need, Detective?"

"A patrol unit to meet me at these coordinates," she said, and rattled off the address Aiden had texted.

She waited for their response. She knew that once they verified her identity, their next step would be to call her superiors, who would pitch a fit and tell them to forget it, probably before deciding to fire her.

"Detective Sorenstam, roger, we will dispatch a unit to meet you at the address," the dispatcher said. "Be advised the nearest unit is currently forty miles away, and responding to another call."

Forty miles? She muttered, "Christ."

Oscar said, "Welcome to the desert."

The dispatcher said, "Advise when you reach the address."

She peered around at the rugged hills. She didn't like her chances of getting radio or phone reception on the fire road behind the factory. "Will do."

She replaced the radio in its cradle and put the car in gear. "Buckle up, kid."

Two minutes later, Sorenstam found the fire road. A mile along it, she pulled into a protected hollow, where the car would be invisible from the factory. She turned it around and parked facing back down the road.

"Have a feeling that when we leave, we may be heading that way at high speed," she said.

Oscar said, "What are you expecting?"

"Don't know if we'll leave here in pursuit."

"Or running."

Neither the radio nor their phones had been able to contact the Kern County Sheriff again. She trusted that deputies were responding, but she couldn't wait for them to arrive.

She got out and took the Remington shotgun from the trunk. She opened a box of shells and loaded the magazine. She put more shells in the pocket of her fleece and zipped it. Oscar was staring.

"I don't plan to run," she said.

"You don't know what these guys are capable of. You'd better be sure of that."

She paused, cold in the night. His words sent a deeper chill through her. She answered by racking a shell into the chamber. The noise cracked and Oscar inhaled.

"Let's go," she said.

45

Sorenstam stuck to the walls of the ravine, trying to glimpse the factory complex while staying below the line of sight. She told Oscar to keep low.

"Don't present a silhouette on the ridge," she said.

"It's dark."

"The moon is up. A moving human form will be identifiable." She sidestepped when the slope steepened. "For all we know, they have night-vision capability. You'd stand out from the background like an electric green frog."

She knew that Aiden and Harper were on the approach road to the complex, probably a mile and a half downhill to the southeast. From here she could see no lights from Harper's car. She tried again to call, without success. Even if she could see the car, that didn't mean she could call them—her phone needed to connect with a cell tower, and she had no idea where the nearest one was. Her portable police radio would connect with anybody on the frequency, but only if they were in range. And within line of sight. They had come to the empty quarter. California raw and unvarnished and wild.

She crouched low, set the shotgun across her thighs, and opened her fleece. She tucked her phone inside the folds of the jacket and typed.

Oscar said, "What's that all about?"

She continued to type. "For a tech guy and a career criminal, I'm surprised you need an explanation. It's dark and what's the brightest light for miles around?"

"Oh."

She was hiding the display so its light wouldn't be seen down below and give them away, working into position on the uphill side of the plant.

APPROACHING FROM HILL TO WEST. WILL HOLD POSITION 100 YARDS OUTSIDE FENCE. DID YOU GET EARLIER MESSAGE?

She pushed SEND and stood up.

Oscar said, "I'm not a career criminal. That hurts my feelings."

She continued down the hill. "Then prove it. Come on."

⁓

Aiden's phone vibrated. He said, "Text from Erika."

He read it aloud, staring at the screen. "What earlier message?"

Harper slowed the car to a near crawl. When they went through a dip, she turned the headlights on again. They were close enough to the plant that the engine noise might be audible. Leaving the lights off would only give Travis cause to get twitchy.

Aiden stared at the darkened road, pensive. "We should split up before we get to the gate, to prevent us both being ambushed. One of us gets out at the next bend. The other drives up to the gate, parks the car, and ducks out the back, to let Travis think we're still in it."

"And go cross-country to meet Sorenstam on the hill?" she said.

"Yeah."

She was quiet. Her eyes shifted back and forth. "You get out. I'll drive to the gate."

"Roger that," he said.

"I'm going to park half a mile outside the gate and leave it running with the lights on. You recon and I'll meet you." She saw him about to question her and brooked no dissent. "Travis will have to deal with me on my terms. You're right—if I drive through the gate, I won't come out alive. So we have to find Erika and go in the back together. We have to find Piper in there. Otherwise, it's . . ."

She stopped, unable to bring herself to utter the words. She knew there was no such thing as spell-casting or talismanic protection, but she couldn't bring herself to say *They'll kill her*, not within sight of the place Piper was being held.

"It's a risk," Aiden said.

"Motion sensors, night vision, yada yada. You run. I'll be a minute behind you."

After a moment, he nodded. "We only have a couple of minutes. Once I find a place where the line of sight to the factory is broken, I'm going to jump out. I mean jump, too. Get going before they can notice that the car has stopped. We can't let them think anything hinky is happening."

"Agreed." She downshifted into second and slowed to ten mph.

"I need you to tell me every scrap of information about the complex you can remember. Perimeter security. The layout of the buildings. Access, egress, blind spots."

"The complex had a cyclone fence surrounding it. Six feet, no barbed wire. Don't know if it's been upgraded."

"I can climb a six-foot fence."

She stayed quiet. He read her thoughts.

"If my leg holds," he said, "and even if it doesn't, I'll make it over. But I don't expect any of the doors to the factory to be unlocked."

"I was only in there a couple of times," she said, "and it's a big shambling place."

She tried to remember it. What came back was the dim and dingy light, the smell of dust and grease, the scale of the place.

"It's a multibuilding complex. Factory and warehouse. The factory is as big as a football field. It has a main factory floor and two basement levels. Underground, it's got long corridors where trucks and forklifts could drive to load and unload components," she said. "Belowground, it's concrete construction and highly compartmentalized. It's a maze. Multiple staircases, plus ladders between floors in a few access tunnels."

"Access tunnels—any that run beneath the perimeter fence and come up outside it?"

"A couple."

She thought of the rat run—a narrow series of tunnels that ran between walls and above the lowest basement ceiling, before burrowing beneath the fence to a transformer building.

"But I only crawled through the tunnels one time, with Oscar, when we were kids. There's no way I could find the entrance point outside the fence tonight in the dark. Sorry."

They could see the outline of the complex in the distance, a boxy set of buildings inside the dull shine of the fence. Harper inched along the road, waiting until they could get out of sight in a dip or behind an outcropping of rock.

Aiden said, "When we go in, we'll try for a door along the back side."

"If it's locked? Don't break a window. They'll hear."

"You don't have a set of lock picking tools, do you?" he said. "Bolt cutters? Glass cutter?"

She shot him a cool glance. "No. Don't, won't, not ever." At least, not ever again.

Aiden nodded, slowly. "Good thing I do."

The road began a brief downhill and rounded a bend where it dipped behind a ledge of rock. The headlights hit the middle of the uphill but didn't reach the top.

"Ready," he said. "Do this quick."

Harper downshifted sharply, sending both of them lurching against the seat belts. At the bottom of the dip, she nearly skidded to a stop and yanked the parking break. Aiden jumped out. He ran around the back of the MINI to the driver's side. She lowered the window.

He grabbed the window frame and bent down. "What did they make at this factory?"

She put the car in gear. "Rocket fuel."

46

Silhouetted against the rocks in the moonlight, Aiden laughed humorlessly. "Figures. Why not?"

He banged his palm on the roof of the car. When she looked again, he was gone.

Heart pounding, she drove up the hill toward the factory. She crested the rise and it came into sight. Dark, entirely, seemingly abandoned behind the chain-link fence. It looked like a ghostly prison.

The road ran straight the last half mile, directly at the gate. Her fears grew sharp barbs inside. The last time she'd been in that building, she'd been fourteen. It had smelled of chemicals and mossy water.

She turned on the high beams. The gate was open. Inside, the road continued straight ahead, fifty yards to a heavy garage door. On either side of the road, yards were fenced off and piled high with pallets and abandoned equipment. Jesus. Driving in there would be putting herself in a shooting gallery.

Harper stopped, well back. She set the parking brake and felt a dry heave trying to roll up her throat.

She could turn and run. So many people had insisted that Piper wasn't here, wasn't in trouble. Who was she to disagree? She could drive back to L.A. and wait for the cops to investigate the situation. She didn't need to be here, in the last place she ever wanted to be: playing vigilante. Outside the law once again.

Screw that.

She put the car in neutral and took a breath. Phone in her back pocket. Swiss Army knife in her front. Heart jammed high in her throat. She climbed into the backseat, cracked the tailgate, and rolled out of the car to the ground. She silently shut the tailgate and ran across the desert slope toward the hill to the west, hoping Aiden had made it there ahead of her.

Aiden found Sorenstam and Oscar in the rocks on a knob of hillside at the back of the factory complex. They were taking cover behind a welter of boulders.

Erika eyed him in the dark, her hair catching the moonlight. She was chilly and intense. "Where's Harper?"

"Figure ninety seconds behind me."

He explained the plan to leave the car outside the gate.

Erika nodded. "Makes sense."

"There's worse to tell."

He told them Piper's wrist had been slit. Erika inhaled. Oscar shook his head. "That sucks."

Aiden said, "Back door, we get inside, we find her, get her out."

Erika said, "You strapped?"

He nodded.

"I have worse to tell, too," she said. "Travis Maddox works for Spartan Security, under an alias. God knows what resources he has deployed down in that factory."

"You gotta be freakin' kidding me," Aiden said.

"Not kidding at all. He's been working in disguise."

For a second, just a second, Erika looked wry. He ran the back of his hand across his forehead.

She said, "We wait for Harper, then we do it." She pointed at Oscar. "You stay here. I mean it. You try to run, you'll get nowhere. The coyotes will get you before you reach town. And by that, I mean Eddie Azerov and his canine companion. You made it once, and you should presume that used up your luck. I could cuff your right hand to your left ankle and leave you here. Or you could trust that I can track better than the bad guys, and when I find you, I'll run you over. It's dark. Oops."

Aiden said, "Take her at her word. You don't want to cross this woman."

They waited until Oscar said, "Okay."

Erika turned and peered between rocks at the darkened complex below. Aiden knew she was feeling the heat, but she had been overtaken by the urgency of Piper's dire situation. She had decided she had to throw the dice on rescue.

He should never have doubted that she'd do so.

Aiden felt her nearness, and felt a swell of emotion. She didn't have to be here. She was risking her career, risking herself, and largely because he had asked her to.

She hadn't given up on him. He felt a catch in his chest and he shut his eyes, fixing her in his mind, letting that thought flow through him. Then he exhaled, opened his eyes, and caught her looking at him.

"You're the best," he said.

She smiled, cool as ever, a pearly presence in the moonlight. "Cheesy pep talk, Coach."

A second later, they heard pebbles skitter across the ground. He and Erika both raised their weapons.

Harper appeared at the edge of the rocks. She brought herself up short.

"Jesus," she said.

They lowered their guns. She stood breathing hard, hands at her sides, staring at them darkly. "Guess you're ready. Remember, point the shooty end at the bad guys."

Erika holstered her pistol. "Got it. Now I have bad news for you. Travis works for Spartan Security. Presume he has a significant surveillance capability and God knows what kind of booby traps inside that factory."

Harper slowly went down on one knee, as though she'd deflated. She looked at Sorenstam, seemingly hoping it was a joke.

"Tell us everything you know about that factory," Sorenstam said.

Harper crouched down. On the dirt, she drew a rough outline of the complex with her index finger. "Front gate here. If they have somebody watching, they should be able to see the road and the MINI . . ."

She stopped. Her phone was ringing.

⁓

Hunched over behind the rocks, down on one knee, Harper took the phone and answered it. "See me?"

"This isn't Red Rover, Red Rover," Travis said. "You don't have to ask. Drive through the gate."

Her head came up sharply. She gave a nervous thumbs-up. Travis apparently believed she was still in the car.

"Not going to do that," she said. "Y'all come out."

"Don't be such a coward."

"Don't play dumb. Walk out the gate and meet my car."

There was a pause on his end. She held Aiden's gaze. She couldn't believe Travis was actually stumped, or trying to figure out how to play things. But all she could do was hold her ground.

"Call me back when you're ready to come out," she said, and hung up.

Sorenstam and Aiden stood and checked their weapons. They gave each other a look and some connection fired up between them. Partners, sworn, ready to breach the building together.

Sorenstam said, "If the Kern County deputies get here, they get here. But Piper doesn't have time for us to wait."

Harper realized they were ready to leave her there behind the rocks with Oscar. That was Aiden's plan to protect her: misdirection. Use the MINI as a distraction while he and Sorenstam went in the back.

Gratitude and sheer relief filled her. She put the back of her hand to her lips and reached for him, but he was already stepping out of reach, chambering a round in his HK.

He turned. "How many connecting hallways in the factory building? Stairs, blind spots? Everything you got, Harper. Quickly."

They both eyed her tensely. She turned back to the square she had begun to scratch in the sand. "It's . . ."

It was a rat's nest of passageways and dead ends and crawl spaces.

"Piper sounded like she was in a small room, not the main factory floor. It could be . . ."

Staircases that doubled back, catwalks where a sniper could lie in wait.

Her breath caught harshly in her throat. "I have to go with you."

There was no other way, no time to get in and out and reach Piper unless she herself led them inside.

Sorenstam said, "You're not a sworn officer."

"That's right, I'm not," Harper said. "I don't know how to protect and defend. I know how to intercept and steal. So I'm going to steal Piper back."

"Harper?" Aiden said.

"Quick, before I change my mind." She started down the hill and gestured for them to follow.

There was no going back now. Even if Travis did as she was asking, it would take only a few minutes for him to realize that he'd been duped. The clock was ticking. They quietly broke cover and began working their way down the slope to the fence on the back side of the factory.

⁓

By the time they reached the fence, Aiden was limping. He was running without complaint, but his stride was noticeably uneven. They crossed the last fifty yards across open ground, in the dark but still visible to anybody on the roof or spotters patrolling the perimeter.

A placard hung on the fence at eye level. PROTECTED BY SPARTAN SECURITY SYSTEMS. That answered that question, then.

Aiden paused and locked his fingers together in a stirrup. Harper looked at him briefly, saw the pain on his face, and said, "I'm okay."

She stuck her toes between the diamond links in the fence and climbed. Sorenstam took Aiden's offer and got a quick lift. She heard him exhale, hard, as he boosted her. Sorenstam slickly reached the top and rolled across like an old-school high jumper. She landed lightly. A moment later, she took the shotgun as Aiden passed it over the top of the fence. By the time Harper dropped to the ground, Sorenstam again had it in her hand. She waited while Aiden climbed over. He dropped, and tried to make it look as if it didn't hurt when he landed.

The factory building ran for more than a hundred yards to the east, about ten yards inside the fence. The space was mostly bare. At a couple of places, fifty-five-gallon drums stood rusting on concrete pads.

There were only a few windows along the back wall. That reassured Harper. There had been, at one time, razor wire along the top of the chain-link fence, but it was long gone, rusted or stolen—at least along the section of the fence they had climbed. It was too dark for her to see whether there were cameras on the building, but it was certain when they landed that there weren't motion-sensing lights. They remained in the dark. All she could hear was her own breathing, her own fear trying to leap out.

Aiden took the lead, hurrying to the wall, gun in his hand. Harper followed and pressed herself against the wall beside him. Sorenstam closed up behind her.

Sorenstam held the shotgun across her body, muzzle aimed at the concrete. Her pistol was holstered. Harper glanced at it, and Sorenstam gave her an excoriating look in return.

"No," she said.

Harper grit her teeth. Sorenstam was not about to give up her service weapon. Sorenstam and Aiden exchanged quick hand gestures. Aiden moved out. Harper followed. In her hand, she held her Swiss Army knife.

They walked silently along the wall until they came to a door. Aiden tried the handle. Locked. Sorenstam whispered, "Window, twenty yards farther."

Harper ducked low and ran to it. It was securely locked. She ran back, shaking her head. "Only way to get in is to break the glass. And what we need isn't access. It's surreptitious access."

From his back pocket Aiden took a slim black case. He dropped—painfully—to one knee and withdrew two slim stainless-steel implements. They looked like they'd been liberated from a dentist's office. He inserted their tips one after the other, carefully, into the lock. He manipulated them back and forth. Harper heard every scratch and click. She scanned the view, her skin practically throbbing with the sense that they were about to be discovered. Sorenstam watched. Aiden whispered, "Light," and she cupped her hand around the display of her phone and directed it toward the door handle. He murmured, "Almost . . ."

This was taking too long. Harper said, "Let me."

With reluctance, Aiden moved aside. His kit was a basic five-pick set, but the old factory had a basic lock. She inserted the tension wrench along the bottom of the lock. Then she slid in a rake. She felt it move along the pins inside the lock. She gently applied tension, sliding the rake back and forth. One by one, the pins fell into place along the shear line.

With a sharp click, the lock tripped. She turned the handle. Eased it open an inch. No alarm.

Pressing a hand to the wall for support, Aiden stood up. The burglar's tools went quickly back in the case and into his pocket. He held the door, nodded, and silently counted to three.

If Sorenstam had any qualms about silent entry without a warrant outside her jurisdiction, she quashed them. First through the door, she disappeared inside. Aiden and Harper followed her, into the dark.

47

Inside, they paused. From the pocket of her fleece, Sorenstam took a roll of electrical tape. She tossed it to Aiden. He tore off a strip with his teeth and strapped it across the latch on the door. He silently pulled the door closed. With luck it would appear locked, should anybody come patrolling. They waited while their eyes adjusted to the darkness. It was almost no adjustment at all. Just dark.

Sorenstam clicked on a mini Maglite. The beam, pinpoint bright, illuminated the hallway.

It smelled of mildew. Closed doors, carpet chewed and bunched up in places. Drop-panel ceiling, with panels missing. Fluorescent light tubes above. On the walls, light switches, some pulled loose and hanging by the wires.

Aiden whispered, "Foragers have been here. Stealing the copper from the wiring, probably."

So, poor security, as if Harper needed any confirmation. "Normally, I would hope the plant has a hard line to the security company, maybe we'd trip an alarm and get a response. But since it's Spartan, I guess we don't want that."

Sorenstam said, "No way."

They crept forward, stepping over the bunched carpet. Harper listened and heard nothing.

Aiden said, "The layout."

"Offices along this side of the building. The factory floor takes up most of the ground level, with a high ceiling and ventilation windows at the top."

"Basement access?" he said.

"Stairs on either end."

They progressed along the hall. At each office, Sorenstam paused, opened the door, and checked the interior, barrel first, the shotgun a black glint under the Maglite. All were empty.

They wanted to work their way to the center of the vast building. That, they had agreed, was where Piper was most likely to be held if she was on this floor: farthest from any doors or windows that could be breached. As far as possible from the exits. She was either near the factory floor, or deep in the guts of the place.

Harper checked her watch. Two minutes, nineteen seconds since they'd left the cover of the rocks outside. Five minutes since she had left the car running. Her arms itched, her scalp, her nerves.

Where was Travis? Where was Zero? Out front, she hoped, staring at the idling MINI. But even if they were, the deception couldn't last much longer.

Aiden paused at a corner and raised a hand, signaling *stop*. He put his back against the wall and inched out to glance around. After a second, he waved them on. Sorenstam snapped the Maglite into a mount atop the shotgun, and she carried it shoulder high, aimed down the hall, with the light tracking her path.

Halfway down the hall, Harper's phone vibrated. She put a hand against Aiden's shoulder. He did the same to Sorenstam. The three of them stopped short.

Harper checked all her nerves. If she answered too loudly, and Travis was nearby and heard her voice . . .

She pressed the key. "Where is she?"

They all held absolutely still. She had spoken quietly, with a note of menace.

Travis said, "This isn't a negotiation. Drive through the gate."

The demand in his voice was absolute. So was something else. Mockery, maybe.

"I can wait all night. I have a full tank. Piper comes out and then Oscar goes on his merry way."

"Pull forward. Piper's in no shape to walk eight hundred twelve meters."

She felt a chill. To know that precise distance, he had to be looking at the MINI through range-finder binoculars. The high beams would keep him from seeing inside the car, but he was sending her a message.

In the white glare from the Maglite, Aiden and Sorenstam looked ghostly. Harper pointed down the hall. Gestured for them to keep going. The three of them hurried, Harper with the phone to her ear, Sorenstam in the lead. Aiden glanced at Harper and made a circling gesture—*keep talking.*

"I need to see Piper. Right now," Harper said.

The offices along the darkened hallway gave way to workshops and labs, some with interior windows, most with broken glass. Then there was a sense of sudden spaciousness. Sorenstam clicked off the Maglite. Aiden inched forward.

They were at the doorway to the vast factory floor. High up, above the catwalks and hoists on rails overhead, a row of windows leaked moonlight. A disused assembly line ran parallel to one wall of the room. Bizarrely, it reminded Harper of the bar at Xenon.

She listened closely and still didn't hear Travis. "Send Piper out."

"Where's Oscar?"

She turned, thinking she heard his voice. Aiden and Sorenstam did likewise. Aiden pointed at the front of the building.

She waited, as silent as she could be. She tried to see in the dark.

Travis still didn't put Piper on the phone. Harper had two thoughts, both of which tightened her stomach. One, Piper couldn't come to the phone because she was unconscious or dead. Or two, Travis couldn't put her on because he wasn't with her. She was someplace apart from him in this complex.

She scanned the rafters, and stopped. A tiny red light glowed from a top corner of the building.

"Come out, Zannah, or I'll bring Piper to you at the end of a chain being dragged behind my car," he said.

It was a camera. She knew then: They were out of time.

She frantically scanned the factory floor. Across it she saw the stairs heading down to the basement. She saw that the staircase had pipes running overhead, and wiring, and conduit. She nodded at Aiden and Sorenstam, and ran out onto the factory floor, heading directly across, aiming for it.

Travis said, "It's time to say good-bye."

48

Harper ran, past empty assembly lines, around ruined and rusting equipment. A second later, she heard Aiden at her side, his boots hitting the concrete. Sorenstam was behind them. The stairway loomed across the factory in the moonlight, a mouth leading down into more darkness.

Travis said, "You can't outrun me, Flynn."

The call went dead.

She might have stuck her hand into a live electrical circuit. "He knows. He's coming."

She sprinted to the stairs and pounded down. Aiden and Sorenstam were a step behind her. Sorenstam's flashlight veered back and forth, illuminating the staircase in flailing streaks.

Halfway down, at a landing, the stairs turned. Harper swung around. Aiden was a silhouette a couple of steps above her, sporadically outlined by the swerving Maglite.

Behind him and Sorenstam, across the factory floor, came two more swinging flashlights.

Harper's skin shrank. "They're coming."

Sorenstam glanced back. Harper and Aiden careened down the stairs two at a time, sinking into the dark. Sorenstam's flashlight barely illuminated their path.

They reached the bottom of the stairs and Harper ran, hands out now, feeling for obstructions. Her knife was in her hand, blade open.

She said, "Light. Put it on the ceiling, Erika."

Sorenstam swung the barrel of the shotgun upward. The Maglite illuminated a trail of thick electrical cabling and conduit and rusting pipes bolted to the ceiling.

Pied Piper. Hansel and Gretel. Ariadne.

"Follow it."

The cabling and pipes were what Piper had cryptically spoken about on the phone earlier. They were the bread crumbs in the forest. They were Ariadne's silken spider's thread—the trail Piper had seen as they brought her in. The girl had the presence of mind to note her surroundings and to recognize the conduit that would lead her out again.

"This way."

Harper ran along the corridor. After fifty yards, the pipes and cables rounded a corner to the right, into another hallway. It was dark, but at the end, some hundred yards distant, light was leaking from around another corner. A shadow wavered within it.

Harper kept running and slipped on something slick. On the floor ran a thin trail of what looked like blood.

She inhaled sharply and pointed. "Gotta be."

Aiden said, "If we find her, we have to get her out. Where's another exit?"

"Second staircase at the opposite end of the building."

Sorenstam took the lead, sweeping the Maglite across the walls and ceiling as she ran. The passageway was deep within the guts of the old plant. Twelve-inch pipes rose vertically along the walls, with rusted valves and joints. The pipes disappeared into the concrete.

Sorenstam drew up. "Stop."

Harper saw that they had not, in fact, come to the end of the rainbow. "God."

Directly ahead, the floor vanished. There was a ten-foot break in the concrete. They approached and looked over.

Below, down at least twenty feet, was a platform that seemed to have been lowered on a hydraulic piston.

Aiden said, "Platform ram lift—for heavy pallets or rolling loads. Looks like it's stopped on the floor below."

They looked around for a switch to activate it. Aiden saw the button on the wall and slammed his palm against it. Nothing happened.

Beyond the gap, around the corner at the end of the passageway, the light spilling onto the floor continued to flow with shadows.

"Piper," Harper called.

There was shuffling and a weak cry. The shadows slid again. They heard the unmistakable clink of a chain.

"Harper?"

Her heart raced. "We're coming."

Behind them, back by the stairs, came the sound of men moving at speed.

"We have to get across," Harper said.

Abandoned equipment was stacked along the walls. Aiden pulled a drop cloth from a humped pile and said, "This."

He lifted a ladder, his face striped with pain.

Harper helped him extend it. They dropped it across the gap in the floor. It clattered and landed on the far side with just inches to spare.

Aiden knelt and braced it. "Erika, you first."

Sorenstam slung the shotgun across her back by the strap. She stepped onto the ladder and walked carefully across. The aluminum creaked. She reached the other side and knelt down to brace the ladder for the next person.

"Harper, go," Aiden said.

Pulse thudding, Harper stepped gingerly onto the ladder. It was flimsy and vibrated with her weight.

"I got you," Aiden said. "Walk."

She put her fingertips against the wall for balance and stepped out over the drop. The rungs felt insubstantial beneath her feet. Her entire body seemed to clench and rebel against what she was doing. Holding her breath, she began walking across. *Jesus.* Her heart pounded, ready to jump out of her chest.

"You got it," Aiden said. "Keep going."

From around the corner at the far end of the hall, Piper called, "Harper, are you coming?"

Harper looked down. The pit beneath her telescoped. Ready to vomit, she stepped off the ladder onto solid concrete, realizing she was close to passing out. She turned around and knelt next to Sorenstam, helping to brace the ladder so Aiden could cross.

He stepped onto the ladder without pause, even though one shoulder was higher than the other, tight with strain, and his leg looked like it might buckle.

Behind him at the distant end of the hall, where it turned, flashlight beams careened.

Sorenstam said nothing, but drew her pistol.

Aiden crossed quickly and stepped off. They pulled the ladder toward them across the gap, stood, and rushed down the hall.

Behind them, at the end of the hall, two men came around the corner. They didn't say anything. They started shooting.

49

Harper stared back down the passageway. At the far end, two forms materialized, running around the corner. Men, slight and lithe, wearing all-black tactical gear, holding automatic pistols. They both fired. The shots hit the wall and the floor. She turned and ran with Aiden and Sorenstam toward the next turn, toward the leaking light and Piper's fading voice.

"Hell are those guys?" Harper said.

They were sure as shit not Travis Maddox and Eddie Azerov.

Harper careened down the corridor around mothballed equipment and fat pipe works. A shot echoed and pinged against metal. Her skin felt alive with nervous sparks. Aiden put a hand on her back and urged her onward. At the end of the corridor, Sorenstam stopped, pressed herself to the wall, and peered around the corner. Then she ran. Harper and Aiden pitched around the corner behind her.

The sparks seemed to jump from Harper's skin. She caromed off the wall, thinking, *Christ*. Five feet ahead was an open office door—the source of the leaking light.

"Piper," she said.

Painfully, with the sound of a clinking chain, Piper crawled into view. She collapsed to a sitting position just inside the door.

Harper threw herself into the room and dropped to her knees at Piper's side.

"Girl, girl," she said.

Piper held her right hand pressed against her chest, clutching it with her left. Blood ran down her arm from her wrist. Her blouse was soaked. Strips of fabric torn from its hem were cinched around her wrist as a makeshift tourniquet. In the dim light, they were iron red. Her face was the color of newsprint, more gray than white.

Harper put her hands on either side of Piper's face and tried to see her through her stinging eyes and pounding pulse.

"Told you," she said.

Piper nodded, quick and fearfully. "You came."

Piper's face was cold. Harper reached for Piper's arm, but the girl inhaled and shrank from her, a cry falling from her lips.

"Hurts. Bad."

Harper backed off. "Just keep the pressure on. We're going to get you out of here."

Piper clutched her right wrist with her left, pressing it against her breastbone. From the hallway, around the corner, they heard men's voices, harsh and guttural. They couldn't make out their conversation, but the men seemed to be hunting for a way to get across the gap in the floor.

Aiden said, "Not much time, Harper."

A handcuff was locked around Piper's slender ankle. The second cuff was locked through a chain, and the chain ran to a standpipe along the wall, where it was padlocked.

Sorenstam crouched and examined the cuffs. Piper eyed her as though Sorenstam had dropped in from outer space.

"The cops are here?" Piper said.

"I am, and Detective Garrison. More are coming." Sorenstam got her handcuff key and freed Piper.

Outside, the men in the hallway were arguing. Harper heard them throwing stuff around, trying to find something to use to bridge the gap in the floor. She caught snatches of their debate.

"*Speshite.*"

"*Oboydite?*"

"*Nyet, tam net vremeni.*"

Hurry. Go around? No, there's no time. They were speaking Russian.

"Who are they?" Harper said.

Piper said, "They're from Spartan Security."

Harper and Aiden looked at her sharply, and at each other.

"Fuck," Aiden said.

Harper said, "Let's get you up."

She worked an arm around the girl and helped her to her feet. Piper sagged. Her legs held, but she leaned over and lowered her head to restore blood flow to her brain.

Sorenstam said, "We can't retrace our steps. Harper, if we keep going down this hallway, will we get to that second set of stairs?"

Harper tried to picture the layout of the building. "If we go down the hallway, we'll be heading for the center of the building. We should find a main corridor that runs the entire length of the basement. It'll take us to the stairs."

Outside the room, around the corner where the floor gapped, a motor hummed to life. The hydraulic lift had been activated.

The Russians had jerry-rigged a battery to the switch, or Travis had restored power. The platform was on its way up. They wouldn't have to jump across. Once it reached floor level, they would just stroll.

Harper pulled Piper tight against her side. "We're going out the door behind Detective Sorenstam, and we're not stopping."

Aiden ejected the clip from his weapon, checked it, and reinserted it in the butt of the gun with a hard slap. "We're going to push them back with covering fire and run down the hallway to the next junction. On my mark."

The hydraulic lift continued to hum. In Russian, a man said, "Go—now." They heard scuffling feet and the sound of men jumping, landing, and pulling themselves up again.

Piper straightened and looked at Harper. "I don't want to die."

"Me neither. So we won't."

All Piper's snark and feistiness had drained away. Harper wanted to cry.

Say something. Something ridiculous and hopeful.

"Ding-dong, motherfuckers. Your doom's here," Harper said.

Piper stared at her with amazement. Footsteps pounded in the hallway.

Aiden spun into the doorway, aimed, and fired. One shot, two. He moved his arm ten inches right. One shot, two.

He ducked back inside the room. An instant later, return fire bellowed from the corridor.

He huffed a breath. Ducked low and rolled into the doorway, firing again.

There was a scream in the hallway, retreating.

He rolled to his feet, charged out the door, and said, "Now."

50

They ran into the corridor. The echo of shots reverberated. Sorenstam led, the Remington up. Harper followed, pulling Piper with her. Aiden brought up the rear, HK at shoulder height, covering the field of fire behind them.

They advanced down the corridor, into the deepening dark, following the swinging light from Sorenstam's Maglite toward the center of the building. Piper drooped against Harper. Her eyes were the size of quarters.

They reached a turn. Sorenstam approached the corner carefully, barrel of the shotgun up and flat against her chest. She stopped, leaned around, and pulled back.

"It's a wide tunnel. Looks like the main passageway through the basement."

Aiden said, "Hostiles?"

"No sign, but there are emergency lights on."

He edged to the corner and looked. Harper peeked over his shoulder and down the tunnel. There was enough light to see, barely.

The tunnel floor was slick concrete, wider than a two-car garage, and had a yellow line painted down its center. It was designed so forklifts and flatbed trucks could drive directly to and from the road to load and unload chemicals. It ran straight as a gun barrel more than two hundred yards to a loading ramp with a rolling door that was down and locked. Next to the door, an emergency exit sign was glowing. The way to the stairs.

The sound of men arguing behind them around the corner at the end of the hallway grew louder. They were planning their next move. Piper whimpered. Harper wanted to crawl out of her skin.

Aiden and Erika looked at the tunnel, and at Harper, and at each other.

They needed time, and cover. They didn't have it.

Piper nearly shuddered. "We can't . . . we won't make it." Her voice was little more than a whisper. "What if we surrender?"

Erika shook her head. "Surrendering would be bad."

"Better than getting shot," Piper said.

"The choice isn't between surrendering and getting shot."

Harper knew it, too: The choice was between surrendering, in which case they would be shot in the back of the head while bound and on their knees, or running for it.

Aiden seemed to both coil and grow six inches taller. Sorenstam went completely still.

"I'll cover the three of you," she said.

Aiden said, "No."

She turned sharply. "Shut up."

There was no way the four of them could run down the length of the tunnel and reach the stairs before the hostiles regrouped and came charging. Two hundred yards: Harper had never covered that distance in less than thirty seconds. Piper could barely stand. Even if she and Aiden each slung one of Piper's arms over their shoulders, they wouldn't get out of this tunnel in under two minutes.

"I'll stay here and cover you," he said. "You're faster than I am right now, Erika."

Determination filled her eyes. "No. You have the strength to carry Piper if need be. And I'm the better shot," she said. "You know it. And you know that's what's going to count."

From two feet away, Harper felt the electricity crackle between them. They were no longer officially partners, but their training and history and bond had come alive and held them poised, together there.

It would take two people at a minimum to exfiltrate Piper. The girl was severely injured. Neither Harper nor Aiden could carry her by themselves, not if they were going to respond to an armed attack.

"No," Sorenstam said. "If you stay here, Harper and I will never be able to get Piper out alive."

He held Sorenstam's gaze. His eyes seemed to fill with a depthless despair.

"It has to be me," Sorenstam said.

The only way for any of them to get out alive was to stop the opposition before they got into the tunnel. If men with guns got around the corner, she and Aiden and Sorenstam would have no chance. The tunnel was merciless: no equipment nor the ubiquitous barrels to hide behind. A couple of doors, but only to closets. To get to the far end of the tunnel, they would have to run, without protection, without stopping.

The only way to do that was for Sorenstam to make a stand.

"Go, and don't look back," she said. "No matter what. I'll stop them when they come around the corner."

She had the shotgun and her pistol. She snapped the Maglite free from the Remington's barrel and tossed it to Aiden. Harper understood: Sorenstam didn't want to give the attackers a target. She turned and jammed the butt of the weapon against one of the emergency lights high on the wall. It shattered and the tunnel dimmed.

"Erika," Aiden said.

"On three," she said. "One, two—"

He caught her arm. She looked at him, fierce and otherworldly.

"Three," she said.

Hanging on to Piper, Harper and Aiden ran down the tunnel toward the bloody shadows and whispers in the far, faded dark.

51

Harper ran down the tunnel, trying to sprint on the hard concrete, through dim and reddish light, toward the distant turn that would bring them to safety. Aiden pounded along, his stride ragged, a syncopated tattoo. The gun in his hand swung back and forth, flashing dully under the emergency lights. Piper hung between them.

Harper focused on the telescoping tunnel and the distant wall, now a hundred fifty yards ahead. The very air behind her felt full of sparks. It was her fear. It was her knowledge that they were coming, and that they were armed.

Aiden didn't look back. But his face was open terrain, his emotions plain even in the nightmarish light of the tunnel.

Behind them, waiting, was Erika Sorenstam. She was all that stood between them and being in the middle of an open field of fire. Harper's throat felt the width of a straw.

Sorenstam was covering them. But there was no cover for her. Only exposure.

The corridor stretched ahead. It looked like a tunnel from a locker room to the playing field at a stadium—but longer. Harper was going flat out—as flat out as she could run, half hauling an injured teenager. Aiden was barely keeping up. She realized he was running close to empty. Still, he kept going.

She'd seen Aiden exchange an aching look with Sorenstam. Harper knew: Sorenstam was doing this to save all their lives but especially that of the man she still loved. Erika was keeping Aiden alive.

She counted in her head, as Sorenstam had told her to. *Six, seven, eight, nine . . .*

⁓

Ten.

Erika stepped out, away from the wall of the tunnel, and swung to face the exit from the hallway. She waited for the shrouded gunmen, the breathing shadows who lurked in the dark. Footsteps scuffed on the concrete. She held, waiting, waiting. The stock of the Remington was snugged against her right shoulder. Her left hand supported the action. The gun had warmed in her hand. It was hers, it was ready, it was ten more seconds of sight and sense and life. Her trigger finger held just short of firing.

A man rounded the corner and came into sight.

"Los Angeles County Sheriff. Drop the weapon," she shouted.

He raised his own gun. She leveled the shotgun, leading him, and fired.

Red fire sparked from the barrel of the Remington. The recoil smacked her shoulder. The man slammed backward, hitting the wall and crashing to his knees. He toppled and fell.

She racked the action, ejected the spent shell casing, and loaded the next shell. The thunder of the shot echoed off the walls and rang in her ears. It filled her head. The smell of gunpowder filled the hallway. She heard only her heart and the ringing of the shot. She couldn't hear Aiden and Harper running down the tunnel. But they had Piper. They were going. With each heartbeat, they got farther away, got a better chance of moving out of range, got another second's blessing, another chance to rescue the girl. Another breath, another chance to live.

The man around the corner ahead in the hallway was nothing but a silhouette. A darkened form, moaning, grunting. Moving. He still had the gun in his hand.

"Sheriff. Drop the weapon," she repeated.

Her hair fell in her face. She held the barrel of the shotgun level on the hallway. The man didn't drop his weapon.

"Now," she bellowed.

He raised it. His hand caught the light. She fired again.

The gun in the man's hand dropped and clattered to the floor. He no longer moved or moaned.

One down. One left.

She retreated around the corner into the tunnel. Her ears rang.

A shot boomed from the hallway. *Okay, then. Number two. Let's do it.*

Footsteps rushed toward her, fast. She had four shells left in the Remington and her Glock in its holster, plus ten more shells and a second full clip in her pocket. She once again raised the shotgun.

And saw. Saw them coming, all of them, into the light, guns in their hands, saw a MAC-10, and an AK, and at least two carrying shotguns of their own.

For a split second, a vast and eternal breath, she considered turning to run. In her mind's eye, she saw herself spin and dash down the tunnel, could feel herself draw her semiautomatic and fire blindly behind her at them as she escaped. She pictured herself reaching Aiden and Harper and bolting themselves behind a steel door, barricading themselves, comrades in arms, a team ready to fight back. She saw it, felt it, could nearly feel Aiden's body against hers as they stood back to back, covering the entire field of fire.

For that moment, she was not alone, facing the onslaught. For that moment only.

They came around the corner. She stood in the middle of the tunnel. She leveled the shotgun and fired.

⌐

They heard it behind them: the roar of the Remington, firing again. Harper was running, breathing hard and crying at the same time. Aiden, his stride ever more ragged, hesitated.

"No," Harper gasped.

Behind them, at the far end of the tunnel, the return fire was devastating. Shot after shot, the deep boom of another shotgun, the flat crack of pistols, the *crack-crack-crack* of a rifle firing in a three-shot burst.

Piper cried out. Aiden stumbled, and for a moment, Harper thought he had been hit. He started to look back. She grabbed his arm.

"Aiden."

Behind them came another gunshot, this time from a pistol, and a shout from Erika. It was wild, the most fearsome and terrifying cry Harper had ever heard.

"Run," she said.

They had to. Sorenstam was standing strong, knowing the consequences and doing it anyway. Giving Aiden and Harper every vital second they needed to survive and get Piper out. One hundred yards to the far end of the tunnel. Ninety.

Harper's heart seemed half ready to tear. She couldn't let Aiden turn around. Turn around and it would be him next, then her and Piper.

"Come on," she said.

He looked as though he couldn't get any breath. He looked as if he wanted to put the muzzle of his own gun to his forehead and pull the trigger. Seventy yards to the turn. Sixty. Piper was fearfully quiet.

"God, run, we gotta run," Harper said.

Then Aiden put his back into it and pumped his arms and paced her again, bolting along the tunnel. They heard return fire. They heard Erika fire her weapon again and again. The cacophony rose, concrete snapping as bullets hit it.

Forty yards. Thirty. The firing stopped. Harper kept going, knew men were coming behind them. She heard shouts, commands, sounds of voices bouncing off the concrete floor and walls.

Men's voices. More than one. Maybe more than two.

Don't look back. She pounded along. Twenty yards.

A final single shot reverberated in the tunnel. She heard the clatter of metal against concrete, as though a long gun were being kicked away from the fallen hand that had held it. Sorenstam was silent. Ten yards.

Aiden reached the corner, limping hard. He grabbed her elbow and slingshotted her and Piper around it, into a passageway that was dark and smelled of rust and chemicals.

She kept going. Realized he had stopped. He had literally hit the wall, leaning his head against the concrete. His eyes were squeezed shut, his teeth gritted.

"Aiden," she choked. "Come on." She pulled on his elbow.

The sound of men running in the tunnel finally got him to push away from the wall. He turned back to face the tunnel and raised his pistol.

Harper felt a sensation in the center of her forehead, like a drill. She yanked on his arm. "No."

He was ready to charge the men head-on. Harper held tight to his arm.

"Don't. Aiden, *no*. Piper—both of us have to get her out. Come on."

He resisted a moment longer, breathing hard. Then he nodded. "Go."

Harper swept the Maglite along the passageway. And she saw that the emergency exit sign hadn't led them to the stairs—ahead was a fixed steel ladder, bolted to the wall, going both up to the factory floor and down to a subbasement. She aimed the flashlight at the ceiling.

The ladder was broken off a few feet overhead. They couldn't climb up.

Piper moaned, a high, desperate sound. Her legs wobbled. Harper feared that she barely had enough blood left to circulate in her system. She feared that Piper's heart was empty.

"Come on," she said.

In the semidark, they reached the ladder. Harper leaned over and looked down.

Aiden said, "Have you ever been down to that level?"

She kept looking. "Yeah. It's all narrow tunnels and pipes and chemical storage tanks. But this isn't the only ladder. I'm sure of that."

Piper said, "I can't."

Harper put her hand to Piper's face. The girl's cheek was warm. "We can. Together."

Aiden was half-shadowed under the Maglite. He looked at her and blinked, as though he was having trouble seeing her clearly in the near dark. She could see the intensity on his face, and pain. She held out a hand.

He took it. She squeezed.

"We're getting out," she said. "We're getting out and taking Piper home."

He pulled her close, and when he looked at her, he seemed to see her clearly, to see the path out.

"Follow me," he said.

52

Aiden hurried down the ladder, boots clanging against the rungs, and stepped off one story below. Harper edged her way down ahead of Piper, ready to catch the girl if she slipped or, God forbid, passed out. The rungs were cold. With each step, the metal rang and the darkness increased.

Harper dropped to the floor. The ceiling was low. Aiden stood close by. She could feel his chest, rising and falling.

Piper worked her way down, awkwardly, using her good hand. When she got within reach, Aiden pulled her in. Her eyes were shimmering and hot.

She nodded and said, "I can stand by myself."

Harper aimed the Maglite. They were in an access tunnel for pipes and gas lines. The ceiling was an inch above Harper's head. Aiden was ducking.

He said, "Which way?"

She pointed toward the west end of the building, the side they had entered from, and cinched an arm around Piper's waist again. "Drive it like you stole it."

"What?" Piper said.

"Balls to the wall."

Aiden led them along the tunnel. After about ninety yards, he stopped. Harper saw why: Ahead lay an open pit. Below them, under flickering emergency lighting, they saw two gigantic pressure tanks. Twelve-inch pipes ran from them horizontally into the walls, spanning the pit. Nearby were several dozen upright gas storage vessels topped with needle valves. Harper didn't know if they were rusting hulks or filled with combustible vapors. A catwalk bridged the room, leading to a narrow ledge and a hatchlike exit opposite.

Behind them on the ladder came footsteps. Urgently, they stepped onto the catwalk. It dipped and groaned.

"Shit," Harper said.

"Shit," Piper said.

Aiden said, "Too much weight. You two first."

Holding Piper, Harper took tender steps out above the pit. The metal quivered beneath her feet. Rust from the railing came off on her hand. Ahead, the bolts that held the catwalk to the wall vibrated with their steps. Crumbling bits of dust and concrete spilled from the wall. She had a wicked fear that the whole thing was seconds from shaking itself loose. The drop to the thicket of tanks was at least twenty feet, the spill to the concrete floor so far that it was all but invisible.

They reached the far side and stepped onto the ledge. The second they stepped off the catwalk, Aiden ran onto it. His feet rang on the metal. The catwalk's bolts creaked and shimmied—they were working their way out of the wall. He was halfway across when she realized why he was going all out.

Black-clad gunmen appeared in the entrance on the far side. Aiden came on, nodding her to move, move, move *now*.

She maneuvered Piper through the hatch into the passageway beyond. Aiden thundered across the catwalk. The gunmen fired at him.

Piper screamed. Aiden leaped off the catwalk and dropped and rolled.

The gunmen rushed together onto the catwalk. They were heavy men in body armor. Harper sat down on the ledge and raised her foot and kicked at the bolts holding the catwalk to the wall.

One of the hostiles shouted. He raised his weapon, but Aiden fired at him. The shot hit the man in the chest. He fell backward, grunting— winded but alive, the round buried in his vest. Harper kicked again, harder. Aiden fired another shot and grabbed the railing on the opposite side from Harper. She yelled, "One, two—"

He pulled and she kicked. With a squeal and a snapping sound, the bolts broke free.

The catwalk screeched and the near end swung down hard. The men turned and tried to run back, but the ancient metal, thin and corroded, twisted and snapped. Shouting wildly, the men flipped over the railing and plunged into the tank forest below. A scream ended abruptly as one of them hit the stack of compressed gas cylinders topped with needle-nosed valves. He lay like a fish embedded on a rack of straight pins.

The other man hit the top of one of the big tanks. He landed on his back and held on to his gun. Then the catwalk crashed on top of him. It slapped down across his chest like the blade of a paper cutter. The sound reverberated. He lay motionless, until the echoes died, and with them his last moans.

Aiden and Harper looked down, Harper on her knees, head hanging low. She was shaking.

He put a hand on her back. It felt more than reassuring. It was telling her: Get up.

Piper edged forward. "Jesus." She stared, her bright-quarter eyes even wider than before. "Did you kill them?"

Harper struggled to her feet. Her hair was hanging in her face, stuck to her forehead with sweat.

"Are they dead?" Piper said.

Aiden raised a hand to nudge Piper back. "They aren't coming after you anymore."

She shrank from him and protected her sliced wrist. "Jesus."

He raised his hands, giving her space, and turned again to the pit. "One minute."

Stuffing the pistol in the small of his back, he lowered himself over the ledge. With apparent pain, he edged down until he was hanging by his fingertips.

"What are you doing?" Harper said.

He looked down. It was about a ten-foot drop to the wrecked portion of the catwalk, another fifteen to the floor below. He kicked out from the wall without a word and dropped noisily to the twisted bridge. He crouched quickly to grab hold.

Harper leaned out, her nerves thrumming.

Lowering himself cautiously from the catwalk, he dropped to the top of the big storage tank. Harper watched anxiously. Behind her Piper stood half-shadowed in the hatch exit, breathing rapidly.

Aiden worked his way to the man who had crashed onto the tank and been crushed by the broken section of the catwalk. The man lay staring sightlessly into the recesses of the ceiling. Aiden pried the pistol from the man's hand and took his earpiece and radio transmitter. A few feet from the body, he picked up a shotgun. Then he scrambled across the top of the tank into the shadows. A moment later, Harper saw him climbing on a stacked set of cylinders, packed tightly in a shipping crate. He groaned but pulled himself up, leaped and pulled himself back onto the ledge.

He limped up, carrying the hostile's shotgun. He twisted the man's earpiece into position and tucked the radio into his shirt pocket.

"Anything?" Harper asked.

"Chatter. Not in English."

Piper's face was blank, apparently with shock.

Harper said, "Probably Russian. Let me have the earpiece." He handed it to her and she put it in. She squeezed Piper's shoulder. "We've gotcha. Ready?"

Piper's voice was surprisingly hard. "Yeah."

She had stopped shivering. Harper didn't know whether that was good or bad.

Harper looked at Aiden. He didn't even have an expression on his face.

"What's wrong?" she said.

"Those cylinders down there?" He nodded at the pit. "They're leaking. I don't know what's in them, but it's high-pressure gas and we don't want to hang around."

Holding Piper tight, Harper started down the tunnel.

Side by side, flanking Piper, Harper and Aiden rushed down the access tunnel. Aiden ducked beneath its low ceiling, gripping the shotgun, the weapon held low. Piper dragged under Harper's arm, moaning every time Harper tried to lug her tighter. The light was almost nonexistent, but she could see Aiden's face in gray scale, a worn and determined outline against the tunnel walls. Behind them came a hissing from the damaged gas cylinders.

Sixty yards along the tunnel, they came to another access ladder, this one ascending. Harper stared up into gloom, listening. Heard nothing.

Aiden said, "Me first."

He climbed to the opening in the floor above, peered out, and waved them up. Piper climbed without complaint, hooking her injured elbow over the rungs of the ladder to stabilize herself. Halfway up, Harper pressed a hand to the radio earpiece.

"Chatter," she whispered. "Somebody's trying to contact those two hostiles we left back in the tank room."

Aiden pulled himself through the opening onto the floor above. "ID? Names? Maybe I could respond in English and make them think it's one of those men?"

He reached down for Piper. "Come on, let me help you."

She flinched. "I'm okay." She climbed awkwardly out and slumped to the floor.

Harper scrambled out behind them into an office hallway lit with fading emergency lights. She recognized the fallen ceiling tiles and torn-up carpet.

"Aiden—we're just around the corner from the hallway where we came into the building."

She pointed. He rushed to the corner, checked, and waved for them to follow.

Cinching her hand around Piper's waist again, Harper headed for the corner. The girl was wheezing now, and stumbling over her own feet. Aiden saw her struggling and put an arm around Piper as well.

In the earpiece, Harper heard static, then a man's voice in Russian.

"Echo One, come in." The voice was muffled and tinny. "Echo One, come in. Zhurov, respond."

Aiden was limping more severely. He pulled them around the corner, into the hallway they'd entered not long before with Erika. The door was directly ahead of them.

"We're almost there," Harper whispered. "Come on, come on."

Aiden pulled them all toward the door. Five feet from it, he stopped.

The tape he'd placed over the lock had been removed.

The door was securely shut again. A lock had been flipped: a Yale dead bolt. To open it took a key.

They were trapped.

From the earpiece, a voice fuzzed. "Echo One is not responding. Check the back exit."

53

Harper's legs felt all at once like loose string. Her vision went fuzzy. "They're coming this way. We have to find another way out."

They started back down the hallway, fast.

"Has to be an exit out the front, across the factory floor," Aiden said.

Piper's feet tangled again. Her head lolled to one side.

"No, girl," Harper said. "Walk. You have to."

They rushed down the hall with everything they had, but Harper could tell they were moving more slowly than they had even five minutes earlier.

In the earpiece, she heard Zero's voice. "Found Zhurov and Rodchenko. Dead."

"Fuck," Travis answered.

Aiden kept going. "Don't slow down."

A second later, the hallway emerged onto the factory floor. It was spooky with moonlight. There was a large set of double doors on the far side.

Harper said, "Those doors have to lead to the exit to the front gate. If we can get through them, I can run for it. The MINI's there. I can drive it back and pick you two up."

Aiden nodded.

They rushed onto the factory floor. They were five feet from the double doors when the first shouts echoed behind them.

She looked back. At the far end of the factory floor stood a dark figure in a hoodie. Every hair on her head stood to cold attention.

Piper turned her head.

"Don't look," Harper said.

They shoved through the double doors, into a hallway that led to the front entrance. Aiden found a metal broom handle and jammed it through the door handles. It was better than nothing but wouldn't stop them for long.

Twenty yards ahead was the rolling garage door that led to the driveway, the gate, and the road. It was open. Outside was the chilly desert night, and freedom. Piper gasped, almost a cry of desperate joy.

Behind them, the doors Aiden had jammed shut rattled. They hurried toward the rolling door. On the wall beside it, a red warning light began to flash. The door started to roll down.

Behind them came sounds of battering, something heavy smashing against the jammed doors. Ahead, now just ten yards away, the rolling door creaked down. There was room for them to get under, but it was diminishing fast.

Piper slid in Harper's arms like a sack of rice. Aiden rushed to Harper's side and started to pick her up.

"No." Harper said. "You stop anybody coming at us. I can carry her."

She crouched. With Aiden's help, she got her shoulder under Piper's midriff and slung her over her shoulder in a fireman's carry. Groaning, she stood up. Her legs were shaking.

She hunkered toward the rolling door. Piper's arms hung limp, hitting her in the back. The door rolled lower, creaking and clattering.

She let out a manic gasp and hugged tight to Piper's legs. Together with Aiden, she bent low and ran beneath the door as it fell. They stumbled out into the cold darkness and Harper fell hard to her knees.

Piper crashed off her shoulders to the concrete. "Jesus."

Harper said, "We're out. We have to keep going."

The rolling door groaned down and hit the floor and stopped. The silence outside was all at once vast and welcome and terrifying.

Harper said, "Arm over my shoulder. Let's go."

Moaning, Piper sat up. With an effort that seemed like she was moving through molasses, Harper got to her knees, bearing Piper's weight. She groaned to her feet.

They heard more smashing sounds deep in the building, Zero trying to get through the doors. Aiden turned to the wall beside the garage door, where there was a large switch. With his HK, he fired at the mechanism. Twice. Sparks ejected and smoke curled out, sizzling.

Harper had never felt so relieved and scared all at once. Aiden backed away from the door. Harper turned toward the gate and the run to freedom.

The MINI was gone.

~

She stared blankly at the desert, and the darkness beyond the gate, and a part of her thought: *It's there. I just don't see it. It has to be there. Why am I not seeing it?*

She heard a sound she took too long to understand was her own half sobs. The car was gone.

Behind them, an engine buzzed to life again and the rolling door began to crank open. Aiden's shots hadn't fried the interior circuitry. Zero and Travis were coming.

"Oh, my God." Harper's breathing stuttered, until she said, "We have to run."

Piper whimpered. "I can't. I can't walk. I can't go any farther."

Harper tightened an arm around Piper's waist, but the girl sagged and resisted. "I can't."

Aiden said, "Sorenstam's car."

Harper said, "I'll go."

Piper grabbed Harper's shirt. "No. Don't leave me. Don't go, please."

Aiden said, "Take shelter." He looked around at the factory complex. "I'll find a way around the outside and get the unmarked car. I'll be back."

He looked at Harper. She was trying not to cry. He took off.

Harper said, "Piper."

She turned and knelt and told the girl to climb on her back.

Without a sound, Piper threw an arm around Harper's neck and leaned her weight on Harper's back. Harper wrestled Piper's knees up against her elbows. Leaning forward for balance, carrying Piper piggyback, she tried to continue. The gate loomed but didn't seem to get any closer.

Piper said, "Wait."

Harper didn't slow down. If she slowed down, she would never get back up to speed. If she slowed down, they were dead.

"To the left," Piper said. "There's a storage yard behind an interior fence. Look—the fence has a break in it."

She weakly lifted a hand and pointed. A section of the fence leading to the storage yard had been torn open. Arms burning with the strain, Harper veered left and squeezed through.

The light was nearly nonexistent here, the ground dusty. Harper looked for a place to hide. Behind a clutch of fifty-five-gallon drums and a six-foot stack of rotting wooden pallets, she sagged and went down on all fours.

Piper slid off her back to the ground. Harper tried to rise, but her legs wouldn't straighten. She crawled back to the fence and shoved the torn section closed, awkwardly.

They were out. Outside, alone, unseen, as far as she could determine. No security lights came on. Moonlight whitened the walls of the factory. She peered around for telltale cameras but saw none.

She crawled back to Piper's side, fell to her butt, and pulled Piper against her in a hug.

"Almost home. We just have a little farther to go."

Piper nodded. They leaned back against the pallets. Harper caught her breath and listened for the sound of a big block engine.

Instead, she heard a clinking chain.

From the shadows near the building, the dog appeared.

54

The dog padded from the shadows. Its eyes glinted in the moonlight. Its leash scritched on the concrete behind it.

A buzzing rose in Harper's head. Her mouth felt full of cotton.

She got to one knee in front of Piper. "Hold still."

The dog walked with predatory deliberation, its steps full of restrained energy, its head low. Its teeth seemed to take up the horizon.

She needed something long and heavy and blunt. A two-by-four. An RPG launcher.

Piper slowly got to her feet.

"Shh," Harper whispered. "Don't move. Don't run."

Piper put a hand on Harper's arm. "No. It's okay."

Harper turned to her in confusion. Piper was staring at the dog. In the moonlight, the girl was as pale as a crushed lily. But her grip on Harper's arm actually was a grip. She took a step.

"Hey, boy," she murmured. "Hey, dog."

She spoke soothingly. The dog stood, ears flat, eyes on her.

Piper inched closer. "It's okay, boy. I'm your friend. You're a good boy, aren't you?"

The dog's ears pricked up. Piper crept forward and slowly picked up its leash.

"Sit," she said.

The dog sat.

Harper gaped. The dog sat, breathing fast. The leash hung loose from Piper's hand. She had seemingly mesmerized the dog. It stretched its neck, sniffing at the blood on her shirt, but stayed sitting. Still, un-less she could control it, she might as well have pulled the pin on a grenade.

Harper murmured, "I'll find something we can tie the leash to."

Something heavy, that it couldn't drag while chasing them. It looked strong enough to pull a tractor.

"Don't bother," Piper said.

"Careful. It's not a normal dog." It was a chain saw with four legs and a tail.

"I've got him."

Piper softly whistled. The dog rose off its haunches. She twisted the leash around her good hand to remove the slack. Harper's skin prickled again. Her nerves were vibrating at some quantum frequency, invisibly quick.

"Hold still," Piper said. "He'll attack you. I can feel it through the leash. He's nothing but a bullet, and I'm holding the trigger." She tugged again on the leash. "Eagle, heel."

She raised her chin, a signal. A motor ground into action along the wall of the factory. Somebody had thrown a switch that activated a rolling door.

A chasm seemed to open. The rolling door slid wide, giving a view into a half-illuminated assembly room at the east end of the factory building. Through the door, out of the shadows, came Travis Maddox.

He swaggered across the concrete paddock, backlit by the factory lights. Harper tensed to run. The dog strained against the leash.

Piper said, "Unh-uh."

Travis raised a finger and wagged it at Harper. A lament rose toward her lips.

It was the first time she had seen him in ten years. The decade had worked a transformation on him.

He may have grown a couple of inches. He may have been wearing motorcycle boots. His heels clicked on the cement. He looked lean and cut, with shoulders broadened by prison weight lifting, and all the baby fat burned away. In the light angling from the factory door, his eyes were deep-set and lined. His corporate haircut looked like a bad joke. He was wearing the same black tactical gear as his dead Spartan Security goons.

Piper handed him the leash. "You were right. Harper and Garrison and Sorenstam—they killed your men. No warning, no chance to surrender. They just took them out, like it was their privilege." She sounded semi-stunned.

"Piper," Harper said, her voice half-racked and breaking. "Why?"

Standing beside Travis, Piper no longer looked wounded and weak. She no longer looked injured at all. In her right hand, she held Harper's Swiss Army knife. She had swiped it from Harper's back pocket, probably while she was slung over Harper's shoulder in the fireman's carry.

"Nobody cut you," Harper said. "The kidnapping wasn't a kidnapping."

Travis petted the dog's cement-block head. "You're slow, but you got there."

Her strength drained from her fingertips. She was backed into the last space on the chessboard. She knew it was half a minute from checkmate.

So make them take you down.

Don't give it to them. Aiden was coming. The local sheriffs were coming. If she had half a minute, she would use it. Every second was a chance for rescue. She stood, her fists slowly drawing tight. *Fight.*

"Good one, Travis. Kudos. You punked me good," she said.

Piper handed the dog's leash to Travis and walked up to Harper. Her face was dirty, but even in the moonlight, she looked flushed. She eyed Harper for a long second, then inhaled and spit in her face.

Travis laughed.

Hot spit dribbled down Harper's cheek. She wiped it off. Her vision had seemingly gone out of true. Piper looked like the same girl who'd been clinging to her all night, but something else was animating her. Something inside, snakelike and venomous.

Travis walked over, stopping directly behind Piper. He was giving her room, maybe to throw a punch, but Harper could sense him pulling the invisible strings.

Harper stared at the girl. "You have permission to speak?"

Travis spread his arms. A grand gesture, as if he were giving Piper permission to fly.

"I yield the stage," he said.

Piper stared at Harper. "You get it now?"

"No."

Say it isn't true, Harper thought. But she knew that betrayal was the way of the world. It was the way she had been raised. It was every lost weekend with her mom. It was being left in a wrecked car on the highway downhill from this godforsaken compound, alone and facing the law for a crime her own mother had committed. It was caring for this girl, and seeing hatred spin in her eyes.

"Tell me this is a joke," Harper said.

For the length of a breath, Piper stayed quiet. Then a fault line seemed to slip inside her.

"A joke? How could I make a joke? Drew is dead. How could I ever find anything funny again?"

Harper stood and listened. *I know.*

Piper glared at her, searching every facet of Harper's face. "That's it? Silence? You have nothing to say?"

Harper didn't move.

Piper stepped closer. "You don't, do you? Drew is dead, and you made it happen. It's your fault. And you have not one word to say."

She didn't. Speaking would get her nowhere. Her face heated and her heart thundered.

"You thought you got away with it," Piper said. "You still do, don't you? Look at you. You're just taking it. You're not even reacting. You're the one who's responsible for my brother being dead and it doesn't even matter to you?"

Harper raised her hands, helpless. It seemed only to enrage Piper all the more. In the background, the dog stirred.

"I know all about you, *Susannah*. Travis told me. All this time, you've been playing innocent. The goody two-shoes, Navy veteran, Miss A-student. What bullshit." She leaned toward Harper's face. "You're a thief and a whore."

"Not a whore, honey. Never."

Piper seemed to get knocked back at that. Her mouth parted.

"I loved Drew," Harper said.

Piper swung an open palm at Harper's face. Harper blocked it. Piper pulled back to swing again before she remembered that her other hand held a knife. She raised it, rigidly, at Harper's neck.

"I will. I will do it," Piper said.

Harper held still. "And I love you, Piper."

For the smallest moment, Piper seemed to process that, and Harper had hope.

Then Piper seemed to ingest it, and the words hit her nervous system, and she didn't relax, or soften. She crouched and gripped the knife tighter, and Harper realized she was going to lunge.

Harper raised her hands defensively, but as Piper drew back the knife, Travis stepped forward and grabbed the girl's arm.

"No," he said.

Piper bared her teeth. "Why not?"

"Because I run the schedule."

Piper was leaning forward in Travis's grip, like the dog straining at its leash. He took the weapon from her hand. She backed off. Then pointed at Harper. "Eye for an eye," she said. "You for my brother."

Harper felt a weird shift in the air behind her. A heavy presence drew near, silent and abrasive. Eddie Azerov stepped into view.

"Hello, Zannah. Let's go."

55

He smelled the same. Fifteen years on, Eddie Azerov smelled the same as he had when they were fourteen, same as he had the night he told Harper she worked for him or she got eaten by the wolves. He smelled like sweat and cigarettes and fear.

He moved in on her, a shadowed face behind the drooping hood of his sweatshirt. A chain clinked, the dog collar he attached to his wallet in the pocket of his sagging jeans. The guy hadn't changed his style since he was twelve. She knew he was stuck, knew he had the emotional maturity of a middle schooler, and knew that meant nothing good when it came to the next few minutes. He was a violent felon with the impulsivity and vindictiveness of a child, and the amoral wants of a sociopath.

He tilted his head, sharply, and lifted his chin as though to sniff her. "We're going now."

"Zero, I won't ever go anyplace with you again," she said. "Whatever we do, we do it right here."

He was so close that his breath moved her hair. His teeth had worsened in the last decade, growing more crooked inside lips that looked gray in the moonlight.

He leaned in. His eyes had a dark sheen, almost glazed. She held his gaze, but her left leg began to twitch. He was not there, she realized. Whatever made a person a human being had turned to sand and blown away. What was left in its place was a spirit that was somehow void, antimatter, a thing that fed on light and blotted it out. It was chaos, entropy, and it was looking for fuel.

He tilted his head the opposite direction, a quick swerve and snap. And then he clacked his teeth.

"Su. San. Nah."

The twitch in her leg worsened. She realized that Aiden was probably dead.

Travis snapped his fingers. Zero stayed up in her face for a moment longer, then stepped back.

Travis took her arm. "We're going for a walk."

And he didn't smell of sweat and fear. He smelled of leather and aftershave and gun oil. He smelled of certainty. He marched her toward the open door of the factory building.

⁓

They walked in the rough moonlight across the dusty storage yard, Zero and Travis on either side of Harper, Piper walking ahead, half turned so she could look back.

Zero leaned in again from her left, and for a second, she thought he might take a bite out of her shoulder. The dog bulled along at his side, shoulders switching, head low.

"Why are you doing this, Piper?" Harper said.

Travis said, "You should know exactly what's going on."

She knew but didn't want to believe it. "When?"

"When did Piper see the light?" he said.

Piper said, "Six months ago. I found out what you are. I found out what you did. After that, who could be real friends with you?"

Harper seemed to feel a fish hook embed itself behind her heart. She couldn't get away, could only feel its barbs tear at her. No matter which way she pulled, no matter what she said to Piper, it would make no difference. This wasn't about logic, or reason. It was about grief speaking through the language of rage. Piper didn't have ears to hear her right now. She only had pain, and was going to give voice to it through hateful words and violence. Harper walked along, Travis's hand tight around her biceps, Zero a cold absence on her left.

Piper said, "You were nothing. You had to put on somebody else's name even to feel like a person. Because you were ashamed. You knew what you'd done. But you shouldn't have changed your name to Harper. The name that fit you is Judas."

Harper said, "Travis, you've become your dad, only worse."

His hand tightened around her arm. "You know nothing, Flynn."

He said it brusquely, and she knew she'd hit a nerve. His breathing turned heavy.

His jaw was tight. "You think Piper is a gofer? That she snivels around shoplifting like you did fifteen years ago? You haven't seen the new world, Zannah."

Piper said, "She's clueless. She can only see the inside of her own head, her own wants." She turned to her. "I'm not some thief like you, taking for myself. I'm a chaotic actor."

Harper looked at her sideways. Piper raised her chin.

"You don't even know what I'm talking about."

Travis adopted a tone of cavalier superiority. "A chaotic actor—"

"I know the term," Harper said. "White hats, black hats. And you convinced Spartan Security Systems that you were one of the good guys."

Piper said, "You're so simplistic."

Travis said, "White hat and black hat are convenient labels."

Piper said, "They're children's names. I'm not white or black. What I am is an adaptive persistent adversary."

She was gaining energy now. She was drawing strength from the air and her own fury and self-righteousness.

Harper understood, at a painful gut level. Travis had lured Piper with talk and God knew what else into the fairy tale of becoming a chaotic actor—convincing her she'd be an anonymous folk hero, a rebel outlaw. He had made her into what his dad wanted Harper to be when she was a teen.

Piper was Travis's victory.

They entered the factory assembly room, and Zero hit a power button. The door rolled shut behind them. Travis turned on the lights, harsh halogens that hung from the ceiling. The concrete floor was cracked and stained iridescent colors from past decades of chemical impregnation.

Travis shoved Harper to the center of the room, to a drain at the low point of the floor. Dead center.

He pointed at her. "Don't move."

He walked around her, slowly, finger aimed at her face. He seemed to be surveying her, as for a taxidermy display. Maybe he wanted to mount her on his wall.

Overhead, a catwalk ran around the edge of the room. There were tracks along the ceiling and chains hanging from them.

Travis continued circling her. Zero joined him, going the opposite direction, the dog at heel.

Piper stood staring at her. Then she took hold of one of the hanging chains. She leaned on it, as though preparing to climb it.

"You betrayed me. You get what you give." Piper pulled on the chain. It was heavy, with huge links, almost as large as stirrups. "You used my brother."

"Never."

"Who were you? Some bartender he met one night. You saw his wallet, and you wormed your way into his life. Hooked up with him in the hopes he'd give you stuff. Same way you wormed your way into Travis's family."

"That's not what happened. Not with Travis, not with Drew."

Piper turned lazily toward Travis. Her expression was halfway between disgust and a smirk. "Just like you predicted. Almost down to the word."

"Piper, I loved your brother," Harper said.

"You knew he was rich. That's what you loved. You found out he came from money, and you were going to get it. God, you sicken me."

Harper stood on the drain, knowing that at the very least she was going to get a hot dose of Piper's bile. She couldn't win here. Defend herself, and Piper had been prepared by Travis with a twisted bingo card of hateful responses. Stay silent, and Piper would assume she was conceding or worse.

Travis walked to the wall and flipped a switch. Overhead, a motor activated. It began drawing up the chain Piper was holding. After a second, she jammed her foot in one of the links and held on. It lifted her off the floor.

"What goes around comes around, Harper."

The chain cranked up, clinking harshly. Piper drew near the catwalk overhead. Nimbly, she grabbed the rail and hopped over. Travis shut down the motor.

From the rickety walkway, Piper nodded at the room below, grandly, as if she were about to make an Eva Perón balcony speech. Her expression twisted into something bleak and eager. Momentarily, she smiled.

Travis nodded at Zero. "Chain Flynn up."

56

Harper shied when Zero approached her. He bounced on his toes and tilted his head again. He clacked his teeth once more, and Harper flinched.

Under his breath he said, "Waited for this a long time." He stopped inches from her. "Take off your—"

"Fuck you, Eddie."

His eyes flashed in the harsh lights. He shoved her, hard, sweeping her ankle with his foot and knocking her down. She shouted, but he spun, dropped onto her legs, and tore her shoes off.

"Stop it," she said.

Travis sauntered past. "He's not going to rape you. He doesn't want the stink."

Zero said, "Take off your jacket."

She felt then that she was going to lose it, that a swarm of hornets was buzzing inside her head. Travis grabbed her from behind and hauled her jacket off. She felt close to hyperventilating.

Kneeling on her, Zero pulled his hoodie over his head. He threw it at her.

"Put it on."

The hoodie smelled like him. It was warm, and she wanted to fling it away.

He put his hand around her throat and leaned close. "Put it on."

When she pulled it over her head, Travis yanked the hood up and as far forward as it would go, nearly obscuring her face. Zero stood, pulled off his boots, and tossed them at her.

"Those, too."

She stared at him. She had a terrible feeling she knew where this was going.

"Now," he said.

She pulled the boots on. He indicated that she should lace them up. Travis pulled her to her feet.

From a pile of debris, Zero picked up a five-foot length of heavy chain. With a zip tie, he secured one end of the chain to the drain cover in the floor. With a second zip tie, he secured the other end around Harper's left ankle.

"This won't work," she said.

Travis slowly circled in front of her. "How do you know what's going to happen next?"

"You think you're going to pull this off? Chaining me to the floor is the last thing you want. That will leave the wrong kind of evidence."

He continued to circle her. "You always thought you were so smart. The getaway driver. Well, guess what." He leaned close. "You can't get away this time."

He looked up to the catwalk. "Piper."

She leaned on the railing. "You betrayed Drew. You betrayed me. And so did your lover."

Harper's stomach gripped. "Piper . . ."

"*Be quiet.*"

Travis and Zero continued to walk around her, the circles widening, widening.

Piper leaned over the rail. "He was there that night. Aiden could have saved Drew."

Harper tugged on the chain. It didn't budge from the drain cover.

"Aiden and Erika Sorenstam—they were there, they were armed. They were the law. They should have handled the situation."

Harper looked up. "They tried."

"Shut *up*." Piper rocked back and forth against the railing. "Aiden could have saved Drew, but he didn't even try."

"That's not true, Piper."

"Liar. Liar, liar, *liar*. They were so busy saving each other because they were screwing each other, they did *nothing* to help my brother."

Piper gripped the railing. This was her moment. This was what she had been building up to for god knows how long.

Harper said, "There were a thousand people at the club. It was mayhem. Aiden and Erika were the only two cops there, trying to get a handle on chaos. Aiden stopped two of the gunmen, but there were so many people running around that he couldn't fire again without hitting them."

"Bullshit. He could have fired at any time. He could have laid down a line of fire. Emptied his magazine. He didn't. He held fire to save himself."

"Where did you get that? I know you read the investigative report. That's not what happened."

"I saw the video," Piper said.

Harper's head snapped up. "What video?"

"Travis showed me."

"The video was all destroyed."

"It was in the cloud," Piper said. "All the data was uploaded wirelessly to the servers. Travis recovered it."

Harper held still, but part of her had doubled over inside. "If you saw the video, you saw . . ."

Jesus.

"Piper, you saw edited video. You saw what Travis wanted you to see . . . if Travis showed you the video, you saw the shooters. You have to know who was behind this whole thing."

"What matters is that Aiden was there. You were there. You two were in a position to stop Drew from dying. Instead, Drew had to pull you across the bar and try to get you out. Instead, Aiden was trying to keep his girlfriend from getting hurt." She leaned back, rocking hard. "Instead, he started screwing you. As soon as it looked convenient, you forgot all about my brother and started banging the cop who survived. That's disgusting."

"Piper," Harper said, trying to keep her voice under control. "Travis ordered the attack."

"Shut *up*," Piper yelled. "Travis was at Spartan's HQ, trying to stop it. He couldn't. He knew Xenon was inadequately protected. The guards were unarmed. When the shooting started, there were only two people who could have stopped it, and they did *nothing*."

"Listen to me, Piper. I'm not talking about what Travis told the security guards that night. I'm telling you that Zero led the attack on Xenon. He was the shooter who escaped. He started the shooting spree, Piper. He's the reason your brother died. He shot Drew."

But she realized, even as she said it, that Piper would never believe it. She wouldn't even admit a particle of doubt into her new and fiery narrative. She might think of herself as a chaotic actor, neither black hat nor white but a force remaking the world to suit her disintegrative rage. But she was as blinded to the truth as somebody who'd stared into the sun. She was under the force of a delusion, and sinking in it.

The dog growled. Harper knew now why she had seen it at the memorial service at the park, and outside her window immediately after Piper had driven away. Zero had been shadowing Piper. Working with her. Making sure she did what she was supposed to: Keep Harper caring.

Travis said, "Save your breath, Susannah. Piper knows who you are, and how you lie, and what the consequences always are."

Piper called down, "You're a killer, Harper. You betrayed Travis and Eddie, and because of that, Travis's dad died. The man who took you in and treated you like his own daughter after you ruined your mom's life. You set him up to die."

Even though she should have expected it, Harper still felt the words hit her like a cascade of ice water.

She shook her head. "No."

"You got Drew killed. You're a double dose of death." Piper rattled the railing. "And then you went off and slept with the guy who did nothing to help him. You pissed on Drew's body. You reveled in it. Well, now you're both going to get back what you did to him."

Piper looked at Travis. "Do it."

He took out a phone and began punching numbers. Zero appeared again at Harper's side. She heard a ripping sound. A second later, he tore a length of duct tape with his teeth, stuck it over her mouth, and wound it around her head as a gag.

High above, Piper leaned back, raised her head high, and screamed.

The sound ricocheted off the metal walls of the room, a slicing shriek, loud enough to hurt Harper's ears. Piper drew breath and screamed again. Then she spun and ran along the catwalk toward the door that led to the main factory floor.

"Help me," Piper screamed. "Help."

Her feet pounded on the metal catwalk. The noise was surely audible for long distances. Harper wondered what the purpose was. Then she didn't.

"Help me—*Aiden.*"

Zero shoved Harper to the floor and grabbed her right arm and stepped on it, holding her down. From the waistband of his jeans, he took a gun and tried to place it in her hand. It was a chrome-plated pistol. She balled her fist. He ground his heel into her forearm, then knelt and put his knee there instead.

"Fight me and your arm gets broke," he said.

She fought. She snarled and squirmed and head-butted him. He turned his black shiny eyes to her. He looked five hundred years old, not thirty.

"'Kay."

He grabbed her by the throat and squeezed. She clawed at his arm with her free hand, but he was too strong. She kicked at him but felt her vision constricting. Someplace overhead, Piper was screaming. Travis stood near the door, calmly watching Zero strangle her. She couldn't get air. The view seemed gray, and darker.

Then she was back. On the floor, dizzy, gulping air. Zero still knelt on her right arm. The ripping sound of tape grew clearer. She raised her left hand halfheartedly, woozy, aiming to punch Zero in the head, and couldn't move her fingers. Her hand was taped into a useless ball, and the ball was taped inside the sleeve of Zero's hoodie, and the sleeve was taped through the pocket of the sweatshirt.

Zero continued binding her right hand, as though he were a rodeo cowboy roping a calf.

He stood up. She saw, in her gradually brightening vision, that the pistol was taped securely to her hand. Her finger wasn't on the trigger, but she knew already that the gun was unloaded.

Zero backed away, waving to her, almost childishly, little finger waves, and whispered, "Bye-bye."

Above on the catwalk, Piper's footsteps continued to pound. The girl was still screaming, and her sloppy words came gradually out of the static in Harper's head.

"Aiden, where are you?" Piper shouted. "Help me."

Harper's eyesight came back, throbbing yellow as she fought for breath. Her throat felt raw. The ice-water sensation had abated when she blacked out, but it was back now, fiercer, stinging.

Travis's voice turned from muffled noise to clearish words. His tone of voice was off. It was breathy and girlish.

"My emergency—yes, it's . . . omigod, send help. I mean—the sheriffs. I need the police."

Harper tried to stand up. Dizzy, she felt herself tipping. She leaned over again, on both knees, and instinctively put her right hand on the concrete to steady herself. The pistol, which entombed her hand, kept her from bracing herself. The barrel scraped along the floor.

"My name is Harper Flynn," Travis said. "Yes, please, oh, God, hurry. He's locked the doors. I can't get out."

She lowered her elbow to the floor and let her head hang until oxygen returned to her brain. Her ears cleared. Her world stopped pulsing yellow.

"The old Powerdyne plant off of Highway 14," Travis said. "Omigod, please hurry."

Harper looked up. Travis stood with the phone to his ear, staring at her. His face was nearly glowing with triumph. It looked like waves of heat were pouring off him, as though he were about to combust.

She knew what he was doing. He was spoofing a call to the authorities.

"I'm so scared," he said. "I'm in a back hallway and there's no way out."

Travis had not just drawn her and Aiden out here to kill them. He had arranged for Aiden to take the blame.

"Everything you've got, please, hurry. He's a maniac, and he's armed."

Travis was talking to 911. And he wasn't just claiming to be Harper. He was undoubtedly using voice-altering software so that, to the dispatcher, it sounded like a woman's voice. There was no voiceprint of Harper's own voice anywhere to compare it to. Though it was illegal, arranging it didn't take a hall pass at the NSA. It just took access to software that altered the phone number displayed as the caller, to misidentify who was on the line. And if things went as Travis planned, there never would be a way to disprove that Harper was calling, because she would be dead.

"Everything you've got," Travis said, desperately. "Everything."

Travis was the security expert. He knew how spoofing worked. He knew how phone freaks and chaotic actors liked to mess with systems. He knew exactly what to do. This was a SWAT.

Travis was preparing the coup de grâce. He was doing to Harper what she had done to him as a teenager: calling the cops.

"You have to understand," Travis said. "Aiden has gone nuts. He killed Detective Sorenstam."

The floor was cold, the concrete rough and scalloped. Harper slowly raised her head and got one knee up and leaned on it until she was steady.

"Killed her—he shot her. Oh, God." Travis let his voice unravel. The bastard was terrifically convincing.

"No, no . . . if I move from here, he'll find me. He's insane. Detective Sorenstam tried to warn me, and I didn't listen. And when Sorenstam got here and tried to pull me out, Aiden *turned on her*." His voice was scoured by tears and terror. "He gunned her down. He kept saying he loved her, that if she wouldn't come back to him, she wasn't going anywhere."

Harper balanced and stood up.

"He just stood there and shot her with a shotgun, and she put up her hands and tried to protect herself and . . ."

Travis drew a sobbing breath. Harper steadied herself.

"Now he's trying to kill me, too . . . yes, I'll stay on the line, but I might have to be quiet for a while because I don't know where he is. Yes, he's *heavily* armed—he has that shotgun and an ax and he probably took Erika's weapon, too, and oh, God . . ."

He paused. "I'm not alone, no. There's another girl here, Piper Westerman. She's hurt." Another pause. "No, she's not with me. She's hiding in a closet in the basement, but if he goes door to door, he'll find her, it's only a matter of time. . . . Yes, I'm hiding in the basement, *please send SWAT, Aiden's going to kill us all*."

Piper stood on the catwalk above, listening. She was going to be left alive to confirm Travis's lies.

She put her ear to the door and nodded to Travis. "He's coming."

Travis lowered his voice. "He's coming. Oh, my God."

He shut off the phone. He gave Harper one last look. Then he smiled up at Piper.

"Now," he said.

She inhaled. "Aiden, hurry. They're coming. Help me."

Harper raised her right arm and rubbed it against her face, trying to work loose the duct tape gag. But Zero had run it all the way around her head, through her hair, with another layer over the exterior of the sweatshirt hood. Without use of her hands, she couldn't get it off, not anytime soon. She looked around, wondering how to make some noise. She kicked at the chain but it only clanked.

Distantly, from beyond the door where Piper stood, came the sound of uneven footsteps. Pounding along, but struggling. Harper tried to yell from behind her gag, but there was no hope of making any sense.

Above her, Piper tensed. She raised a hand, signaling Travis. Then she unlocked the door.

Simultaneously, Travis flipped a switch. Overhead, the emergency lighting came on, white-blue and harsh. It strobed. Flashing, flashing, quickly, God knows how many times a second.

Then Aiden crashed through the door, and Harper knew exactly how many times a second. Exactly the right number to trigger a seizure.

57

Aiden stopped outside the door, pulling up sharply. His leg was a hot bolt of pain. The catwalk above the main factory floor swayed as he ran, his footsteps too loud. But Piper's shouts sounded desperate. He had a shotgun slung over his back by a strap and his HK in his right hand.

He should not have left them. He should have stayed with Harper and Piper—because, as he ran toward Sorenstam's police car, he had seen a shadow patrolling the fence line. Then he'd heard voices raised, in Harper's direction. He had quickly backtracked, slipped in a window, and worked his way toward the sounds of arguing, finding the ladder to the catwalk. But not fast enough. Now he held the rail and focused on the doorway ahead.

Piper screamed again. *"Aiden."*

Outside the door, he flattened himself against the wall. He stuck the HK in the small of his back and pulled the shotgun over his shoulder. It had a full magazine. He breathed to calm his heart rate, to still the pounding in his head, so he could hear what was happening on the other side of the door. He couldn't go through the door deaf and blind. Not if he wanted to keep from shooting Piper. And Harper.

She had given him a look, before she ran, that had been like a flaming arrow between the eyes. She had seen what was in him, seen that he didn't care if he got out. She'd said nothing—just taken Piper and gone.

That look. He couldn't decipher it. She had let him head off into what could have been a trap. Could she possibly have lured him and Erika here to get rid of them, out of sight, in the dead of night, and leave them for the coyotes? To clear herself of any taint, destroy the last source of testimony against her in the attack on the club?

No. She couldn't have. Harper had not turned on him.

"Aiden—*please.*"

Piper was yelling as loudly as a sideline cheerleader in a packed stadium. She was coherent and definite and had the lung capacity to keep screaming as if she could single-handedly carry the team across the goal line.

It wasn't right.

He gripped the shotgun, his finger on the trigger.

Piper, screaming to raise the roof, when for the last twenty minutes she had been so drained from blood loss that she could barely lift her voice above a whisper.

This was wrong. Piper, yelling. And where was Harper?

He leveled the barrel of the shotgun at the door. He listened.

"Help me. *Hurry.*"

Piper's voice was nearby. Echoey, but it sounded like she was on the same level as he was. So maybe on a catwalk on the other side of the wall.

Where was Harper? What had happened to separate them?

Nothing good. But Piper wasn't talking about that. She wasn't asking him to help *them.* She kept calling, Help *me.*

That was a mistake.

His breathing picked up again. He tried to listen.

And in the background, he heard it. A man's voice.

"*. . . He has that shotgun and an ax and he probably took Erika's weapon, too, and oh, God . . .*"

Aiden tightened his grip on the shotgun.

"*If he goes door to door, he'll find her, it's only a matter of time. . . . Yes, I'm hiding in the basement,* please send SWAT, Aiden's going to kill us all."

Shock pulsed through him, then anger, pure and white, like a phosphorous grenade exploding.

Travis Maddox—had to be. He was imitating Harper. Aiden didn't fully understand it, only knew two things: Harper had been telling him the truth all along. And death waited on the other side of that door. It would be thrown open by Piper Westerman.

Piper was in there, with a liar, and she wasn't coming out. Talking about Erika. Not true, none of it.

And Travis was blaming Aiden for things that were about to happen.

Aiden tried to breathe, his chest tight. He seemed to feel hands squeezing his head, trying to crush him. He eased his finger more securely against the trigger.

He leaned his head back against the wall, just for a second, until he could draw a full breath. In his mind, he saw an image of flashing eyes and a slow smile, her hand reaching out to him. A laugh, the surprise of it. Her willingness to embrace him despite his great and dismaying faults. Her lips on his, her chest rising and falling with his, skin against skin.

She'd been there for him all along.

He straightened and took one more breath. He swung around, leveled the Remington, and kicked the door open.

He saw Piper standing on the other side, straight-backed and bright-eyed and so brimming with loathing that she seemed to shine. The barrel of the shotgun centered on her and she didn't even flinch.

Then the strobe flashed on, and his world dissolved in twisting light.

58

Harper saw it with brutal clarity.

Chained to the grate in the floor with only a small radius of movement, she peered up and saw Aiden kick the door open. It slammed back against the corrugated metal wall. He aimed the shotgun at Piper, who stood before him on the catwalk without so much as tensing. Then the strobes unraveled him.

Harper screamed behind the duct tape, but the sound didn't even reach the walls.

Aiden held on to the Remington for a couple of seconds longer, but he was all at once gone, the strobe lights causing a slow rolling blackout. He didn't fall to the floor, didn't jerk or convulse. He blinked and looked away and then wasn't looking. The strobes flashed *fast fast fast*, whatever pulse that aligned with electrical signals in the brain, and short-circuited him. He turned, slowly, to the right, losing his balance. His grip on the shotgun loosened. Piper lunged and grabbed the barrel, and she didn't even have to wrest it from his hands. He kept turning, the spin coming in horrible black-and-white snapshots under the fiercely strobing lights.

Harper yanked on the chain, trying to yell.

Travis stepped away from the wall and whistled to Zero. Upstairs, Aiden went down on his knees, hard.

Piper, under the strobe, looked like a vampire who had been unearthed, white and fast moving. The shotgun seemed to pop with light in her hands.

"Not the plan," Travis said. "Put it down. We're going."

He strode to the ladder and climbed up. Piper set the shotgun on the catwalk at Aiden's side.

"We'll watch," Travis said. "Now let's get clear. It won't take long."

He pulled her through the door Aiden had kicked open. Then they were gone.

Harper watched the shattering light. Aiden was on all fours, head hanging low, looking into the distance like a wolf. Harper yanked on the chain.

Then Aiden was crawling, trying to get one hand on the rail to pull himself up. He was propping his hands on the rail. The lights flailed, white-black-white-black.

He was standing up.

He had the shotgun in his hand.

He was aiming it over the railing, unsteadily, at her.

⟶

Harper backed up. She didn't do it consciously. Her feet just moved. But after five feet the chain caught her. She stumbled. Her left hand was bound inside the pocket of the sweatshirt, but she raised her right hand.

Then remembered. *Oh, shit.*

The big silver pistol duct-taped to her right hand. As soon as she raised it, Aiden swung the barrel of the shotgun downward. She screamed, as hard as anything she'd ever done, not even trying.

He pulled the trigger.

She fell backward and hit hard on her butt. The strobe lights turned the room into a firefight all by themselves.

The shotgun failed to fire. She lowered her hand and tried to stick the barrel of the gun into the links of the chain, to somehow loosen the tape and tear free of it. Above her, Aiden swayed. He knew the gun had not fired. He looked stunned—maybe in a fugue state. He was there but he wasn't. And she knew what he thought he was seeing.

And if he didn't, the next second changed his mind. The dog padded across the floor, its nails clicking on the concrete. It stopped at her side. In the strobe, every time the lights flashed, the dog seemed to be in a different place, as though it were three dogs, four, teeth and slobber. It sniffed Zero's sweatshirt.

Above her, Aiden regained his footing. He was slowly coming out of the postseizure state.

He racked the slide on the shotgun. The noise was ungodly. If there was any ammunition in the magazine, he had just pumped a shell into the chamber for certain.

At the sound, the dog snarled and raised its head toward the catwalk. It bared its teeth and barked.

For a hard second, Aiden looked like he was trying to locate the source of the barking. The strobes flashed, the dog seeming to jump and change size with every spark of the lights. White-black-white-black. Aiden tracked the sound with the barrel of the gun.

She inhaled and jumped away from the dog.

The blast of the shotgun filled the room. The slug slammed into the floor. Chips of concrete flicked through the air. They hit the back of her legs. She skittered, her leg chained to the floor, circling away from where she had been.

He thought she was Zero.

His brain injury had left him open to seizures, especially seizures triggered by flashing lights and flash photography. She'd seen it several nights earlier, at Joe's Cafe, when he turned away from strobing camera flashes. He had hinted at it, tried to explain. She understood that he hadn't suffered a grand mal seizure, but what a doctor friend had once explained to her as a complex partial seizure. The brain had fired uncontrollably. Now he was coming back.

Coming back badly. Because complex partial seizures unwound slowly, and during that time, the person was in an altered state of consciousness. Going through that kind of seizure sometimes resulted in delusions.

The shotgun racked again. He fired. The sound seemed to fill her entire life.

The dog was dauntless. It ran to the foot of the ladder and jumped, barking wildly. The lights blanched the room, making Harper nauseated and disoriented. But if she didn't keep moving, she was dead. He wouldn't keep missing her. He didn't have to. He didn't have to keep firing from thirty feet away. All he had to do was climb down the ladder and walk over to her.

She had to find a way to communicate.

He fired again. The shot hit the chain near her foot. She cringed. She was shaking, head to toe. Keep moving. *Think.*

At the foot of the ladder, the dog jumped and snarled. It raised up on its hind legs and put its paws on the rungs, snapping feverishly.

Aiden was coming down.

59

Aiden gripped the ladder. He swung around and began to descend. A strange ringing filled his head, swelling and diminishing over and over, cyclically. The lights continued to flash, *blackwhiteblackwhite*, and an aura spit at the edges of his vision, a fiery electric tracer, a sine wave that danced like dry lightning in a black thunderstorm. The taste in his mouth was metallic.

The shotgun in his right hand was heavy. Three shells left before he had to reload.

He needed to climb down as fast as possible. Zero was below him, and Zero was always armed.

Beyond the ringing came another sound, something animal, something violent. Below him, in the strobing pit.

He didn't know where he was exactly. How he'd gotten here. The walls were moving, *whiteblackwhiteblack*. His hands were in front of him, and the pain in his leg seemed to be from a heated iron bar.

Go. Zero was there.

Zero, who had screwed his life, killed people, set Xenon ablaze, and turned loose his thugs on Erika.

He continued to climb down, painfully, the shotgun clattering against the rungs.

Somebody else. Here. Should have been.

Piper. He had heard her. Voice, she was screaming. His name. Where was Piper?

He felt as if he were caught in a stream of air and electricity. Buzzing noise. Something had happened to him. He seemed to be made of pain, and so vague that he didn't know where his body ended and the air and walls began. He should be able to see colors, but the lights—*whiteblackwhite*. He was in a tunnel, racing through a focused stream of lights and energy. His hands were half-numb. He kept climbing down the ladder.

Sound beneath him, growing louder. Through the sine wave thrum, barking. He worked his way down the ladder, his hands flashing in the light, moving with jerks, not seeming attached to him.

He half jumped, half fell to the ground. When he turned, he saw Zero.

His breath jammed in his lungs. Ten yards away, Zero crouched on the floor. *Whiteblackwhite*. The piebald room was etched with shadows and pitiless light, on and off, *blackwhite*, and his perspective wasn't 3-D, somehow both flat and stretched, warped and zooming. Zero crouched on the floor close to rusting machinery, one hand jammed in the pocket of his gray hoodie, hiding Aiden didn't know what. The other hand, right hand—on the concrete. Gun in it.

Drop the weapon.

He tried to say it, heard the words with painful clarity in his mind. No sound came out of his mouth.

Drop the weapon. "Dro . . ."

He stumbled. His feet didn't seem responsive, and the room was throbbing *whiteblack*. Zero had moved. Slipped sideways. Now looking up at him. That gun.

How much time had passed? There was a lapse. He felt a slicing sense of urgency. Time gone, how much?

From a million miles away, a million years, he seemed to know he was back on the floor of the club at Xenon, lights stroking, music droning, shapes shifting in panicked flight. *Whiteblackred*, blood misting the air. *Whitegoldorange*, the swoop and spill of flame before it caught the wall behind the bar and erupted in ravenous rapture.

He saw Zero, facing him this time, right there. Hood pulled over his head, shadowing his face. Not the gas mask now, not the shining flame eyes, but the same slight form, armed and eager, face almost glittering in the shifting light *whitesilver*, a strip of mask around his lower face.

He walked toward him, two steps, the shotgun coming up in his hands, the ringing rising to a wail.

He saw the dog half a second before it lunged at him.

Harper crouched, ready to throw herself one way or the other like a soccer goalkeeper facing a penalty shot, knowing it wouldn't matter as long as she moved. Aiden was going to fire at her, twelve-gauge from fifteen feet, she would either guess right or not. She couldn't wait, couldn't try to judge it. The sickening strobe light made it impossible to see his movements smoothly. By the time she could tell which way he was swinging the barrel, it would be too late.

Then in the flash of white light, the dog was a snapshot of furious movement. Muscle and its torn face, teeth, midair.

It launched at Aiden. In that moment, she thought it was salvation and death, putting an end to this and ruining her only hope, her heart. Darkness, another blast of jerking light.

Aiden swung the butt of the shotgun. It hit the dog in the side of the head. Eagle cried out hideously, and his flight continued to a limp collapse on the floor.

Harper backed up, giving herself a foot of slack in the chain. Another flip of the light and Aiden was facing her again. He braced himself and held the shotgun with the assurance of an experienced soldier and lawman.

And he wasn't going to ask her to surrender herself.

Not like this. *Not this end*, she thought. If she had only a hundred heartbeats left, let them not end in terror.

Not at Aiden's hands.

He didn't see her. He couldn't. He thought she was a killer, the killer of his hopes, of people who deserved a chance at wonder, of people he had loved. He thought he was avenging all the destruction wreaked by a psychopath. He thought Zero was ready to kill him with the gun taped to her hand.

Not death. Not death. And if she died, she knew that Aiden would be next. Once he regained his senses, if he found her dead on the floor, he would use the next shell in the shotgun on himself.

He turned, unevenly, then braced himself, feet shoulder-width apart. The shotgun came up, came around, centered on her. The end of the barrel, a dark eye, a portal, aimed dead at her.

"Drop . . ." he said. It was all he could seem to get out.

She couldn't run. Couldn't yell. Couldn't even speak up for herself. Aiden couldn't see her, not right then. He could only see the killer who'd plagued his days and nightmares for the last year.

She stilled. She stopped moving altogether.

She held her right hand high overhead, the gun aimed at the ceiling. But that wasn't enough. He took a step toward her. Her left hand, taped inside the sweatshirt, might look as though it held another weapon.

Slowly, inch by inch, she lowered her right hand.

~

Aiden stepped toward Zero. Every inch of him hurt, muscles tense to the point of aching. His head screamed. He felt as though he'd spent ten minutes in an industrial dryer with ten pounds of rocks. The metallic taste in his mouth was running with blood. He had bitten his tongue.

He had blacked out. He knew that and tried to narrow his eyes so that the flashing lights wouldn't trigger another seizure.

Time lost. He couldn't remember what he'd been doing before this thing began. There was only darkness, only clouds.

Harper. Aiden seemed to hear her name in his head, flowing through him. Something about Flynn.

Kicking open the door *blackwhitelightninggray*. Harper—she had looked at him. He knew why now. He understood, and it poured over him like the snaking aura that flicked its tongue at the edges of his vision: Harper had been telling the truth all along.

Piper. She wasn't here. Shit, what had Zero done with her? He remembered her . . . in the heat of a chaotic and dangerous moment, he had heard her screaming.

She and Harper weren't here. Zero was.

He had a shotgun in his hands. Zero was straight ahead, blocking his path. Why? He had Piper, had . . . did he have Harper? Zero was trying to stop Aiden from getting to them. Standing there goading him, holding a gun, a pistol and . . .

Aiden blinked, trying to clear his vision. The ringing in his head sounded suspiciously like sirens. Zero looked small and large at the same time, and his hand was a silver bundle that enveloped the pistol.

"Drop it," he said, and knew that wasn't going to happen.

But Zero didn't fire. He had a clear shot, but Aiden had the drop on him. Zero couldn't lower the gun and get off a shot before Aiden pulled the trigger on the shotgun.

He took another step. *Blackwhitesilver.* He held the Remington low and pressed the stock against his hip, left hand beneath the barrel, right finger on the trigger. Three left in the chamber.

Zero stood absolutely still while he advanced. Then Zero put the barrel of the pistol to his own head.

60

Chained to the floor in the factory assembly room, Harper held the pistol roughly against her temple. She heard the distant wail of sirens in the empty desert night.

Aiden stood fifteen feet from her. The Remington shotgun was snugged low against his right hip. The muzzle was pointed at her chest. His face, flipping between white and black under the strobe lights, grew ever more focused.

He looked like the cop he had been, the soldier he once was, walking into what was going to be a trap. And he looked like a man who'd just lost his partner and believed he was facing Erika Sorenstam's killer. He looked like an executioner.

She pressed the barrel of the pistol against her temple. Even under the strobe lights he had to see that.

Didn't he? He took another step toward her.

The sirens grew clearer. It should have been the sound of rescue. Instead, it was a countdown to destruction. Zero was somewhere nearby, watching. If Aiden didn't fire, Zero would. Half consciously, she wondered if Travis cared about the evidence the cops would find here. But it wouldn't matter, not if Aiden killed her and SWAT killed him—or Zero killed them both and made it look like murder-suicide.

She had only minutes before a tactical squad would make a dynamic entry, blasting open the factory doors and coming after Aiden.

She had to convey that to him. But he had taken the equivalent of a massive blow to the head, from the inside out. So she stood with the barrel of the empty pistol against her temple. She held so still she thought she might become stone.

Aiden gritted his teeth and said, more clearly this time, "Drop it."

She'd never felt so scared. Not even when she'd been about to double-cross Travis and Zero, driving full speed toward a police roadblock.

She slowly dropped to her knees. It was impossible to make it look like smooth surrender, but she had to try. Her left hand was still bound to her midsection inside the pocket of the sweatshirt. Keeping the gun pressed to her temple, she lowered herself to the concrete and lay face-down. Then she slowly, oh so slowly, moved the gun away from herself, in a broad arc along the concrete, pointing it away from Aiden. He approached. In the flashing lights, he was hot light and shadow, a kaleidoscopic nightmare.

His shadow passed over her. The barrel of the shotgun pressed against the back of her head. She flinched and let out a stifled sob.

Aiden didn't react. She didn't know what happened in his mind at these times, whether a screaming filled his head along with the visual miscues. The sirens were no longer a hint on the night air but a rising wail. And now, mixed with the freakish black-white strobing, were blares of red and blue, pounding in through the windows at the top of the building. The cops were closing in.

She could see nothing but his shadow. The lights had become another version of noise. Aiden had to know it was only a matter of moments: This was his last chance to kill Zero without witnesses.

The barrel of the shotgun pressed heavily against the base of her skull. Aiden dropped to the concrete beside her, pressing one knee on her right forearm, as Zero had done earlier.

He looked at her right hand. "The hell."

He pulled the hood of the sweatshirt off her head.

For an eternal moment, he did nothing more. He stared at her. Even with the vicious strobe of the lights, he should have been able to see that she wasn't Eddie Azerov, that she was the woman he had held skin to skin. But he didn't move, didn't say a word.

Outside, the sirens swelled to full volume and the blue-red spin of lights filled the windows. The cops were outside. They would deploy snipers around the perimeter. A forced-entry team would prepare to bring out the battering ram and the flash-bang grenades.

Then she heard a flick and felt a warm blade slip under the duct tape that encased her right hand. *Thank God.* Aiden sliced through the tape that bound the pistol to her hand and tugged the gun from her grip. He tossed it deep into the shadows, clattering it across the concrete floor.

Next he brought the knife up to the tape that gagged her. It slipped beneath the tightly wound strands. Aiden flicked it, ripping the edge and nicking her cheek.

He sliced the tape through and yanked it roughly from her mouth.

"Aiden," she said. "It's me."

He breathed. His knee remained on her arm. The barrel of the shotgun remained against the base of her skull.

He said, "They'll be here soon. You tell me what I want to know and I'll let SWAT take us both down. They'll kill you clean. You lay there grinning and lying to me, I'll kill you dirty. Your choice."

Harper lost it then. The room seemed to crack under the force of the strobing lights. She opened her mouth and couldn't even draw breath. The shotgun pressed against her head. Aiden breathed heavily above her.

Then she cranked it all down. "Aiden, listen to me. You know what's happening. It's your nightmare. Meet the new dream, same as the old dream."

He went still.

"This is the zombie dream. It's not real," Harper said.

He paused another long moment, then removed his knee from her arm and rolled her over. In the strobing lights, she saw his ferocity and despair.

She had nothing, not a weapon, not even her own face. Nothing but to empty herself in front of him.

"It's me, Aiden. Earlier tonight, at your place, you held on to me and told me I was not alone. I said the same to you. It's me," she said.

He blinked and stared at her. She wanted more than anything to scramble and run, or grab him and hold on. She lay still.

"It's me." She knew he still couldn't see it. "Close your eyes."

He didn't look anywhere close to doing that. Not when it would give Zero the jump on him. He glared at her.

"Please. Close your eyes. Listen to my voice. Feel my face."

He struggled, seemingly debating, and then, staring her in the eye, shut his own.

"Can you hear me? I love you," she said. "I loved you the first moment I saw you at Xenon, when you came through the crowd toward me. I knew you were coming to help me. I saw it in everything about you."

He opened his eyes. He looked at her for an excruciating second. Then he took the gun from her head. He exhaled as though he couldn't get any air.

"Oh, God." He knelt on one knee, staring at her with horror.

"If we don't get out of here," she said, "it gives Zero and Travis everything they've wanted since day one. They'll get away with killing us, and with killing Drew, and burning down Xenon. If we die, nobody will know you were right, that there was a third shooter. They won't know the phantom is real."

"You—it's really you."

"Really."

He reached out with an unsteady hand and brushed his fingers across her cheek. He seemed to be fighting with himself. As though he understood that all his sensory inputs were giving him one set of data, and his brain was giving him another.

Tears leaked from Harper's eyes and ran down her face toward the floor. "Trust me. Please."

His face was torn. She put her hand on his.

"Hear me. Even if it seems crazy to you. It's me. Really me, not him in disguise."

She put her hand around the back of his neck and pulled him toward her. He resisted, then he didn't. She lifted her head and put her lips to his ear.

"You don't have to hide from me. I see you."

She kissed his cheek, shaking. Then he turned his head and kissed her on the mouth.

A second later, he set the shotgun down and clutched her in his arms. He scanned her face. He looked like he was fighting himself, like his heart and his sight were scraping against each other. Behind him, at the high windows, the police lights swirled.

"We're out of time," she said. "Zip tie. Cut my foot loose from the chain."

He slipped the knife under the plastic and slit the tie. Then he cut through the duct tape that bound her left hand inside the pocket, and she shucked off Zero's sweatshirt.

"Zero's still here someplace," she said. "Travis took Piper. He said they were going someplace where they could watch. And we gotta get going before the cops come in."

She scrambled to her feet. Aiden picked up the shotgun. He was slowly recovering his balance and bearings.

A second later, she realized why she didn't need to hear the sound of a battering ram to herald the cops breaching the room. The rolling door to the outside droned into action and started to clatter open. The cops had found the controls.

She hesitated. If they surrendered, could they withstand the SWAT team storming the building? The strobes were insane. Seeing them clearly, discerning their intentions, would be difficult.

"Aiden, put down the gun and raise your hands."

Aiden bent to set the shotgun on the floor—just as the flash-bang grenade rolled through the door. A second later, from the catwalk above them, Zero began firing at the cops.

61

Zero's gunfire raked the air above their heads. One shot, two. Harper ducked and clawed her fingers into Aiden's arm. The noise from the flash-bang had disoriented her, but she was already so oversaturated from the strobe and the fear that it almost didn't matter. She ran toward a door at the back of the room. Lagging, he came along with her.

Seconds later, the cops thundered through the rolling door. In the scarred and freakish light, Harper saw the track of a laser sight appear on the wall ahead of her. It moved from left to right, settling on the door they were aiming for. She dropped to the floor, pulling Aiden down with her.

He resisted. She didn't know if his impulse was to lay down his gun and shout surrender, or to turn and fire upward. Then he dropped, rolled onto his back, and swung the barrel toward the catwalk.

"No," she shouted.

Zero was nothing but a shadow, flickering in the strobe light, jumping from spot to spot as the lights flashed.

Harper yelled, "Fire and they'll shoot you. Let the cops get him."

He resisted an instant longer before she yanked hard on his arm and pulled him to his feet and through the door.

She slammed it. A shot clanged into the door from the far side. Though it was solid metal, a blister formed at Harper's eye level.

"Jesus shit," she said.

In the hallway, the abrupt absence of the strobing light left her dizzy. The walls spun. Aiden shook his head as though clearing it and braced his legs to steady himself. Another shot blistered the door.

He looked around. Pallets were stacked along the corridor.

"Grab one of these."

They pulled a pallet to the door and jammed one side under the handle. The other end nearly bumped the opposite wall. It would keep the door from being easily opened.

Aiden slung the shotgun over his shoulder and put a hand on her arm. "We . . ." He looked unsteady. She held on to him. "Gotta get out."

"You're telling me."

Inside the factory assembly room, Zero was no longer firing. Not now that the cops were inside.

"They won't take us peacefully, will they?" she said. "Not even if I surrender myself."

"You could surrender. You could tell them all the tactical information they wanted, badge them, tell them you were the Queen of All Assault Teams, and they'd still come gunning for me. Once Zero— when he opened fire . . ."

She understood. "It's open season."

"You can get out."

But if she got out, he wouldn't. The only way to keep him alive, she saw, was to keep herself at his side.

"We'll both get out. Run," she said.

They hurried down the corridor, Aiden brushing his free hand against the wall for balance. The hallway scoped to darkness. Her dizziness was abating, though the adrenaline depletion, the utter exhaustion, was taking hold.

But he was hanging on to her. He had an arm around her waist and was supporting her. With what strength, she didn't know.

"Zero and Travis have a way out. You do, too," he said. "You talked about tunnels."

She felt a little strength return. When they thought Piper was desperately wounded, she'd rejected the possibility of belly-crawling through tunnels and filthy vents. Not now.

"The rat run," she said.

She had to find it. Behind them, the doorknob rattled. The wooden pallet shrieked as someone tried to force the door open.

As they ran raggedly down the hall, she tried to orient herself. She tried to remember. The darkness had to become familiar once again before she brought it back.

She slowed. Aiden tried to pull her along.

She pointed. "Ahead. Should be an intersecting hallway."

Behind them at the door came a metallic banging sound. SWAT had found a use for the battering ram. She looked back and saw the door slam open a few inches. The pallet held in place, but a second jolt from the ram sent the door flying open.

"Hurry."

She pulled Aiden around a corner into a near-black hallway. Behind them, they heard curt, muffled conversation—tactical commands, gruffly issued.

"Your phone," she said breathlessly.

She'd lost the Maglite. He lit the display and they stumbled along the hall. A minute later, she found the utility closet door. If it was locked . . .

She pulled it open. "This way."

They ducked inside and closed the door. Aiden swept his phone around the cramped room. A ladder bolted to the wall dropped into an access tunnel that ran between the two basement levels.

Through the crack beneath the door, flashlight beams swung back and forth. So did the red laser targeting light of a tactical rifle. Shadows and sliding footsteps passed outside in the dusty hallway. They held their breath.

In the hallway, in a low voice, a man said, "Flynn's still on the phone with the dispatcher. Says the shooter has explosives—this place manufactured fuel for solid rocket boosters. If he gets a chance, he'll set them off. Engage at will."

Harper squeezed her eyes shut, trembling. After another moment, the footsteps faded.

Aiden whispered, "And you said I was paranoid."

She slipped her arm around his. He was breathing hard. He was nothing but muscle and grit and, somewhere inside him, a compass that had returned to true north.

She whispered, "Can you climb? Can you crawl?"

"I'll do whatever I have to."

They climbed down the ladder to an access hatch. Aiden flashed the light from the phone. They saw the tunnel, a two-foot-by-two-foot vent that ran horizontally through a conduit between the two basement levels. She dropped to her belly and began to eel through.

"When I was twelve, I came here with Travis and his dad and the others," she murmured. "We explored and found the way out to the hatch beyond the fence. It still has to be there."

They crawled, Aiden breathing heavily behind her. Her feet scraped along the concrete. And gradually, a new sound invaded her headspace: hissing. Somewhere, gas was still escaping from a pressure vessel. She didn't smell anything, but odorless gases could still asphyxiate her and Aiden and the cops.

Sixty feet down the tunnel, the concrete changed to plywood. Their elbows and knees and feet knocked against it. Aiden's phone flashlight illuminated only a few feet ahead. Beyond the light was nothing but coal-dark echoes—until the sound stopped rebounding. Harper's heart dropped to the pit of her stomach. Ten feet ahead, the tunnel dead-ended.

"No," she said.

She seemed to unwind and run down. This far, and there was no farther. A heavy bolus of tears and despair swelled inside her, a black wave about to crest.

"We'll find another way," Aiden said.

But his voice was flat. There was no other way.

She turned to him, wondering if he was ready to let go. If he wanted the cops to come in, for the night scope to target him, to put an end to the echoes and phantoms and the half-lit world he had fallen into.

Then a new light appeared a few feet ahead, a panel being pulled off the side of the tunnel. She crouched, instinctively, though taking a defensive position couldn't possibly protect her in the narrow confines of the tunnel.

Aiden tried to shield her, though he was behind her. "Move." He couldn't get by.

They heard a shuffling sound. Two hands appeared at the edge of the panel, and with a grunt, somebody boosted himself up.

Oscar appeared.

62

Oscar stuck his head through the gap in the paneling. His dark curly hair was stuck to his forehead with sweat. Harper tried to stay silent, but a sound of shock and joy slipped from her lips.

Oscar said, "Don't just sit there staring at me. This way."

They crawled to the gap. Oscar jumped down and Harper wriggled out headfirst, tumbling into his grasp. Aiden followed.

Oscar had a flashlight in his cell phone. He directed it along the corridor where they stood. It was a crawl space between the walls of the lower basement level, eighteen inches wide, dusty, covered with protruding nails from the timber construction, bricks on the floor, left-behind detritus.

He said, "You were getting lost. Jeez, I thought you'd remember the way."

"I was fourteen, and—Oscar, Christ, what are you doing here? I thought you'd . . ."

"You're complaining?"

"Not on my life," she said. "Zero's here. Travis may be, too. And earlier, I heard a storage tank hissing. Stay inside and we only have three endings."

He nodded, understanding: get shot, get blown up, or choke to death on escaping gas.

He said, "None of the above. Let's go."

She heard the bravado in his voice but could see that he was flighty, moving with the desperate nerves of a deer that knows it has been scented by predators. He was in a big damn hurry to get out of there. Fine with her.

He raised on tiptoe to look behind Aiden, into the plywood tunnel. "Where's Detective Sorenstam?"

In the silence that stretched then, Oscar's face crumpled. "Oh."

Harper nodded. Aiden stared through the walls.

Blinking back his emotions, Oscar turned sideways and sped along the crawl space. They followed. She glanced back at Aiden. In the near-dark, he looked focused.

"Oscar, how'd you get in?" he said.

Oscar flicked a look over his shoulder. "Transformer box on the west side of the complex beyond the fence. Harper should remember it."

"That's where we were trying to get to," she said.

"You hit a dead end. And you weren't exactly silent."

"I'm all out of silent. All I got now is two feet and whatever fuel is left in me."

They reached a T junction. Oscar put a finger to his lips and turned an ear to listen to the building. Harper could hear only her heart pounding, and Aiden's labored breathing.

Oscar raised a hand, a *hang on* gesture. "We go left for a minute, then lower ourselves through a ceiling vent. It comes out onto a catwalk in a tank storage room."

"Then?" Aiden said.

"Cross the catwalk, get back into the conduit on the far side of the tank room, and slide along like greased pigs till we pop up outside the fence. After that, we're gone."

"Gone back to the unmarked car?" he said.

Oscar looked at him. "To the MINI. I parked it behind a boulder just on the other side of the fence. Damned little thing, you can hide it anywhere."

Oscar took a big breath, like a swimmer about to dive deep. Harper touched his arm.

"This . . . I never thought. Oscar, I—"

"Not now, cuz. Don't make me lose my shit."

I misjudged you, she wanted to say. A sense of shame overcame her. The words jammed in her throat.

"Thank you," she managed.

"You're gonna owe me, massively, when we get out. I'd negotiate my fee right now except I don't want to get my ass shot off before I get what's due."

He said it with gusto but an utter lack of conviction. She pointed at the T junction.

"Go."

They rounded the corner and gingerly wedged their way along the passage. The crawl space lowered. They dropped to hands and knees.

Keep going, Harper thought. She tried not to think about how close they were. Never consider the journey ended—not till you cross the finish line. Oscar's cell phone flashlight swung as he scurried.

"Ceiling vent's just ahead," he whispered.

She inched along. Then she felt the floor give way, undermined by something—a crowbar, the butt of a gun—and they crashed through the ceiling beneath the crawl space.

Below, Zero was waiting for them.

63

When the bottom of the crawl space gave way, Harper, Aiden, and Oscar plunged six feet into a tank room and hit the catwalk where Zero was standing. The catwalk hung from the ceiling, loosely connected by rusted bolts. Their crashing weight pulled the bolts loose and the catwalk dropped another eight feet before slamming to a sudden stop.

Harper landed on her hands and knees with the wind knocked out of her. She tried to catch her breath. Holding as still as possible, she carefully turned her head to look back.

The catwalk had fallen across a twelve-inch pipe that spanned the tank room. Its far end was loosely touching the wall of the room, keeping it from tipping completely, but it was wildly unstable. One entire railing had ripped off. The drop was deadly.

So was the catwalk. Zero crouched on the far end of it, a cut-down pump-action shotgun in his hands.

He reached into his back pocket and pulled out a road flare. He lit it and tossed it over the edge. It dropped, insanely white, into the depths of the tanks below and clattered onto the floor. Eerie light and shadows snaked around the room.

Harper saw: Oscar had crashed in front of Zero and lay on his back, groaning. Aiden had landed in front of Oscar, five feet from her. They were like passengers lined up on a giant gangplank. Then the catwalk wobbled. She and Aiden were on one side of the pipe, Oscar and Zero on the other. Harper felt the catwalk begin to seesaw.

She grabbed the remaining railing. It tilted. Aiden, on his knees, grabbed for the railing, too—but not quick enough. He slid off the side of the catwalk.

Harper shouted, "No—"

She lunged for him, but he pitched over the edge.

And was caught on a broken piece of metal by the strap of the shotgun.

He hung, swinging back and forth, before grabbing the strap and trying to steady himself.

But as soon as he raised his arm, the strap slid along the metal strut it was hooked over. The strut was a ten-inch piece that remained from the broken railing. It had bent horizontal, and Aiden's weight was slowly bending it further. It was beginning to tilt toward the floor far below. The strap of the shotgun slid an inch toward the end before stopping.

Harper froze. The cavernous room amplified the sound of the rusty catwalk grinding against the pipe, and of metal groaning as it bore weight in ways it was never designed to.

Cautiously, she looked around. Behind her, there was a ledge that led to the doorway out of the tank room. It was maybe three feet beyond the end of the broken catwalk. If she backed up a step, she could turn and leap for safety.

She knew what would happen if she did. This end of the catwalk would swing upward, like a seesaw when a kid jumps off. The far side—across the pipe—would plummet. Zero was at the farthest end. He would swing fastest, hardest, take the most vicious whack.

But Oscar would go down just as badly. It was worse here than in the other tank room where the goons had fallen. This was deeper, older, with machinery more rusting and sharp. If Oscar fell, that would be it.

Aiden would have little chance either. If she jumped, the portion of the catwalk where he hung would rise. He would swing toward it and might be able to grab hold as it rose upright. But only for a second. Because the catwalk wasn't secured to the pipe, the entire thing would slide off the far side like a dropped javelin. She held still.

Zero grasped the railing with one hand. With the other, he held the sawed-off shotgun. He stared past Oscar, past Aiden, at Harper.

"You gonna jump? Again?" he said. "You always do, don't you?"

"Eddie, you don't know me. You never did," she said.

"I know you, bitch. Don't matter if I call you Harper or Zannah or Fuck Me. You jump. You all do."

Aiden stopped reaching for the strut. With every effort he made to grasp it, the strap of the shotgun slid closer to the end. Oscar lay on the catwalk, facing Zero. In the eerie light from the flare, Harper could see that his head was bleeding heavily. He steadied himself and tried, slowly, to scoot backward away from Zero, toward her. Zero swung the shotgun toward him. One-handed, he pumped the slide. The noise was like bones cracking. Oscar stopped crawling.

"I shoot you, yeah, it'll change the balance and we'll probably all fall," Zero said. "So what? By then, you'll be dead. So hold still."

Oscar held still. Aiden hung beneath the catwalk, his arms straining. The strap of the shotgun slid another inch. Maybe three inches left before it ran off the end of the strut. And gravity didn't give time-outs.

"SWAT's thirty seconds away," Aiden said. "Put down the weapon."

Zero's eyes widened. His teeth clicked. Rage or amusement, she couldn't tell.

Harper held her balance. The catwalk moaned, complaining of the weight it was bearing. Zero continued to level the sawed-off barrel of the shotgun at Oscar.

An immense wave of emotion hit her. All this time, she had thought of Piper as the little sister she wished she'd had. But Oscar was the real thing, a brother to her. And she understood that she loved him like family: unconditionally.

She couldn't just stand there. Standing still was begging for time and entropy to do their work, in the form of Eddie Azerov. But she felt the seconds being sucked away, and knew that she couldn't save Oscar and Aiden both. Zero was waiting for Aiden to fall. Once the strap of the gun slid off the strut, the balance of weight would shift in Zero's direction. To even it up again, Zero would blow Oscar off the catwalk. And then he'd run toward the fulcrum, the pipe in the middle of the whole precarious contraption, and he'd empty the magazine at Harper.

Aiden hung, both hands gripping the strap on the shotgun. He looked up at the strut, and at the strap, a millimeter thick, working its inexorable way to free fall. Then he looked at her.

"Go," he said. It was nothing but air and desperation.

She was five feet from him. It was close enough that maybe, *maybe*, she could throw herself to the floor and grab his arm, maybe hang on to him so he could get hold of the strut. She inched her foot forward and slid her hand along the railing.

The catwalk shimmied and started to twist. She backed up again. Checkmate.

She tried to believe it, even as her mind fought the idea. *Do something. Jump. Scream. Call down a rain of spikes and claws. Change the balance.* Nothing. That was the answer the air was sending her. Nothing.

Aiden was slipping. Zero stared at her. He was waiting. That was all he had to do now. Wait, and it wouldn't be long.

"Now you know how it feels," he said. "Watching the inevitable. Feeling it all come down on you."

She never knew when it became clear to her. A sound, or a visceral memory—instinct making clear what had lurked nearby all along, vague and so wrong.

It was the sound of a chain, dragging on concrete. And as her nerves fired, this time she didn't cringe and want to run. This time, she felt a jolt of electricity.

She whistled.

From the doorway above Zero's side of the catwalk, at the entrance to the tank room, the dog padded out of the shadows. It stopped and looked over the edge at them. Then it looked up, across the room, at the doorway leading out. Harper's hair stood on end.

"Eddie," she said. "Did you go into Xenon that night planning to shoot Drew? Did Travis order you to kill him? Or was that you, free-styling?"

He cocked his head. "Shit happens to targets of opportunity."

His words seemed to echo in the pit. Overhead, she heard scuffles and breathing. The dog growled. In the spitting light from the flare, Zero's teeth were visible. He was smiling at her.

She held his gaze. Slowly, she extended her arm. A broken stump of metal protruded from the catwalk railing. Gritting her teeth, she jammed her forearm against it and sliced.

The pain leaped on her. Blood spilled in a jagged tear up her forearm. She pulled it against her chest and let it bleed onto her shirt. Oscar looked at her with dull disbelief.

Then she whistled, little more than air and spit, and raised her arm again, and said, "Eagle. Sic."

The dog gathered itself in the doorway, tiny eyes fizzing in the light from the flare. It jumped nimbly onto the catwalk.

Zero said, "What?"

Eagle had eyes, and teeth, only for her. But a hundred pounds of brindled muscle instantly tipped the weight on the catwalk. The balance swung in that direction.

Harper threw herself down and reached for Aiden. She got his left arm in both her hands and held on. When she took some of his weight, the strap of the shotgun slipped from the end of the strut.

Zero was off balance, arms wheeling. Oscar was sliding, trying to grip the catwalk but too bloodied and disoriented to manage it. The dog was charging. Zero grabbed the rail and brought the barrel of the shotgun up, finger on the trigger. Harper held on to Aiden's arm, thinking her gamble was the wrong one, all wrong. Oscar was going to lose.

Aiden swung, and in his right hand, he brought up the Remington. The barrel swept toward Harper's face and she closed her eyes and then the roar of the shot took everything. The seesaw continued its arc. The echo of gunfire filled every space around her.

There was a clatter of metal, and the sound of something heavy hitting the tanks and equipment far below. The seesaw stopped its arc. It slowed and swung back toward balance.

Harper looked. She was still holding on to Aiden's arm. Beyond the pipe, Oscar was flat on his belly, grasping the catwalk. The dog had crouched in front of him.

Zero was gone. Aiden had shot him.

Even as emotion arced through her, she tried to hold on to him. She had little strength left. Blood dripped from her arm. The pain throbbed.

"Hurry," she said.

He swung his right arm up and dropped the shotgun on the catwalk. Then he grabbed hold, taking some of his own weight. He looked up at her.

"He's gone. We're there."

He pulled himself up as the sound of the SWAT team drew nearer, men running through the corridor outside. Harper held still, close to him, eyeing Oscar and the dog, holding her breath so a flood of tears wouldn't send them over for good.

She looked up at the exit from the tank room. For a second, she saw them: Piper and Travis, eyes shining from the shadows. Piper's face was riven with some kind of horror. Harper thought she knew what it was. Piper had heard Zero confess. She knew she'd been fooled.

Travis leaned out and, for a moment, locked eyes with Harper. Frustration and anger spilled from him. She raised a finger and pointed it at him.

She mouthed, *I'll find you.*

Beyond the entrance to the tank room, flashlights and laser sights appeared, coming quickly. Travis grabbed Piper's arm and vanished.

Harper turned toward the entrance. "Don't shoot."

They all had their hands locked behind their heads when the cops finally found them.

64

In the end, it took two hours before the Kern County Sheriff's deputies uncuffed Harper's hands and declared her a witness, maybe a victim, instead of a threat.

The night was a blitz of headlights and crane spotlights. Beneath them, detectives and the coroner and forensics teams were examining the abandoned factory. Above the sterile glow, the Milky Way spilled its trail of blazing stars.

Zero was dead. Aiden's shot had blown him off the catwalk. The sheriffs weren't saying what had killed him, the shot or the fall, but it didn't matter. He was gone.

He was there.

Everything they'd had to fight to prove was there in the factory and could no longer disappear. It was justice, rough and ugly and a vindication that she hoped Aiden could see. But she knew: Everything he'd been battling for the last year had, tonight, turned to ashes and grief. Because the deputies had found not only Zero's body, and those of the Spartan Security goons, but that of Erika Sorenstam.

Aiden was across the dirt outside the perimeter fence in front of the factory, leaning against the hood of a patrol car. They'd removed his cuffs, too. He had a bottle of water in his hand but wasn't drinking. He was looking at the mountains, in the direction where they'd started out on foot with Erika. The place where their lives diverged.

Erika was the reason he was alive to mourn. She was the reason Harper could ache for him. If Erika hadn't stood and fought in the tunnel, they would all have been captured and executed. Harper pressed her fingers to the corners of her eyes.

A minute later, Oscar came up to her. He had a bandage wrapped around his head, gauze over the gash in his scalp.

"You look drained," Harper said.

He was slumped, hand to his head. His hair hung limply over his eyes. He looked about eleven. He was practiced at affecting that look: the hangdog kid, wide-eyed, scrappy, and oblivious. It was all a front, but tonight it was endearing.

"There's no reason they'll hold you," she said. "I told them you were a friend of mine who was along for the ride."

"That's lame," he said.

"You mean, give you an hour, you'd create a legend and a digital trail that showed you were somebody else who's never been anywhere near any of the dirty fingerprints on this shit show?"

"You may say you're so long removed from the life that you're a clean skin, but you're still Zannah to me." A sly shine broke through the facade. Then, just as quickly, it was gone.

"You gonna be okay?" he said.

"I always am."

"What a bullshitter you are."

He turned her forearm to examine the bandage the paramedics had wrapped around it. She would need stitches and a tetanus shot, but she hadn't sliced any arteries or nerves.

He stretched his arms and hugged her. When he pulled away, he walked off, looking at the ground. She thought he might simply slip into the night. Quickly, she checked her pockets. Good. She had her wallet. The keys to the MINI were where she'd stuffed them after he handed them back earlier. She watched him amble away.

To her surprise, he stopped by a sheriff's cruiser where Zero's dog, Eagle, was penned behind the wire mesh. He leaned his palms on the window and whistled. The dog came to the glass and sniffed. It looked lost and harmless. When she turned away, Oscar was talking to a deputy, pointing at the dog, making entreating gestures. She shook her head. He'd take the thing home and rehabilitate it if given half a chance.

Aiden was talking in exhausted tones to another detective. After a minute, the woman nodded, shook his hand, and walked toward Harper.

"We'll need to talk to you again, Ms. Flynn, but for now, you're free to go."

Harper nodded. "And Detective Garrison?"

"Him, too. We don't know who exactly SWATted us, but—"

"I do. I heard him do it," Harper said.

"As I said, we'll talk to you again."

Aiden looked up and walked over.

"Travis is gone," he said.

"He probably had an escape plan prepared. For if things didn't turn out the way he planned."

The detective glanced back and forth between them. "You two certainly saw to that."

"We're a helluva team," Aiden said.

A pep talk had never sounded so dispirited. She tried not to wince. But he looked at her with something akin to relief.

"Piper Westerman, the girl who went with him," Harper said.

The detective glanced at the desert. Piper was out there, presumably running with Travis. Harper felt a pang, like being kicked in the gut with steel-toed boots.

"I planted a seed," Harper said. "Piper heard Eddie Azerov confess to killing her brother. She's smart, and she's got a fistful of rage in her heart. If she figures out that Travis isn't the savior she thinks he is, we might have an opening to get her back."

She looked at Aiden. He nodded. She thought about Oscar's ability to perform online magic, and her contacts with spooks and cryppies from her Navy days, and how nearly impossible it was to disappear completely.

She wasn't going to let Travis go, not as long as he had Piper. "There has to be a way to find her."

Then she looked south, toward Los Angeles. "I'll talk to her parents," she said. It was going to be one cold sunrise.

The detective nodded again, maybe a cop-to-cop glance for Aiden, and headed off.

The night had drawn a chilly cloak around it, one that clung hard. In the wretched lights, Harper could see her breath. It faded into the air almost instantly. Everything seemed insubstantial.

Or not. Aiden was standing in front of her.

For a moment, she sought for words. Then he stepped forward and pulled her against him, wrapping her in his arms.

She rested her head against his chest. Around them, the noise and lights seemed to fade. They were left standing, last ones. In wreckage, but standing.

He bent his head to her ear. "Never should have doubted you."

"You had every reason to doubt me."

"You have every reason to doubt me. But somehow . . ."

"You saved my life tonight."

"You saved mine."

"So we're even?"

It was weak, even to her own ears. The most tentative of first steps. But for the moment, it was enough. He pulled her closer.

"Back there, inside," he said, "what you did, what it took—you were incredibly brave. And I thought you were dead. When I thought that . . . it nearly killed me."

She held tight to him. "I'm right here."

"Whatever happens, this has told me to cut through all the bullshit and get real."

He put a hand around the back of her head. He kissed her forehead and kept his lips there, hungry and grateful. "Never again. I won't leave you." His voice was almost gone.

"I'm not going anywhere."

"I love you. I do. You've gotta know that."

She shut her eyes and held him, and his scratching whisper reached her ears, a promise and a plea. He repeated the words *I love you*, and he whispered her name. It was a murmur, in time with his heartbeat.

She tightened her arms around him. She opened her eyes, heard his heart, heard his promise, her name like an incantation. Her own heart stuttered, and the words she wanted to say were held in abeyance. She turned her face to his.

"Aiden, look at me. Really look."

He did. Behind the warmth in his gaze lurked something disconcerted, like déjà vu.

"Do you know who I am?" she said.

The cold spotlights threw their shadows downhill across the sand. A crack appeared in his gaze, and the light seemed to flood in, and wake him up again. The pain returned to his face.

He took her face in both his hands. "Yes."

His voice fell away into the night.

She knew then that she had heard him right. The name he had whispered wasn't hers. For a gleaming moment, he had lived in a parallel world, and let slip a dream. *Erika.*

"I see you, Harper," he said. "Forgive me." Broken. "Do you see me?"

His arms were tense. He was waiting for her to jump. To run, to turn again.

"I see you," she said, and held on.

ACKNOWLEDGMENTS

As always, friends and colleagues provided me with invaluable assistance as I wrote this novel. For their insights, knowledge, and support, my thanks go to Tom Cooper, Michelle Bailat-Jones, Nate Shreve, Nancy Freund Fraser, Jessica Renheim, Jamie McDonald, Ben Sevier, Brian Tart, Sheila Crowley, Deborah Schneider, Mary Albanese, Adrienne Dines, Kelly Gerrard, Justine Hess, Tammye Huf, and David Wolfe. And, as ever: Paul Shreve, you make it all possible.

ABOUT THE AUTHOR

MEG GARDINER is the author of *The Shadow Tracer, Ransom River*, and four Jo Beckett thrillers, as well as five novels in the Evan Delaney series, including the Edgar Award–winning *China Lake*. Originally from Santa Barbara, California, she divides her time between London and Austin.